OUT FOR BLOOD

LAURA LAAKSO

Copyright © 2024 Laura Laakso

The right of Laura Laakso to be identified as the Author of the Work has been asserted by her in accordance with the Copyright, Designs and Patents Act 1988.

Published in 2024 by Bloodhound Books.

Apart from any use permitted under UK copyright law, this publication may only be reproduced, stored, or transmitted, in any form, or by any means, with prior permission in writing of the publisher or, in the case of reprographic production, in accordance with the terms of licences issued by the Copyright Licensing Agency.
All characters in this publication are fictitious and any resemblance to real persons, living or dead, is purely coincidental.

www.bloodhoundbooks.com

Print ISBN: 978-1-917214-82-7

*For Louise Walters, who has walked this path with me from the
beginning.*

JANUARY

ASSIGNMENTS

Sinta whimpers on my lap, and her back paw beats a rhythm against the edge of my desk. I lay a hand on her shoulder, murmuring soothing words, and she settles back into a peaceful sleep. She barely fits on my lap now. I watch her for a few moments before turning my attention back to the emails.

A potential client is due to arrive in a few minutes. While making sure the office is habitable in the January chill, I decided I ought to deal with some paperwork. One task led to another, and I have not left my desk for nearly two hours.

Footsteps descending the stairs to my front door signal the arrival of my visitor. Sinta yowls at the doorbell, and I shush her. She stays in my arms as I close the laptop lid and answer the door.

The woman standing at the threshold is in her late forties, with dull greying hair, understated make-up, and wearing a faded blue coat. She looks worn and tired, but upon spotting Sinta, a smile brightens her plain face. I borrow Sinta's nose by habit and identify her as an East Mage. Then I usher her in and introduce myself.

'Aleson Hampten,' she says in a husky voice. Her hand is cold in mine.

'Do you mind dogs? I can take her upstairs.'

'Not at all.'

Aleson offers her hand to Sinta, who leans forward to sniff it and then glances at me with clear disinterest. But when I set her down, Sinta takes her time inspecting Aleson's shoes. Aleson strokes Sinta's back and is rewarded with a wagging tail.

I show Aleson to a chair opposite mine, and she declines my offer of a hot drink. Sinta lies down at my feet. With no Karrion here to take notes for me, I retrieve a notepad and a pen from the top drawer. I find taking notes on paper while speaking is less impersonal than hiding behind a laptop.

'How can I help you?' I ask, pen poised over the blank page.

'I think my husband is having an affair and I'd like you to prove it.'

I fashion my features into an expression of sympathy. Thanks to the work we have done with New Scotland Yard and a few cases of our own, I have begun thinking about my business in the same terms as Karrion does. But simple infidelity cases will put food on the table long after high-speed car chases have ended in speeding tickets, and after clandestine meetings in shadowy alleys have moved elsewhere due to better street lights. The assignment from Lord Ellensthorne is almost finished, which will mean a significant drop in income for Wilde Investigations.

'How long have you been married?' I ask.

'Nearly eighteen years.'

'Is this the first time you've suspected infidelity?'

'No, but it's the first time I think it might be serious.'

'What makes you say that?'

Aleson sighs. 'In the past, it was a late night at the office here, an overnight business trip there. The usual kind of excuses. But now he's working late almost every night and most weekends too. We don't talk like we used to, and the other day, I noticed a strange credit card in his wallet. It's from a bank we've never used, and the statements don't come in the post like they do for our other accounts.'

'A separate credit card is a handy way to avoid suspicious entries on the joint accounts,' I say, and jot down a note.

'My guess is the statements are electronic, as I've found no trace of them.'

'Is there a particular person you think your husband is having an affair with?'

'Probably a twenty-something floozy from the office. That is the stereotype, isn't it?' The sharpness of her words is at odds with her weary demeanour.

'What does your husband do for a living?'

'He has an international courier company specialising in transporting magical items. His company handles normal antiques and artwork too, but items of power are his expertise and where the big fees are.'

'I didn't realise international artefact dealing was so popular.'

Aleson gives me a bemused look. 'The large magical communities are known for trading items and rituals from different countries. How else could developments be made and traditions of power preserved?'

Feeling like I have just exposed myself as the country bumpkin that most Mages of Old London regard me as, I clear my throat. 'Do you have a photo of your husband?'

'I can email it to you.' Aleson reaches into her purse for her phone. 'Together with some photos I took of his calendar for the next couple of weeks.'

'That's very helpful, thank you.' I write down the office email address.

An icon appears at the top of my phone screen, indicating that I have received a new email, but I ignore it for now.

'What precisely do you want me to do for you?' I ask.

'Follow him, figure out his routines, find out who he's cheating on me with, and take photos.'

'Photos of them together in general, or photos of them...' I leave the question unfinished.

Aleson's expression crumples, but she squares her shoulders and stares up at the ceiling until she gains control of her emotions. 'Both, if possible. Anything I can use against him when I file for divorce.'

'Very well.'

I detail my charges and go through the standard paperwork. She sits through it, impassive and with her hands resting flat on the scarred surface of my desk. When she opens her chequebook to pay for two days of fees in advance, I notice the cheque has already been signed. After all the paperwork is completed, she removes a business card from a silver case and writes a mobile number on the back in indigo ink.

'Call me any time of day or night, if you have any questions or have found the proof I'm looking for.'

'Of course.'

Heavy footsteps approach the door, and in their cadence, I recognise Karrion. A key turns in the lock. He walks in and then pauses.

'Sorry, I didn't know you had a client meeting.'

Sinta trots to greet him, having finally decided that he is part of the pack. Karrion strokes her head and, after she has rolled over, tickles her belly.

'Don't be sorry.' I stand and introduce Karrion to Aleson. 'We're done anyway, unless you have any further questions for me?'

Aleson shakes her head. We say our goodbyes, and she leaves.

'Do we have a new case?' Karrion asks after the door has closed.

'Yes.' I pick up my laptop and notebook. Karrion lifts Sinta into his arms, and we go upstairs. 'How was the driving lesson?'

'It was all right. You know how it is. Be careful of the kid on the bike. Don't forget to look left and right. Leave plenty of time to brake before a red light. Only a fool would ignore the two-second rule. It's not that difficult, though if birds had been made to drive cars, evolution would have given us opposable thumbs.'

'You do have an opposable thumb, Karrion.'

'That's not the point. Why drive when you could fly?'

'It sounds like you should have taken helicopter lessons instead.'

'Trust me, if I could afford them, I would.'

Laughing, I head to the kitchen to put the kettle on. I pause. Outside my lounge window, an unspoilt winter landscape stretches far beyond my field of vision. When I bring my hand close to the glass, the cold causes my fingertips to tingle. Calling upon Sinta's ears, I listen out for the constant noise of Old London. The city rumbles on around me, and yet I am looking at an impossible sight.

A chill creeps away from the window, inching along my arms and down into my torso. I am frozen to the spot, mesmerised by the winter wilderness and its implications.

'Yan?'

Karrion's hand on my shoulder cracks the ice encasing me. I tremble, my teeth chattering as feeling returns to my body. Turning away from the window, I stumble and Karrion catches my elbow.

'It's getting worse, isn't it?'

'What?' I ask, struggling to form the words with my numb lips.

'That curse the Winter Queen put you under.'

Anger flashes through me, sharp as frost splintering a tree. How dare he refer to my Cwēn in such a way?

'It's not,' I say.

'Yes, it is. I hate seeing you like this. We need to find a way to put an end to it.'

'There's nothing we can do. The mark will remain until the Winter Queen chooses to call in the favour I owe her. I can't go to her for a task because the Summer King banned me from the Unseen Lands.'

'I get that, but how long will it be before you freeze to death for real?'

'She'd never let that happen.'

My worth lies in being able to provide something she needs. At least, I hope so. The alternative is joining the pack of Fey hounds, and that thought scares me more than I can put into words.

'Let's talk about the new case,' I say, to banish the growing terror in my mind.

'Anything good?' Karrion's expression brightens.

'It sounds fairly straightforward.'

I tell him about Aleson and the assignment while we make tea and carry our mugs to the lounge. The remains of a small fire smoulder in the hearth. Although the winter's cold no longer bothers me, I continue heating the flat for Sinta's comfort and to keep the damp at bay.

'We have a bit of legwork to do, but taking the photos for our client shouldn't be a problem.'

'Sounds good,' Karrion says.

Sinta whimpers by the window, and I realise that I meant to let her out when the winter landscape distracted me. Now I glance towards the glass, reluctant to witness the unnatural sight a second time.

'Shall I let her out?' Karrion's voice is gentle.

'Please.' I force a smile, which grows more genuine while I watch Karrion tickling Sinta. Her tail wags and she jumps up to lick Karrion's cheek, missing by a foot.

Karrion opens the window and lifts Sinta out. I worry briefly that the cold rolling in is the sharpness of the Unseen Lands, but Karrion's posture remains relaxed. He must sense my thoughts for he offers me a reassuring smile.

'It's just your back garden. Nothing more.'

'Right. Good.'

When Sinta barks to be let in, I push past the reluctant tension in my muscles and stand. Sooner or later, I will have to face the window when Karrion is not here, so I might as well tackle the fear head-on. But all I see is the view I have been used to for over a year. Whatever spell the Winter Queen cast over me is gone.

'How are your side projects going?' I ask after I have washed our mugs.

Karrion opens his bag and pulls out a second-hand laptop. He bought it as a Christmas present for himself and his siblings, though I gather he has hogged it for the most part.

'Do you want to talk about Shamans or Lifelines first?'

'Let's start with Lifelines.'

'Okay. For a relatively small charity, it's got a lot of press attention over the years. I'm sure Viola Braeman's association helped a great deal with that. While the High Council of Mages never publicly backed the charity, the fact that their chief celebrity fundraiser was the Speaker's wife implied a lot. From the various news articles I've read, several Council members volunteered with them or took part in gala dinners and auctions.'

'Anyone interesting?' I ask, feeling more alert.

'As potential Leeches? No. We've vetted them all and they are who they say they are.' He pauses. 'Well, in so far as their magical powers are concerned.'

'So that's a dead end.' I make no effort to stop disappointment colouring my voice.

'Not necessarily. There are an awful lot of photos from Lifelines events showing people I couldn't identify. Any number of them could be Leeches.'

'With nothing to compare the photos to, how are we going to figure out who they are?'

'I haven't figured that bit out yet. But I reckon the more we keep digging, the more information we're going to uncover, even if some of it will be inadvertent.'

'I'd love to get my hands on the Lifelines volunteer lists, but that's not going to happen unless we obtain a court order,' I say.

'Which we can't do because we have no concrete proof that Lifelines has done anything wrong or is in any way enabling Leeches to climb Old London's political ladder.'

'Exactly.'

'There is something I want to share with you,' Karrion says, a delighted grin appearing on his face. 'You're going to love it.'

'Go on.'

'Lifelines have a gallery of photos from past events on their website. I figured I'd take a trip down memory lane as far back as I could, seeing as I'm pretty familiar with the movers and shakers of Old London's politics these days. You'd be surprised by how many public figures turned up. It seems that dying kids are a political goldmine.'

'That's awfully cynical of you. Next you're going to tell me you have photographic evidence of Lord Ellensthorne kissing babies and playing hopscotch.'

'I'd pay good money to see that, but no. What I found is even better.'

Karrion clicks on a file on his laptop. The photo shows an indoor riding arena with several children on small ponies. A young man is standing next to a grinning little boy and holding a small oxygen tank. At first, I cannot see anything out of the ordinary about the photo, but then I frown. I know that man. He is older in the photo I have of him, in the photos I saw in his flat, but there can be no mistake: the young man is Gerreint Lloid.

'Good spot,' I mumble, still trying to recover from my shock.

Though why should I be surprised? We already know Lloid was connected to Gideor Braeman and volunteered with Lifelines. That could even be how they first met.

'That's not the interesting part. This photo was taken seven years ago. As far as I can figure out from the information available online and a few sneaky phone calls Jamie made for me, it was at least two years before Lloid began his political career. And almost a year before Lloid started receiving payments from Braeman's secret Leech trust.'

'Another good spot,' I repeat, this time with more conviction. 'The question is, why would a Leech be volunteering with a children's charity before he became a politician?'

'Isn't it obvious? It gave him access to children who were dying. Who's going to notice a Leech is stealing their power if they're already that sick?'

While it is a conclusion I, too, have reached, hearing it spoken out loud gives me pause. It is one thing for a Leech to steal magic from adults, but to prey on terminally ill children seems too monstrous to contemplate. Can Leeches be so lacking in fundamental human morality? Or does Lloid lack empathy? Was his happy and loving relationship with Leina Parez a mere sham? Could my original instincts about Lloid being innocent of Leina's murder have been incorrect?

Or am I reading too much into an old photograph?

'It's a scary conclusion to reach,' I say when the silence has gone on for too long. 'I doubt we can prove or disprove it while Lloid remains missing.'

'What else could it be?'

'I don't know, but we don't know that much about him. Would we be so quick to jump to such an alarming conclusion if we didn't know he was a Leech?'

'If he wasn't a Leech, we wouldn't know about his existence at all. How likely is it that Leina would have been murdered without her association with Lloid?'

'Not very. Still...' I search for the right words, but they elude me. 'You're probably right. Sometimes I wonder if we're too quick to see the worst in people, but I suppose that's one of the hazards of the job. Be sure to send that photo to Jamie. It may yet prove important.'

Karrion grins, proud of his achievements, and I smile. He no longer asks if I am sure he should contact Jamie direct. With every case we work on together, he becomes less my apprentice and more my business partner.

'What about the Circle of Shamans?' I ask.

'Unfortunately, Lord Ellensthorne spoke the truth when he told you last month that Phillep Marshell lost his job right before Ellensthorne hired you. Two days earlier, to be precise.'

'Do you buy his claim that the list he gave us was updated to exclude Marshell?'

'I'm more than happy to think the worst of Lord Ellensthorne,' says Karrion, 'but it makes sense for him to give us up-to-date information. Otherwise, he's wasting our time and the High Council's money.'

'The latter is all he cares about, I'm sure. It's a shame we couldn't find a connection between Marshell losing his seat in the Circle and Lord Ellensthorne.'

'Funny you should say that.' Karrion clicks on another file on his computer. 'I've been looking through the statements published by the Circle of Shamans over the past year and I found one where Phillep Marshell criticised the new direction of the High Council in spending less money on essential services like schools and the NHS and expecting charities to pick up the slack.'

'When was this?'

'Three weeks before he lost his seat on the Circle.'

'Coincidence?' I ask.

'Doubt it. It gets better. I've become quite familiar with Old London's political machinations over the past month and I've learned to read between the lines a bit. It turns out that the Circle of Shamans is nowhere near as far under Lord Ellensthorne's thumb as he'd like everyone to think. The Council is starting to bend to his will – I don't even dare to speculate what methods he's used to persuade them – but the Elder Shamans are resisting.'

'Good for them. Any sign of how Lord Ellensthorne is dealing with the quiet rebellion?'

'Two other long-standing members of the Circle have lost their seats, one in late December and one last week.'

'Lord Ellensthorne is ridding himself of the resistance,' I say. 'It's a bold move, but not out of character. He's going to have to be careful or else people will start talking.'

'He could do with being the subject of greater scrutiny. It might do away with some of his pompousness. Either way, I'll keep an eye on the Circle meetings. If anyone fails to raise their seat, we'll know.'

'Is there a way to find out the names of the Shamans who've lost their seats?'

'Of course. While no one can hear what's said during the Circle meetings, attendance is a matter of public record. The local government's website notes the attendants for each session, including any who attempted to raise a seat and failed.'

'Are there many of those?' I ask.

'Usually a few. Most Shamans don't realise how much raw power is required to wrench a seat from the square. There are always some who attempt it as a dare without any intention of serving in the Circle. It's a flaw in the selection process, but the Elders argue that anyone prepared to sacrifice so much power to raise their seats possesses, by default, the necessary altruism to become one of them.'

'The realities of the Circle work might come as a shock for many younger Shamans. Keep track of the names. It would be interesting to speak to them to find out if they were inflicted by the same mysterious bug as Marshell was when he lost his seat.'

'Do you still think Lord Ellensthorne is using a Leech to get rid of his political rivals?' Karrion asks.

'You tell me. Have you ever had a genuine illness that has sapped your power?'

Karrion hesitates, covering the silence by running his fingers along the laptop keys. His power has not been the same since Baneacre killed a flock of birds around him and Karrion tried to bring them back to life. Twice I have asked him whether something is hampering his recovery, but both times he has dodged the question. I have to trust that whatever is going on with him, he will confide in me when he is ready.

'No, there's no such illness.'

'That's what I thought, and it's worrying. But there's something that concerns me even more.'

'What's that?' Karrion glances at me, teeth playing with his lip piercing.

'If the cases we investigated in December are part of a

Shadow Mage conspiracy and Lord Ellensthorne is behind Lloid's disappearance, that still doesn't explain which Leech attacked Marshell. He lost his seat five weeks before Lloid disappeared. At that time, Lord Ellensthorne didn't yet know about Lloid's true nature.'

'Where could Lord Ellensthorne have found another one?'

'Where indeed? If Lord Ellensthorne has a supply of Leeches from a different source, his motives for asking us to vet the High Council and the Circle become more genuine.'

'More to the point, what's Lord Ellensthorne doing with a steady supply of Leeches? We need to get our hands on his world domination plan so we can meddle as much as possible. Sinta can help too. Meddling is much easier with a dog in tow.'

I reach across the table to poke his shoulder. 'You've been watching too much television again, haven't you?'

'Let's just say that catch-up services and YouTube have not been my friends since I bought this laptop.'

'Time to get to work then. We have an adulterer to catch.'

2

___

GROUNDWORK

Aleson Hampten has sent me two photos of her husband; one looks like a formal picture from a website, another a holiday snap from somewhere warm. The quality of both is poor. Maerk Hampten has a round, friendly face, with grey eyes and brown hair, which is greying at the temples. He looks more at home in a suit and a tie than in a garish yellow shirt on a beach.

The other photos appear to be from an Outlook calendar. Most days are filled with appointments, but the majority are scheduled as telephone conversations. I point this out to Karrion.

'If he's in the import/export business, he's bound to have clients all over the world,' he says. 'He must have to get in touch with people at all hours of day and night.'

I click through the photos of the calendar. A pattern catches my eye, but I double-check it twice before opening a map. The address I type in points an arrow to Fowler Road in Ilford.

'Hampten goes out to an industrial estate in Ilford twice a week, every week.'

'To do what?'

'I've no idea. Perhaps he stores packaging materials there. Or it's his distribution centre. We need to find out whether his company owns a warehouse on Fowler Road.'

'And if it doesn't?' Karrion asks.

'It could be a cover for an affair, or a rendezvous with a lover.' I jot down the address and hand it to Karrion. 'Find out everything you can about the company, including any property they own. Companies House must have records. Work your magic, even if it means flirting with people over the paintings of Salvador Dali.'

'If it works, it works.'

'Only for you, my friend.' I laugh.

Karrion draws his laptop closer and opens a search engine. Soon the only sounds in the room are the occasional crackle of wood in the fireplace and the tapping of our keyboards.

Although I find Hampten's company on social media easily enough, they themselves are less present than I had expected. Their wealth means that they appear in the photos for various charity galas and public events, but I cannot find any indication that they have an affiliation with a specific charity. For once, there seems to be no connection to Lifelines.

I study a photo of Aleson dressed in a purple ball gown and adorned with glittering diamonds. She seems so different from the defeated woman who hired me to help her divorce her husband, but I know not to draw conclusions based on surface veneer. I need only to remember Reaoul and Eolande Pearson to recall what a beautiful shell can disguise.

None of the articles mentioning the Hamptens gives me any insight into their personal lives. All I discover is that they split their time between a luxury flat in Old London and a villa in the Caribbean. The photos reveal no awkward moments where

Maerk is paying attention to another woman while Aleson looks on, leaving me none the wiser about the realities of their relationship.

'What have you got?' I ask when Karrion has finished reading.

'Let me digest for a moment,' he says, and heads to the kitchen.

I hear cupboards opening and closing before Karrion returns with a packet of custard creams. He makes a second trip to fetch us each a glass of water. Finally, he sets a strip of painkillers in front of me.

'What are these for?' I ask.

'You look a little uncomfortable.'

He is right. Although I have remained injury-free for the past month and have recovered well from the wounds Cathwulf inflicted on me, chronic pain is a reality I live with every day. I have been aware of my pelvis beginning to ache, and Karrion must have noticed my attempts to ease the pain. A year ago, his perceptiveness would have made me uncomfortable, but now I swallow two tablets with my water and smile when he refills my glass.

We eat a couple of biscuits in silence, and I am about to suggest lunch when Karrion decides he is ready to share.

'The company is bigger than I expected. In addition to Old London, they've got offices in New York, Berlin, and Tokyo, with plans to expand to China and India as well. Reading between the lines, while they run a courier service for regular antiquities and valuables, the big money is in transporting magical artefacts and ingredients. Several auction houses use them as their chosen courier and they have a similar relationship with some big international suppliers of spell components.'

'Magic is a bigger business than I had realised,' I murmur.

'It's nice for those with the capital to set up a business like that. You can't put mana gems and volatile potions in a regular cardboard box and send them in the post. They need special crates and insulation. Also, not everything can be shipped in a plane because of the explosion risk.'

'Typical Mage magic, always so flashy.' The corner of my mouth lifts as I repeat Karrion's criticism of the Mages entertaining crowds at One Magic Change.

'Tell me about it. In any case, Mercury Deliveries is doing very well. The majority of the customer reviews I read were positive and the firm was quick to resolve any problems. I even went on a website that lets employees leave anonymous reviews of the workplace for others to see, but there was nothing about the company there.'

'What about the warehouse? Does it belong to Mercury Deliveries?'

'It does. But the thing is, I don't see why the CEO would visit a warehouse regularly. They don't take part in stocktaking or packing items. Even if they were shipping something especially valuable, I'd expect Hampten to wine and dine the client instead of getting his hands dirty.'

'You're right. We need to check out that warehouse,' I say.

'A road trip to Ilford? You're spoiling me.'

'Never let it be said that I don't look after my employees.'

'I'd compare notes if there were more of us,' Karrion says with a laugh.

'Let's take it slow for now. Did you find out anything about the company finances?'

'As far as I can tell from the annual accounts, the profits have grown every year. There's no sign that the company is in financial difficulties. Also, Aleson and Maerk own the majority of the shares in Mercury Deliveries. If she does divorce him, she's going to be very wealthy.'

'Based on the photos I've seen, I don't think she's short of money now.'

I recount the few observations I gleaned from my research, but between us, we have discovered nothing suspicious aside from the visits to the warehouse; so that needs to be the starting point for our new assignment.

'How do you feel about some clandestine surveillance work?' I ask.

'You mean skulking in darkened doorways with a cup of stale coffee and a hand-rolled cigarette? I already have the leather duster, but I might need to buy a fedora. Unless you have one in a cupboard somewhere?'

'No such luck. Also, your mum is going to kill me if you take up smoking on my watch.'

'I'm a grown man and free to make unwise decisions.'

'Not on my time, you aren't.'

Karrion crosses his arms in mock irritation. 'Before you crush any more of my dreams, what is it that you'd like me to do?'

'Go to the Old London office of Mercury Deliveries and find a quiet spot to watch the front door. If Maerk Hampten leaves the office at any time, follow him at a discreet distance. If that doesn't make you feel enough like a spook, you're free to take as many photographs of him as you desire.'

'Awesome, Yan. I'm on it!' He leaps out of his chair with such enthusiasm he almost knocks his laptop off the table. Casting an apologetic glance my way, he throws on his leather jacket. 'I'll keep you posted on my progress. Will you be manning the command centre?'

'No. The Circle of Shamans is meeting in an hour and there are two Shamans I haven't been able to check before. I'm hoping they'll turn up today and I can complete that part of our assignment.'

'Lord Ellensthorne will be so pleased. But do you really think a Leech could masquerade as a Shaman, especially one strong enough to raise a seat in the Circle? It requires more than just raw power. It needs sheer strength of will.'

'Don't you think a creature determined to hide so publicly in Old London possesses an above average willpower?' I ask. 'If they're capable of casting enough magic to be given a seat on the High Council of Mages, it stands to reason that they would find a way into the Circle as well.' I pause, closing my eyes as the medication takes effect and the pain blurs around the edges. 'Karrion, I need to know for certain. I screwed up with Gerreint Lloid and I'm not going to do that again. If there are more Leeches in the Council or the Circle, I need to find them.'

'If you do, what then?'

'Then we're going to put arrangements in place to protect the Leeches before I tell Lord Ellensthorne and Mr Whyte about them.'

'Okay. Let me know where you're at and we can decide when and where to meet.'

With a wave, Karrion leaves. I tidy away the glasses and the remaining biscuits. Sinta stirs at my movements, and after a quick trip outside, I spend five minutes working through basic obedience training. It's enough to tire her out, and she offers no howled protests when I strew the lounge with chews and toys and close the door behind me.

A chill January wind stings my eyes as I leave the shelter of the Guildhall and step on to the square of geometric stones. While the Mages serving on the Council all wear silk cloaks identifying their school of magic, the Shamans bear no emblems of position or their spirit animal. All I see are men and women wrapped tight against the elements as they wait for the allotted time.

The Guildhall clock tower strikes once in a shower of orange sparks. It is fifteen minutes until the Elders begin their meeting. All around the square, Shamans approach, ready to choose their seats. Two Paladins in full armour usher tourists away from the centre of the square and the Shamans. I circle the group at a safe distance, checking the faces partially hidden by hats and scarves for the two supposed Shamans I am here for.

Luck is on my side. I recognise a young woman just as she takes her place next to one of the black stones. While a middle-aged woman in a pink parka raises her seat with practised ease, I shift between the onlookers, inching closer to my target. A group of Japanese tourists and their cameras block my path. I hurry around the group, concern fuelling my steps, but I need not have worried. Eiva Langden has not moved.

I watch her as I approach, keeping several people between us. Eiva bites her lower lip as the ground beside her shudders and groans. The stone rises in reluctant jerks until about two feet of the pillar stands above ground. Despite the cold weather, beads of sweat slide down her temples and her face takes on a greyish tinge. A gust of wind blows past her, and I tilt my chin up. The familiar sour tang sends a shiver of fear down my spine. She is a Leech.

Eiva sits on the pillar, bracing one hand on her knee, while the other remains in her coat pocket. She must be using mana gems, though that ought to be impossible. Tinker Thaylor told us that only Mage power can be stored in gems, though she was wrong about only Mages being able to access that power. Or could it be that Eiva has stolen enough magic from a Shaman to raise her seat? If that's the case, is the Shaman still alive?

Little by little, her pillar rises higher. While there are others, most likely the more recent members of the Circle, who take their time in raising their seats, she is by far the slowest. But she joins the others at the correct height within the set time limit. I cannot help wondering what benefit she gets from putting herself through such an ordeal. More than that, Eiva still has to lower the pillar from its height of approximately fifty feet. It will be a long drop to the square if she fails.

The woman in the pink parka raises her hands, signalling that the meeting has begun. No one outside of the Circle can hear what is said when the seats are raised. I have never thought to ask Karrion whether it is a side effect of wrenching stones from the square or whether Mages have set a permanent silence ward around the Circle. Either way, when the meetings are in progress, the weather has no impact on the Shamans and they have absolute privacy.

Careful to keep myself behind Eiva, I weave between people on my way to the edge of the square. I find myself a discreet spot around the corner of a small church. While the meeting continues, I call up a copy of the file on the Circle of Shamans I have on my phone and check Eiva Langden's details. She is down as a Rabbit Shaman and lives near Barbican, not far from my flat.

I have enough time to pick up a coffee and check in with Karrion before the pillars begin to descend. He offers to come and help me, but watching Hampten is more important if we are to close the case quickly. Delaying it would be better for business, but increasingly I have felt that the bread and butter cases that help us stay afloat don't matter. So what if a rich Mage is having an affair, when we are yet to solve a Shaman girl's kidnapping and Lloid is still missing? Old London is my home, and as a Wild Folk, I have a strong instinct to look after it.

Eiva is among the first to leave the meeting, and I follow her at a discreet distance. She stops to buy groceries and to browse in a bookshop, but otherwise she makes her way home on foot. Her flat is in a newer building, which looks a step up from where Lloid lived, but it is by no means fancy. I hang around the building for half an hour, keeping a careful eye on the windows, but when my legs begin to ache and nothing happens, I leave.

My stomach tells me it's high time I had lunch, and I pick up a sandwich on my way to the Mercury Deliveries' head office. When I arrive at the right street, I expect to find Karrion huddled in a doorway to fulfil his PI dreams, but opposite the office building is a vegan café. Karrion is in a window seat. He grins and waves me inside.

'Hi, Yan. You need to try these turmeric lattes. They're pretty tasty.'

An empty plate is on the counter next to him, and he is tucking into a piece of chocolate cake. He shows me a mug containing steaming yellow liquid. I take a tentative sip. The taste is better than I expected, and I walk to the counter to order myself a cup and a slice of carrot cake.

'This isn't quite the dingy doorway I was expecting,' I say when I take a seat next to him.

'True, but let's face it, it's bloody freezing outside. There were only so many times I could stamp my feet and blow into my hands before I drew attention to myself.'

'Any sign of Maerk Hampten?' I ask, keeping my voice low enough that the other customers cannot overhear us.

'Not yet. There was a mass exodus at lunchtime, but as much as I kept a close eye on everyone, I didn't see him.'

'I wonder...' Unlocking my phone, I search for the main office number and dial it.

'Good afternoon. Mercury Deliveries.'

'Hi, is it possible to speak to Maerk Hampten, please?'

'I'm afraid Mr Hampten is out of the office today. Can anyone else help you?'

'That's okay. I'll send him an email,' I say.

'Have a good afternoon.'

'You too,' I say, and end the call.

'Maybe we should have started from that,' Karrion says, but he does not appear perturbed by the wasted morning.

'It never occurred to me that he wouldn't be there. Isn't the boss supposed to be in the office all the time?'

'Possibly not if the boss is busy shagging a secretary.'

'Perhaps. But it looks like we're going to have to catch him at the warehouse.'

'What time was the meeting in the calendar?' Karrion asks.

'Seven o'clock.'

'We've got a few hours still, even taking into account driving to Ilford. What are we going to do until then?'

'I'd like to give your surveillance skills a bit more practice. One of the Elders of the Circle is a Leech.'

Karrion straightens in his seat, almost sweeping his plate off the counter in the process. 'I was wrong and you were right. Are we going to tail him?'

'Yes, we are, as much as we're able. And the Leech is a her, not him.'

'A female Leech? That's a first.'

'There's been nothing to suggest being a Leech is specific to one gender. Though if Gideor Braeman was as much of a letch as Ilana suggested, I'm not sure why any woman would choose to trust him with the secret of their true identity. Perhaps ambition overruled common sense.'

'Or perhaps he knew about her already?' At my puzzled look, Karrion elaborates. 'What I'm saying is that just because we don't know anything about Leeches' sense of community doesn't mean they don't have one. I can't think of a single magical race who isn't drawn to others of their kind. Even Feykin work together when it suits them.'

'You may be right. Most people in Old London think Leeches are an urban myth. That probably makes it easier to hide in plain sight. If a person feels low on power, they'd assume their recent activities have tired them out, not that a Leech has stolen magic from them. You'd have to be aware of Leeches to notice them. I'd heard the rumours, but I still didn't spot what Jans was doing until he attacked me.'

'Yet one of the first things Lord Ellensthorne said to you was about Leeches,' Karrion says.

'Yes, but he was blackmailing Braeman. My guess is, as soon as he figured out that Braeman wasn't a Light Mage, Lord Ellensthorne did as much research into Leeches as he could. Aside from magic, knowledge is the ultimate source of power in Old London.'

'Is it just me or is the prospect of Lord Ellensthorne knowing more than we do a frightening thought?'

'It is, but so far, it's also true. He's been several steps ahead of us for the past few months. Try as we might, we've not yet caught up.'

'But this new Leech changes things, doesn't it?'

'It does,' I say. 'And this time, we're not alone.'

I give Eiva's address to Karrion and finish my coffee. The health benefits of the turmeric are not immediately apparent, but Karrion tells me to be patient as he leaves. I linger just long enough to find Jamie's number in my contacts. He answers after just two rings.

'Afternoon, Yannia.'

'Hi, Jamie. Do you have a moment?'

'Sure. What's going on?'

While the traffic noise in the street goes a long way towards keeping the call private, I lower my voice just the same. 'I found another Leech.'

Jamie's chair creaks in the background, and I imagine him straightening in his seat. 'In the High Council?'

'No, in the Circle.'

'But isn't it harder for them to pretend to be a Shaman, given the entry requirements into the Circle?'

'I've already had this conversation today with Karrion,' I say, resisting a smile. 'It would appear not.'

'Fair enough. Have you told them yet? You know, your employers in this.'

He must be somewhere with people around him. I lower my voice again, mindful of the people walking past me.

'Not yet. We know where she lives and we'll keep an eye on things for a little while first. That way she'll be under observation when I break the news. If someone tries to take her, we'll be there to witness it and even step in.'

'Good plan. I can do some digging into her past, if that would be of use to you? Unofficially, of course.'

'Yes, that would be very helpful. She may well be living under a false identity, like Lloid. I'll message you her details.'

'Thanks. I'll let you know what I find out.' A door closes in the background, cutting off some of the noise. 'And, Yannia? Be careful. There's a good chance every Leech in Old London recognises you by sight these days. Given what happened to Lloid, they may be feeling twitchy. I'd hate to see you or Karrion get hurt. Especially when the Leeches don't know that you're trying to protect them.'

'Up to a point, we are. The sooner we can eradicate them from Old London's political structure, the safer we'll all be.'

'Regardless, keep a safe distance between you and her at all times. If she spots you, it's better to let her go than give chase.'

'Agreed. We're not going to do anything stupid.'

Jamie and I say our goodbyes. I send him the information straight away, relay his warning to Karrion, and head home.

———

Sinta is waiting at the lounge door and she wriggles in my arms as I carry her to the window. After she has been out, I pack her bowl and food in a bag. She knows what this means and parks herself firmly in front of the door. I scoop her up on my way past and carry her first down and then up to the street level.

The pub is quiet; only a few regulars sit at the bar. An older couple is finishing cups of coffee in a nearby corner, and the landlord, Funja, is carrying a tray of sandwiches to a larger group. Behind the bar, in the darkest corner of the pub, Wishearth is exactly where I expected. It may be my imagination, but the tables around his seem to have shifted a little further away.

Sinta rushes to Boris, Funja's Irish wolfhound, whimpering as she tries to lick his nose. Boris tolerates her attention with the grace and dignity of greater age, although, in truth, I know he adores her. I unclip Sinta's lead, certain she will be safe in the pub, and continue to Wishearth's table.

'I see you've decided my evening plans for me,' he says with a chuckle.

The scent of wood smoke curls around as Wishearth watches me with dark eyes. Even in the warmth of the pub, he is dressed in a mariner's peacoat and the heat does not seem to bother him. I would like to ask him about that and many other things, but he has a habit of either answering with another question or distracting me altogether.

'Hopefully Funja won't mind,' I reply, not wishing to prolong the silence. 'Karrion and I have work to do tonight and

I'm not sure how long it's going to take. If you can have Sinta for the evening, it will give her a change of scenery.'

'We're glad to have her anytime.' Wishearth takes a sip from his pint of Guinness and leans forward. 'You don't have to worry about a thing when it comes to Sinta.'

While I am familiar with Wishearth's penchant for cryptic remarks, they always give me pause. Is he just talking about tonight, or does he mean something else? Before I have a chance to ask, he winks.

'New year, eh? You can find all sorts of new ways to get into trouble, if I'm not mistaken.'

'I think I've done a pretty good job at staying out of trouble so far.'

'Perhaps, but we're only halfway through January. How long do you think this trend is likely to continue?'

'Why does everyone think I'm accident prone?' I ask, tugging my coat-sleeve further down to hide a bruise from walking into a door-frame this morning.

'Wasn't it Jamie who suggested last month that Old London's hospitals needed to start offering you frequent bandage miles?'

'Do you eavesdrop on my every conversation?'

'Only on the ones that matter.' Wishearth drains his glass. 'Time for another, I think. Would you mind?'

With a dramatic put-upon sigh, I take his glass and walk to the bar. I order a brandy for myself and another pint for Wishearth. Although his Guinness is always on the house, I set down enough money for both drinks. Funja is often generous, and I want to repay his generosity when I can.

When I return with our glasses, Wishearth is greeting Sinta. She is on his lap, front paws against his chest, while he rubs her sides. Uncomplicated love shines between them, and I swallow down my envy. Nothing is that simple in real life.

As if sensing my thoughts, Wishearth looks up and smiles. There are sparks in his eyes, but none fall. Instead, it's as though a tendril of smoke connects us, tempting me towards him. I take half a step forward, bumping against the edge of the table without really noticing, and open my mouth to speak. Before I have figured out what I want to say, a shard of ice slices through me. In its wake comes hatred so pure that it leaves me feeling inhuman. This man would see me burn and he would laugh while I suffer.

I gasp and take a step back, all but falling into my chair.

'Are you all right?' Wishearth asks, the sparks vanishing from his eyes in an instant. He sets Sinta on the floor and stands up.

The hatred melts away as quickly as it came, leaving only confusion and fatigue. My thoughts are no longer my own, and I hate the feeling of being out of control. But I cannot explain this to Wishearth; the words refuse to form, and I force a smile instead.

'I'm fine. It's just pain.'

Wishearth frowns, but he says nothing and reaches for his pint. I follow suit and relish the burn of the brandy as it slides down my throat. This sort of fire I can handle.

Rather than sit back down, Wishearth circles around the table, each step measured. He stops behind me, and I resist the temptation to twist so I can see him. Instead, I relax back into my seat, intent upon conveying my trust in him. Heat comes off him in waves, seeping into my muscles and bones. It suffocates me, and without thinking, I shy away from him. The heat disappears, and I exhale my relief.

When Wishearth returns to his seat, his frown has deepened into a scowl. I want to explain that it's not his fault, that it's not personal, that something has changed in me; but the words do not come, as if someone has gagged me. Perhaps she has. I have no experience with Fey marks, and the Winter Queen's must be the most powerful of them all.

'I packed everything Sinta is likely to need,' I say, nudging the bag at my feet.

Wishearth nods, but says nothing. His troubled expression remains in place when he moves the bag closer to his chair. Unsure what else to do, I rise and whisper a goodbye. I am no further than a couple of steps away when he calls my name, causing me to turn.

'Be careful. The pawns are closing in.'

___

3

CRY FOR HELP

I pick up Karrion a few streets from Eiva Langden's flat. He cranks the heating up and presses his hands against the blower. I pass him a Thermos of tea, which he all but yanks from my hands.

'You're the best.' Karrion unscrews the top and breathes in the steam. 'But don't think I haven't noticed how I have to do all the cold and boring stuff. Without an audiobook to keep me company, I might have died out there.'

'You're the one who wanted to emulate the PIs of old by watching criminals from shadowed alleys. I never claimed it would be in any way glamorous or exciting.'

'Being a gumshoe is much more fun during the summer.'

'I'll remind you of that when you don't want to wear a leather duster and a fedora during a heatwave.' The light turns red, and I brake. 'There are sandwiches for you in the bag by your feet. Smoked salmon and cream cheese.'

'Wow, you don't often make an effort.'

'I'm full of surprises.' I grin. 'Also, I bought them from a café.'

'That's more like it.'

Karrion eats while I tell him about my phone call with Jamie and Wishearth's parting words. After pouring a second cup of tea, he passes it to me and I take a sip.

'Do you think Wishearth has taken up chess?' he asks.

'It's possible. He must pass his days somehow.'

We pass through the invisible barrier between New and Old London. I feel the difference immediately. It is as though all background noise has been cut off. Some part of me is always aware of the echoes of rituals, spell graffiti, and magical auras brushing mine. They all form part of Old London's lure, but I am a rarity among the residents in being conscious of it. I once described the sensations to Karrion, whose response was puzzled curiosity. Perhaps it is a Wild Folk ability, like detecting auras or identifying other magic users by their scent. We are more attuned to our surroundings, even in the city.

'Are you worried about what Wishearth said?' asks Karrion.

'If I had a better idea of what he's hinting at, I might be. He's always been right, but never all that specific.'

'How do you expect him to maintain his air of mystery if he gives you clear and helpful advice?'

'There is that.' I switch lanes. 'Did you see Eiva?'

'No, and I'm convinced there's nothing glamorous about our job now.'

'That's the spirit.'

Slowed by the evening rush hour, we reach the industrial estate just after half past six. I park a few streets from the warehouse, and we walk the rest of the way. As we round the corner to Fowler Street, a taxi stops at the far end and a woman steps out. Beneath her long coat, flashes of a red dress show when she moves. She disappears between two buildings.

'Damn, she's early,' I say. 'Let's go.'

With a glance around the quiet street, we quicken our steps. By the time we reach the correct address, the woman is nowhere to be seen. I curse under my breath and look around.

'Is this where she came?'

'I think so, though I'm not sure,' Karrion says.

The warehouses along the street are all about the same size and most are emblazoned with company logos and adverts, but the building we are after has a discreet plaque with *Mercury Deliveries* on it. A main entrance appears to lead to a small office at the front, and there are signs indicating that lorries dock at the back. The sticker next to the door tells us that the warehouse closed at five.

'Let's take a look around the back. Maybe we can find windows or another way in.'

'It occurs to me that a warehouse is a pretty good place for an illicit affair,' Karrion says, keeping his voice down. 'Not the most romantic, but definitely a good way to keep people from seeing something they shouldn't.'

'That's not good news for us.'

A small lorry is parked on the side of the building with no one in the cockpit. As we pass it, I hear the faint ticking of a cooling engine, but I dismiss it as unimportant. I doubt Hampten drove here in a lorry.

The loading docks are at the back, with enough space between the fence and the building for small lorries to turn. Two roll-down doors are closed and locked. An electronic keypad next to each glows in the darkness. In one corner of the dock, a narrow window set high on the wall is slightly ajar.

'Can you check round the other side?' I ask, and peer at the window.

'Sure. Just don't go anywhere.'

'Where would I go? I can't fly. You're the Bird Shaman here. If anyone's going to sprout wings, it's you.'

'Working on it,' he mutters.

I cast a curious glance at him, but he leaves without looking back. There is something I am missing about him, something he is choosing not to share. I feel a flash of disappointment. Why doesn't Karrion trust me?

A sound from within the warehouse draws my attention back to the task at hand. Was that a cry for help? I move as close to the wall as I can and call upon the ears of a fox. The sound comes again.

'Help! Somebody help.'

It is a woman's voice, faint but still recognisable, and it comes from somewhere further inside the building. I can barely hear her. Looking around, I search for something to stand on, but the area is clear. I test the rolling doors and find them both locked. With my heightened hearing, I track Karrion's approaching footsteps and climb down from the loading bay.

'Did you hear her?' I ask, a little breathless.

'Hear who?'

'The woman calling for help.'

'I didn't hear anything, but there're no windows or doors along that wall. What did she say?'

'She asked someone to help her and she sounded really scared.' I pace, filled with nervous energy. 'We need to find a way in.'

'Should we check the front door?'

'Let's.'

We jog around the building, and I ignore the small aches blooming in my joints. The front door is locked, and there are no windows on this side of the warehouse. I crouch to peer through the lock, but see nothing.

'Help! Somebody help.'

The plea comes again and without my magic, I would have missed it. I am not certain whether the call is getting fainter or if we are further away from her. Either way, she sounds terrified.

'Did you hear that?'

'No. I don't have your ears.'

'We need to help her.' I curse myself for never having asked Fria to teach me how to pick simple locks. We could use a professional thief at the moment.

'Shouldn't we call the Paladins? Or Jamie?'

'It's going to take forever for them to come here. What if Hampten spotted us and thought his mistress was entrapping him? Or what if this has nothing to do with an affair and she's being attacked by someone other than Hampten?'

'Sounds like a huge coincidence.' Karrion silences my frustrated retort by raising his hand. 'But I'm not saying we shouldn't do anything. We need to figure out a way in.'

'That window at the back,' I say straight away. 'If you can boost me up, I might be able to fit through it.'

'And what, take on a murderous Mage by yourself?' Karrion crosses his arms.

'No, I'll open the door for you, of course.'

'Oh, all right then.'

'Less talking, more moving. Come on.'

We hurry back the way we came and climb on to the loading dock. I pat my jacket to check that the torch Karrion gave me for Christmas is safely in the inside pocket. Even if the warehouse is lit, the cold iron blade hidden within the grip may come in handy.

'Once I'm inside, call the Paladins. And call Jamie. While I think this is likely to be a magical affair and therefore the first responders ought to be Paladins, he may be able to help. At the very least, he can smooth the way after I break into this building.'

'Got it.'

Karrion leans against the wall and laces his fingers together. I place my foot on his hands, and he lifts me far easier than I expected. Caught off guard, I have to grab the window ledge to avoid falling backwards.

Luck is on my side. The window opens inwards and the gap is large enough for me to squeeze through. I peer into the room, but no lights are on. With a whisper of magic, the darkness resolves into shapes. The space beyond is dominated by stacks of flat-packed cardboard boxes and piles of wooden pallets. A line of light shines from beneath a door at the far end of the room.

'Hurry up,' Karrion hisses behind me. 'You're not light as a feather, you know.'

I draw myself up and wriggle my torso through the window. There is no room to twist around, so I have no choice but to use the agility and stealth of a lynx as I drop down, landing on my hands and knees. Even with the use of my magic, the fall still sends shocks of pain up my wrists. Hands raised and ready to defend myself, I rise and listen. The only sound I hear is Karrion calling the Paladins.

When no one barges into the room, I inch forward to inspect the rolling doors next to me. Another electric keypad glows in the darkness of the room. Without a code, I have no way of letting Karrion in. I shoot him a quick text. Gliding forward on soft lynx paws, I cross the room to the door with light shining from beneath it. Almost without conscious thought, I find the torch inside my jacket. I am about to touch the door-handle when my ears register a sound, fainter this time.

'Help! Somebody help.'

The door opens at the slightest tugging, and I keep it shielding me until the gap is wide enough to slip through. I drop on to all fours and peer around the door, ready to dive for cover.

The corridor ahead of me is dark and empty. The door to my left and another on the right stand closed, as does a third at the end of the corridor. A faint light is shining from under the one to my left.

My skin prickles from the presence of magic, though I have no way of identifying it. Have I triggered an alarm ward by opening the door?

'Help! Somebody help.'

Now the words sound quiet and distorted, but there is no mistaking their source: she is behind the left door. I slide forward until my ear is pressed against the wood. A faint rustle is the first sign of movement, followed by the scuffle of shoes against the floor and a low growl. The door has no lock, and I ease it open.

This room is smaller. Two lamps on the floor cast giant shadows across the windowless walls. A man is standing in the centre, dressed in black and with his back to me. There is no sign of the woman we saw, but the walls are lined with indistinct shapes. My heightened vision suffers from the glare of the lamps, and I let go of the magic. Straight away, I wish I hadn't.

Along the walls, shadows form into large black dogs, which rise to their feet. At the first sight of them, I am back in the Unseen Lands, pursued by the dark Fey hounds. My breath catches in my throat as I recall their burning eyes and terrible bays.

A low growl reverberates around the room, and the man whirls around. The lights are behind him, leaving his face in shadows, but his build and hairstyle match those of Maerk Hampten.

'How are you here?' he asks, words slurred and uncertain.

Something about his demeanour feels off, but the thought is drowned by my concern for the woman and my fear of the hounds. I step into the room, fumbling for my torch, and look around for her. She is not here. Confusion worms through my fear. I heard her voice from this room. I am certain of it. Where could she have gone? There are no other doors or any windows.

'How are you here?' Hampten repeats, beginning to sound angry.

As if responding to his emotions, the dogs' growls deepen. The sound echoes around the room, and mixed in with it is raw power. Their wildness entices me, tempting the primal part of me to join their pack. I shake my head to try to clear it, but I am caught in an expanding web of savage magic. The hounds' anger sweeps me down a rapid of primitive emotion, and my fury finds its target.

'Where is she?' I growl at Hampten.

Hampten's face twists into a grimace. 'I'll never tell.'

The hounds are closing in, but whether to help or hinder me, I am not certain. I try to call upon my enhanced senses to aid me, but all I smell is the foul breath of the Fey hounds, all I hear are the jeering calls of the Fey, and all I taste is Cathwulf's blood sliding down my throat. What need have I for logical thought when my instincts serve me well?

My numb fingers let go of the torch, but it takes an eternity before I hear the metallic thunk of it hitting the ground. I am swept away by the rising tide of power in the room, unable to resist the anger and hunger that vibrate through my body. When Hampten flexes his fingers into claws and drops into a crouch, it is all the invitation I need. Moving as one, the hounds and I leap forward.

4

____

AWAKENING

My consciousness returns when someone picks up my hand and presses two fingers against the inside of my wrist. I am lying on something cold and hard, and my face is wet. My body aches, as if I have battled a Wild Folk and lost. When I try to open my eyes, it takes me a few tries before my lashes separate.

The first thing I see is a Paladin's sword pointed at my throat, the jewels glowing with menace. Hairs at the back of my neck prick up at the proximity to deadly spells waiting to be unleashed.

A second Paladin is checking my pulse, but she draws back when she notices that my eyes are open. The hand she was holding is covered in blood, and I become aware of a rich salty taste in my mouth. I swallow, and my power stirs at the taste of magical blood.

A dark lump is lying on the floor next to me. As I struggle to a sitting position, my eyes focus and I recognise Maerk Hampten. Or, more specifically, what is left of him. His hands are torn and bloodied and his throat is ripped open. Before I woke up, I had been lying in the pool of blood spreading around him.

Did I do this? Did I lose control of my wild instincts and kill a man?

The taste in my mouth takes on a new meaning, and I turn away. Nausea rises like a wave, but although I gag, I manage to avoid vomiting. I wish I could wipe away the awful taste from my mouth, but my hands are equally bloodied. Shivers run through me, and I hug my knees to my chest. As I do so, a pain lances through my side, where the silver Fey scar is a permanent reminder of the battle I fought in the Unseen Lands.

A whisper of metal against metal is the first warning of what's to come. A third Paladin enters with chains forged from cold iron, true silver, and heart copper. As much as my instincts tell me to get as far away from the magic-nulling metals as I can, I offer no resistance when the Paladin closes manacles around my ankles, wrists, and throat.

'Yannia Wilde,' he says in a formal tone, 'I hereby detain you on suspicion of murdering an as yet unidentified male. Your case will be fairly investigated and if sufficient evidence against you is found, you will face judgement by a Herald of Justice.'

They help me up, and I am grateful for the support when my legs buckle. I raise my hand as much as the chains allow, and the Paladins give me a moment to find my footing. We leave the room, and it is only in the corridor that I realise the hounds are gone. Were they ever there, or did I simply imagine them? Could the Winter Queen's mark be wreaking havoc with my perception of the world to such an extent that I have lost control of my powers?

My thoughts are beginning to clear, and I recall the reason why I entered the warehouse in the first place.

'Did you find a woman anywhere?' I ask.

'A woman?' The Paladin to my left frowns. 'We didn't find

anyone else in the building. Are you saying there's a second victim?'

'I...' Struggling to make sense of my jumbled memories, I think back to the last clear image. It was Karrion boosting me up towards the window. 'I heard a woman calling for help. That's why I came here. Inside, I mean.'

'That's what your apprentice told us.'

My stomach lurches. 'Where's Karrion? Is he all right?'

'He's fine. Worried about you and angry we wouldn't let him into the building. He seems to think that his New Scotland Yard consultancy ID is as good as a badge or a Paladin's sword. I believe he was trying to persuade your detective friend to vouch for him.'

'Jamie?'

'Could be. I didn't catch the name.'

The pain in my side intensifies. Weakness seems to leech from the epicentre and it spreads through me until I struggle to walk. The Paladins notice this and they slow their pace. Even though they suspect me of murder, they are still prepared to show me compassion.

'Can I rest for a moment?' I ask, my voice barely above a whisper.

'We have a van right outside the main door. You can rest there.'

Although I feel like every step is too much to bear and I will soon collapse, we manage to shuffle down the echoing corridor, through another door, past the office, and into the sharp winter air. The scent of frost refreshes me, and the last two yards to the van are easier.

'Yan!'

At Karrion's frantic shout, I turn to watch as two Paladins stop him from approaching. They have to grab his arms and hold him back, and still he struggles. It is only when Jamie appears from behind the van to lay a hand on Karrion's shoulder and murmur something in his ear that Karrion relaxes.

'It's fine,' Jamie says. 'He's not going to do anything stupid. Right?'

His last word is directed at Karrion, who nods.

The Paladins release their grip, and Karrion straightens his leather duster. He is like a cockerel rearranging his ruffled feathers. Jamie and Karrion approach.

'Christ, Yannia, are you all right? Whose blood is that?' Without waiting for a reply, Jamie turns to the Paladins. 'Have you checked her for injuries?'

'The blood is not hers.'

'Then whose blood is it?' Jamie asks at the same time as Karrion speaks up.

'Did you find her, Yan? And why are you in chains?'

At their worried stares, the true extent of my predicament dawns on me. Shame heats my cheeks as tears well in my eyes.

'I think I killed someone.'

The Paladins drive me back to Old London and to the Brotherhood of Justice. There, with the help of scenes of crime officers from the Metropolitan Police, they take my clothes, swab my face and hands, dig under my fingernails, comb through my hair, and photograph everything. I receive a grey tracksuit and white socks before I move to the next room, where a Paladin healer examines me. When I mention the pain in my side, she checks the scar, but it's no different from the usual silver colour. Other than that, I only have scrapes and bruises, but no serious wounds.

'I need my regular pain medication,' I say as the healer has finished treating my hands.

'What medication do you use?'

Her eyebrows rise when I list my medications until I explain that I have EDS. She promises to contact my doctor and organise prescriptions.

'Do you feel well enough to give a statement?'

'I might as well get it over and done with.'

She escorts me to one of the interrogation rooms, where two Paladins are waiting for me with a woman I assume is a human detective. I am still chained and my ability to identify people by scent is gone. There is a two-way mirror on the wall opposite the door, and I wonder whether Jamie and Karrion are watching from the other side.

The woman identifies herself as Detective Inspector Hughes and explains that she will be conducting an investigation into the death of the man who is presumed to be Maerk Hampten, but who has not yet been positively identified.

'These Paladins are present as independent witnesses and to ensure that you receive fair treatment throughout the investigation. If you would like to have a legal advocate or a support worker present, you can request one at any point. Do you understand?'

'Yes.'

'Can you confirm your name, address, and date of birth?'

I rattle off my personal details without bothering to explain that my birthday is an estimate. The conclave does not record births and deaths in the same way as the rest of the country. We keep track of the turns of the seasons, the slow dance of stars across the sky, and cycles of the moon, but not days and dates.

'Please tell us in your own words what happened. As you do so, please be aware that the Paladins have cast a truth zone in this room and they will know if you are being dishonest. If at any point you don't wish to continue, you can say so. Likewise, if you want representation, we can pause the interview.'

Once again I confirm that I understand, and I take a moment to gather my thoughts. My voice is steadier than I was expecting as I relay the assignment I received from Aleson Hampten, the background work we did, and how Karrion and I arrived at the warehouse. My narrative is clear as I talk about how we investigated the outside of the building and when I first heard the woman's cries for help; but everything after I went through the window is fragmented, as if I am holding shards of a broken mirror and the picture is distorted beyond recognition.

'There was a door, a corridor, and another door. The woman's voice was growing fainter, but I was sure it came from the other side of the door. I opened it and someone was there. The shadows turned into dogs, or possibly Fey hounds, but I can't remember if they were threatening or helping me. After that, everything is a jumble of anger, fear, and magic. Until I woke up, surrounded by Paladins.'

'Did you kill Maerk Hampten?' DI Hughes asks.

'I don't know.'

She looks to the Paladins, who both shake their heads. I can't figure out whether that means they know I am lying or that I am telling the truth. Exhaustion washes over me, and I struggle to keep my eyes open. The emptiness of being separated from nature strikes me for the first time. I pull at the manacles around my wrists, but they offer no give. Without a key, there is no way out of these chains.

As if sensing my discomfort, DI Hughes closes her notebook. 'We can finish for today. As we process more of the evidence, we may wish to interview you again.'

'Of course. I want to find out what happened as much as you do.'

Some of the tension around the Paladins' eyes leaves, and I guess they have dropped the truth zone. They escort me out of the interrogation room and through the labyrinthine corridors to the prison wing. Only people waiting for judgement or execution are housed within the Brotherhood. My cell is identical to the one in which I interviewed Jonathain Marsh. It has a table with a single chair, a small bathroom cubicle, a bed, and a narrow wardrobe. One of the Paladins removes the chains and unlocks the manacles around my wrists and ankles while the other stands guard. Only the collar remains.

'There are toiletries in the bathroom, a change of clothes in the wardrobe, and someone will bring you a light meal soon. Do you have any dependents you need to make arrangements for?'

I silently thank Wishearth that I took Sinta to the Open Hearth for the evening. She will be in good hands there, and I trust Funja and Wishearth are happy to keep her for longer than overnight.

'No, everything should be fine. But am I allowed to make a phone call?'

'You can do so tomorrow. There will also be visiting hours in the morning and evening. We understand that Detective Inspector Manning and your apprentice have been keen to see you.'

The thought of having to see Jamie and Karrion inside a prison cell fills me with shame so strong all I can manage is a nod before I turn away. A small window overlooks the Thames, and I stare out without taking in any of the details.

How could everything have gone so wrong? This morning, I was exasperated because we had a boring adultery case to work on, and now I may have a matter of weeks to live. I have no way of knowing how long it will be before I appear before a Herald, but once judgement has been passed, the execution happens within a week. If I am guilty.

In all my mad plans about leaving the conclave and turning my back on Dearon, I never thought I would do so through dying. Not just dying because I risked my life for a friend and the gamble did not pay off, but dying as a punishment for murder.

I glance at my hands resting on the windowsill. Despite the Paladins processing me, my nails are stained brown with dried blood. For the first time in my life, the sight does not evoke hunger. With desperation bordering on violence, I yank off my clothes and stumble into the bathroom.

The water is unbearably hot, but I welcome the discomfort and angle my face up. When I have all but drowned under the needle-like spray, I reach for the shower gel. It has no scent, and for that I am grateful. I scrub my skin until it is raw, all but tear off my nails, and wash my hair until it is nothing more than a snarl.

When at last I stagger out of the shower, I use half of the toothpaste tube, trying to burn the lingering taste of blood from my mouth. Then I have just enough strength left to dress in the spare clothes the Paladins have left me and crawl into bed. While I was in the bathroom, someone left a tray of food on the table, but I ignore it. Every time I close my eyes, Hampten's torn body floats from the confines of my mind, and bile rises to my mouth.

Why didn't I allow myself to vomit at the warehouse? At least then I would know for certain whether the wild hunger took over and I ate some of Hampten. Now it has been so many hours that my stomach will be empty. I will never know.

I fix my eyes on the opposite side of the cell, searching my memories for any way to clear my thoughts. Finally, I settle on reciting lists of poisonous mushrooms and plants over and over. The lights stay on, for tonight I fear the darkness.

5

___

LOYALTIES

I wake before dawn, disoriented and searching for Sinta's warmth. Pain throbs from the Fey scar, indicating that I have been lying on that side too long. When I roll over, an ache spreads to my joints. I did not check the food tray for pain medication, nor did anyone bring me any.

My stomach rumbles. Hunger has no regard for my mood or my situation. I push myself up, groggy from disturbed sleep and the pain. The sandwiches on the tray have gone stale, and I leave them untouched. Instead, I drink three mugs of water and wish for a cup of coffee.

By the time the morning visiting hour arrives, I have tidied away the clothes I scattered across the floor the previous evening, made the bed, and forced myself to eat the bowl of porridge the Paladins bring me for breakfast. They do not seem to believe in coffee, for breakfast is accompanied by a mug of milky tea, but it goes some way towards easing the headache pressing against my temples.

Karrion and Jamie arrive together. Neither is wearing a coat, but Karrion is holding a notebook and a pencil. He rushes to me, drawing me up from the only seat in the cell, and envelops me in a tight hug. I bury my head in the crook of his neck and will myself not to cry as I breathe in his scent. It is not the scent of a Bird Shaman, but rather the man himself, and it offers me more comfort than I can put into words.

'Is Sinta okay?' I mumble against Karrion's shirt.

'Perfect. Wishearth and Funja both send their love and said that they'll look after her until you're released. She's in great hands.'

'Thank you.'

'How are you?' Karrion asks as he pulls back. 'Other than the obvious, that is.'

I offer them both a watery smile, for I cannot think of anything to say that would even begin to describe the turmoil raging in my mind. Before the silence turns awkward, I direct Jamie to sit on the chair and perch on the edge of my bed. Karrion sits next to me and drapes an arm over my shoulder. I lean against him, savouring his warmth.

Now I have a chance to look at them closer, both Jamie and Karrion appear tired and worried. No doubt they didn't sleep much more than I did. They each have a magic-nulling collar around their neck, which seems like an odd precaution to take with Jamie.

'What can you tell me?' I ask. Treating this as just another case is the only way I will stay sane.

'Not a lot,' Jamie says. 'It's not my case and they're not letting me anywhere near the evidence. The only thing I heard was that the room where you and the body were discovered was full of bloody dog prints, but none were leading in or out.'

Jamie's words trigger a foggy memory.

'There were dogs in the room. Or were they hounds?'

'Hounds?' Karrion grips my shoulder a little tighter. 'Are you sure?'

'No.'

'Hounds, dogs, what's the difference?' asks Jamie.

'I think by hounds, Yannia is referring to the Cù-Sìth, the huge Fey dogs known for hunting humans for sport. According to folklore, hearing them bay three times in a row means certain death.'

'And you think the Fey dogs were in the warehouse last night?'

'I don't know. Everything after I climbed through the window is fragmented. I can't tell what was real and what wasn't.'

'Do you think someone put a spell on you?' Karrion asks.

'It's possible. I think there was a lot of magic inside, but I'm not sure what kind and what it was directed towards.' Resting my head on Karrion's shoulder, I twist to look at him. 'Can you tell me what happened after I went in?'

'Bugger all, that's what. Nothing happened. You texted me. Then I stood on the loading dock after I called the Paladins and Jamie, and tried to listen for any sign that you were in trouble. The Paladins found me there a couple of minutes later.'

'That can't be right.' Jamie frowns. 'Can you remember what time you called me?'

'About five to seven,' says Karrion.

'The Paladins didn't arrive there until at least forty-five minutes later,' Jamie says.

'No,' says Karrion. 'It was only a couple of minutes.'

'Did you check the time?' I ask.

'Well, no, but I can tell the difference between a few minutes and nearly an hour.'

'And you didn't hear anything after I went in?'

'Not a damn thing. I tried channelling my inner owl for a while, but then I developed a hankering for mice and had to give that up. At least when you fought Cathwulf, you made so much noise I knew you were in trouble. But this time, it was like the earth had swallowed you whole.'

Snippets of words spoken in anger rise from the maelstrom of my mind. Was it me who spoke or someone else? Who was I arguing with? What has happened to my memories?

'What about the woman?' I ask. 'Did you hear her calling for help while I was inside?'

'No, Yan. I never heard her.'

Jamie shifts in his seat. In a sudden flash of premonition, I know I'm not going to like what he is about to tell us.

'The thing is, Yannia, no one but you heard a woman calling for help.'

'So what?'

'There could have been a different reason why you wanted to go into the warehouse alone.'

'Such as?'

Rubbing the back of his neck, Jamie studies the scratches on the table's surface. Next to me, Karrion shifts, as impatient as I am.

'Apparently, Mrs Hampten gave a statement to the Paladins about her meeting with you yesterday morning.'

'Why is that so bad? I told the Paladins myself what she hired me and Karrion to do.'

'But you met with her alone, didn't you?' Jamie asks.

'Yes. Karrion had a driving lesson and he arrived just as my meeting with her was ending.'

'It means it will be your word against hers.'

Easing Karrion's arm off my shoulder, I stand. Pain flares in my side, and I rub the area of the Fey scar while I pace to the window and back.

'What did she say?' I try to keep my voice steady, but there is a tremor I cannot hide.

'That after she said she wanted evidence to divorce her

husband, you pointed out that a divorce would mean she'd get half of everything at best, whereas an inheritance would give her everything. You mentioned certain extra services you provide to select clients, but she said no. Apparently, that made you angry.'

'Yan would never–!' Karrion says. His attempt to emphasise his words by leaping up is hindered by the low bed, but with some difficulty, he manages to stand. The glare he directs at Jamie has not lessened as a result of his undignified clambering off the bed. 'No fucking way.'

'I never said any of that,' I say, but my objections are drowned by Karrion's indignation.

'How can you even suggest that?' Karrion advances on Jamie, a finger pointed at Jamie's chest. 'Have you learnt nothing about Yan's character in the past few months? Do you really think she's capable of murder? Don't you know her at all?'

Jamie stands, raising his hands in an attempt to appease Karrion. 'I'm only relaying what I heard. But you must appreciate that I'm looking at this from the perspective of a detective, not as Yannia's friend. And at the moment, I must say things are bleak.'

Lacing my hands with Karrion's, I draw him away. He resists at first, then relents.

'It's fine, Jamie,' I say. 'I understand where you're coming from. But I hope you know I would never offer to assassinate someone or even hint that murder would be an appropriate recourse for infidelity.'

'Her statement goes against everything I know about you. That said, the evidence against you is significant. Unfortunately, my superiors also think so. This will be the only time I am allowed to visit you before the judgement.'

'I thought she was your friend,' Karrion growls.

Jamie glances my way, but avoids eye contact. 'She is. But

given the situation, I must be a police officer first and a friend second.'

'That's a stupid choice.'

'It's fine,' I repeat. 'I don't blame you for thinking about your career even when it looks like I've just ended mine.'

Karrion opens his mouth to argue, but I tug his hand and shake my head. He huffs, but slumps back on the bed. Jamie also sits.

'There's something I don't understand. How could Aleson Hampten lie about our meeting when she gave her statement to the Paladins? Didn't they use a truth zone?'

'They're only reserved for interrogating suspects,' Jamie says.

'Why?'

'It takes a great deal of power to invoke the Heralds' ability to sense human deception, or so I'm told. Think about it: have you ever given a statement on any of your cases with a truth zone in place?'

Karrion and I exchange a glance.

'No, we haven't,' I say.

'There you go. She can say whatever she wants, just like anyone reporting a crime outside of Old London. If she's lying, as you say, she must assume the evidence will support her statement.'

I sigh. 'Which at the moment it does.'

Jamie nods. 'DI Hughes is an excellent detective. She's going to find the truth, whatever it is.'

'Let's hope so.'

Before the mood turns even gloomier, Jamie stands and offers me his hand. When I shake it, he squeezes my shoulder with his other hand and tries to smile.

'I hope we find that this has all been a misunderstanding. Until the judgement, this is goodbye. If I find out anything important, I'll let Karrion know, but everyone at New Scotland Yard knows that I have a conflict of interest on this case.'

'Thanks, Jamie. I appreciate your support,' I say.

'Such as it is,' mutters Karrion.

Jamie flinches, but he does not admonish Karrion. After a final wan smile in my direction, Jamie knocks on the cell door. A Paladin lets him out and locks the door behind him.

6

DEBRIEF

'Jamie is a moron,' Karrion says, glaring at the door.

'He's in a difficult position. We've helped him out several times, but by organising the consultancy position for us, he put his reputation on the line. His superiors no doubt use this as an opportunity to question his judgement on the whole.'

'Speaking of which, Jamie took away my consultant's ID. When I tried to suggest that he could have a discreet look at the case file and we could conduct our own investigation, he told me to mind my own business. Apparently, he's not letting me anywhere near New Scotland Yard or this case.'

'Perhaps it's best if we let the police and the Paladins determine whether I had any involvement in Hampten's death.'

'Bollocks to that,' Karrion says, his jaw set in stubborn defiance. 'Remember how they "investigated" Braeman's death and put the wrong man in front of the Herald? No way am I going to let that happen to you. If anyone is going to get to the truth, it's you and me.'

'There's not a lot I can do at the moment.'

'No, but I can do some digging on my own. While you're

here, I'll be your eyes and ears. I'll report back every day and we'll solve this together.'

'It's going to be difficult without any help from Jamie.'

'So what? We're the dream team. If anyone can find the truth, it's us.'

'Okay, you win.'

'Good.'

Karrion hugs me, and I relax against him. In this moment, it is easy to forget the cell and the charges hanging over me, but the numbness that separates me from my magic is a nagging sensation at the back of my mind. The lack of power is like a missing limb, and a part of me is constantly searching for the threads of nature that would grant me heightened senses, greater strength, and faster speed.

Without my magic, am I still a Wild Folk?

As if sensing my thoughts, Karrion directs me to the chair. 'The sooner we get you out of that collar, the better.'

'I'm not going to argue with that. Let's start from the beginning. Before we arrived at the warehouse, what did we do wrong?'

Karrion opens a new page in his notebook, pen poised over the paper. 'We expected Hampten to be in the office all day, and as a result, I wasted a couple of hours watching the front of the office.'

'What could we have done instead?'

'More background research? A proper dinner break?' He grins when I roll my eyes. 'What do you think?'

'It would have been interesting to find out where Hampten was all day, if not at the office. We could have watched his house to see if he was there before arriving at the warehouse. Perhaps it would have been wiser to delay investigating that regular appointment until we had built a better picture of the man we were trying to spy on.'

'Patience. Is that something we've struggled with in the past?'

We laugh at that, and it feels so good I want to prolong it as much as possible, but a spike of pain in my side causes me to wince and cough.

'Are you hurt?' Karrion asks, amusement changing to concern in an instant.

'I must have suffered a knock to my ribs last night. They've been bothering me ever since.'

'It's not the rib Cathwulf fractured, is it?'

'No, that was on the other side and healed quickly thanks to the Paladins and Lady Bergamon.'

'Did you tell the healer?'

'Yes. She checked the Fey scar, but it looked normal. I'm sure this will pass in a day or two.'

'I can hassle someone to check you again, if you want?'

'No need. If it worsens, I'll speak to the Paladins.'

Karrion nods, but he picks up a plastic cup from the table and fills it with water. I accept it with an understanding smile. It has been some time since I gave up telling Karrion I would be fine on my own and began accepting his help with quiet gratitude. The water sliding down my throat refreshes me, though I experience a stab of longing for the cold spring water at the conclave.

I would be safe there; protected not just by the sentry spirits and my fellow Wild Folk but by the laws of our kind. Justice would be swift, and there would be no need for collars and cells and Heralds of Justice. However, I cannot help wondering what sort of punishment Dearon would mete out to his chosen mate for a crime she may or may not have committed. Would he put me to death or choose clemency?

'Is there someone you'd like me to call?' asks Karrion. 'Lady Bergamon? Or Dearon, perhaps?'

'Lady Bergamon will already know. Wishearth will have told her. As for Dearon, absolutely not. He doesn't need to know anything is going on unless I appear before a Herald and he declares me guilty. Then you may call Dearon.'

'You know, even in a Paladin cell, you're not an island.'

'I'm not trying to be an island. I have you to help me. But what purpose would calling Dearon now serve? At best he'd worry for weeks, at worst he'd insist on coming to Old London. If he wanted to visit me, he'd probably punch a Paladin when they tried to put a collar on him and he'd end up arrested too. Also, do you want to babysit an irritable Wild Folk with questionable social skills?'

Karrion grimaces. 'Point taken. When it comes to people, he seems to have the patience of a carrier bag.'

I put the cup back on the table and lean against the wall. 'Let's get back to the more pressing matter at hand. So we could have done our preparations better. If they don't execute me, I'll do better next time. What about the warehouse? I know you didn't hear the woman's cries for help, but was there anything else that struck you as strange?'

'There was the time I seem to have lost. What's up with that?'

A memory stirs, bringing with it the sensations of unrelenting rain, nausea from cold iron, and decaying flesh. It takes me back to Lord Ellensthorne's study, where I watched him slowly choking to death as I stood over Baneacre, my gun aimed at his face. It was the first time I killed a sentient being in cold blood, and there have been many a night when Baneacre's gaunt ghost has hovered over my bed, his eyes burning with the fire of plague fever and his long fingers creeping to stroke my hair, as one might a faithful hound. In those moments, only building a fire and hugging Sinta close allowed me to soothe my racing heart and slide into a dreamless sleep.

'Can you recall any other instance when you've lost time?'

While he thinks, Karrion rolls his lip piercing backwards and forwards, his teeth clicking against the metal. 'At the Fey Mound,' he says at last.

'That's what I thought too. Did you have your cold-iron necklace on last night?'

'I don't go anywhere without it.' Karrion shoots a glare towards the door. 'Except apparently a cell at the Brotherhood of Justice.'

'If you still lost time, that must mean there was a Fey present at the warehouse. Your necklace should protect you against glamour, even one cast by a first- or second-generation Feykin.'

'What would a Fey have done there? Do you think Hampten had one working for him?'

'I can't imagine what a mortal would have to offer a Fey in return for services rendered, or at least I can't until I find out what the Winter Queen wants from me. Given that she saved my life, I expect she's going to demand a significant reward.'

Dropping the pen on top of his notebook, Karrion strides around the table. He runs a hand through his hair until his blue-black plumage sticks up in every direction.

'Did you have any cold iron on you?' he asks, his gaze sharp with meaning I do not yet understand.

'I had the torch you gave me for Christmas, but I don't recall whether I had a chance to draw the blade. Probably not.'

Karrion turns a full circle, and I can almost hear the rustle of feathers as he preens like a raven.

'Then you had no protection against Fey glamour.'

The implications of Karrion's words spread through me like seedling roots in tilled spring soil. My memories remain jumbled, but there is logic to their fragmentation. An image of a Fey hound rises from the darkness, eyes blazing as it regards me, but it fades without ever evoking the fear I am accustomed to feeling.

'That's why nothing makes sense,' I whisper.

'Exactly. They could have made you see and feel anything they wanted. I'd bet you anything that there were dogs in that room, not Fey hounds, and the glamour confused you.'

'If that's the case, why didn't the Paladins find any dogs when they entered the warehouse?'

'A teleportation circle?' Karrion shrugs. 'It could have been in a dark corner somewhere and it's not like using one causes a shaft of light to shoot to the sky.'

'Let's say a teleportation circle is the right answer, and I'm not saying it is, why would anyone go through the trouble of removing dogs from a crime scene by magical means? What's the point of all this? And what's the point of having a Fey there casting a glamour over us? To what end?'

Karrion opens his mouth, but closes it again with a sheepish smile. 'Yeah, I've no clue.'

'Me neither. There's a whole side to this picture we're not seeing at the moment. All we know for certain is that Maerk Hampten is dead and I was somehow involved in his death.'

'There's another thing we know: Aleson Hampten had her part to play in this. She gave you those photos of the calendar, no doubt knowing that we'd consider the warehouse the best place to start our investigation.'

'And then she lied about my meeting with her,' I add. 'But why?'

'We're going to figure it out. And then we're going to prove you're innocent. Meanwhile, should we discuss how we're going to break you out of this cell?'

'No, Karrion. I'm going to stay here and face the Herald.' When he looks like he wants to argue, I lay a hand on his upper arm. 'I need to find out the truth. I need to know if I lost control.'

'There's no way you could,' Karrion says.

I shake my head. 'We both know how close I came with Cathwulf. Maybe I was going to back off anyway, or maybe I needed you throwing half a tree at me to come to my senses, but the result was the same. I was prepared to tear open her throat.'

'But you didn't.'

'No, but it doesn't mean I couldn't do so under different circumstances, especially if Fey glamour played its part.'

'If a Fey put a spell on you, then it wasn't your fault.'

'Had it been anyone else, would Hampten have ended up with his throat ripped open? There's a reason why we spend so many years learning control at the conclave. We're wild creatures and it's our instincts that allow us to thrive in nature.'

Frustration flickers across his features, but he exhales slowly. 'I understand. We'll do our best to figure this out while we wait to see whether you're called before a Herald or not.'

'Thanks, Karrion.'

A key turning in the lock causes us both to face the door. The same Paladin that let Jamie out steps into the doorway.

'You have five minutes,' he says, and eases the door shut.

'Time flies when we're trying to solve yet another impossible case,' Karrion says, his rueful smile not quite managing to hide his disappointment.

'I appreciate you coming as soon as you could.'

'I would have camped right outside the door if the sodding Paladins would've let me.'

'Pity they're sticklers for rules and regulations.'

'Someone has to be, I guess.' Karrion runs a hand through his hair again. 'Listen, Yan, there's something else you should know.'

'What's that?'

'The newspapers found out about Hampten's death and your subsequent arrest. You made front page headlines in both Londons.'

Rubbing my eyes, I groan. 'Great. That's my career as a PI done for sure.'

'Not necessarily. Admittedly you may have more demand as an assassin going forward, but I'm sure we can turn this around somehow. And if it turns out that you're not guilty, it's free advertising.'

Karrion remains optimistic, no matter the obstacles in his way. There are times when his youth leads to naivety, but at the prospect of being left alone in the cell, his faith gives me great comfort. I hug him, breathing in his scent and enjoying the strength of his arms around me. When we hear the door open again, Karrion steps back.

'I'd better go, but I'll see you first thing tomorrow morning.'

'You don't have to come every day,' I say, fighting to keep my voice steady.

'Rubbish. As if I'm going to leave you here alone. I'll see you tomorrow.'

'Okay.'

With a final squeeze of my hand, Karrion leaves. The door closes behind him with a finality that spreads a chill through my limbs.

7

DOCTORS

By noon, my restlessness about being confined has led me to pace around the cell until the pain in my legs forces me to stop and I slump on the bed. I am expecting lunch when the cell door opens and two Paladins enter, one of whom is carrying a set of chains and a long cloak.

'Would you like to go outside? Prisoners have two allotted exercise times a day.'

'Sure,' I say, eyeing the chains with weary disinterest.

I allow myself to be chained, and one of the Paladins drapes the cloak over my shoulders. They lead me slowly through the prison area and down to a small inner courtyard away from the gleaming marble façade of the Brotherhood. The strip of sky visible high above me is grey and heavy with dark clouds. My breath creates a stream of fog, and I wonder whether it will snow. If it does, will Karrion still come tomorrow?

The Paladin attaches a long chain to the manacles around my wrists, thus giving me a measure of freedom to roam around the courtyard. I take a few tentative steps and the chain clinks. The sound irritates some part of me, where anger smoulders and demands to be stoked into a raging blaze.

Rather than give in to the temptation, I grit my teeth and walk a circle around the courtyard first one way and then another. After the second lap, my whole body pulses with incandescent hatred.

This is how it must be for predators living in zoos. An enclosure, no matter how large, is a pale imitation of freedom, and seeing the walls only makes the confinement all the more real. I tilt my head back, drawing the winter air deep into my lungs, but all I can smell is moisture and pollution. The world I know, the world I belong in, is everywhere around me and yet out of reach.

A sudden urge to tear at the collar and the manacles until I bleed flashes through me, but I remain still, standing in the centre of the courtyard. I appreciate anew the fate I condemned Cathwulf to by allowing the Paladins to imprison her rather than killing her myself. She will have spent her last weeks as much a prisoner as I am now. The irony of the situation is not lost on me.

Certain that my mood will not improve by the meagre exercise available to me, I indicate to the Paladins that I would like to go back inside. We retrace our steps to my cell, and I am glad to have the manacles removed. Having to wear the collar is bad enough. As the two Paladins are leaving, a third brings me a lunch tray.

I look at the food with weary disinterest, but drink the cup of tea that comes with it. Lunch is a warm chicken salad with a small roll and a bowl of fruit. I pick at the salad, eating about half of it. A part of me hates wasting food, but I cannot stomach any more. The pain in my legs is getting worse, and I curl up on the bed, wishing the Paladins would hurry up with obtaining my medication. I will have to ask again when someone comes to take away the tray.

My questions are pre-empted, however, when a Paladin

arrives half an hour later. As she picks up the tray, she glances towards me.

'Your doctor from the north has arrived to examine you.'

I frown, but she has gone before I have a chance to voice any objection.

The man who enters the cell is in his late thirties and dressed in blue jeans and a blue-collared shirt. He is carrying a small black bag, which he opens. He places a blood-pressure cuff on the table. Glancing back at the Paladin in the doorway, he smiles.

'I'll knock when we're done,' he says in a melodious voice.

The Paladin nods and locks the door.

All the while, I have remained on the bed, balanced on my elbow in a half-sitting position and staring at the man I have never seen before. When he turns to me with a placid smile, I resist the urge to bare my teeth.

'Who are you?'

'I'm your GP from the conclave.'

'No, you're not.'

'I could be. Shall we start by taking your blood pressure?'

Now I do bare my teeth. 'Stay away from me.'

Doing my best to keep the pain hidden, I scramble off the bed and stride towards the door, ready to summon the Paladin back. A hand touches my shoulder; a little more than a fleeting brush. I whirl around, and the man raises his hands to placate me as he takes a step back.

'Wait. My name is Jack Lincoln. I'm a reporter working for the *New London Courier*.'

I relax a little.

'Why are you pretending to be a doctor?'

'It was the only way I could think of to be allowed to visit you. They don't exactly invite reporters in. Obtaining the fake paperwork cost a pretty penny, but I know it'll be worth it.'

'But why are you here?'

'To hear your side of the story.'

'What story?'

'The murder of Maerk Hampten.' Jack reaches into his bag and retrieves a notebook and a pen. 'I didn't dare try to bring in a Dictaphone, so we have to do this the old-fashioned way.'

Too shocked to speak, I can do nothing but stand and stare at him. Perhaps later I will admire his audacity, but that will have to wait.

'Would you like to tell the story in your own words or shall I ask questions?' When I do not answer, he smiles. 'Please, sit. One of my sources indicates that you have a chronic illness. I'd hate to cause you any discomfort by hogging the only seat.'

Shaking my head to free myself from the stupor, I circle the table and lean my back against the windowsill, thus forcing Jack to twist around if he wants to look at me.

'What makes you think I'm prepared to tell you anything?' I ask.

'Don't you want to tell your side of the story? Perhaps garner some goodwill among the residents of both Londons? Our paper has a strong readership in Old London. You might even have some sway over the police investigating your case.'

'Why would I want to influence the investigation?'

'Are you looking forward to being executed? I hear it's not the most pleasant of endings, no matter how quick the Paladins make it. Have you harboured thoughts of suicide long?'

'Don't be ridiculous. I'm not suicidal, never have been. And you seem to be awfully certain a Ierald will judge me guilty.'

'So you maintain you're innocent. Interesting. But weren't you found covered in the victim's blood?'

'I want you to leave,' I say, crossing my arms.

Lincoln smiles, unfazed by my tone or my words.

'Look, I think you and I can help each other. If you give me an exclusive interview, I'll make sure you'll be portrayed in the best possible light. We could really do with some informal photos as well. Is there a friend I can contact? Your apprentice perhaps? Neither of you seem to have much of a social media presence, and the photo from your driver's licence is hardly flattering on the front page of a national newspaper.'

The anger swells like a wave within me, leaving me trembling. Collared and bereft of magic, I am all but defenceless, and the knowledge only increases my fury.

'I have no intention of sharing anything, be it my story or photos of me, with you and your newspaper.'

Deaf to his objections, I stride past him and bang on the door. The Paladin looks taken aback when I glare at her from the threshold.

'This man is a reporter, not a doctor. Get him out of here. And unless you make a habit of torturing your prisoners, find me an actual doctor so I can have some fucking pain meds.'

The release of anger leaves me panting while the Paladin calls for more guards. One stands at the door while two grip Jack's arms and remove him from the cell. He shoots one last look in my direction, but I stare past him, as I try to bring my breathing back under control.

'On behalf of the Brotherhood of Justice, I apologise,' the Paladin at the door says. I offer her no reply.

It is only when the door has closed and been locked that I slump against the wall and slide down to the floor. A shaking begins in my arms and spreads to my hands until I have to clutch them close to my chest for I cannot bear the physical sign of the releasing emotions.

The vulnerability I now feel takes me back to the night when Jans broke into my home. While my magic was of little use against a Leech, it nevertheless remained my armour and my greatest weapon. Since then, through my increased power, I have found a defence against the demons of the world, even the Fey. Yet here I am, confined to a tiny room, utterly powerless. A journalist was able to gain access with relative ease, and my only recourse was asking someone else to deal with him. That Jack Lincoln meant me no physical harm does not matter. He made me feel helpless, and that wounds me more than an assault ever could have done.

After a while, the shaking in my limbs subsides. I stumble to the bathroom and splash cold water on to my face. It helps to clear my thoughts, as if I am washing away the emotions Lincoln left in his wake. I return to the bed and curl up on my side, staring at the wall.

I have little idea how much time has passed before the door opens again. Drawing in a slow breath, I roll over. The man standing by the table bears the grey hair and eyes of old Paladin bloodlines, but instead of armour, he is wearing a white coat. Perhaps he chose not to enter the Brotherhood in favour of studying healing, or perhaps he is one of the many who leave before taking their place among the Paladin ranks.

'Ms Wilde,' he says, placing his bag on the table, 'my name is Doctor Iaison Venter. The Brotherhood has asked me to visit you to talk about your regular medications.'

Relief surges through me. I push myself up and indicate that he should take the chair. He opens his bag and sets a notepad in front of him, much like Lincoln did earlier.

'Why don't you tell me about your medical history.'

'I have Ehlers-Danlos Syndrome.'

'And what are your particular symptoms?'

'Frequent injuries, some dislocations, disrupted sleep, and constant pain. I also bruise easily and seem to be forever walking into things.'

'Poor proprioception.' He nods.

I do not bother to explain the rest of the symptoms; fatigue, frequent nausea, brain fog, the intolerance to cold. He is not my doctor, nor do I expect him to treat my condition. All I want are painkillers.

'What medication do you take?' he asks.

With the ease of someone used to dealing with medical professionals, I explain the different medications I take, the dosages, frequency, and the side effects I experience.

'That's quite a list.'

I shrug. 'It's still a work in progress, but the current regime works well enough.'

'And how do you feel in yourself?'

The question throws me, and I frown. 'What do you mean?'

'What does your mood tend to be like? Do you often feel low? Does your mood change depending on the time of day? Do you have someone to talk to?'

'My mood is fine,' I say, feeling the first sliver of unease. 'Aside from being imprisoned here, of course.'

'Are you in contact with your family?'

'No. I'm an only child, my mother is dead and my father is dying.'

'I understand you're the only one of your kind living in Old London. That must be difficult.'

'It's fine,' I reply, not understanding what this has got to do with my illness.

'Do the medications you take help with the feeling of isolation?'

'What? No, they're for the pain.'

'Yes, but there are many different kinds of pain, both physical and emotional. Which kind are you treating with all the pills you take?'

'The pain from my EDS.' I cross my arms, even though I know it will make me look defensive. 'I'm not depressed.'

'Are you sure you're not embellishing your symptoms to gain access to opioids?'

'How do you fake a dislocated shoulder?'

'But you yourself just said that you only suffer injuries some of the time.'

'I'm still hypermobile.' To prove my point, I hyperextend my elbow until it bends backwards.

'There's a great deal of evidence to show that hypermobility in itself does not automatically mean that those affected suffer any more pain than an average person.'

'Not everyone who's hypermobile has EDS. But I do.'

'It's a difficult condition to diagnose given that there is no definitive test for it. Could your GP have mistaken simple hypermobility for EDS? It happens more frequently than you might guess.'

My growing frustration demands that I jump up and pace the room, but I force my muscles to relax as best I can. Once again, I want to bare my teeth at this man who threatens the foundations of my world, but I choose diplomacy.

'I was diagnosed by a rheumatologist who specialises in connective tissue disorders.'

'Still, even specialists make mistakes at times.'

'Why are you so convinced that I *don't* have EDS?' I ask, unable to keep the sharpness from my tone.

'In my opinion, you display all the symptoms of someone mistaking the feelings of isolation and loneliness for physical pain and treating them with inappropriate and often addictive medications. This habit can cause serious long-term harm and does not in any way deal with underlying mental health problems.'

'I'm not depressed,' I say, louder than I had intended.

'Then why so defensive?'

'I don't like being called a liar.'

'That's going too far. I'm merely suggesting that you are confused between your mental and physical well-being.'

'Which I'm guessing means that you're going to ignore the medication regime my doctor prescribed me.' I uncross my arms, flexing and contracting my fingers as a cat might.

'It would be unwise to deny you any medication, but given your current situation, I doubt there will be much here that will cause you pain. This cell is a safe environment for you, both physically and emotionally, and I hope you see it as such.'

I want to tell him that chronic pain is not dependent on activity and that being confined in this tiny room will, in fact, make things worse for me. I want to explain that I rely on my magic as a distraction and a way to tolerate the constant ache in my limbs. I want to point out that by refusing to believe me and by belittling my experiences, he is doing far more damage to my mental health than struggling to adapt to life in the city ever did. But I choose to remain silent. It will make no difference whether I shout at him or argue my case with logic. He will not listen.

Dr Venter closes his notepad and searches through his bag. From a clear bottle, he shakes out two white pills and places them on the table. I resist the urge to snatch them up.

'I'm going to prescribe you with paracetamol up to three times a day. I'll inform the Paladins that you are to receive one more dose today and then starting from tomorrow, one in the morning, one mid-afternoon and one in the evening. Given that I feel you score fairly high for risk of self-harm and suicide, I will ask the Paladins to look after and administer the medication.'

'Paracetamol isn't going to touch the pain,' I say, hating the way my voice cracks.

'Then I suggest you find a way to deal with the underlying cause of your perceived pain experience. I know your current situation may make it difficult, but try to think positive. Smile and laugh as much as you can, and the pain will get better.'

Dr Venter picks up his bag and walks to the door. As soon as the cell door closes behind him, I snatch the pills from the table and rush to the bathroom. My hand trembles as I fill the plastic cup and gulp down the medication. Half of the water spills down my chin, and when I glance at myself in the wall mirror, my eyes are wild. But it is the wildness of a caged animal, not that of a Wild Folk.

8

CREEPING FROST

The paracetamol, when it kicks in, smudges the edges of my perception a little. The pain has established an iron grip, and I have no choice but to let it consume me. The cell offers no distractions, and my muddled brain will not focus enough for me to examine the details of the mystery surrounding Hampten's violent end. Thus I let the pain pulse through me in time with my heartbeat, and the agony flows and ebbs like the winter tides, never releasing me from its grip. Each swell erodes my sense of self a little more until I am the pain and the pain is me and nothing else exists in the world.

When the Paladins offer to take me outside again, I turn them down. The last thing I need is to be walked around in chains like a dangerous dog. Dearon's words about a wolf who chose to live with men and who became a dog flash across my mind, but they only add to my despair.

What would Dearon think if he saw me now, caged and collared like the domesticated pet he accused me of becoming? Would he despise me, despise my weakness, or would he find it in his heart to understand?

The answer seems obvious: why would Dearon want a feral city dweller when he could have a Wild Folk as his mate?

These thoughts haunt me while I brush my teeth. This time, I switch off the light, though a faint glow from the street lights outside the Brotherhood casts a pale strip across the opposite wall. I stare at it until sleep blurs the pain into dreams of cages and huge, angry dogs surrounding me, ready to attack.

I wake up early again, my limbs heavy with fatigue. The warmth of the cell feels oppressive in the pre-dawn stillness. It takes me a long time to persuade myself to rise, but once I do, I limp to the bathroom. A cold shower eases my discomfort.

Breakfast is waiting for me when I step out of the bathroom, still drying my hair. I take the pills and force myself to eat the porridge, but after a few spoonfuls, I give up. Although it is still early, I make the bed, knowing that Karrion will visit soon. When the Paladins fetch the tray, they bring me a fresh towel and two changes of clothes.

When Karrion arrives, the first thing he does is hug me as thoroughly as yesterday. Seeing him lifts my spirits, and I find myself wishing that he could stay with me for the duration of my incarceration. Even the thought of him leaving wet towels dotted around the room does not dissuade me.

'How are you?' he asks.

'I'm okay. How are you?'

'Not bad, though I completely forgot I have my driving test in two days. But I'm going to see if I can reschedule it for later. I don't have time right now, what with you being here and all.'

'Don't. You've worked hard on learning to drive. It's not like a few days' delay is going to make any difference to the case.'

'I hate the idea of you being here any longer than you have to be.'

'Me too, but it was always going to take time to conduct our own investigation. We need solid proof if you want to convince the Crown Prosecution Service not to put me in front of a Herald.'

'I'm going to find that proof,' Karrion says, pushing his hands in the pockets of his black jeans.

'I know.'

He grins at my ready show of faith and guides me to sit down. My pelvis crunches, but I hide the wince by smiling.

'How's Sinta?'

'She's fine. I stopped by your place yesterday to pick up her food and toys and anything else she might need. From what I saw at the Open Hearth, she's basically running the place. I wouldn't be at all surprised if when you get released she'll refuse to eat anything but the finest fillet steak and venison sausages.'

A lump appears in my throat as I imagine Funja and Wishearth spoiling Sinta rotten. She has no idea how loved she is. It occurs to me that perhaps I don't, either.

'I've been digging around online some more, but I haven't found anything much yet,' Karrion says. 'I'll keep trying and I do have a potential lead to follow.'

'What's that?' I ask, perking up.

'Mum thinks that one of her friends might have worked as a cleaner for the Hamptens a while back. She's trying to track down this friend at the moment. Maybe we'll find out something interesting about the affair or why Mrs Hampten would lie to the Paladins.'

'That's brilliant, Karrion.'

'I haven't done anything yet. So far, it's been all Mum. Apparently, the name rang a bell and she mentioned it to me. Mum sends her love, by the way.'

'Thanks.'

'There's something else, but you're not going to like it.' Karrion reaches into his back pocket and pulls out a folded piece of newspaper. 'This appeared in today's paper.'

I unfold the paper to reveal a full page from the *New London Courier*. There are two photos: one is my driving licence photo, the other is grainy and lacks detail, but it seems to show me in chains in the exercise yard, with two Paladins in the background. The headline reads *London's Most Savage Killer*.

The first part explains the basic details of Maerk Hampten's death, presumably what little has been shared with the press, but it then continues on a profile piece on me. It describes me as volatile and aggressive. One section in the middle catches my eye.

Yannia Wilde calls herself a Private Investigator, but she has little in common with most members of the profession. She lacks all but the most basic education, has no relevant qualifications, and seems to have missed the memo about professional behaviour. A source that chose to remain anonymous even hinted that Ms Wilde has been known to sleep with clients in return for them overlooking the serious errors she has made.

If that is not worrying enough, it would appear that Ms Wilde is deep in the quagmire of substance abuse. The author of this article himself heard Ms Wilde protesting her innocence of the murder of Mr Hampten, all the while screaming for more drugs. Aside from the murder she is awaiting trial for, who knows what other crimes Ms Wilde has committed while chasing a high?

I stare at the article, my cheeks burning with anger and embarrassment. The rage I felt yesterday resurfaces, so strong I want to rip to shreds every part of this cell until my hands bleed and I am too tired to move. My hands flex, nails scratching the surface of the table in a vain effort to contain my fury.

'I don't get how this is possible,' Karrion says, giving voice to the thought reverberating around my stuttering brain. 'Who the hell is Jack Lincoln? Have you ever heard of him?'

At the sound of the name, some of my rage coalesces into molten steel.

My countenance must change, for Karrion takes a step back. 'If you're going to murder someone, please let it not be me. But I'm going to take that as a yes.'

'He came to see me yesterday, pretending to be my "GP from the north", and wanted an exclusive interview. He used fake papers to get in. This must be his revenge for my throwing him out.'

Karrion half picks me up and plants a kiss on my cheek. 'You're my hero. If I ever grow up, I want to be just like you.'

'A disgraced PI whose name has been dragged through the mud? Or a suspected murderer?'

'Even then, there's no stopping you. And by the way, I'm going to kill a few Paladins for this, even if I have to storm the Paladin General's office single-handedly. Heads are going to roll even if I have to steal one of those posh swords to do it.'

'I have a horrible feeling you already resemble me far more than is good for your continued health and freedom.'

'Freedom, shmeedom. I'll sort this out right now.' Karrion is halfway to the door when he turns around. 'Or we could hang out. I don't have anything more to report, though.'

'No, you go ahead and start preparing for your driving test. Though could you do me a favour?'

'Anything.'

'Could you see if I can have a few books to read? This cell isn't exactly filled with activities. I'm bored.'

'Of course, no problem. Jonathain Marsh had a book, so I don't see why you couldn't have some as well.'

'Thanks. Say hi to your Mum and siblings for me. I'm practically an honorary Bird Shaman now I'm a jailbird.'

Karrion laughs and we hug goodbye. I bury my face in the warmth of his T-shirt, inhaling his scent, and then force my arms to let go of him. Watching him walk out is no easier the second time, but the thought of him raising hell with the Paladins brings a ghost of a smile to my lips.

It is late afternoon, and the pain has forced me to stop pacing and return to the bed, when the cell door opens. I will myself to turn my head, but once I do, I rouse myself to better take in my unexpected visitor.

The Paladin General stands less tall than when I was last in his presence, and the lines around his eyes and mouth are deeper. I can only imagine how much the burden of letting an innocent man die for the safety of Old London must weigh on his shoulders, and I do not envy his position.

He is carrying a stack of books under his arm and he sets them on the table. When he looks at me, his smile is tinged with sadness.

'They are from my personal library. I chose a couple of mysteries, but mostly tales of wilderness and nature. I realise it is like trapping a bird in a cage and expecting it to sing upon seeing pictures of its habitat, but I hope you find even a sliver of solace within the pages.'

'Thank you,' I say, keeping my voice neutral while my brain is in overdrive trying to figure out why he is in my cell.

'You should know that your young apprentice caused quite the scene in the entrance hall earlier today. He was so angry I expected him to turn into a phoenix. But he had every right to be angry. I apologise for the security breach and Mr Lincoln's intrusion. The Brotherhood will take action, and you may rest assured that it will not happen again. I hope these books are a small token of my personal apology.'

'Thank you.' There is more I would like to say, but I have no right to shout at the Paladin General just because I am angry or frightened. Too many people already consider me a savage. I have no intention of proving them right.

With the slightest of nods, the Paladin General leaves with a soft rustle of his grey robes. I wait until silence has returned to the cell before rising to inspect the books.

I flick through the pages, pausing occasionally to inspect drawings of animals and plants. Now that I have something to read, I feel no inclination to do so. With a mixture of indifference and frustration, I lie back on the bed. The throb in my pelvis receives no more than a cursory acknowledgement, nor can I force myself to shift position.

A small part of me knows that I am in danger, not from journalists or Paladins but from confinement in this cell. While living in Old London has smoothed some of my primal edges, I am still wild at heart. Not a wild animal, but the next best thing. I have made a life for myself in the city, but no Wild Folk can be caged for long. To be cut off from nature will kill us as surely as the Paladins' swords will.

The worst part is that while I know all of this on a rational level, I cannot will myself to care.

I raise my arm and trace a finger along the invisible mark on my forehead. A sliver of frost runs through me, and it brings with it a spark of life. I repeat the action. The temperature seems to drop a few degrees, but it causes me no discomfort. Spurred by the new sensation, I rise long enough to pick up one of the books of nature stories and begin to read.

The words of the pages conjure images of deer herds, packs of wolves, and skeins of geese. In everything I imagine, the landscape is shrouded in a blanket of frost. The air is cold enough that my breath creates plumes of fog. When a breeze strokes the trees, ice crystals on the branches chime in a melody so delicate, only a being of winter can hear it.

My feet plunge into a deep snowdrift, and I pitch forward until my front paws find balance. I shake myself, sending up a cloud of powdery snow. The scents of a forest tempt me to explore, and I inhale the smell of pines and spruces. It is not the scent of the home I have known since birth, but an echo of a homeland from the distant past. We were free here, once, hunting in the woods and plains of a vast wilderness, living in harmony with nature, knowing no other existence. I long to be there now, and every thump of my heart is a cry for a life forever out of my reach.

A soft growl draws me back to the present. The pack is gathering for a hunt, excitement causing our tails to quiver. I know all the wolves around me, not by name but by scent, touch, and sound. They are my kin; siblings and lovers and offspring. Only together will we survive the harsh winter and bring down the prey that will feed us for many changes of the sun and the moon.

We move along the forest edge in a single file, moonlight casting long shadows across the unbroken snow to our right. In the play of light and darkness, my spirit separates from the wolves and speeds forward, no more than a whisper among the trees.

Now I am an elk, tall and graceful in a landscape that is as much mine as the wolves'. I hear them coming, not in the sound of their paws breaking through the hard crust overlaying the softer snow but in the silence of the woods around me. My long strides widen the distance, fear spurring me on, but they possess the tenacity of a hungry predator. I reach a shallow stream, which flows too fast for it to freeze even in the heart of winter. Thirst burns my throat, but I dare not drink for fear of it slowing me down. My hooves clatter against the wet stones as I cross the stream.

Time has no meaning during the pursuit. There is only predator and prey, hunting and fleeing, the whisper of paws in soft snow and the crunch of hooves on ice. One moment I am alone in the woods, the next, low shadows flit between the trees, surrounding me. I have a choice: fight or flee.

I plant my hooves firmly on the ground and lower my head. The crown of antlers is heavy and has caused me many a tangle during the autumn months, but now I am grateful for every prong. One swipe will kill a wolf. If I maim enough of them, perhaps they will seek easier prey.

The attack comes from above. I missed the boulder in the shadow of a tall spruce, and as the thought registers, a weight lands on my back. Teeth clamp down on my neck and the sharp pain is like a tiny lightning bolt down my limbs. I whirl around, intent upon dislodging my assailant, but another wolf leaps at my throat.

It is a battle rehearsed over millennia. The wolves leap, bite, and snarl, while I kick, twist, and stamp. There is no certainty over the outcome, but this time, their weight and sharp teeth bring me to my knees. The snow around my head melts and turns red, but I bear them no grudge. We are all part of the same cycle of life and death, and it is my time to lose.

My spirit rises from the carcass and spreads wings the colour of moonless nights. I soar in the clear air until I find a branch I like. There, with my claws digging into the bark, I watch while the wolves tear open the elk's belly. Steam rises from the entrails spilling out, and growls echo between the trees while the wolves fight over the organs. I feel no sadness as the being that was me turns into meat and fur and bones to be gnawed.

In a flicker of shadows, an unkindness gathers, waiting for the pack to have their fill. The wisdom of the world is in the eyes of a raven. That wisdom assesses the wolves, counts the distance and strength of a leap, and its likely ferocity. One of my kin swoops down and lands on the snow, hopping towards the elk's head. A wolf growls, then lunges. The raven finds safety in a nearby pine.

The vigil continues until the growls subside to satisfied whines and the wolves have licked the blood off their paws and one another's necks. They move only a short distance before settling down to rest in a loose group. We keep one eye on them as we claim the carcass in a cascade of shadows. The elk's eye stares at the stars far beyond its reach. I find a precarious balance on the cooling cheek and reach down to claim my prize.

My mouth waters from the smell of meat. I crane my neck to peck at the empty eye socket, but my teeth clash together. The unexpected sound shatters the illusion, and my eyes fly open. I am back in the cell, staring at the white ceiling far above me. The corner of a book digs into my ribs. The smell of meat remains strong and when I let my head fall to the side, I see a tray of food on the table.

Whatever trance I was under, it was strong enough that I never heard the door open and close.

Some trace of the wild instincts remains, for I push the book aside and all but leap off the bed. My dinner consists of a steak, grilled vegetables, and a slice of cake. Ignoring the cutlery, I tear into the meat, licking juices off my fingers while I chew. It is burnt rather than bloody, but it satisfies the primal hunger gnawing at my belly. I eat it all and growl when there is no more to be had. The rest of the food is of no interest to me.

I drink straight from the bathroom tap and the droplets of

water landing on my cheeks restore my self-awareness. My experience of the winter landscape is as clear in my mind as if I was there. I feel the snow crunch under my paws, the pain of teeth on my flank, and the wind caressing my spread wings. Whatever ancient magic I invoked through the book and the Fey mark, it made me wilder than even embracing the conclave life ever could.

I carry on reading the book, but keep my hands well away from the Fey mark. But as the darkness outside deepens, my thoughts stray time and time again to wondering how my experience of the wilderness was possible. It is as though a barrier has been breached, but to what purpose, I can only guess.

My answer comes as gradually as the change of seasons. The stale cell air gives way to the crispness of frost. A shiver runs through me, then another. The shadows by the wardrobe deepen, coalescing into a distinct figure. The Winter Queen steps forward in a flurry of snowflakes. Although the distance to my bed is two yards at most, time slows as I watch her approach; muscles paralysed with cold and fear.

As much as I want to ask her why she is here and how she got past the cold iron encircling the cell, no words come. The air has vanished from my lungs, replaced by frost. I lie on my bed, gasping for breath as the Winter Queen reaches me. She sits on the edge of the bed, and a layer of ice crystals spreads over my blanket. When she leans forward, her eyes show a desolate landscape of midwinter, where survival and death balance on a razor edge of ice. I forget that I cannot breathe.

The Winter Queen reaches out with a slender hand. Despite being unable to move, I brace myself against pain. Instead, she strokes my hair. With each movement, more of my stress and anxiety slip away until I am at peace. Was I able to move, I would curl at her feet, as a faithful hound should.

My consciousness begins to slip away as my vision blurs to the blackness of a raven's feathers. The last thing I am aware of is her lips caressing the shell of my ear with the bite of midwinter frost.

'Soon.'

9

———————

DISCREPANCIES

I wake to an empty cell. The pain that roused me is so strong I feel like my pelvis is being crushed. Fighting to keep my movement steady, I roll on to my side and sit up. Changing position eases the pain a little, but not much. I stand and pace across the cell and back while I wait for the worst of it to subside. Gradually, I become aware of how cold I am. Working as quickly as my shaking hands allow, I put on all the clothes the Paladins have provided and crawl back under the blanket. My pelvis protests, but I curl into a ball, all the while trying to figure out which is worse: the pain or the cold. I reach no conclusion before I slide back into unsettled sleep.

———

When I wake again, fear arrives before awareness. My gaze skitters around the cell, searching every inch of it many times over. The Winter Queen is nowhere to be seen. I am hot under the layers of clothes and blanket, but the relief of being safe overrides any discomfort.

How could she have been here? The walls, the door,

even the mesh over the window, contains cold iron. A Fey should not be able to enter under any circumstances. Yet I am certain she was here. Did I summon her through the mark and with my exploration of her season? Did my wildness create a bridge for her to use? Or was the encounter nothing but a nightmare dreamed up by an overwhelmed mind?

The grey walls have no answers to offer. The spark of me I regained last night sputters and fades. I roll on to my side as before, pack the blanket between my knees to offer support for my aching pelvis, and slide back into restless dreams.

How much time passes before I next open my eyes, I am not certain, but as I blink my eyes into focus, a Paladin is leaning over me. She is carrying a set of chains. A second Paladin stands in the open doorway.

'It's your exercise time.'

The idea of going outside robs my limbs of what little strength they have. I rub my face in the blanket and shake my head.

'I don't want to go outside.'

'Our healer advises against prolonged inactivity such as you're currently undergoing.'

Anger surges through me, yanking me off the bed as surely as if I were a puppet whose master had picked up the strings. The Paladin takes half a step back.

'I'm not your pet dog, content to trot on pavements in chains,' I say, voice trembling with fury. 'I'm of the Wild Folk, a creature of untamed forests and the open skies, who roams free and far. Put me in chains and you will take away what makes me wild and therefore me.'

'There's no need for hostility.'

'Locking a wild animal in a cage doesn't make them tame.'

'Our healer is concerned that your mental health is

deteriorating and it's having an impact on your physical health too.'

'What do you expect when it was the quack you picked who told me it's all in my head.' I bare my teeth. 'So leave me the fuck alone until I'm released or taken before a Herald.'

The Paladins exchange a glance, unsure how to proceed. I choose for them and lie back down. If they want me to go outside, they can drag me in chains. Seconds tick by until eventually the footsteps move away and the cell door closes.

Once I am certain they will not return, I slink to the bathroom and make the mistake of glancing in the mirror. My hair lies in snarled tangles around my shoulders and my eyes burn with a feral gleam. The water from the tap is cool as it slides down my throat, but it is not the icy perfection of a mountain stream. With a dissatisfied snort, I return to the bed.

For two days I hover in the twilight zone between sleep and wakefulness, doing my best to ignore the armoured people invading my den. When the leaden blanket of bleakness threatens to smother me, I use the Fey mark and the books to transport myself elsewhere. I explore the winter landscape as a fox, a stoat, a bear, and a deer, swim in the mountain brooks, and soar over the valleys and peaks on thermals.

Each time I do so, I lose a little more of my humanity. The words in the books no longer mean anything, nor do the cutlery and crockery on the food trays. I consume the meat while leaving the rest. What need have I for cups of milky liquid, or soft vegetables?

There are times in the feral haze when I feel like I have forgotten something, but the thoughts are as insubstantial as a handful of morning mist. It is only when a corvid disguised as a young man steps into my cell that the idle meanderings coalesce into recognition. Karrion takes one look at me curled up on the bed and rushes over.

'Heron's tail feathers, Yan, you look terrible!'

I shrug and look away. At least my first instinct is not to growl at him.

'Honestly, I leave you alone for two days and this happens. What's wrong? Are you in pain? Are you ill? Have you eaten?' Karrion wrinkles his nose. 'And when was the last time you took a shower?'

When I try to recall, my mind goes blank. I shrug again.

'Okay, first things first. You'll feel better after a shower. I'll find you some clean clothes and something to eat. Do you need help getting up?'

My instinct is to say no, but when I rise, the room spins in slow loops. Karrion takes hold of my elbow and guides me to the bathroom. Once I am safely gripping the sink for balance, he closes the door with the promise that I only need to holler if I feel faint.

The shower refreshes me, but it also settles a blanket of exhaustion over me. All I want is to sleep until I feel better, no matter how much a rational part of my brain yells that my condition will not improve with more rest. It takes me a long time to work the knots out of my wet hair and when I glance in the mirror, I see that the dark circles under my eyes are like bruises.

What has become of me and how has the transformation been so quick? I have been imprisoned for less than a week. How long will I survive like this?

I am losing the battle against my desire to lie back down when Karrion returns carrying a tray. A stack of clothes is pinned under one of his arms. I take them from him and return to the bathroom to dress. When I step out again,

Karrion draws me to a chair and drapes a blanket over my shoulders.

'Eat.'

At the sight of the bowl of porridge, bile fills my mouth. I push away the tray and stare at the grey ceiling.

'Yan, you've got to eat something.'

'I'm not hungry.'

A hollowness gnaws at my insides, but I cannot tell whether it is because of the lack of food or because of my dark mood. Either way, breakfast does not interest me.

'Did I ask you whether you were hungry? Until you are capable of perfecting photosynthesis, you can bloody well eat breakfast like the rest of us.'

'But–'

'If you don't eat something, they're going to tie you to a hospital bed and stick a feeding tube down your throat. Does that suit your wild tendencies better?'

His decisive tone causes the corner of my mouth to twitch. I pull a slice of ham out of the roll on the tray and force myself to eat it. The saltiness eases the nausea enough that I manage most of the porridge. By the time I push the tray away, the heaviness in my belly has spread exhaustion to my limbs. I eye the bed with renewed interest, but Karrion sets two pills in front of me. Doing my best to keep my hand from trembling, I swallow them with tepid tea.

'Is that all the meds you're taking at the moment?' he asks.

'Paracetamol is all the doctor would give me,' I say, eyes fixed on the tea mug.

'What? Why?'

'He didn't believe me.' My voice cracks. 'Said it was all in my head.'

Karrion leaps up. 'What kind of a moron can't tell the difference between faking and real pain?'

I shrug, blinking rapidly to keep the tears from falling. His anger mirrors mine, yet no words can escape past the lump blocking my throat.

He is beside me in an instant, wrapping gentle arms around me. I breathe in his warm scent, on the verge of letting go. But if I allow myself to fall apart now, I am not certain I'll ever be able to put the pieces back together. I lean against Karrion's shoulder, but instead of letting the tears fall, I focus on the memory of Sinta's shining eyes and wagging tail. There is so much love in her, and I have to believe that I will see her again.

When the swell of emotions subsides, I draw back and offer Karrion a wan smile.

'How did your driving test go?'

Karrion ducks his head as he stands and shoves his hands in his pockets. 'I failed.'

'How come?'

'I reversed into a gravestone,' he mumbles, barely audible.

'You what?'

'I reversed into a gravestone,' he says, a little louder. The tips of his ears turn pink.

'Did your test form part of a zombie apocalypse survival training?' I ask, fighting to keep my expression neutral.

'Obviously not. Stupid church didn't have a boundary around the cemetery and the car didn't have reverse sensors. How was I supposed to know they had graves so close to the road?'

'That is a well-known problem in the city,' I say, and dissolve into laughter.

The force of my mirth takes me by surprise. It lifts my spirits and dispels the gloom that has been hovering over me. For this brief moment, even the pain is not as severe and I relish the relief.

When my giggles subside, Karrion is glowering by the door. Wiping tears from my eyes, I rise and hug him.

'Don't worry. You're never going to make the same mistake again.'

'Yeah, but what if I fail again because I make a different mistake?'

'Isn't that how life seems to work in general?'

He looks like he wants to argue, but he sighs and wraps an arm around my shoulder. 'I guess you're right.'

'Are you taking more lessons before you try again?'

'Yes, though I can't afford too many.'

'Is your employer paying you enough?' I ask with a wink.

'Well, she's in jail at the moment, so I reckon dealing with payroll is not a priority.' Karrion leads me back to the chair and picks up the blanket that has ended up on the floor.

'I need to add you as a signatory to the business account.'

'Aren't you afraid I'll run off with all your money while you're here?'

'No.' I flash Karrion a grin. 'You forget that I know where you live. If you run off with my meagre savings, I'll ask Fria to cover all your stuff in cat hair. How many times would you have to wash your boots to get the smell of cat urine out of them?'

Karrion shudders. 'You're a cruel woman. Point taken.'

'Have you found out anything about the Hamptens?' I ask, eager to get my mind back on the case.

'Not as much as I had hoped.' Karrion rubs the back of his neck. 'The past couple of days have been pretty hectic.'

'It's fine,' I say, tamping down my disappointment.

'Not really. I know how hard it must be for you to be stuck here with nothing to do and no control over your fate.'

'Isn't that what apprentices are for?' Even I can hear the forced lightness in my tone.

'Well, yours could do with more hours in the day. But in

between helping Mum with the brood and studying for the driving test, I have been digging into Aleson Hampten's past.'

'Did you uncover any skeletons?'

'Not really. The only interesting thing I found was that Aleson's father committed political suicide by having an affair with the wife of the then Speaker. He held one of the Light Mage seats on the Council, but he had to step down after some sordid photos made their way to the tabloids. His divorce was messy and very public. Afterwards, the whole family dropped off the media radar. Given some of the comments I read online, I can't blame them for wanting to keep a low profile.'

A detail niggles at the back of my mind, and it takes a moment before I grasp it. Even as I begin to speak, I wonder if I am misremembering something.

'Aleson's father was a Light Mage?'

Distracted by the book of bird tales on the table, Karrion takes a moment to look up. 'Yes, everyone in the family is a Light Mage.'

'Not Aleson. She's an East Mage.'

'That's not possible. Two Light Mages can't produce any other kind.'

'Unless her mother was having an affair with an East Mage.'

Karrion considers this, tapping a fingernail against his lip piercing. 'It looks like we may have uncovered an adultery scandal from several decades ago. But what's that got to do with Maerk Hampten's death?'

'Maybe nothing. You didn't find any old tabloid articles about the affair, did you?'

'No, but I can keep digging if you want.'

I nod, still trying to put my finger on why this bothers me so much. 'Everyone in the family must have known about the affair. While Mages don't have the Wild Folk ability to identify people by their scent, they must be able to tell the difference between Mages from all six schools of magic.'

'No doubt you're right, but I still don't understand what an old affair has to do with our current predicament.'

'Don't you mean *my* predicament?'

'Oh, no. We're in this together or not at all. How many times do I have to repeat that before you believe me?'

'A few more times wouldn't go amiss,' I say with a small smile. 'But in all seriousness, the more we find out about the Hamptens, the more chance we have of figuring out who would want to set up a trap in the warehouse.'

'I'm on it. And from now on, I'm visiting you every day even if it means having to ask the Paladins to babysit the goslings during the visiting hours.'

'Thanks, I appreciate it.'

For the rest of the visiting hour, Karrion chatters about inconsequential matters, as if even a moment's silence would cause me to slip from his grasp. Perhaps it would. As it is, I prop my chin on my palm and let his words wash over me. They tether me to life outside the cell, to joy, and to the feeling of being part of a family. Memories of Christmas Day spent with Karrion's family thaw some of the ice within me, but I fear that the effect will not last once I am alone once more.

When the Paladins open the door, Karrion drags out the goodbyes as long as he can. I assure him that I will be fine; and he leaves. Shortly after, the Paladins bring my lunch. Still troubled by the revelation of Aleson's parents, I absently eat most of the food. Karrion's visit has energised me, and I pace across the cell, relishing in the stretch of my muscles. The exercise brings its own pain, but I ignore it in favour of counting my steps. If I walk far enough in this confined space, perhaps my thoughts and dreams will take me to the conclave so I may run free among my kind.

I have lost all track of time in my efforts to escape beyond the grey walls, and the door opening catches me by surprise. A Paladin stands in the doorway, carrying a familiar set of chains, and I prepare myself to tell him again that I have no interest in going outside.

'Your friend pointed out that we have neglected to provide you with the opportunity to observe your religious practices. On behalf of the Brotherhood, I apologise.'

'My religious practices?' I have little idea of what he is talking about, but I refrain from saying so.

'Your kind prays to Hearth Spirits, do they not?'

The prospect of seeing Wishearth lifts some of the lingering gloom. It will not be the same as sitting opposite him at the Open Hearth, but just being enveloped in his smoky warmth will be enough to reaffirm our bond. Now, for the first time, I am eager for the Paladin to chain me.

'Yes, please.' I hold out my hands.

Once I am shackled, the Paladin leads me out of the cell and down a corridor to a large room containing tables and chairs. From the casual air, I take this to be a break room for the Paladins on guard duty. At the far end, a small fire is already burning in an ornate fireplace. From the size of the branches, its sole purpose is to allow me to make an offering to Wishearth.

'Your friend wasn't clear on what you use for an offering, so we gathered together a range of plants and branches. If these are not suitable, we can postpone this until we have found the right materials.'

'No, this is perfect.' I take the bowl from him. 'Thank you.'

The Paladin retreats to the end of the chains and turns his back to me. It is as much privacy as he can give me, and I am grateful. From the bowl I select long stalks of lavender, an oak branch, and dried holly leaves. My fingers tremble as I bind them together and kneel on the hearthstones.

'Hearth Spirit, the guardian of the home and hearth, the protector of the wildest among us, bless these flames. Accept this offering and grant me the strength to survive my imprisonment.' The offering ignites, and I let it fall on to the flames. 'Please, Wishearth.'

My eyes sting from the brightness of the fire as I search for familiar eyes amid the blaze. A sudden bloom of smoke causes me to cough. Once I have caught my breath, I turn back to the flames, expecting to find Wishearth laughing at me. Instead, all I see are fire and embers glowing orange.

Wishearth didn't come.

Tears spring to my eyes, and I swallow around the lump in my throat. I dig my nails into my palms, unwilling to cry in front of the Paladin. Could it be that the fire is an illusion, something created just to fool me? But to what purpose? The Paladins are keepers of justice and thus rarely cruel. Perhaps Wishearth could not hear my prayer, or he is busy elsewhere.

Another thought burns through my mind, leaving a sick feeling in the pit of my stomach. What if Wishearth was watching me at the warehouse and saw what I did to Hampten? Could it be that he has left me at the mercy of the Herald, having already judged me guilty?

My racing thoughts threaten to spiral into panic, and I push myself up. Blood rushes to my numb legs and the pricking sensation causes me to groan. At the sound of the chains clinking, the Paladin turns. Upon my nod, he leads me towards the door. I glance back over my shoulder, but the fire has already died, leaving behind only glowing embers.

Wishearth didn't come.

10

A TRAIL OF DECEPTION

For the next five days, Karrion visits without fail, drowning me in cheerful chatter for two hours. He makes sure I eat breakfast, and it feels less like a chore while he talks about his siblings and the birds he saw on the way to the Brotherhood of Justice. Even pigeons get a mention. His presence soothes an ache within me that catches and bleeds in the hours between his visits, when the cell echoes with my loneliness. It is a hurt that defies definition, and each day, it grows a little more, until it becomes a miasma of anger, fear, hopelessness, and betrayal. Distinct from the physical pain of my illness, it occupies all the space in my chest, pushing aside the rest of me. Only in Karrion's presence does breathing become a little easier, and I love him all the more for it.

No amount of arguments from him will convince the Paladins to bring in another doctor to assess my pain, but he does persuade them to let me have a hot-water bottle. Three times a day, they bring me a fresh one, and I come to reach for it with eager hands. The heat of it is oppressive to the point of physical pain, but the relief is strong enough that I would rather tell the Winter Queen to sod off than give it up. A single hot-water bottle cannot erase the agony of EDS, especially after so many days without adequate medication, but it quells the fire in my pelvis and relaxes muscles that have grown stiff during my inactivity.

Each day, a Paladin offers to take me to the fireplace. I follow the guard out of the cell with less and less enthusiasm. The words of the prayer to the Hearth Spirits, words I learned by rote as a child until I needed no conscious thought to speak them, now stick in my throat until I watch the offering burn in silence. Wishearth never appears amid the flames and each day, the rejection stings a little more. The conviction that he has abandoned me because I am a murderer grows until he may as well be a Herald declaring me guilty.

I keep quiet about the daily offerings and Wishearth's absence whenever Karrion visits. He has had a go at enough people on my behalf, or so I tell myself. Another, secret, part of me fears that were Karrion to confront Wishearth, he would learn the truth about my guilt and also abandon me. I would not survive losing them both.

The shadow of my guilt hovers over me whenever Karrion is not here. My mind conjures scenario after scenario of how I tore Maerk Hampten apart, how I feasted on his flesh, and how I guarded his body against the Paladins. My dreams become filled with gore and warm meat until I am frightened to close my eyes. It is easier to focus on the suffocating heat of the hot-water bottle and the agony splintering my limbs than to be reminded, yet again, of the wild animal within me.

A more rational part of me knows that the pain, the lack of sleep, and my non-existent appetite are causing me to grow weak. But such is my certainty over the verdict of Wishearth's unspoken judgement that this imprisonment becomes part of the punishment. A man is dead because of me. Do I not deserve to spend all my remaining days trapped by pain and fear?

I'm sitting at the small table contemplating my breakfast when Karrion struts into the cell under the disapproving glare of the guard. My stomach lurches, caught between hope and fear. He waits until the Paladin has closed the door, twirls a full circle, and grins at me.

'If you eat your whole breakfast, I'll tell you something amazing.'

'That doesn't seem fair,' I say, glancing at the unappetising cheese roll on my plate.

'The choice, my dear boss, is yours.'

No amount of meaningful throat clearing or repeated pointed looks has any effect on Karrion, and I have no choice but to eat the roll. It tastes stale, but I wash it down with the last of the lukewarm tea, set down my mug with more force than necessary, and lean back in the chair.

'Start talking, Karrion.'

With deliberate care, he folds my blanket and plumps my pillow. When I throw a teaspoon at him, he casts a reproachful glare over his shoulder.

'Was that really necessary?' he asks. He passes the spoon back and sits down.

'Why aren't you talking?' I ask.

'Wow, prison makes you crabby.'

'Can you blame me?'

'Point taken. Okay. I didn't want to tell you about this earlier in case it led nowhere, though after all the work, I would have been a bit miffed if it didn't, but I've been looking through the old records of Mageia.'

'The Mage Academy? Why?'

'What you said about Aleson being an East Mage kept niggling at the back of my mind. I couldn't find any aristocracy gossip about her mother having an affair, so I guess I was looking for proof that she really is an East Mage. If I could've got my hands on her transcripts or even just a list of grades, I would've seen straight away which was her primary school of magic.'

'Makes sense.'

'It was a wonderful theory, but Mageia refused to release the personal information of a former student. That was that. But it got me thinking about the sort of information that would be in public records. It led me to the lists of past prize winners, recipients of merit awards, scholarships, and so forth. No surprise that there are lots of prizes for Mages, unlike us mere mortal Shamans. But I digress. I found something.'

'What?!' I ask.

'Aleson won the Illumination Prize for two years running.'

'I've never heard of it.'

'Join the club. But the clue is in the name.'

Karrion's grin tells me he enjoys being cryptic, and I wish I had a fork to threaten him with. Waving a pillow or a hot-water bottle does not have the menacing effect I am looking for in a potential weapon.

'Illumination Prize sounds like something you'd win for Light magic.'

'Exactly. More than that, it's the prize for the highest exam marks across all years for a Light Mage.'

'But that's impossible. She's an East Mage.'

'Not when she completed her magical education she wasn't.' Karrion leaps up, his face brightening into a grin. 'Yan, I don't think the woman you met was Aleson Hampten.'

A dozen thoughts whir around my brain as I try to make sense of Karrion's words. It both makes sense and feels impossible.

'Why?' I ask, giving voice to the first coherent word that emerges from the chaos.

'I haven't a clue. But it makes sense, right?'

'I don't know.'

He is pacing now, up to the window and back, and his energy leaves me feeling dizzy. Is this what I look like when I am chasing the truth?

'Are you sure?' I ask before I get distracted by admiring how far Karrion has come in a few short months.

'As sure as I can be. The photos taken at the prize ceremony for both years bear a close resemblance to the pictures of a younger Aleson I found online. But there's more.'

'Go on,' I say. An echo of Karrion's excitement resonates within me.

'I've also looked into Maerk Hampten and the company. Truth be told, I wasn't making much progress until I decided to call the main number for the company and try my luck at charming the secretarial staff. A lovely lady at the reception desk told me two very interesting facts.'

When Karrion pauses for dramatic effect, I throw the teaspoon at him again. This time, he dodges.

'Get to the point, Karrion.'

'This would be a lot more fun if you played along.'

'At this rate, I'll die of old age before you'll divulge all your information.'

Karrion's grin indicates he would like to continue the banter, but my raised eyebrows persuade him otherwise. 'Fine. First of all, two months ago Maerk Hampten fired his secretary of ten years. Secondly, he's not been to the office in those two months.'

My exasperation vanishes while I try to wrap my mind around this latest piece of information.

'Why not?' I ask.

'According to the receptionist, he's been working from other offices and from home. All his meetings have been via conference calls. No one at the head office has seen him in those two months.'

'That's weird, though I'm not sure I see how firing the secretary fits into the picture.'

'I have an idea, but there's something I need to ask you first: when you confronted him at the warehouse, did you check what kind of magic user Hampten was?'

Instead of saying no straight away, I force my thoughts back to the jumbled memories from the warehouse. Time has made them no clearer, nor can I understand why everything is such a blur. There must be more going on than simple Fey glamour. Try as I might, I cannot remember what Hampten looked like, let alone what sort of a magic user he was.

Wait. I am searching the wrong part of my memory. While waking up next to his body was no less confusing, at least those images are clear in my mind. In fact, they are so vivid I have avoided going anywhere near them for fear of having to confront what I did. Could they contain the answers I am now looking for?

Without offering Karrion an explanation, I walk to the corner of the cell by the window and slide to the floor. My pelvis and the Fey scar protest when I pull my knees close to my chest, but I ignore the pain as I force myself to relive those moments after waking up, sticky with Hampten's blood. A distant part of me is aware of Karrion, faithful and trusting, standing guard by my side while I am lost in a nightmare of blood, swords, and grim Paladins. When it does not offer the insight I need, I sink even further into the memories until I recall the taste of Hampten's blood on my tongue. Although I am cut off from my power, the thought of lapping up magical blood sends a small thrill of pleasure down my spine.

Just as I am about to gag and lose my breakfast, it comes to me: alongside the rich bouquet of blood are wet fur, bones, and the sweetness of puppies. Hampten was a Dog Shaman.

My eyes fly open, and I push myself away from the wall. Karrion reaches for my hands and helps me up. I hurry to the bathroom and gulp handful after handful of water straight from the tap to banish the taste of blood that lingers in my mouth. When at last I turn to Karrion, the softness around his eyes tells me he understands something of my inner struggle.

'He was a Dog Shaman.'

Karrion nods, the stillness in his expression hinting at prior knowledge.

'If you knew that already, why did you ask?'

In his smile, I see a man who is no longer my apprentice but rather my partner. Despite my circumstances, my heart swells with pride as I regard him. We have worked together for less than six months, but already he has shown himself to be more than capable of handling anything a case might throw at us. More than that, he has not given up on me, like Jamie and Wishearth have.

'Actually, I didn't know,' he says, the smile remaining on his lips.

'But you suspected.'

'Yes, though I had no way of knowing what sort of magic user he was. All I was certain of, or near enough certain, was that he wasn't a South Mage.'

'Was he supposed to be a South Mage?' I ask.

'According to his family tree and school records, yes. You realise what this means, don't you?' Karrion rocks on to the balls of his feet, eager for my answer.

My thoughts remain in the echoes of the warehouse, and I shake my head to try to clear them. Power types and labels swirl around, confused and out of order.

'Hampten is a South Mage?' I ask at last.

'Yes.' Karrion's voice is gentler now, as if eager to guide me to the conclusion he has already reached. The balance of power between us has shifted, but I do not begrudge him for the knowledge he possesses or his new-found confidence.

'Which means that the man I... the man who died in the warehouse wasn't Hampten.'

Karrion's face splits in a grin. 'Exactly.'

The implications of this rush over me in a sensation so powerful I, too, rise and pace the length of the cell. All of a sudden my situation, while still dire, changes to a picture far more complicated than I'd first thought.

'If the woman who hired me wasn't Aleson Hampten and the man who died wasn't her husband, then who are they?'

'Yeah, not a clue.' Karrion's grin falters.

'But wait, the police and the Paladins are still holding me on suspicion of murdering Hampten, aren't they?'

'As far as I know, but it's not like Jamie answers my calls anymore.'

'They must have figured out that the man who died wasn't Hampten,' I say.

'Fingerprints or DNA ought to prove it. Though if the detective in charge asked the fake Aleson to identify the body, that could have prolonged the deception for a time. You'd think they'd compare him to photos of the real Hampten too, though they must have shared a reasonable likeness if Aleson directed you to real photos of Maerk. Did you think there was anything off about the man's appearance at the warehouse?'

Once more I return to my chaotic memories and to the dance of shadows around the walls. The lights were low, and behind the man, and all I recall is his general height and build. Those match Hampten's, but they are not much to go on. It's as though the lights were placed in a way to make it impossible to identify the man, and I say as much to Karrion, who nods.

'Now the secretary getting the sack makes perfect sense,' says Karrion. 'It's one thing to fool people from afar, quite another to convince someone who you've worked with every day for the past ten years. It also explains why he hasn't been to the office for the past two months.'

'I don't think it does. In fact, I think the whole pathologist figuring out the body isn't Maerk Hampten's point is moot. Where's Maerk Hampten himself in all this? Where is the real Aleson Hampten? Surely they would have got in touch with the police as soon as the papers plastered the murder across the front page?'

Karrion pauses, then shakes his head with a rueful chuckle. 'Damn. I was so caught up in the conspiracy that I forgot the basics. Sorry, boss.'

'Don't apologise.' I laugh. 'From the sound of it, you're on your way to solving the whole mystery while I'm rotting in jail. It's good to see that I still have my uses, even if it's just as your sounding board.'

'There's no way I could ever do this without you.'

I bite my lip before I point out that one day he must, assuming he wants to make a name for himself as a private investigator. Even if the Paladins choose not to put me in front of a Herald and execute me for murder, there will come a time when I am to return to the Wild Folk conclave that was once my home. If that happens, it will be up to Karrion to keep Wilde Investigations going. Envy sets my stomach churning as I imagine Karrion solving cases and chasing culprits around the dark streets of Old London while I play Dearon's obedient mate. I would much rather stay in Old London, much rather pursue criminals side by side with Karrion. But am I brave enough to abandon everything that makes me Wild Folk, everything that defines me?

Silence has settled between us, and Karrion clears his throat. I look up, realising that I have been staring at my toes.

'I think something's happened to Maerk Hampten,' he says.

'Like what?'

'It doesn't make sense for the real Hampten to fire his secretary and disappear off the face of the earth, but it's the first thing I'd do if I was impersonating someone. That's why he hasn't come forward now.'

'Do you think the wife was in on it? Maybe the company is in trouble and they were dodging creditors. They could have both disappeared off into the sunset, leaving impostors behind to lay a fake trail.'

'It's certainly possible. Who's looking for them on a beach somewhere if Maerk's murder makes the front-page news?'

'That would explain something else I thought was odd,' I say slowly, tugging at a loose thread in my memory. 'When the woman who hired us wrote a cheque for the retainer, it had been pre-signed. So, I think, was the cheque below it.'

'Makes sense. If someone is taking over your life, they'd need funds and it would keep the bank from growing suspicious if all activity on the Hamptens' accounts suddenly stopped.'

'We need to figure out who the imposters are. Have you checked the contact details that the woman gave me when she hired us?'

'Yes. The phone number is no longer in service and the email is from a free provider. Unless you know a hacker, we can't access her emails. The address is real in that it's the Hamptens' place.'

'If she gave me a burner phone number, there's a good chance she created the email account just to communicate with us. I keep coming back to thinking that the police must know by now that the victim wasn't Hampten.'

'I wouldn't count on it. They don't have us to aid their

investigations.' Karrion silences my protests with a wave of his hand. 'We're more awesome than you give us credit for. But seriously, there's been nothing in the papers about the victim not being Hampten.'

'The police and the Paladins may have chosen to keep that detail from the press if they're conducting a fraud investigation.'

'True.' Karrion thinks for a moment, drumming his fingers on the side of the wardrobe. 'Mum gave me the name of her friend who used to be the Hamptens' cleaner. It came as no surprise that she was dismissed two months ago without a warning or an explanation. But what's weird is that she was sacked by email.'

'That seems a bit informal,' I say.

'My thoughts exactly. She got three months' pay in return for not working her notice period, which is far more than stipulated in her contract. She was quite happy with that, but did think the whole situation was weird.'

'Two months ago fits with our timeline of the Hamptens disappearing. My guess is, your mum's friend was sacked via email because she would have realised the people now occupying the Hamptens' home weren't the real deal.'

'I'll keep digging into the company's finances. Perhaps I can find some indication that it's struggling, which might explain why the Hamptens took off.'

'Thanks, Karrion.'

We speak of other inconsequential matters until the guard opens the door to indicate that the visiting hour is at its end. Karrion hugs me close and for once, I do not complain about crushed ribs or my inability to breathe.

'I'm not giving up hope,' he whispers, 'and neither should you.'

His words focus my thoughts while I examine everything he has told me. My inability to do anything from the cell is frustrating, but I know Karrion is doing his best and more, perhaps even more than I ever could. The notion brings a smile to my face.

That smile disappears an hour later when another Paladin appears in the doorway.

'Ms Wilde, the Crown Prosecution Service and the Brotherhood of Justice have decided that the case against you is strong enough for you to appear before a Herald of Justice.'

FEBRUARY
WEDNESDAY

11

THE PULL OF THE OCEAN

The murmur of many conversations turns the courtroom into a cavern of echoes. A cascade of noise washes over me as I am ushered in, flanked by two grim Paladins. I stop beside the summoning circle, careful not to touch the true silver symbols carved on to the floor. The marble is cold under my bare feet, but the dull ache it triggers barely registers against the backdrop of agony which consumes me. The Paladins chain me to the iron pillar next to the summoning circle and leave, taking their positions on either side of the enormous double doors.

Seating is arranged in a semicircle in raised galleries, and a sea of people looks down. I spot Karrion and his mother in the front row. Aderyn flashes me a watery smile, while Karrion studies me with intense concern. As much as I would like to reassure them, I can't.

A few rows behind them, Lady Bergamon and Wishearth sit side by side, heads bowed together. My heart clenches at the sight of Wishearth. Why did he come? I keep my attention on them, a little disappointed that neither acknowledge me in any way. There are other familiar faces in the crowd: Fria and

Tinker Thaylor sit at the opposite ends of the gallery, which strikes me as odd, and even the librarian from the Royal Exchange, Fortnem, is present, though without his spirit raven. It seems that my reputation as a PI has extended further than I realised. Or are they here to satisfy their curiosity and to watch me fall from grace?

Behind me, the double doors open again. The officials representing the High Council of Mages, the Circle of Shamans, the Brotherhood of Justice, and the Metropolitan Police file past me. Even in my dazed state, I am shocked to see Lord Wellaim Ellensthorne, the Speaker for the High Council and the First among the Shadow Mages, turn to face me behind the officials' table. Our eyes lock, and his lips curl up in a slow smirk. His warning about Wild Folk killers from last December echoes in my ears. I am the first to look away, and my gaze slides along the table to rest on Jamie. His attention is fixed on a point somewhere near my feet, and my stomach lurches. I both feared and hoped he would be present.

The Paladin takes her place next to the summoning circle. She is not someone I recognise from my dealings with the Brotherhood of Justice, but the Paladins have strict rules about keeping those serving at the judgements separate from those guarding the prisoners. Her expression betrays no emotion as she nods to Lord Ellensthorne, who indicates that she should proceed.

Unable to look away, I watch as the Paladin kneels on the far side from the iron pillar and begins the summoning. Power flows outward from her. Secured with magic-nulling chains, I cannot sense her aura, but the magic slides along my skin like the caress of sea mist. The smell of true silver and ozone fills the air. One by one, the sigils begin to glow. My gaze locks on the empty space in the middle of the circle.

The portal shimmers into existence in a burst of electric-

and-azure-blue light. The colours are so bright I see nothing beyond the figure stepping through, though my vantage point should offer me a glimpse of another plane. In his wake, the gateway collapses into a sphere of power, which roils and changes every moment. Staring at it for more than a few seconds makes me feel so dizzy I have to look away. The Herald straightens in front of me. His long hair could be white or black, and like his robes, it shifts through every shade of grey. Both the robes and his hair billow in a wind that only affects him. Up close, his features, too long to be human, are sharp and severe. The solid azure eyes give the impression that they see everything at once.

Lord Ellensthorne unwinds a scroll and reads: 'Yannia Wilde, you are hereby accused of the murder of Maerk Hampten, a South Mage, and engaging in an act of cannibalism to obtain power. Stand ready to receive the judgement of a Herald of Justice.'

A silence has settled over the courtroom, and Lord Ellensthorne's smug words echo in the cavernous space.

The Paladin rises to her feet and bows low. Although I cannot understand the language, the respect in her tone makes the message clear. Lifting her gaze to address the Herald towering several feet over me, she relays the charges to him.

The fear begins as a tremor in my hands and develops into shaking so powerful I lean against the iron pillar to remain upright. My face is flushed and my breathing is ragged. Black spots swim across my vision, and I will myself not to faint, grateful I chose not to eat breakfast.

Lost in the terror, I miss the Herald stepping closer. A myriad of scents washes over me, each more bizarre than the previous one, each impossible to define in terms of human existence.

The Herald looms over me. I tilt my chin up so he may look into my soul and hold my breath as I wait for the verdict.

An eternity passes as the Herald stares at me. All that I am is laid bare before him, but I feel no sense of intrusion, only a burning desire to finally know the truth. He will answer the question I most need answered: am I a murderer?

The Herald utters a word. So deep is the connection between us that I expect to understand him, as if the ritual has granted me wisdom I never yet possessed. But the sound is as alien as when the Paladin translated the charges. She must surely do so again. Or are we expected to guess the outcome? As I begin to turn my head, she speaks.

'Innocent.'

A wave of murmured conversations erupting all around the galleries washes over me while I try to process the verdict. Innocent? Does that mean I didn't kill anyone?

I barely notice the portal opening to accommodate the departing Herald or the officials stepping away from the long desk. Lord Ellensthorne arches an eyebrow, but I have no time to make sense of his expression before the same Paladins who escorted me in release the chains binding me to the pillar. The last things I see before the guards lead me out are Karrion sprinting towards an exit and Lady Bergamon smiling at me. Wishearth is nowhere to be seen. I'm glad.

The Paladins take me along unremarkable corridors to the main guard post outside the prison cells. They unlock the manacles and set out a bag containing those few personal effects the police did not retain as evidence. A distracted part of me listens to them explaining that I need to sign various forms regarding my release and that I should return the grey tracksuit at my earliest opportunity. The police took all the clothes I was wearing when I woke up in the warehouse. How am I to catch the bus home without shoes? Perhaps Karrion thought of it, though I cannot call him because my phone was also evidence.

Once I have signed my name half a dozen times, all that remains is for one of the Paladins to remove the collar. I tremble in anticipation of becoming whole again and I have to grip the counter in front of me to stay still. Instead of reaching for a key, one of the Paladins whispers words of power behind me, and the two sides of the collar come apart.

I have no more than a second to feel relief before I collapse like a puppet whose strings have been cut. The impact with the marble floor is a distant echo of pain compared to the awful hollowness in me. My limbs are all separate, disconnected from my spine by the absence of magic. I am empty, powerless, and I roll on to my side as nausea sweeps me away.

Strong arms gather me close, while smooth and rough fingers stroke my forehead. Some of the vomit dribbles down my cheek and tears of shame spill down to join it. A white cloth embroidered with small yellow flowers is used to clean my face. When I look up, my gaze finds eyes in the exact shade of summer skies in Lady Bergamon's garden.

'We've got you,' Karrion whispers from my other side.

He lifts me with enviable ease and carries me out of the Brotherhood. After three weeks indoors, even the polluted air of Old London tastes heady, but I have no time to take in the different smells before Lady Bergamon opens a car door and Karrion eases me into the back seat.

'Do you still feel sick?' he asks.

I shake my head, not trusting my voice. Lady Bergamon slips into the front passenger seat and twists to watch me.

'Good, because it's your car you'll be hurling all over,' Karrion says. 'Also, you should feel fortunate to know you'll be my first passengers since passing my test yesterday.'

'It's only a short ride,' Lady Bergamon says. 'Soon you'll be feeling much better.'

A flash of light nearby causes me to screw my eyes shut to control the rising nausea. Karrion swears and starts the car. Even with my eyes closed, I feel the hesitation in the way he drives and the way the car shudders before every acceleration. We reach our destination in one piece, and Karrion sighs before unclipping his seat belt.

It comes as no surprise to me that he has driven us to Lady Bergamon's house on Ivy Street. Karrion opens the car's passenger door and I shuffle out. The world tilts. He catches me before I fall, and carries me to Lady Bergamon's door, through the house, and out into the back garden. Lady Bergamon hurries past him and spreads a blanket on the lawn. Karrion lays me on it. My hand rests on the grass.

'Let the garden restore your power,' Lady Bergamon says, and drapes another blanket over me.

Despite it being only early February, here in Lady Bergamon's garden the spring is further along and the sun is warm on my face. My skin prickles as I absorb the rays and become aware of hushed voices nearby. I have no power to enhance my hearing, but I can just make out the words.

'She shouldn't be this low on power,' Lady Bergamon says.

'Could it be because of the collar? She was imprisoned for three weeks.'

'The collar prevented her from accessing her magic, but it shouldn't drain it away.'

'Then what's going on?' Karrion asks.

'I'm not sure.'

The voices slip away as I focus on the garden. I feel no better than when Karrion laid me down. Is Lady Bergamon correct that there's something wrong with me? Did the pain and the isolation break me? No. In the past, all I had to do was open myself to the power within the garden and it restored my magic. This should be no different.

With that thought in mind, I reach out, seeking the fine web of power that connects everything in Lady Bergamon's domain. But rather than finding the familiar weave, I feel searing pain. I curl into a ball, my mouth open in a wordless scream as I struggle to draw a breath. While my lungs burn for air, my mind sings with an agony so pure that nothing I have experienced over the past three weeks comes close to touching it. The only clear thought that forms is a certainty that any moment now, my heart will stop beating. I welcome the solace death promises.

Lady Bergamon strides to me, speaking words of power in a voice that resembles the crack of thunder. Clouds obscure the sun; the shadow of winter is upon me. The ground trembles with the echo of distant hooves. A gust of wind slams against my face, bearing with it whispered words of a language both ancient and inhuman. Water floods my veins, filling my lungs and separating me from the agony. Lady Bergamon straightens my limbs and rolls me on to my back. I am helpless to resist. The arms of the ocean lift me to the surface, allowing me to draw a breath of salty sea air.

'My lady.'

Bradán's familiar voice comes from somewhere nearby. Both Lady Bergamon and the wind have grown silent, but I remain buoyed by the rise and fall of the waves.

'Something's wrong with Yannia,' Lady Bergamon says. 'Can you help?'

A grey horse head appears in my field of vision and Bradán's red eyes bore into mine. Salt water drips on to my face from the seaweed tangled in his mane. He inhales longer than any mortal could and reaches to brush my fingers with his muzzle. No sooner do I feel the velvet softness of his skin than he recoils with a gasp of pain, a black burn forming on his upper lip.

'She's being poisoned.'

'What with?!' Karrion asks.

'Karrion, can you fetch a bucket of water from the well?' Lady Bergamon asks.

'There's water right here.'

'Yes, but it's not from the garden. Please? We need it urgently.'

'Fine,' he says, and hurries away.

'Yannia,' Lady Bergamon leans over me, 'can you tell me the source of the pain?'

The question confuses me. I am floating in water that is neither hot nor cold, somewhere near my beach. There is no pain in this place, nothing but the swell of waves and the overwhelming peace that beckons me away from the figures gathered around me. I am so tired it would be easy to close my eyes and let go.

'She's fading,' Bradán says.

'We must adjust the spell to keep her here. But be careful, unravel it too much and her heart will give out.'

The agony returns, so sudden that I arch my spine and cry out. A distant part of me resents Lady Bergamon and Bradán for inflicting this suffering on me. Why will they not let me go, when the ocean is calling me with the promise of rest at last?

'Yannia, where's the pain?'

If I answer her question, perhaps she will grant me peace. She has the power of life and death, over blood and plants, the soil and the stars. All of this I know, just as I know the wildness and its call. But the agony comes from a different world.

'Tem,' I gasp.

'What?' Lady Bergamon asks, but Bradán leans forward.

'The wound on her side.'

Lady Bergamon pulls my shirt up, exposing the Fey scar. 'This is old.'

'That is how it appeared moments after the Winter Queen's healer finished her work.'

'If one of your kind can achieve this, so could another.'

Hurried footsteps and panting announce Karrion's approach. He sets the bucket next to me and leans closer.

'Is someone going to tell me what's going on?' he asks.

Lady Bergamon ignores him and turns to Bradán. 'Can you hold the spell? I need to fetch supplies from inside.'

'Yes, though not indefinitely.'

'I won't be long.' Lady Bergamon kneels next to me and strokes stray locks of hair off my forehead. The pain eases again, leaving me lying in the shallows. 'Don't stray too far out to sea, otherwise you'll be lost forever.'

Before I have a chance to protest that I cannot move my limbs and thus have no control over the water, she is gone. Karrion takes her place next to me, murmuring words of comfort. Is it me he is trying to convince or himself? I should find the fear in his voice upsetting, but he is only partly here and the water is soothing against my skin.

I drift until Lady Bergamon returns and a reflection off the heart-copper bowl she is carrying stings my eyes. She pours some of the water from the bucket into it and adds herbs.

'You're going to need to change form,' she says.

At first I think she is talking to me and I struggle to find the words to explain that I have no power for shifting, but then I see Bradán's outline shimmer and contort. Soon, a naked man crouches next to me, seaweed still entangled in his long hair.

'What would you have me do, my lady?'

'Hold her legs.'

Bradán shifts until he is crouched over my legs and presses his hands on my thighs. It is as though a brick wall has settled on me, though it causes no pain.

'Wait, what are you planning to do?' Karrion asks.

'We need to extract the poison from Yannia before her heart gives out,' Lady Bergamon says.

'You're not seriously suggesting cutting her open out here, are you?'

'There's no choice.'

'Hospitals exist for this very reason.'

'She'd never reach one alive.' Lady Bergamon leans closer to my face, as if concerned about my reaction though I have not made a sound. 'The only thing keeping her alive is the spell Bradán and I wove around her and it will snap if we try to move her away from the garden.'

'So you're going to perform surgery on your lawn?'

Even in his outrage, Karrion does not move, though his hand squeezes my shoulder. I wish briefly that I could take his hand and tell him that everything will be all right, but the scent of wet sand steals the thought away.

'This is the source of my power,' Lady Bergamon says, and softens her voice. 'She will feel no pain, but we must act quickly. The longer we wait, the greater the chance that the damage will be permanent.'

Karrion hesitates for what seems like an eternity, then nods. 'What do you need me to do?'

'Brace her shoulders like Bradán is doing with her legs.'

'Fine.' He grips my shoulders.

Cool water trickles over my abdomen, unlike the lap of the waves, and I begin to protest when Lady Bergamon speaks in a language I do not recognise. The moon waxes and wanes, stars wheel across the sky, and green shoots push through the dark soil. I wish I could see the skeins of magic she gathers around me, connecting us both to every plant in her domain. Thus distracted, I barely feel the blade splitting open my skin.

The beach is all around me, beckoning me to run like I used to. It has been too long since I have sped across the dunes and the flat expanse of sand, all of nature running with me. In my mind's eye, my legs morph into wolf paws and deer hooves, my arms into wings, until I am nothing but the wilderness. Perhaps there I could find my power again.

Beyond the expanse of sand, the sea calls out to me, no longer content with an invitation to play in the shallows. The deep water whispers a promise of solace and freedom. I could disappear, be truly wild, if only the weight on my shoulders and thighs would lift.

A shadow falls across me as Karrion leans closer to Lady Bergamon. 'What's that?'

'It is cursed cold iron,' says Bradán in a low growl.

'Doesn't your kind regard all cold iron as cursed?'

'A fair observation, Man of the Sky, yet in this instance the object bears a Fey curse.'

'Do you know what kind?'

'One for binding power,' Lady Bergamon replies. 'It sapped Yannia's magic when she was imprisoned and turned her natural ability to draw power from the world around her into pain so severe it would surely have killed her without intervention.'

'Who could have done it?' Karrion asks.

'I'm afraid you'll have to do the detective work; I am merely a healer.'

Silence falls around me while Lady Bergamon works. There are times when I feel tugging at my side, but there is no pain and the seagulls wheeling across the sky make concentration impossible. Their cries speak of the sea, fish, and wind in their feathers. Karrion must hear them too, but he never looks up. I would like to ask why, whether he has something against gulls as well as pigeons, but it would be impolite to interrupt the birds.

'Bradán, I will need your help in sealing the wound,' Lady Bergamon says.

Sunlight heats the top layer of the water I am floating in. The crashing waves contain an incantation, but I cannot discern the words. When the heat intensifies, it reminds me of a smoky presence in my life. I shy away from the memories of Wishearth's arms around me and think instead of the campfires of my youth. Dearon and I lay under the stars, listening to the moors and woods around us. Life was uncomplicated then, and I had no notion of the pain and suffering that would follow.

'It is done.'

The pressure against my legs and shoulders eases. Karrion sits back. In the periphery of my vision, Bradán steps clear of me and returns to his equine form. He tosses his head, sending a spray of droplets over me.

'We are even, Wild Woman.'

I would like to respond, but my attention is drawn to the invisible web connecting each blade of grass beneath my fingers. It takes all of my strength to shift my hand, but the movement is enough to connect me to the threads as fine as spider silk.

A wave lifts me high and carries me to the shore. I lie on the wet sand, clear of the ocean, and allow my eyes to slip closed.

12

EMPTY

The sky is fading to indigo when I next open my eyes. I am lying on my side, facing the orchard, and someone has draped a blanket over me. The cooling air is filled with rich scents, and without thinking, I reach out to my magic to sharpen my senses. All at once, I smell the soil beneath me, the grass wet with rising dew, and a hint of blood somewhere nearby. An owl hoots in the distant forest. The moisture in the air caresses my face, and I taste the velvet edge of it on my parched tongue. A cloaked figure sharpens into the approaching Lady Bergamon. She is carrying a basket, and a single inhale tells me it is filled with wild garlic.

Upon seeing that my eyes are open, Lady Bergamon crouches next to me and strokes my forehead with fingers stained green. The scent of garlic intensifies.

'How are you feeling?'

I remain still while I consider the question. The terrible agony is gone, leaving behind only a memory of itself; a shape within me that was once occupied by pain. My hip aches from lying in the same position for too long, but the discomfort is tempered by an echo of distant waves.

In this twilight moment, nothing beyond the boundaries of the garden feels real. I know that were I to turn my thoughts elsewhere, my mind would be filled with memories of fear, guilt, and uncertainty, but I fix my eyes on the intricate weave of Lady Bergamon's basket, and I struggle upright. A wave of dizziness washes over me, and I hang my head while I wait for it to subside.

'Better, thanks.'

With Lady Bergamon's help, I stand and stagger indoors. In the kitchen, she draws out the nearest chair for me and I sit down. My toes prickle, and I glance at them, half surprised that my feet are bare. I had forgotten that I am still dressed like a prisoner. More than anything I want to be rid of the clothes and scrub my skin until the stench of the cell is gone. But I merely sit there, watching Lady Bergamon brew a mug of her pain-relieving tea. She adds half a teaspoon of white powder from a jar bearing a drawing of a poppy, and three teaspoons of honey.

'Drink this,' she says, and sets the cup in front of me. 'It's not as strong as I might have otherwise made it, but I understand that you've had no proper medication for weeks. This shouldn't make you too drowsy.'

Heedless of the heat of the tea, I drink it in long swallows. Some honey remains at the bottom of the mug and I scrape it into my mouth. The sweetness brings a familiar nausea, and I grit my teeth while I stare at the faded green cupboards.

Lady Bergamon sets a plate down on the table. On it are two cheese and pickle sandwiches.

'You should eat something, you look half-starved. Did the Paladins not feed you?'

Trying to find the words to explain is too much effort, and I pick up the first sandwich. The bread is dark and filled with seeds; one of Lady Bergamon's homemade loaves. I eat with little regard for taste, but the tartness of the pickle dispels the nausea.

'Karrion left your car here,' Lady Bergamon says, and I realise my silence unnerves her. 'He assumed you'd like some peace to settle back in at home and said that he would stop by first thing tomorrow morning. I've put a pair of gardening shoes by the front door for you. Return them when you next visit.'

I nod as I carry my mug and plate to the sink. There is much I should thank her for, an explanation I should offer for the silence I wear as a mantle, but the lump in my throat blocks any words I might utter. Perhaps she senses this, for Lady Bergamon draws me into a hug. Her hold is stronger than a month ago, and beneath the numbness encasing me, I rejoice in her gradual recovery. Like her plants, she is healing.

'If there's anything you need, even if it's just company, I'm here. Or you can ask Wishearth to pass me a message.'

Hiding my flinch at Wishearth's name by brushing hair from my face, I step back and nod. At the door, I turn to find Lady Bergamon watching me.

'Thank you,' I say as I slip my feet into the unfamiliar shoes and leave.

My flat smells musty and damp. Karrion must have visited regularly, for the mail is arranged neatly on my desk. Notes are attached to each opened envelope, but I ignore them and make my way upstairs. My living area is tidy, and I make a mental note to thank Karrion tomorrow. A couple of dog toys lie abandoned near the window. I should walk to the Open Hearth to pick up Sinta, but I remain rooted to the spot. We have been apart for too long, and yet I am not certain I can face Wishearth tonight.

The sound of a door closing above me alerts me to the fact that I have stood in the empty lounge long enough for my legs to begin aching despite Lady Bergamon's medicine. I return downstairs and to the bathroom, which is also cleaner than I remember leaving it. Perhaps cleaning has been Karrion's way of dealing with the frustration of seeing me imprisoned.

Now I am free, and yet I still feel the manacles around my wrists and ankles. When I swallow, the collar remains firm against my skin. Yet, I was declared innocent.

I stand under the cool water for a long time, savouring the droplets hitting my upturned face. When I reach for the shower gel, I give in to my earlier desire and scrub my skin until it is pink. Even as the scent of mint fills the small space, I fancy I can detect a remnant of the cell at the back of my nostrils. It is this notion of futility in my actions that drives me to switch off the shower and reach for a towel. The feel of my wet hair clinging to my skin reminds me of my most feral moments in the cell, and I reach for the hairdryer. Anything to feel normal again.

My fingers drift to the scar on my side. It is the same silver colour as before, even though I have a vague memory of Lady Bergamon cutting into me to remove something. Perhaps this is what Bradán meant when he said we were now even. I trace the irregular line with my fingertips, but it feels no different from before. A memory of agony echoes through my mind before fading into the steady song of the waves.

After returning upstairs, I pace; listless and restless. My steps slow near the fireplace. Karrion has stacked logs in it, ready for a new fire, but I cannot bring myself to light one. Wishearth ignored my calls at the Brotherhood of Justice. How, then, can I invoke the old rituals here? Even if he came, how could I look him in the eye and see his certainty of my guilt reflected among the flames? Better to stay away from the fire and allow the ice to numb any feeling of abandonment.

After my fifth circuit around the lounge, I walk to the wardrobe and survey its contents. I own no dresses, and a white shirt tucked into my tightest jeans will have to do. The bathroom mirror is still fogged up from my shower, and I dry it with a towel. After pinning my hair up, I check my reflection in the mirror. The eyes staring back at me are empty. My fingers drift up to release one of the shirt buttons, revealing the top of my black bra. I leave before I lose my nerve.

The club is busy. Most of the tables are occupied, and the dance floor is a mass of people. The music is loud enough to discourage conversation, which suits me well. I make my way to the dance floor. A Mage is standing on a platform next to the DJ, swaying to the music as she sends a dozen glitterballs spinning over the people. The display of light is dazzling, but when I see the glimmer of sun on fresh snow in it, I tear my gaze away. Tonight, I am not me.

At first, I hesitate before the sea of beautiful people. Countless insecurities rear up, but I refuse to confront them. The beat thumps through me, and I embrace it; body and mind. My feet move on their own accord. I am rusty to begin with, a little too self-conscious, but soon my muscles recall old dance moves and the joy of the movement takes over. The scar on my side remains painless. Magical auras press against me from all sides. I ignore them, just as I ignore the scents of power. Closing my eyes, I drown myself in the music.

Time loses meaning. I dance until thirst drives me to the curve of opaque glass serving as the bar. My words are barely audible, but the woman leaning forward appears adept at reading lips. She soon places a glass in front of me and accepts a folded note in return. I tilt my head back and drain the glass, savouring the burn of rum and the buzz of caffeine. The bartender arches an eyebrow, and I shake my head. She clears away my glass and flashes a flirtatious smile at two men standing at the far end of the bar.

I smell her first: sweat, lipstick, and vanilla. Overlapping them are cinnamon, clouds heavy with rain, mud, and coconut. An East Mage. Closing my eyes, I let my imagination run wild. My lips are already curving up when I turn and lean my hip against the bar. Her black hair glows in the light of the spells, and her dark eyes draw me in. At the sight of her full lips, I swallow and wish for another drink. She caresses me with her gaze and her smile widens. The hunger I witness in her thaws some of the permafrost holding me captive.

She offers me her hand, the curve of her wrist accentuating the delicate bones and the shadow of veins beneath the skin. I reach out to her. The connection reaffirms silent questions asked and answered all at once. She draws me to the dance floor.

Her skill far surpasses mine, but tonight I refuse to feel intimidated. Instead, I let her guide me until we dance as one. We begin at arm's length, but as one song blurs to the next, an unseen force draws us together until we become a being of eight limbs and two heads. Even then, it is not close enough.

We move around the dance floor, and she guides me to the far end, where the Mage's lights cannot banish the gloom lingering around the tables. It is only there, in the no man's land between movement and stillness, that she kisses me. Her lips taste of cherry blossoms with a hint of tequila. I respond as if I might drown myself in her. Perhaps I can. With the same grace as she showed on the dance floor, she backs into the corner of a curved sofa and draws me on to her lap. I go willingly, running my fingers through her damp hair while I chase something undefined in our kisses. Her hands slip into the back pockets of my jeans, and she pulls me closer. The music fades to the periphery, as do all the people sharing the space with us.

The desire that speeds through my veins awakens something in me that has lain dormant for too long. This woman could be my solace for the night, an antidote against the empty flat and the cold fireplace. If she welcomes me into her home and her bed, I could remain a stranger for a few hours more.

Hairs at the back of my neck prick up. As my eyes open, I catch a glimpse of a prehensile tail swaying to the rhythm of the music. Ice cracks beneath me, sending a spike of adrenaline through my body just as I plunge to my watery death. My lungs fill with water; a current pulling me deeper into the darkness.

I jerk back, flailing in an effort to find my balance. A hand finding the edge of the table behind me keeps me from falling. Beyond my companion, in the darkest corner of the club, Pheonix's lavender eyes glow.

'What's wrong?' the woman asks, confusion and concern competing. She seems oblivious to the Fey behind her.

My breathing comes in ragged gasps as I force my focus on her. The desire I felt only moments ago remains, but it is as though I am staring at her through a clear sheet of ice. She will not provide the warmth I am looking for.

'I'm sorry... I have to go.'

Ignoring Pheonix, who leans against a wall with a smirk, I hurry away. Outside, the air is cool and I draw it deep into my lungs as I button my coat. Perhaps it will snow tonight. The numbness I have been trying to avoid settles over me, and my shoulders sag.

The Winter Queen has won.

My steps are heavy as I make my way up the stairs to the lounge. The shadows of the winter night have coalesced to form a darkness deep enough that I hesitate at the threshold. But I have nowhere else to go and I force myself forward. The yawning emptiness of the fireplace is a silent rebuke, and I turn my back to it to stare out of the window. Most of the neighbours have gone to bed, and there is little to see in my tiny garden.

A glint of orange arrests my attention, and I borrow the sight of a cat I sense nearby to see better into the garden. There is nothing but a shed and shrubbery out there. Another glimmer draws my gaze to the right. It takes me longer than it should to realise that what I am seeing are mere reflections in the glass, and I turn around. The fireplace is filled with sparks, and they ignite the logs with magical celerity. As the flames rise, they grow into the shape of a man. Wishearth steps out, straightening to his full height on the hearthstones.

'Yannia,' he says, and in his voice, I hear a myriad of emotions I am too tired to identify.

'Wishearth.' I cannot think what else to say.

'I was expecting to hear from you earlier.'

With the fire behind him, it is impossible to interpret the expression on his face, but there are no sparks in his eyes now. I turn partly away, for once not comfortable with how easily he reads me.

'Why?' The question falls from my lips with more bitterness than I had intended. 'You lost interest in my offerings.'

Wishearth takes a step forward, keeping one heel in the fire. 'What are you talking about?'

'When I spoke to you at the Brotherhood, you never came.' My voice cracks, and I hate myself for it. 'You always know more about what's going on than us mere mortals, so I figured you knew that I'd be declared guilty and wanted no part of it or my execution.'

'I came every time you called me,' he says, and sits on the hearthstones. 'No matter how much I spoke to you or tried to reach out to touch you, you couldn't hear me. I hoped you'd still know I was there, though I suspected you didn't from the way you sounded later on.'

'You were there?' All the disappointment and bitterness intermingle with relief until they become indistinguishable and fade into the numbness holding me a prisoner. 'You came?'

This could be why few humans follow the old ways. What is the point of making offerings to an entity who never responds?

'Of course. Did you really think I was going to abandon you? Is that how you think I reward a lifetime of loyalty and repay you for your friendship?'

Heat rolls off him in waves. I dig my nails into my palms to keep from backing away, unwilling to offend him when things are just beginning to make sense again. But the warmth is stifling enough that I struggle to draw a breath.

'I... I don't know.' Shifting back, I cover the movement by reaching out to him and letting my hand drop. 'You always seem to know... I mean, were you there that night?'

'When the Mage died?' Wishearth looks away, his lips pressed into a thin line. 'I'm not as omniscient as you think. Watching you constantly beyond the reach of a fireplace would require so much power that even the offerings of every resident in the city might not be enough. So no, I wasn't there and I don't know exactly what happened beyond what Karrion and Lady Bergamon have told me.'

Was I counting on him to offer certainty, or is it better that he did not see me waking up in a pool of blood? Surely of all the people in my life, there is no one except Dearon who understands the wildness of my nature better than Wishearth.

It is that thought, more than anything, that prompts me to approach until the heat radiating from him is all but unbearable.

I want to reach out to him, to ask him to lend me his strength, but the icy hatred forces me back. Balling my hands into fists, I want to scream my frustration at the Winter Queen for creating a barrier between Wishearth and me. Then the frost settles over me and the anger melts away like the first snowflakes of a winter.

'What's wrong, Yannia?'

Wishearth's voice is gentler now and his eyes glow softly in the gloom of the flat. There is a lump of hard snow in my throat, and it takes all my efforts to speak despite the geas holding me captive.

'I can't find my bearings,' I say, trying to find the words to explain the disconnect. 'It's like I'm adrift without an anchor. Dark water surrounds me and a storm is coming. If I don't find something to hold on to, I'll be lost. Wishearth, I don't want to be frozen forever.'

He rises and draws me to the fire, despite my resistance. The blaze burns high in the presence of a Hearth Spirit, and I recoil from the heat.

'You have to fight this,' Wishearth says, and reaches to run his fingers over my forehead.

As soon as he makes contact with the Winter Queen's invisible mark, heat floods through me, banishing some of the ice. We stare at each other across the short distance, and I wish his flames would engulf me. If I caught alight, perhaps I would be free of the Winter Queen's influence. Perhaps then the terrible pain that burdens me in my every waking moment would ease. I could become a being of flame and heat, free at last.

Wishearth's image grows blurred as the desire to no longer be overwhelms me. I slump forward, relieved and surprised in equal measure when his arms gather me close. The scent of wood smoke drowns me in Wishearth, and I bury my face in the crook of his neck. It is not until his coat turns wet that I realise I am crying. My awareness opens the floodgates, and I sob until I am certain my body will break in half and my mind will be lost in endless sorrow. Wishearth coaxes me forward until I am cradled in his lap, and he holds me while all the emotions I have held in during the trial escape.

We stay like that for what seems like forever, but eventually he eases me back until I am lying on my bed, still held in his arms. A feather-light touch of fire caresses my eyelids in turn, then my forehead, and finally, as the darkness draws me into a different embrace, my lips.

THURSDAY

13

BEGINNING ANEW

I wake to the sound of someone moving around in the kitchen. My mouth has a fuzzy aftertaste of rum and my eyes are puffy from all the crying, but I have slept better than in all the time I was imprisoned. I push myself up on my elbows and I realise I am still dressed in last night's clothes, though a blanket is draped half across me. At first I assume Karrion has come in quietly enough not to wake me, but then Wishearth enters, carrying a plate and a mug of tea.

'Does Open Hearth deliver breakfast now?' I ask to cover my surprise.

'You missed supper last night, so this is the next best thing.'

His coat is off and his hair is more tousled than usual. Did he spend the night here? Did he lie next to me, guarding my sleep? There is a vague memory of hot lips on my skin that teases the edge of my consciousness, and I will myself not to blush.

'Do Hearth Spirits sleep?' I blurt out.

'Not in a way that you mortals consider sleeping, but we have our way of resting.' Before I have a chance to ask him to elaborate, he hands me the plate. 'Here. I made you these.'

'Thanks.'

Wishearth runs his fingers over my collarbone visible through the open shirt collar. The gesture conveys intimacy beyond anything I was expecting, and a flush creeps to my cheeks.

'You look like you haven't eaten properly in weeks.'

'I didn't have much of an appetite while I was imprisoned.'

'That's understandable.'

Something about the smell of the toast intrigues me, and I peer between the layers of toppings. 'Ham, cheese, and... marmalade?'

'They're the traditional breakfast flavours, are they not? You don't have any bacon or eggs in your fridge.'

'Right... yes.'

He looks at me with clear expectation, and I take a tentative bite from the toast. Although I expect the combination to be unpleasant, the salty ham offsets the sweetness and creates something resembling a balanced flavour. It is not a combination I would ever choose, but it's edible, especially when my empty stomach makes its presence felt.

'Good effort,' I say, and take a swig of my tea. 'Is this your first time making breakfast?'

'Is it that obvious?'

'I've always assumed you don't eat. All I've ever seen you with is a pint.'

'For the most part, that's true, though I make an exception for Lady Bergamon's cake.'

'Who doesn't?'

The smile I receive in response has a softness to it I have never encountered before. As if reading my mind, Wishearth clears his throat and reaches to press his fingers against my forehead.

'How are you feeling?'

'Better. Whatever you did, it melted the ice.'

The "for now" remains unsaid, but as the smile fades from his lips, I know Wishearth heard it just the same.

'I've told you before that there is no shame in asking for help. Here in Old London, you are surrounded by people who care for you and owe you a great debt of gratitude. I understand that life can be complicated, but you don't have to take the burden of the whole world upon yourself.'

My skin prickles from the tension that forms between us. I search Wishearth's eyes for sparks, but all I see are flames. Without thinking, I reach out to take his hand. To my surprise, he entwines his fingers with mine. Heat spreads up my arm and for the first time in a couple of months, it triggers no discomfort.

'Wishearth,' I swallow, 'thank you for coming to check up on me. I should have had more faith in you.'

'It's easy to expect the worst outcome when the circumstances are bleak.' He squeezes my fingers. 'At least now you know.'

'Yes.'

His eyes drift to my lips. I swallow again, conscious of how dry my mouth is and how his warmth connects us. Wishearth shifts closer, and a hint of a smoky breath caresses my cheek.

The sound of the doorbell ringing causes me to jump and let go of his hand. He pulls back his fingers as the flames disappear from his eyes, replaced by smoke. A moment later, they clear.

'It's Karrion.'

'Right. Good.'

My eyes drift around the room, focusing on anything but Wishearth. I feel cheated, but also a little relieved. Things are complicated enough as they are. Yet I feel the ghost of his breath on my face again and shiver at the memory.

'I should go. You two have investigating to do and Funja will have today's first pint waiting for me. It would be rude to keep him waiting.'

'Yes.'

We both stand. It is Wishearth's turn to reach a hand towards me, only to let it drop before making contact. With a rueful smile, he disappears in a shower of sparks.

Footsteps echo from the staircase, accompanied by a familiar yowling. I smile and move the plate and the mug to the table to save them from being trampled. Karrion opens the door and has just enough time to bend down before Sinta launches herself out of his arms. She shoots towards me, her lead trailing behind her, and leaps against my legs. I try to pet her, but she is too excited to stay still for any length of time and I end up lying down on the mattress. Sinta clambers on to my chest and licks my face, all the while whimpering. Her tail wags so fast that her whole body quivers.

'It's good to see you haven't forgotten about me while you were the queen of the Open Hearth,' I say, and dodge Sinta's tongue.

'Apparently she spent a great deal of time curled up next to Boris, always watching the door. Funja tried to tell her that you were away, but I think she was determined to will you to return.'

A flash of guilt causes my stomach to lurch. I should have picked her up yesterday evening rather than leaving it to Karrion. Being under the Winter Queen's spell is no excuse for being selfish and not putting Sinta's needs first. But the puppy squirming in my arms seems to hold no grudge, and I hug her close.

'I assumed it would be okay for me to just turn up this morning,' Karrion says. 'You don't have your phone so I couldn't call and check what time was good for you. I didn't wake you, did I?'

'No, I've been awake for a little while. Thanks for picking up Sinta and for tidying up around here.'

'The last thing you needed was to come home to a dusty and damp flat.' Karrion sets his rucksack on one of the armchairs. 'How are you feeling?'

'I'm okay,' I say, for the truth seems too complicated.

'Liar.'

Karrion responds to my raised eyebrow with a steady stare. I am the first to look away.

'Seriously, Yan, how are you? You've just spent three weeks imprisoned and yesterday Lady B performed surgery on you on her sodding lawn. If I were you, I'd be rocking in a corner right about now.'

'I may have done some of that last night.' At his concerned frown, I glance at the fireplace. 'But I do feel much better for it. Wishearth helped.'

'That's something, at least. But we have a way to go before normality resumes. And speaking of which, have you had breakfast yet?'

I gesture towards the remaining slice of toast on the plate. 'I'm not that hungry.'

Karrion lifts the top layer of bread. 'Ham and cheese, right? Do you mind?'

'Go for it,' I say, fighting to keep my expression neutral.

He takes a big bite of the toast and pauses partway through chewing. With a suspicious glance my way, he pulls apart the layers again.

'What's with the marmalade?'

'Wishearth made me breakfast. Ask him.'

I regret the words as soon as they leave my mouth. Karrion's eyebrows rise and he grins, looking at the unmade bed and then my clothes.

'Are Hearth Spirits providing room service now? Is that why you've got half your bra showing?'

My cheeks heat as I pull the sides of my shirt closed and stride to the wardrobe. Behind me, Karrion laughs. I turn, fresh clothes in hand, to find him right next to me, arms spread wide. Snaking one hand around him, I step into his embrace and bury my face in his leather jacket. The smell of it is so him that my throat constricts. I missed this.

'You know, the toast isn't half bad,' Karrion says as we draw apart. 'But you didn't answer my question: what's with the marmalade?'

'I don't think Wishearth has much experience with making breakfast.'

'You're the exception, then?'

With my eyes drawn towards the fireplace, a fuzzy sensation of hot lips on mine as I fell asleep teases on the edge of my memory. I keep it to myself.

'Seems so.' I walk to the door. 'Do you mind keeping an eye on Sinta while I take a quick shower?'

'Of course. I'll make coffee.'

Standing under the cool spray, I try to marshal my thoughts. I am no longer a prisoner and I have a mystery to solve. Yet the knowledge I carry with me threatens to draw the cell walls around me once more. Can I really go back to the way things were before all of this happened? Can I still be Yannia Wilde, Private Investigator, or is that part of me lost for good?

When I return upstairs, two mugs of coffee and a plate of sandwiches are waiting on the table and Karrion rises from having rebuilt the fire. Did he make an offering to Wishearth on my behalf? If so, what did he say?

'How's the Fey scar?' he asks.

I lift my shirt to reveal the uneven silver line. 'Exactly as it was before.'

'I wasn't sure if you were still hungry after your special breakfast, so I made extra sandwiches,' Karrion says, and takes his usual seat.

'Thanks.' I am about to say that I have no interest in the food when my stomach growls. Rather than argue with it, I reach for a sandwich.

'I don't know whether Jamie has changed his mind about our involvement in the case now you've been declared innocent, but I figured we could at the very least conduct our own investigation.'

The bread, ham, and cheese turn to glue in my mouth, and I struggle to swallow. Turning to Karrion, I will him to understand so I am not forced to say the words out loud. However, he only sips his coffee and watches me with clear expectation.

'I may not be.'

'You may not be what?'

'Innocent.'

'What are you talking about? A Herald declared you innocent. What further proof do you need?'

While I would like to bring up Jonathain Marsh, Karrion does not need a reminder of the life we failed to save. Another Paladin was present at my judgement to ensure the justice system would not fail a second time, at least not in the same way. But Karrion seems to have forgotten a crucial detail about my case.

'I'm innocent of Maerk Hampten's murder. But you and I know the man in the warehouse wasn't Hampten. I may still be a killer and it is only the victim's identity we don't know.'

Karrion opens his mouth to argue and closes it again without saying anything. There is little he can say when he knows I am right. My heart swells at the knowledge that even now, he does not doubt me.

'Okay, you have a point, but that doesn't mean this can't work to our advantage.'

'What do you mean?' I ask.

'Well, Jamie will think you're innocent. Maybe if we ask nicely, he can get us reinstated as consultants for the Met and we can help with the case. Let's face it, they're not going to figure out who the real victim is and where Hampten has gone without our help.'

'You're awfully optimistic about our abilities.'

'Come on. We figured out the victim wasn't Hampten while you were in prison.'

'You did a raven's share of the work.'

Karrion grins at my choice of words, but he shakes his head. 'I wouldn't have known for certain without your ability to identify all types of magical blood. That's damned handy.'

'That's one of the reasons why we like to keep quiet about it.'

'Extracting secrets from a Wild Folk is about as easy as banishing all the pigeons from Old London.'

'If that's the case, how come you know so much about me?'

The downy feathers of Karrion's aura swell with pride. I have taken my Wild Folk abilities for granted all my life, but now I am grateful for even the smallest reminder that I am still connected to the weave of power running through the world.

'Maybe I just have a special talent,' Karrion says with a grin.

'Then why do pigeons keep following you around?'

He scowls at me, but cannot help joining my laughter. Our mirth continues longer than necessary for such an obvious joke, but in his grin, I see my relief reflected. Although I was imprisoned for only three weeks, I have missed sitting across the table from him as we solve crimes together.

Once our laughter has subsided, I take a sip of my cooling coffee. 'While I appreciate the opportunity to maximise our chances of helping with the investigation, Jamie deserves the truth. After what happened with Baneacre, I promised Jamie I would never again withhold information relevant to a case from him. If he finds out I've kept something back, we can forget about our consultancy work and having Jamie help us in an informal capacity.'

'I guess you're right.' Karrion sighs. 'But I'm not as quick to forgive him for abandoning you as you seem to be.'

'You know the situation was more complicated than that.'

'That doesn't mean what he did was right.'

'He forgave me for not sharing Lady Bergamon's secrets. The least I can do is forgive him for following orders.'

'Some loyalty towards his friends wouldn't go amiss.'

'The true test of that comes now that I'm no longer in prison.'

'If he still refuses to talk to us, he can expect a pigeon or a hundred to crap all over his car.'

'What a terrifying prospect.'

For this moment alone, I find respite from the mystery of the case before us. It is enough to sit here with Karrion in the safety of my home without dwelling on the past three weeks or thinking about what lies ahead. I don't need Wishearth's prescience to know that to find the truth, we will need all our strength and cunning.

14

MENDING BRIDGES

The doorbell rings. Sinta rushes to the door, but I scoop her up and hand her to Karrion before heading downstairs. Jamie stands on the doorstep. I am less surprised to see him than I perhaps should be, though I wonder if us talking about him called him here. Names have no power of summoning, or so I was told as a child; but there have been times when I have wondered whether that is true.

There is no sign of the familiar longing in Jamie's eyes as they meet mine. Rather, I see contrition and perhaps loneliness in the thin press of his lips. His right hand grips the handle of his briefcase, while his left is shoved deep in a coat pocket. He does not maintain eye contact for long before moving to examine our feet.

'Hi, Jamie,' I say, careful to keep my tone light.

'Can I come in? I didn't want to disturb you yesterday, but there are things we need to discuss.'

'Of course. Karrion and I are having breakfast. Perhaps you'd like to join us?'

Jamie hesitates only briefly before he nods and forces a

smile. Silence hangs between us as I lead the way upstairs. Karrion has distracted Sinta with a bone, and she is content to remain stretched out by the window and ignore Jamie. Karrion stands up when we enter and his expression hardens into a scowl. I shoot him a warning glance, while Jamie stops just inside the door.

'I invited Jamie to join us for breakfast,' I say in a voice that discourages arguments.

'Great.'

Karrion stalks to the kitchen and returns a moment later with a third mug of coffee. Normally he would offer the second chair to Jamie, but now he returns to his place and leaves Jamie with a choice of either the corner of my mattress or a wooden stool. He chooses the latter and carries it to the table. Once we are all seated, he opens his briefcase and retrieves a clear plastic bag from it.

'I wanted to bring you the personal effects we took into evidence. Our techs have processed everything and since you're innocent, there was no need to hang on to them.' After passing me the bag, he retrieves two plastic identity cards from his briefcase. 'Also, you're both officially reinstated as consultants for the Metropolitan Police.'

'That's great.' I take my phone to the kitchen and plug it into a charger. The bag also contains my torch, which I set on the counter. 'Though before you reinstate us, there's something you need to know.'

'What's that?' Jamie asks, and reaches for his coffee cup.

'The man who died in the warehouse wasn't Maerk Hampten.'

My pulse picks up speed while I watch Jamie process my words. Will he call the Paladins and have them drag me back to the cell in chains? Will this be the last straw for our friendship?

'How...?' Jamie clears his throat. 'How do you know?'

'I was covered in the man's blood and recognised his magic type. He was a Dog Shaman, whereas Hampten is a South Mage.'

Jamie sips his coffee in silence, and I can almost see the pieces falling into place in his mind. My hand trembles as I reach for another sandwich and I change my mind, pushing my fingers under my thigh instead.

'So when you went before the Herald, you received a judgement for the wrong crime?'

'That's right,' I say, but Karrion speaks at the same time.

'Pretty convenient set-up, wasn't it?'

'What?' Jamie frowns.

'Yan was set up. It's obvious.'

Karrion's power shifts like a quarrel of sparrows, and I lean across the table to lay a hand on his arm. At my touch, his aura settles down and his scowl eases a fraction.

'Do you have any proof about the victim's identity?' asks Jamie.

'Nothing beyond my word.'

He nods, as if this is what he was expecting. 'No one at the Met is going to take your word for it. As far as they are concerned, you were the obvious suspect and now you've been declared innocent, it has made them look like fools.'

'What does this mean for us?' Karrion asks with a little less anger.

Jamie shrugs. 'The Herald declared Yannia innocent. That she suspects the charges were incorrect doesn't change anything in the eyes of the Yard. At the moment, their only concern is figuring out who killed Hampten.'

'Why was everyone so sure the victim was Maerk Hampten?' asks Karrion.

'Aside from the fact that he was found in a warehouse owned by Hampten's company and he matched Hampten's general description? His wife provided a positive identification.'

I lean forward, now fully engaged in this latest mystery. 'Aleson Hampten identified the body?'

'Yes.'

'The same woman who claimed Yan offered to assassinate Hampten?' Karrion says. 'Her word must be super reliable.'

'You forget that we had no reason to suspect her of lying. Why would she say the victim was her husband if he wasn't?'

'Why would she tell lies about her meeting with Yan? Clearly she's in on it somehow.'

'Was the identification based solely on her word?' I ask. 'Was there no fingerprint or DNA match?'

'There was no reason, not when his wife had identified him.'

'And you had no reason to suspect her.'

'I'm sorry, Yannia. The evidence against you was compelling. In hindsight, perhaps it was too compelling, but most murders don't have enough substance to form the plot of a crime novel. If the evidence is pointing in a particular direction, nine times out of ten it's the correct way to proceed.'

The press of Karrion's aura against mine eases as more of his anger slips away. Although Jamie's apology was aimed at me, it seems to hold a greater meaning for him. I never blamed Jamie for following orders. How could I, when I have struggled to break free from my father's promises for years? Even now, they compel me to return to the conclave while my heart remains undecided.

'It's fine,' I say. 'But what happens when we figure out who the man at the warehouse was?'

Jamie hesitates, turning the sandwich he is holding over and over. 'That's up to my superiors. They may decide to put you before a Herald a second time.'

'Hang on a minute,' Karrion says, standing up. 'Are you saying that if we solve this case, the police are going to reward Yan by throwing her back in prison?'

I also stand and lean to rest a hand on Karrion's shoulder. His narrowed eyes are a protest against the injustice of that outcome, and once again, I envy him for the certainty of his views.

'You forget that my position regarding the judgement hasn't changed,' I say. 'I went before the Herald willingly and I shall do so again if it means knowing for certain whether I killed that man or not.'

'It's not fair,' Karrion says, and in his voice I hear an echo of Ilana speaking the same words.

'Few things in life are fair. Karrion, I need to know.'

It looks like he is going to continue arguing the point, but with a final tug of his earrings, he nods and sits down. Jamie relaxes a fraction.

'So what's the plan now?' asks Karrion.

'First things first,' Jamie says. 'I think it's best if we start by comparing notes. You've clearly conducted your own investigation, and I'd be interested to hear your findings.'

Karrion stacks up our mugs and rises. 'I'll make more coffee.'

'Hang on,' I say. 'You did most of the investigating, so you'd better bring Jamie up to speed. I'll make the coffee.'

In Jamie's presence, Karrion does not ask if I am certain. Any lingering wariness towards Jamie melts away as he recounts his investigation and the conclusions we had reached during my imprisonment. The final surprise is our speculation that Aleson Hampten and the man at the warehouse weren't who they claimed to be.

'Bloody hell.' Jamie rubs a hand over his face. 'You figured all this out from a prison cell.'

'Give credit where credit is due, Jamie.' I return with mugs of fresh coffee. 'Karrion did the work. I was merely his sounding board.'

'Now you're not giving yourself enough credit,' Karrion says. 'Only you could have discovered that the victim and his supposed wife were of the wrong magic type.'

I smile. 'This could go on all day, so let's move on. Jamie, what can you tell us about the official police investigation?'

'Not a lot. Your clothes were covered in the victim's blood. His throat had been torn open, and the official cause of death was exsanguination. The damage looked to have been done by large canine or canines, though of course we had nothing to compare the wounds to since you were in human form when the Paladins found you. There were plenty of large paw prints around the room in the victim's blood, but no animals were found at the scene. DI Hughes speculated that you had changed forms many times during the murder, though the soles of your feet were clean. No one could tell whether the paw prints came from dogs or wolves or both. They also found the victim's blood and skin under your fingernails.'

'That could have been self-defence,' Karrion says.

'Yes, it could have been. Since Yannia can't remember what happened, we can only speculate about the events in the warehouse.'

'About that,' I say, and allow my thoughts to stray to the terrible agony for an uncomfortable moment. 'We have a theory concerning the memory loss.'

'Which is?'

'Fey glamour can change perception of the world and the effects can be extraordinary depending on the strength of the Fey.'

'Yeah. Just by being near Baneacre's Fey Mound made me start emptying bins,' Karrion says. 'Or maybe it was his weird lackey that put a spell on me.'

The memory of plunging through ice into deathly water flashes through my mind, followed by Pheonix's cruel smile as he watched me from the shadows. Is it a coincidence that I ran into him the day I was released from prison? Did he play a prank, knowing that I had been marked by the Winter Queen? Or does he answer to her now? Will I ever be free from the threat of the Fey?

'There is also this.' I pull up my shirt long enough to reveal the scar on my side.

'An old scar?' Jamie asks. 'How is that relevant?'

'The wound was inflicted in the Unseen Lands only a couple of months ago and the scar looked like this as soon as a Fey healer finished her work. When I walked into the warehouse, I was fine. But sometime between losing consciousness and waking up, someone had inserted a cursed cold-iron token into the wound and sealed it in such a way that it looked no different. It had to have been a Fey.'

'I thought the Fey were allergic to cold iron.'

'They are. It burns them like acid would a human. I can't bear to be near it either. But there are ways around it. I was able to wield a cold-iron sword just by wearing a pair of leather gloves.'

Karrion sets down his coffee mug and paces to the fireplace. He crouches to throw another log on to the fire and stays there for a while, staring at the flames. Is he searching for a sign that Wishearth is listening, or has he conveyed a message I did not catch? When he turns, his expression is troubled.

'All of this implies that there's a Fey after you and not just a Mage.'

Our eyes meet. 'I know.'

'But why?' asks Jamie. 'Do you make a habit of pissing off the Fair Folk?'

'My actions in the Unseen Lands and the part I played in

Baneacre's demise may have had unforeseen consequences. Then again, I would have thought the Winter Queen would stop her subjects from trying to kill me while I still owe her a favour.'

'That's a cheery thought,' Jamie mutters.

'For the present moment, it matters not which of the Fair Folk wishes me harm or why. Rather, we need to figure out who the man at the warehouse is and why he had to die. That path, I believe, will lead us to the reasons behind this whole affair. What about the woman I heard? Did you find her?'

'Neither the Paladins nor the SOCO team found any sign of a woman there. However, there were indications that the scene had been tampered with before the Paladins arrived.'

'Such as?' Karrion asks.

'Voids in the blood-spatter patterns suggest there was something up against the walls of the room that was subsequently removed. They could have been boxes. Do you remember anything like that in the room?'

Once again, I struggle to force my memories to clear and for the events of that night to make sense. But all I grasp are fragments.

'I remember shadows across the walls and hounds. Or maybe dogs, I'm not sure. Everything after I entered the room is a blur. The woman's calls for help were clearer.'

'What did she say? Was there anything that could help us identify her?'

An idea is taking form, ephemeral at first but gaining substance. At last I realise what has been bothering me about the events at the warehouse.

'She said "Help! Somebody help". But the strange thing is that she said the same thing over and over. I've only just connected the dots.'

'What do you mean?' Karrion asks.

'If you were calling for help, wouldn't you be shouting anything that came to mind? Why repeat the exact same phrase over and over?'

'Yeah, that is weird.'

Jamie braces his fingers against the edge of the table to stretch them. 'That to me suggests less danger than the words imply.'

'Exactly.' I nod. 'What if the whole thing was a set-up?'

'Hang on,' Karrion says. 'How could they have guaranteed the outcome?'

'By manipulating the circumstances.' The more I think about it, the more the pieces fall into place. 'We didn't find out about the warehouse. Aleson Hampten, or whoever the woman who hired me is, told us not just where to go but at what time. When we arrived, right on cue, a woman got out of a taxi. We never actually saw her go into the warehouse, we just assumed she did. As we were checking the place out, I heard a woman's cry for help. We jumped to the conclusion that it was Maerk Hampten's lover. After that, luring me inside was easy.'

'But how could they be certain you'd go in instead of me?'

'The only way in was a narrow window. That alone limited the options. Also, if they've done their homework about me, they'd know I insist on being the one heading into potential danger.'

Karrion huffs and crosses his arms. 'Yeah, we're going to have to have another word about that.'

'We can have a dozen words about it, but it doesn't change what's already happened.'

Jamie examines the contents of his coffee cup, but he sets it down again without taking a drink. 'What I find strange is the purpose of the plot. Why bother if a Herald is going to declare you innocent?'

A shadow threatens to disrupt my focus on this latest

mystery. 'You forget that we still don't know if I'm innocent or not. Even if I didn't kill that man and the scene was staged, appearing before a Herald has done a great deal of damage to my reputation in Old London. Who's going to hire a Wild Folk PI who was the main suspect in a murder that involved a body that had been torn apart? I have some savings, but it's likely that Wilde Investigations is finished.'

'Not if I have anything to say about it,' Karrion declares.

I smile at his certainty. 'Whatever happens to the business, I'm not admitting defeat until we've figured out who's behind all this.'

'Where do we start?'

'Has the victim's body been released yet?' I ask Jamie.

'No. Normally that doesn't happen until after the judgement.'

'Is there any chance we could see the body?'

'I don't see why not, though I'll have to make some calls. Why?'

'Maybe we can find some clues about his true identity.'

I clear away the empty plates and mugs. Washing up can wait. My conscience twinges at having to leave Sinta again so soon after coming home, but she has settled on her bed and her eyes are drooping. A brief search through my freezer yields a hoof filled with frozen mince. I take her to the garden and tempt her back on to her bed with the hoof. When I look up, Karrion is pulling on his long leather coat. He passes me my jacket, and I slip my torch into the inner pocket.

Jamie hesitates and then reaches into his briefcase. 'There's just one thing you ought to see before we go.'

'What's that?'

He hands me a folded newspaper. Karrion comes to stand behind me, and when I reveal the front page of the *New London*

Courier, he swears. Staring at us is a grainy photo of me chained to a pillar at the Brotherhood beneath a headline: *The Beast of Old London Goes Free.*

15

THE SLUMBERING DEAD

Karrion kicks at a stone, which skitters across the pavement and clangs against the railing further along the road. When he moves to go after it, I lay a hand on his upper arm.

'You could kick every pebble in Old London and it wouldn't make you feel any better.'

'It might.'

'You'd be better off kicking that reporter, Jack Lincoln.'

His scowl eases into a hopeful grin. 'Can I?'

'Best not, otherwise the next headline will accuse me of corrupting the youth of Old London.'

'I was plenty corrupt before you came along, but point taken. It just pisses me off that people can write lies like that about you and get away with it.'

'It makes me angry too.'

'You seem a lot calmer than I am,' he says.

'Only because I have more pressing things to deal with. But Jack Lincoln had better hope our paths don't cross anytime soon.'

'We could send some pigeons to dive-bomb him,' Karrion says with a grin.

'I'll help you pay for the bird seeds.'

Jamie, who has been making phone calls next to his car, puts his phone away and approaches us.

'We're all set for a visit to the mortuary. Would you like a lift or would you rather follow me there?'

'A lift would be much appreciated,' I say.

'Hop in.'

The journey takes us away from Old London and along the northern bank of the Thames. The traffic slows as we approach Big Ben and the Houses of Parliament. When we stop at a red light near Westminster Abbey, Karrion leans forward in the back seat.

'It's pretty cool that after all these months of working together, we finally have a chance to peek inside a mortuary.'

I turn my head to grin at him. 'Didn't you tell me a few weeks ago that you'd accepted that there was nothing glamorous about our job?'

'Even if I did, a crow is allowed to change his mind.'

'As long as you're not expecting us to have to take on the undead horde with nothing but a fire extinguisher and a broom handle.'

'About that,' Karrion turns his attention to Jamie, 'what safeguards do they have in place to make sure that the dead don't rise and start snacking on the staff?'

'We don't live in a zombie apocalypse film,' Jamie says, but his voice contains traces of mirth.

'More's the pity. It would be cool to test my zombie survival plan. Plus, we could feed Jack Lincoln to the horde to slow it down.'

'You have a zombie survival plan?' Jamie asks, staring at Karrion in the rear-view mirror.

'You don't?'

'Why would I?'

'Because you never know when a Mage experiment will go wrong and unleash undead horrors upon Old London. It's good sense.'

'Sorry, Karrion. I suppose I prefer to live in the real world,' Jamie says.

'In the real world that contains magic, murderous Fey, and otherworldly beings casting infallible judgements?'

Jamie opens his mouth to reply and closes it again without saying a word. He turns right, away from the river, and slows to manoeuvre around a bike messenger.

'Okay, you may have a point there,' he says.

'Thought so.' Karrion leans back, lacing his fingers behind his neck. 'For the record, a wetsuit and duct tape is the way to go. And a cricket bat, if you don't mind a bit of close contact. Also, you'll need a helmet to protect your head and face, but I reckon you can nick one from the riot police.'

'I'll bear that in mind.' Jamie glances at me. 'Do you have anything to add?'

'Invest in a pair of running shoes and a sniper rifle?'

Karrion leans forward to give me a thumbs up. 'Nice one, Yan.'

'The former is easier to obtain than the latter,' Jamie says.

'You could always take up hunting in your spare time,' I reply.

'If you do, promise me you'll dress in a deerstalker and a black coat.' Karrion laughs.

Jamie chuckles. 'I'm not sure that's a role that would suit me. If I had any medical knowledge, I'd be better suited to the role of the sidekick.'

'You and me both,' Karrion says. 'I guess that makes Yan the famous detective.'

I twist in my seat to look at Karrion. 'You've more than earned your place as a detective over the past few weeks.'

Heat creeps across Karrion's cheeks as he rubs his neck. 'I reckon it's a team effort.'

'Which means that we couldn't do it without you,' I say with a smile.

Jamie parks on Horseferry Road outside the Westminster Public Mortuary. A low iron fence separates the pavement from the raised gardens on either side of the path leading to the doors. Without the signs declaring it as the *Coroners' Court*, the red-brick building with its white highlights looks more like a Mage residence than a mortuary. I am not certain what I was expecting, but this is not it.

We follow Jamie through the main doors and to a reception desk, where we show our ID and sign in. While Karrion is scrawling his signature, I become aware of people staring at me for a little longer than is necessary. When I meet their gaze, they quickly look away. Shame turns my breakfast into acid. Have they read Jack Lincoln's lies about me? Do they see me as the Beast of Old London, or simply as a murder suspect whose name has been cleared?

Feathers brush along the edge of my awareness. I turn to find Karrion watching me, a frown creasing the skin between his eyebrows. The first thing that strikes me is that he didn't touch me to catch my attention. Has he found a way to sense my aura of power, or did he assume I would be aware of his magic?

'Are you okay?' he asks, keeping his voice low.

I force my lips to a line that could be interpreted as a smile. 'Fine.'

The receptionist presses a button to unlock the door by her desk, and Jamie leads us through it. We walk along a corridor and pass through a set of double doors to the mortuary. Karrion cranes his neck to look around with the enthusiasm of a horror-movie aficionado, but we pass no windows affording a view of a room filled with bodies waiting for an autopsy, nor do interns carrying plastic bags filled with severed limbs pass us. There are only ordinary doors, all closed. Karrion's aura flags.

'Not what you expected?' I ask, and wince as my voice echoes in the corridor.

'I was hoping for at least one headless body on a gurney.'

Jamie glances at us over his shoulder, and Karrion spreads his arms.

'Hey, I make no apologies for my zombie theory. They're going to rise one day, it's only a matter of time. When they do, I want to be prepared.'

'This explains why you're so eager to squash graves with your car,' I say, dodging the poke that comes my way.

'If it's all the same to you, please could we never speak of that again?'

'Not going to happen, and you know it.'

'It was worth a try.'

'What's this about driving over graves?' Jamie asks.

'Nothing,' Karrion says, and his tone invites no further questions on the matter.

We walk almost to the far end of the corridor before Jamie stops and knocks on a door. A muffled voice invites us to come in.

The room is a small office, with tall filing cabinets behind a desk. A large light-box is mounted on the wall, and it is currently showing a series of skull X-rays. Behind the desk sits a man in his late forties with thin glasses, a bushy beard, and a receding hairline. He smiles and stands, extending a hand over the desk.

'Jamie, good to see you, mate.'

'Liam, how's it going?' Jamie shakes his hand.

'I spend my days and the occasional night cutting open dead people, so I'm living the dream.'

Jamie grins. 'Your parents must be so proud.'

'They keep telling their neighbours I'm a GP rather than a pathologist. Every time I visit them for Sunday lunch, some old biddy stops me outside their house to ask about their piles.'

Both men grimace, and Jamie laughs.

'Sorry, Liam, but rather you than me.'

'That's the sort of attitude that will see you land on every pathologist's blacklist.'

'Meaning what? You won't let me see cut-up corpses?'

'No, when you die, we're going to spread anatomically inaccurate rumours about you. Come to think of it, why wait until you're dead?'

'It's good to see all those ethics lessons at the medical school haven't gone to waste,' Jamie says.

'Ethics are overrated. Did you know that Hippocrates used to drink wine before treating patients?'

'Is that true?' Jamie asks.

Liam shrugs. 'He was Greek. So probably. Anyway, what can I do for you?'

Jamie motions to me and Karrion. 'These two are consultants for the Met. We're investigating the murder of Maerk Hampten.'

We introduce ourselves, and I see a spark of recognition in Liam's eyes. Lifting my chin, I meet his curiosity head-on.

'Yannia Wilde,' he says, staring at me. 'Weren't you the prime suspect in that murder case? All the papers were talking about a big trial... or judgement, I should say.'

'I was. A Herald cleared me.'

'All right then. What do you want to know?'

Taken aback by his easy acceptance of my innocence, I struggle to think where to begin.

'Can we see the autopsy file?' asks Karrion.

'Certainly. I can email you a copy. Most of the records have been electronic since the city decided to go paperless.' Liam waves at the towering piles of folders on his desk and at the filing cabinets behind him. 'As you can see, no paper anywhere.'

'Did you happen to take Hampten's fingerprints?' I ask.

Liam frowns. 'Let me check the file. I've seen a fair few bodies since Hampten and I can't keep the details straight in my head.'

He spends a few minutes looking at his computer before leaning closer to the screen.

'No, sorry. Identification was provided by the widow. There was no need for fingerprints.'

'And you didn't happen to take them anyway, just to be thorough?' Jamie asks.

'I've been finding myself in frequent trouble for being thorough when I've been told to be otherwise. So in this instance, I'm afraid you're out of luck.'

'The body is still here, isn't it?' I ask.

'Yes, it is,' Liam says after checking the file. 'We can't release it in case we need to run further tests or search for more evidence.'

'Now is the time for that,' Jamie says. 'We need to take his fingerprints.'

'Would you mind telling me why?'

'Some new information has come to light that calls into question the identity of the body you have in the freezer. We're here to either prove or disprove a theory.'

Liam rises and leans in to press a few keys on his keyboard. 'In that case, might I invite you to follow me, my good lady and gentlemen?'

He takes us down a lift to a lower level that holds the autopsy rooms and an extensive laboratory. Karrion's earlier eagerness to see headless bodies returns, and I fear what his reaction might be if he were to come into close contact with a particularly decomposed corpse. Traumatising him is not on today's agenda.

'Will you want to see the body?' Liam asks as he stops outside a heavy steel door.

Jamie looks to us, leaving the decision to me. I pause, wondering what it will be like to come face to face again with the man I may have killed. But the possibility that seeing his body might trigger a buried memory is all the encouragement I need to nod.

'Wait here. I'll need to take him out of storage.' Liam pauses. 'That sounded horrible. But you know what I mean.'

He disappears through the door. I move across the corridor and lean my back against the wall. My skin is crawling with a thousand unseen insects while I try to imagine what this is going to be like. Will Maerk Hampten have my teeth-marks on his neck? Did I rake his face with my claws? Did I feast on his flesh, while he lay helpless in a pool of his own blood? Will seeing him again make me hungry?

My vision blackens around the edges and the floor ripples beneath my feet. Karrion is there in an instant, his hands on my shoulders. He anchors me, but to what, I am not certain. I stare at him, distantly aware that my mouth is hanging open.

'Breathe, Yan. Just breathe.'

I can't. All the air in the corridor has vanished. Karrion should not be able to talk. Why are he and Jamie not lying on the floor, gasping? My lungs heave against my ribs, but nothing happens. There is no air here.

'She looks like she's about to pass out.'

Jamie's words come from a million miles away. Karrion grips my shoulders harder, fingers digging into bones that are always sore to the touch. The pain jolts a spark of awareness in me.

'Do it with me, Yan. In through the nose, out through the mouth.'

I try to copy him, but nothing happens. Panic floods through me as my vision narrows until all I can see is Karrion. Even he is blurring into shadow.

'Come on, Yan. Try harder.'

With what little strength I have left, I manage to pull a miniscule amount of air through my nose. The black spots swimming across my vision slow. I exhale through pursed lips, like Karrion is doing. Copying him, I take another breath, then another. He keeps me at it, long after the worst of the panic has subsided. Only when he is certain my breathing has evened out does he pull me into a hug.

'You're okay, Yan. Everything is fine. I'm not going to let anything happen to you.'

I cling to him as tears prickle in the corners of my eyes. Is this how life will be from now on? Will I always be haunted by what I did, or what I may have done? How can I go on without knowing whether I am a killer or not?

The shaking begins as a tremor in my fingers and spreads until my teeth are chattering. Karrion hugs me tighter, and I am reminded of the way Wishearth held me last night. These two men are my tether and anchor, keeping me safe from the horrors my mind conjures up and keeping me from fleeing to the conclave to face the judgement of my own kind. They are a lifeline, even during times when I am not certain I deserve one.

'It's okay, Yan. It will be okay.'

Karrion repeats this over and over, his lips close to my ear. Little by little, his voice and the calm press of his aura against mine slow my tripping heart. The tremors lessen, then fade away. I ease back, not so far as to break away from Karrion, but far enough that I have room to rub my face. My eyes are gritty, and my body aches like I have attempted to run a marathon with no training.

Jamie is further down the corridor, his back to us, browsing his phone. Were it anyone else, I might interpret that as disinterest, but I recognise the gesture for what it is: Jamie is giving me space and privacy.

I shift so my back is against the wall again and pull Karrion's arm around my shoulders. He settles beside me, leaning his chin against my temple.

'Thanks,' I say.

'Anytime.' He uses his free hand to tilt my head in his direction. 'Honestly, Yan, anytime.'

The smile I offer in return is weak, for the grittiness in my eyes is growing worse. So much has happened in the space of a day, and my emotions are lagging. I would like to sleep for a week, to escape to a cottage by a beach, and to hunt down whoever is behind this, all at once. But for now, all I can do is wait in a corridor to see the body of a man I may have killed.

Beside me, Karrion shifts. His movement alerts me to the fact that my legs and pelvis are aching, like they do when I stand for too long.

'Shouldn't Liam be back by now?' I ask.

'He should,' Jamie says, turning. 'We've been waiting for an hour.'

'What is he doing, defrosting Hampten with a hairdryer?' Karrion asks.

Before Jamie or I have a chance to reply, the door in front of us opens. Liam stands in the doorway, a shade paler than when we last saw him.

'I can't find the body.'

16

―――――――――

VANISHING ACT

'What do you mean, you can't find the body?' I ask.

Liam leans against the doorway. 'I mean I've looked in every drawer of this storage room. Maerk Hampten's body is no longer here.'

'I told you,' Karrion says, a little too eagerly. 'The zombies are about to rise.'

'Even if that was medically possible, which it isn't, there's no way a mindless zombie can open a freezer door from the inside,' Liam says.

'Maybe we're dealing with telekinetic zombies?'

A look from me silences Karrion before he has a chance to come up with more outlandish theories.

'Could the body have been moved elsewhere?' Jamie asks. 'To one of the other rooms?'

'That's what I'm going to check next.'

Liam disappears through a door further along the corridor. We stay where we are, trying to process what this could mean for our case.

'Does this happen often?' Karrion asks. 'The Met losing a body?'

Jamie frowns. 'Are you suggesting we're that incompetent?'

'You did arrest Yan and she didn't do anything,' Karrion says, the edges of his aura shifting like ruffled feathers.

I move between them before Jamie lets loose whatever angry retort is on his lips.

'We don't know that for sure,' I say to Karrion, just loud enough for Jamie to hear me. 'Besides, none of this is Jamie's fault.'

'I just think it's convenient, that's all. We need the body to clear your name and now it's nowhere to be found.'

'And you think I arranged this?' says Jamie. 'That I somehow disposed of the body so we couldn't solve the case? Is that really how little you think of me, Karrion?'

'You're not much of a friend, that much has become clear,' says Karrion. 'If you're not loyal to your friends, maybe you're not loyal to New Scotland Yard either.'

'Don't you fucking dare!' Jamie says, but I stop him by raising a hand.

'Karrion, you're out of line,' I say, doing my best to rein in my temper. 'I understand that you're angry and you have every right to be, but not at Jamie. The Paladins were the ones to imprison me and put me before a Herald. They were doing their duty, just like the detective inspector in charge of the case was by deeming the evidence against me strong enough to justify a Herald's services. It's their job. If you want to be angry at anyone, let it be at the people who set this trap for me.'

'I am.' He clenches his fists. 'Trust me, I am. But he abandoned you.'

'Jamie was following orders,' I say before Jamie replies. 'If he'd been suspended or fired, then where would we be now? We can't solve this case without the help of New Scotland Yard, and you know that as well as I do.'

'But he abandoned you,' Karrion repeats.

'If that was true, we wouldn't be standing here, nor would our consultancy arrangement have been reinstated. Jamie did what he could from afar.'

'Maybe, but he should've done more.'

'You're right,' Jamie says, surprising us both. 'I should have done more. But honestly? I didn't know what to do. This is the first time I've been in a position where a friend has been accused of murder. The higher-ups shut me out of the investigation so thoroughly I didn't know the Crown Prosecution Service had decided to put you before a Herald until hours afterwards. Hell, you probably knew about it before I did. They told me that if I tried to visit you during your imprisonment, it would be considered interfering with the investigation and I would be immediately dismissed. The only concession I managed to wheedle out of them was letting me attend the judgement as the Yard's representative. But I should have done more. I should have thought of something, some way to help you. Every day, I hated myself for abandoning you to that cell and that feeling hasn't gone away since yesterday.'

'I don't blame you, Jamie,' I say. 'I was hurt by your absence, I won't deny it, but it was one hurt among many. But you need to know that I understand and that I forgive you. I would never expect you to end your career for me.'

'Thank you, Yannia.' Jamie rubs his eyes before forcing a smile. 'That means a lot. Hopefully, one day I may even forgive myself.'

After offering Jamie as convincing a smile as I can manage, I turn to Karrion. He is staring at the floor, his face set in a determined frown.

'I'm sorry, Jamie,' he says to his shoes. 'What I said was way out of line.'

'You have as much right to be angry with me as Yannia does.

I'm sorry I didn't do a better job of staying in touch during the past few weeks.'

Karrion nods, dragging his eyes high enough to reach Jamie's knees. He steps past me and offers Jamie his hand.

'Feel free to punch me for being rude, if you fancy it.'

Jamie shakes Karrion's hand. 'I'll pass, thanks. With my luck, I'd break a finger on all the metal in your face.'

They share a tentative smile, and the tension in the corridor slips away. I breathe a little easier.

'But seriously, though,' Karrion says. 'How can a body just vanish?'

'Let's hope Liam has an answer for that,' Jamie replies.

We wait another ten minutes before Liam returns. This time, his mouth is set in an angry line and he is accompanied by a young man in a lab coat. The man is carrying a paper folder.

'The body is actually gone,' he says.

'What do you mean?' Jamie asks.

'I mean this genius signed a transfer order for the body to be released to a crematorium two hours ago.'

'What?' I ask. 'How can that be?'

'Oh, it gets better.' Liam nudges the man none too gently closer to us. 'Tell them the rest, Matt.'

Matt shuffles through the pages, eyes downcast until Liam clears his throat.

'She had all the paperwork, including a letter from the detective inspector in charge of the case saying that the body could be released for the crematorium. All the paperwork was in order, I swear.'

Before I have a chance to ask to see copies, Liam beats me to it.

'Show them the paperwork that's all in order.'

Keeping his eyes fixed on the folder, Matt selects several

sheets of paper and passes them to me. I look through them and frown.

'Is this meant to be a joke?'

'Is it indeed?' Liam asks, nudging at the other man. 'Tell the nice lady whether this is a practical joke you've decided to play.'

'No joke, that's the proper paperwork.'

I fan out the papers for the others to see. Every one of them is blank.

'What's going on?' Karrion asks.

'I'm not sure.'

Passing him the papers, I allow my power to quest outward until I find Matt. My aura slides over him, seeking an active spell. I find none, only catching a fleeting impression of snowflakes melting when my magic touches them. The sensation is stronger around the papers.

'Something's wrong. It's not a spell, but it's something.'

'Hang on.'

Karrion returns the papers to me and reaches under his coat collar to take off the necklace he wears against his skin. It is simple, nothing but a leather cord and silvery disks stamped with skulls of various birds. I take a step back, not wishing to come into contact with cold iron so soon after my imprisonment and Lady Bergamon's emergency surgery.

'Here,' Karrion says to Matt. 'Touch this.'

As soon as Matt's fingers close around the cold iron, his eyes roll back and a tremor runs through him. He shakes his head, as if trying to clear his thoughts.

'What happened?'

'Does this still look like the correct paperwork to you?' I ask, offering the papers back to him.

'But these are blank. What's going on?'

'You were under a Fey glamour.'

A look of revulsion twists Matt's features, and I fight to keep my irritation hidden. This is not the first time a human has reacted thus to magic, nor will it be the last. Perhaps he is more open about his feelings because he has not realised that Karrion and I are not human.

'They put a spell on me? Why would they do something like that?'

'Because it was the easiest way to get what they wanted, which was the body,' I say, my voice a degree colder than is necessary. 'You have no resistance to glamour and didn't even realise anything was wrong.'

He shudders, as if uncomfortable in his own skin. Beside me, I sense Karrion's growing annoyance as a roiling of his aura. He is even less forgiving of prejudice towards our kind than I am.

'I presume there are security cameras everywhere in this building?' I ask Jamie.

He nods.

'Good. We'll need to see that footage.' I turn to Liam. 'You may as well return Matt to wherever you found him.'

'Why?'

'Because he came into contact with a Fey or a powerful Feykin. We can't trust a word he says.'

Matt is frowning, as if noticing me for the first time. 'Wait, don't I know you?'

'No,' I say, lifting my chin and returning his stare with my haughtiest Wild Folk countenance. 'You live in the wrong London to know who I am.'

He grows a shade paler as he realises the implication of my words. Liam takes him gently by the elbow and escorts him away. Matt's expression is one of puzzlement, as if he is only beginning to understand the consequences of coming into contact with magic.

While we wait for Liam to return, I roll my shoulders and

stretch my neck, trying to ease some of the tension that has crept into my muscles. Karrion's aura calms, and he gives up on chewing his lip piercing. Jamie stands a little further away, hands in his pockets.

'Not every human reacts like that,' he says into the silence of the corridor.

'I know.' I force a smile. 'You're a prime example of that.'

He looks like he wants to correct me, but there is no need. I know that Jamie would never be repulsed by the use of magic because he wishes he too had the gift. But despite the time he spends reading books or drinking herbal concoctions aimed at unlocking his hidden potential, he will never have power for the simple reason that his veins are filled with the wrong kind of blood.

When Liam returns alone, he looks a little less sure of himself than before.

'I'm going to have to report the missing body,' he says.

'Of course.' Jamie nods. 'While you do that, perhaps we can view the security footage to see what really happened?'

'After we've done that,' I say, 'would you mind if we went through the autopsy file together? If someone went to the trouble of stealing the body, there must have been evidence on it they didn't want discovered. Perhaps between the four of us, we can figure out what it might have been?'

'Sure,' Liam says. 'I'll set up one of the evidence review rooms.'

He gives us directions to the security station and heads towards his office. Jamie takes us back to the entrance hall and down a different corridor until we find a room with two security guards. It takes only a matter of moments for Jamie to explain the situation and convince the guards to let us review the cameras. Karrion sits behind the controls and begins rewinding the footage.

We focus on the outside cameras first. Three hours earlier, a taxi pulled up next to the loading bay, followed by a hearse. A woman got out of the taxi, then two men in black suits rose from the hearse to confer with her. Despite the low quality of the CCTV images, I recognise Aleson Hampten. But she is not the only thing that catches my attention.

'Look at that,' I say, pointing to the corner of the screen.

The spot is in the shadow of the building. At first I think my eyes are tired, for something is flickering in and out of focus, but I soon realise it has nothing to do with me. A miasma of darkness solidifies and scatters in a rhythmic pattern.

'Is that a spell or a person?' Karrion asks, squinting at the screen. Next to me, Jamie looks nauseated.

'How much are you willing to bet it's a glamour?'

'A pigeon feather?' Karrion grins at me over his shoulder, and I poke him in the ribs.

'When you say it's a glamour, what do you actually mean?' asks Jamie.

'Someone is either disguising their appearance using a glamour or they're hiding something in that spot. My guess would be the former. Magic and technology are an unpredictable combination, as we found out with Melissa's illusions. We're lucky the cameras captured anything at all.'

'It's on the move,' Karrion says, preventing further questions from Jamie.

The miasma moves towards the funeral directors, who shrink back and then relax. As far as I can tell on the screen, their expressions slacken. They walk to the back of the hearse, remove a gurney on wheels, and move up the loading-bay ramp.

'What just happened?' Jamie asks.

I am about to answer when a flicker within the miasma has me leaning forward, a hand on Karrion's shoulder.

'Can you play it back, but slower?'

'Give me a sec.'

The footage rewinds and stops, moving forward at a slower pace than before. There it is again: a long, black tail lashing out of the glamour and disappearing back into it. Ice floods my veins, as if I had plunged through it into dark waters.

'Pheonix. It's Declan Pheonix.'

Karrion twists around in his seat. 'Baneacre's lackey? What's he doing here?'

'I don't know. But don't forget that I met him long before Baneacre forced his way into Old London. I thought he was Feykin at the time, but Pheonix warned me about Melissa, though in such a cryptic way I didn't understand what he meant until much later.'

'Is he capable of the glamour on Matt?' Jamie asks.

'Absolutely,' I say, without hesitation. 'He once charmed me with such ease I didn't realise what was happening until Karrion shook me out of the spell.'

'Bloody hell, Yannia. That means he could've done anything that took his fancy to those humans.'

'Agreed. The question is, what does he want? What's his role in all this?'

'I'm guessing he wasn't exactly pleased when you killed his new king,' Karrion says. 'Didn't you mention that he was planning a coronation and everything?'

'Much of that may have been banter, but I'm certain stopping Baneacre disrupted whatever plans Pheonix may have had. I can understand him wanting revenge, but why wait this long? And why like this? It seems an odd way to go about it, when he could easily kill me in my sleep.'

'That's a cheery thought,' Karrion says. 'Don't you think it's time we warded your flat?'

'What's the point? Baneacre walked through wards like they weren't even there. Pheonix isn't as powerful, since he's not one of the Autumn Champions, but it wouldn't surprise me to learn that he is a Fey lord. A Mage ward isn't going to keep me safe.'

'What about that thing you showed Amitta?' Jamie asks. 'A circle, was it?'

Regret washes over me at the mention of Amitta Pandia. I tried to save her, gave her all the help I could for her to survive the night, but Baneacre killed her anyway. In the quiet moments of sleepless nights, my thoughts often wander the paths of past regrets. Was there something else I could have done for her? Had I stayed with her, would Baneacre have killed us both? Or did warning Lord Ellensthorne doom Amitta?

Realising that Jamie is waiting for an answer, I force my focus back to the matter at hand.

'A circle should keep out a Fey, especially if cast with cold-iron tokens, though that theory remains untested.'

'Not really,' Karrion says. 'Lady B was safe in the circle for two days.'

'But was that because the circle kept her safe or because Baneacre never saw a need to test it?'

Karrion opens his mouth to reply, but shakes his head instead. 'I hadn't thought of that.'

'A circle might work,' I say to Jamie, 'but it would also keep me trapped within it. What sort of a life would I have if I spent my days and nights cowering behind a wall of power, imprisoned in my own home? I couldn't hide forever, especially not from a semi-immortal Fey. If Pheonix wanted to kill me himself, he would have already done so.'

Jamie grimaces. 'That's a cheery thought.'

'It's the reality of the life I've chosen in Old London. I've helped people, but I've made plenty of enemies along the way, some more dangerous than others.'

'Maybe you should train as a ninja,' Karrion says. 'Just to be on the safe side.'

'We'll call that plan N. Let's review the rest of the footage.'

Aleson Hampten, the funeral directors, and Pheonix enter the building via the loading-bay doors. Karrion cycles through the other cameras until he finds them again. We follow their progress along empty corridors until they come to the same place where we waited not long ago. Matt steps out of one of the cold-storage rooms, and Aleson walks forward, Pheonix right behind her.

There is no external sign of the magic Pheonix works, but Matt's expression grows slack. He stands there, arms hanging limply by his sides, much like the funeral directors did only a few moments before.

'Is Matt under his spell?' Jamie asks.

'Yes. They all are, except Aleson,' I say, and frown. 'Why isn't Aleson under his spell?'

'From what we're seeing here, she's a willing participant,' Karrion replies.

It makes sense. There is a possibility I might have detected a glamour affecting her when she hired me. Would Pheonix know I can identify magic users, or that I do so by habit? But why would he have chosen this mortal to help him? Or is the better question why Aleson is working with a Fey? What does she stand to gain from all this?

'That must be safer for them both, given that this case has brought her into contact with both me and the Paladins. Plenty of opportunities for someone to notice something amiss, and I'm not sure how well Fey glamour holds in the proximity of the Paladins' swords.'

'Who the hell is she?' Karrion asks.

'What do you mean?' asks Jamie.

'Well, we know she's not the real Aleson Hampten. Yan is certain of it. Wouldn't it make our lives a lot easier if we knew who she really was?'

'It would,' Jamie says. 'But to find out, we'd need her fingerprints and a DNA sample.'

'We'll add that to the list of things we'd like to have,' I say. 'One problem at a time.'

On the screen, Matt leads the funeral directors into the storage room, while Aleson and Pheonix stay in the corridor. Karrion speeds forward on the footage, fifteen minutes passing in a matter of moments, and lets the video play on when the funeral directors push the gurney out of the door. On it is a body bag, secured down with straps across the chest, waist, and legs. Matt follows them out, arranging papers into a folder. There are the official letters and permissions he needed to see to release the body, neatly set out on blank pages.

We follow the group back to the loading bay, where the funeral directors load the body on to the hearse and close the curtains around the back. A taxi pulls up next to it, and Aleson slides into the back seat. Pheonix follows her to the car, but he pauses by the back door. The miasma clears as he turns to look straight at the CCTV camera. Lifting his top hat, he smiles and bows.

17

DEATH MASK

'He knew I'd be watching,' I say into the silence of the room.

'How could he have known?' asks Jamie.

'Pheonix must have realised that if the Herald cleared me and I figured out that the man at the warehouse wasn't Hampten, one of the first things I'd want to do is see the body. That's why it was removed today and not three weeks ago. Think about it. They've had plenty of time to cover their tracks. Why wait until now?'

'So he's toying with us,' Karrion says, a tremor of suppressed anger clear in his voice.

'He's a trickster Fey. Toying with mortals is what he does best.'

'How the hell are we supposed to beat a Fey who seems to be ten steps ahead of us all the time?' Jamie asks.

'By being thorough, doing all the work, and figuring out what his endgame is.' I take half a step towards the door. 'Let's find Liam. We've seen all we need to here.'

'I'll ask someone to make a note of the licence plates of the taxis and the hearse,' Jamie says.

'Fine, though I doubt they'll lead us to the body or Pheonix. He's too careful for that.'

Karrion rises, and together we return to Liam's office. He is typing away and upon seeing us, detaches a memory stick from the side of his monitor.

'Perfect timing,' he says. 'I've just downloaded the autopsy file. Follow me.'

He takes us further down the corridor to a small room with a light-table at its centre. A row of large monitors is mounted on one wall, and there is a wide light-box on the opposite side. Liam switches on a laptop on a side table and plugs in the memory stick.

'The paper copy of Hampten's autopsy file is gone, no doubt courtesy of DI Hughes's non-existent instructions.' Liam taps away at the computer, speaking over his shoulder without looking at the screen. 'Lucky for us, Matt doesn't have the user rights to delete the electronic files.'

'Can you imagine if he did?' Karrion asks. 'We'd be at square one.'

'Not quite, but retrieving the backup is a hassle. Here you go.' A folder of files appears on one of the monitors. 'Where do you want to start?'

'Why don't you talk us through the autopsy findings first?' Jamie leans his back against the light-table. 'Then we can review the photos and go through any questions we may have.'

'Sure thing.' Liam opens a summary sheet on the screen.

Karrion shifts so he is standing next to me, and his hand finds mine. I entwine my fingers with his, grateful for the quiet show of support and for Jamie's suggestion of leaving the photos until later. The prospect of seeing them is only slightly less terrifying than coming face to face with Hampten's body.

'Maerk Hampten died from blood loss after his carotid arteries were severed. The wound to his neck was irregular and caused by teeth rather than a weapon. Based on the casts made and on the series of prints recorded around the body, the animal in question was a canine, either a wolf or a large dog. The victim also had defensive wounds to his hands and forearms, and he had suffered hairline fractures to the back of his skull, indicating that he fell and hit his head with some force. It's likely to have stunned him enough for the animal to tear open his throat. He will have bled out in minutes.'

A dull ache in my fingers alerts me to the fact that I am clutching Karrion's hand with enough force that I must be hurting him. He makes no attempt to pull back from my grip and simply stands there, chewing on his lip piercing. I want to back away, to run from the room, and keep running until I am no longer in the city. Isn't it time I returned to the conclave? No one there knows what I did. I could hide away in the wilderness until the city has forgotten Yannia Wilde and her crimes.

But even as the urge to flee has me leaning away from Karrion, I know it would do me no good. I would wake up every morning searching for blood on my hands. Running and hiding would not absolve me of the guilt I carry, only worsen it. I must see this case through, even if it means standing before a Herald a second time.

'Was it just one dog?' Karrion asks, his teeth clicking against the lip piercing he is chewing.

'We didn't do any of the paw-print analysis here, but just looking at the crime-scene photos, it's clear there were several. As for the marks on the body, my guess is perhaps three?'

My heart lurches. So my fragmented memories are correct. There were dogs in the room where Hampten was killed. But to what end?

'Can you match the teeth that inflicted the defensive wounds with the canine that killed the victim?' Jamie asks.

'Yes. The same animal that bit the victim's left arm also tore open his throat.'

'What about DNA?' I ask, my voice hoarse. 'Was any recovered?'

'I'd have to check the rest of the case file.' Liam turns to the computer. 'Give me a second.'

We wait in tense silence. After a while, I realise Jamie is staring at mine and Karrion's linked hands, but his attention does not bother me. He has long been dropping hints that he believes there is something romantic between me and Karrion, and I have been ignoring him just as long. If he wants to read something into Karrion's show of support, he is welcome to do so.

'Here we go,' Liam says, and my head snaps up. 'We've got the victim's DNA, of course. They recovered several samples of canine DNA from the scene. Further analysis identified two German shepherds and three mastiff types.'

'Any other humanoid DNA recovered on the scene?' I ask.

'There was a separate pool of blood away from the main scene.' Liam leans closer to the screen. 'That came back as yours.'

That must be where they – perhaps Pheonix? – cut open my side to insert the cursed cold-iron disk beneath the Fey scar, though I leave the thought unspoken.

'If you changed into a dog, would your DNA be that of a dog or you as you are now?' Karrion asks.

'I have no idea,' I say. 'If someone has conducted such research, I know nothing about it, though I can't imagine a single Wild Folk conclave who would be prepared to assist an outsider, especially when it comes to giving DNA samples and allowing ourselves to be studied. We're considered little more than wild animals by most of the country and the last thing we need is being measured and sampled like zoo specimens.'

Liam swivels around in his chair, eagerness lighting his features. 'If you want to find out for sure, why don't you transform into a dog and I'll take a DNA sample. The results won't be instantaneous, but you'll have the answer in a couple of weeks.'

The suggestion is so absurd I have to bite back a laugh for fear of offending Liam. His offer is earnest, but he has inadvertently demonstrated just how little he understands magic and the different types of magic users.

'We're in a man-made building and my power is tied to nature. I could no more transform here than you could cast a fireball.'

'You never know, I might be a Mage.'

Lifting my chin, I lock eyes with him. 'I do know and you're not.'

Surprise flashes across Liam's face, and he turns to Jamie, who is smiling. Caught somewhere between amusement and annoyance, Liam chooses to laugh.

'Wow, you're good. How did you know?'

'Trade secret.'

'All right. What if we go outside? Can you transform then?'

I shake my head. 'I've been in the city too long. My power is too low to assume another form.'

It may not be true, not after sleeping in Lady Bergamon's garden yesterday afternoon, but I am not about to spend what little reserves I have to satisfy a human's curiosity, even if it might offer some insight into the case. Experience has taught me that I cannot afford to deplete my magic, not when we are chasing a trail as confusing as this one.

'Can we see the autopsy photos?' Karrion asks before Liam has a chance to object further.

'Sure.' Liam frowns, as if struggling to recall that we had

been discussing a case until he suggested I transform into a dog. 'I'll put them up on the big screen.'

Karrion's grip on my hand tightens as a folder of photos appears on the wall. Liam clicks on the first one, and the screen is filled with a body dressed in blood-soaked clothes, the zip of the body bag drawn all the way down.

As much as I feared seeing it, I had hoped it would prove to be a thread to unravel my tangled memories. But Liam may as well have chosen an autopsy file at random for all it triggers in my mind. I feel nothing as I take in the torn throat, the smudge of blood across the forehead, and the shredded shirt collar. No, that is not quite true. I frown as I walk around the table to stare at the face of the unknown man.

'Do you have a close-up of the face?' I ask.

'Of course.'

Liam scrolls along the ribbon of preview icons until he finds the photo I am after. Hampten's – no, not Hampten's – face fills the screen. I stare at it, my forehead creasing, while I try to search for something out of place. There is nothing. I turn to Karrion.

'If this isn't Hampten, how can he look exactly like him?'

'How do you know the body isn't Hampten's?' asks Liam. 'The widow identified him.'

Ignoring Jamie's answer to Liam, Karrion digs out his phone and performs a quick search. He brings up a photo of Maerk Hampten from the Mercury Deliveries website and holds it up next to the image on the screen. There is no doubt about it: the two photos show the same man.

'It's not possible,' I say. 'There has to be a difference.'

'He didn't have a twin brother did he?' Karrion shakes his head before I have a chance to reply. 'No, that wouldn't work. They'd both be Mages if they were identical twins.'

'There's something we're missing,' I say, staring at the screen. 'But what is it?'

Karrion walks around the table to be closer to the screen. We stay like that for a minute, both studying the dead man's features, until Karrion cocks his head.

'Hey, Liam, do you have a close-up of the wound on his neck?'

Liam scrolls through the photos again and an image of a torn throat fills the screen. Karrion takes another step closer and points not to the wound but to the skin right above it.

'What do you think that is?' he asks.

Along the ragged edges of the skin around the wounds are faint marks. I follow Karrion closer to the screen, trying to make sense of them. The marks are regular, diagonal slashes that have bruised the skin. One thing is certain: they were not made by a dog.

'I have no idea,' I say at last. 'Could a thin rope have been wrapped around his neck before he died?'

'No way,' Liam says, closing the photos and opening the main file. 'I performed the autopsy myself. The only damage to the throat was caused by the dog. Nothing else.'

'How would you explain the marks?' Karrion asks.

'I... I can't.'

Jamie's hand dips into his pocket and out again. He dials a number and brings his phone to his ear.

'Mery, drop whatever you're doing and come to the mortuary. We need you.'

While we wait for our Mage reinforcements, we scour every photo in the autopsy file for more of the same marks and anything else out of place. There is nothing more. I try to recall if there was a length of rope on the floor when I woke up in the warehouse, but none of my memories make sense. My frustration sends me pacing across the room. I hate that I cannot trust my mind. Shouldn't some part of me know for certain whether I killed that man or not?

Mery arrives in a cloud of cigarette smoke. Her uneven fringe is covering her green eye, but her blue eye flashes as she spots us.

'Well, if it isn't the Met's least favourite PI and her trusted sidekick,' she says, her voice raspy. 'You've caused quite a stir among the powers that be. Poor DI Manning had to do a great deal of grovelling to persuade them to reinstate you as consultants. I'd be on your best behaviour for the next hundred years or so, otherwise it's Jamie's head that will be served on a silver platter to the Commissioner.'

Jamie shifts, shooting Mery a warning glance. Karrion's eyes widen and he turns to Jamie, who waves him away.

'There's something we need your opinion on,' Jamie says.

'If I'm not here to answer your questions, what was the point of getting out of bed this morning?'

'That's exactly what I hoped to hear.' Jamie frowns. 'Liam, can you call up the photo from earlier?'

The close-up of the torn throat returns to the screen. Mery whistles, shoving her hands into the pockets of her black slacks.

'I'm not saying I was expecting puppies, but this is extreme even for you, boss. Looks like someone wild lost their temper.' Mery shoots me a sideways glance. 'No offence.'

'None taken. But you're not wrong. This is from the Hampten autopsy.'

'All right. Someone did a number on this guy. But I don't see why you called me away from my lunch so I could stare at a mauling victim.'

Karrion points to the screen. 'See this?'

'It's a mark of some kind.' Mery shrugs. 'So what?'

'To us, it looks like it was made by a rope,' I say. 'Only there was no sign of strangulation in the autopsy findings.'

'So the pathologist missed something. It wouldn't be the first time.'

'I didn't miss anything,' Liam says, rising from his seat by the computer. 'I dissected the victim's throat to catalogue the animal damage. There was no indication of ligature wounds either in the soft tissues or in the X-rays.'

'Sorry, I don't speak doctor,' Mery says.

'The victim wasn't strangled. His throat was torn by a dog.'

'In that case, why am I here?'

'Because there are a great many details about this case that don't add up,' I say. 'This is one of them and we were hoping you might help us figure out what it means.'

'Okay.' Mery walks closer to the screen. 'So your victim was killed by a dog, but this one part of his neck showed a rope mark. What about the sides and the back of his neck?'

'We've examined every photo, and this is the only one that shows the mark.'

Mery tilts her head back to stare at the ceiling. Her fringe shifts, revealing her mismatched eyes, which gradually widen.

'No way,' she says. 'No fucking way.'

'What?' Jamie asks.

'No. It's proper impossible.'

'What is?' he asks.

'Are you sure that man is Maerk Hampten?' Mery asks.

Her question surprises me. Hope stirs in me, and Karrion grins. We are on to something and my gut tells me it is something big.

'As it happens, we know for a fact the man who died in the warehouse couldn't possibly have been Maerk Hampten,' I say.

Mery nods. 'In that case, this makes perfect sense.'

'Could you share with us mere mortals, please?' Jamie asks, his voice rising in impatient anger.

'Don't get your knickers in a twist, boss. I'm fairly certain what we're looking at is a Death Mask.'

'The what now?' asks Karrion.

'Damn, what do they teach Shamans these days?' Mery asks, but she is grinning, her eyes glowing. 'Though Death Masks are beyond obscure lore, so I suppose I can't mock you too much.'

Karrion crosses his arms. 'If it's so obscure, how come you know about it?'

'I'm special, that's why.' Mery chuckles. 'No, I had an interest in obscure glamours when I was studying, which led me down many a brownie hole.'

'Will you please just explain what the hell you're talking about?' Jamie asks.

Mery raises her hands to placate him. 'Deep breaths, boss. Death Mask is an extremely powerful glamour. The spell enables you to lift the likeness of a dead person and apply it to another body. It only works on facial features, so it can't exactly change a bloke to a chick, but it's bloody effective. Why didn't anyone pick up on the magical residue at the crime scene?'

'No idea,' Jamie says. 'I wasn't allowed anywhere near the investigation.'

Unzipping her leather jacket, Mery takes out her phone and dials.

'Hey, Hughes. Who was the Mage at the Hampten crime scene? Uh-huh. Just Paladins? Uh-huh. With all due respect, Hughes, you're a fucking moron.'

She ends the call and shakes her head.

'The wankers didn't bother with a Mage because they had a suspect covered in the victim's blood. So the scene was processed by the Paladins, who are about as useful as humans in figuring out the magic present. No offence, boss.'

'None taken,' says Jamie. 'But I can't help feeling like you've only given half an explanation.'

'Right. A Death Mask is an effective, albeit extreme way to disguise a body's identity. Think full-works plastic surgery, but for dead people. Without a Mage present to sense the magical residue, the glamour is untraceable by inspection or technology.'

'You said it lifts the likeness of one body for another,' Karrion says. 'Does that mean that Maerk Hampten had to be dead for someone to steal his face?'

'Yep.'

'By glamour, do you mean it's Fey magic?' I ask.

'Not just any Fey glamour, but the most powerful sort. The spell requires the blood from the beating heart of a mortal to create the weave for the mask.'

'But if those marks are anything to go by, Hampten was strangled...' I leave the thought unfinished.

'Meaning a third person died just to create the spell,' Mery says.

'Hang on,' Karrion says. 'We reckon Hampten disappeared about two months ago. Does this mean he was kept alive until Yan was framed for murder?'

'Not necessarily. A Fey powerful enough to create a Death Mask would have the means to store it until it was needed.'

All roads lead back to Pheonix. But why go to all this trouble? Am I receiving my first taste of a Fey vendetta? Could there be something else in play other than mere vengeance?

'So you said you knew for certain that the man who died in the warehouse wasn't Hampten,' Mery says, turning to me. 'How come?'

'Official records indicate that Hampten was a South Mage, but the victim was a Dog Shaman.'

'How do you know?'

'I tasted his blood.'

Mery whistles. 'Those Wild Folk abilities you have are bloody handy. Pun intended.'

'Thanks.'

'Right, so someone went through an awful lot of trouble to make it look like Yan killed Hampten,' Karrion says. 'How do we figure out the real identity of the victim?'

'That's not hard.' Mery shrugs. 'Just take the fingerprints and DNA sample from the body and run both through our system.'

Karrion, Jamie and I share a look.

'What?' Mery asks.

18

GLAMOUR

We leave the mortuary in silence. After a lengthy explanation about the missing body, Mery is as caught up in the mystery as we are. We stop by Jamie's car, and Mery lights a cigarette, tilting her head back to blow out the smoke.

'I think it's time we paid a visit to Aleson Hampten, or whoever the woman impersonating her is,' Jamie says.

'My thoughts exactly,' I reply.

'Are you coming with us, Mery?' Jamie asks.

'As if I would miss it. You have a nasty habit of having fun without me.'

'Do you mind if we stop by my place?' I ask. 'I'd like to let Sinta out.'

'No problem.' Jamie turns to Mery. 'Will you follow in the smoke-mobile?'

'Sure. Only the cool kids are allowed in my car anyway.'

Mery takes her place behind the wheel of her mint-green VW Golf, cracking the window open. The hand holding the cigarette dangles out of the window. Her car leaves a cloud of blue smoke in its wake.

We make a quick stop to check on Sinta and then head over to the Hamptens' place. They live in a penthouse flat with a view of the Thames. This is the third time we have investigated a Mage along the riverfront, and I wonder at which point will the presence of Paladins begin affecting the house prices. Perhaps the Mages living here are too rich to concern themselves with a murder or two in the neighbourhood.

'If Aleson Hampten is home, let me speak to her first,' Jamie says while we are on our way to the top floor. 'She made some serious accusations about you and she may be more willing to talk to us if we don't antagonise her.'

'So it's okay for her to lie about Yan?' Karrion asks, and I lay a hand on his arm.

'No, but we need her to tell us what she did with the body. She's unlikely to cooperate if we go in calling her a liar.'

Before Karrion has a chance to reply, I nod. 'Sounds like a plan. We'll wait in the corridor until you're ready for us.'

We hang back as Jamie and Mery walk the length of the short corridor to the door. Jamie raises his hand to knock and pauses.

'The door is ajar,' he says just loud enough for us to hear.

As we approach, Mery's aura expands. Power crackles between her fingers. Jamie hesitates, then steps aside to let her through the door first. Karrion and I follow close behind them.

The door leads to a small hallway with a floor-to-ceiling mirror along one side. Beyond it opens a spacious open-plan kitchen-lounge. After the experience of the Pearsons' and Hailfaxes' homes, I was expecting a lifeless flat filled with chrome and marble. Instead, the walls are covered in paintings of African wilderness and Japanese sakura. There are tall wooden carvings of animals dotted around the lounge, and above the television hangs a row of carved masks. A low cabinet to one side holds a selection of conch shells and flat stones showing various fossils. The hardwood floors are covered with Persian rugs.

'Is this a home or a museum?' asks Karrion in a low voice.

A cherry-wood dining-room table near the kitchen is covered in stacks of paper. I only glance at them, catching enough to see that they contain various financial documents, before I continue my search. There are three bedrooms, all decorated in tones of sienna, ochre, and forest green. The master bedroom has an adjoining bathroom with a marble tub sunk into a raised dais. The bathroom is bigger than my lounge, but this is not the first time I have encountered evidence of the disparity of wealth among the citizens of Old London.

It takes a matter of moments for the four of us to search the flat and confirm what the initial silence hinted: there is no one here.

'I see no sign of a break-in,' Jamie says as we all return to the lounge. 'Do you?'

We shake our heads. Although I leave the thought unspoken, a small part of me had hoped we might find the body here. But I see now how illogical that is. Smuggling it past the doorman would be difficult enough, and without the benefit of the mortuary's cold-storage rooms, the body would soon begin to decompose.

'Do you think Pheonix did something to her?' Karrion asks.

'I don't know,' I say. 'But it's more likely than the other way round.'

'Maybe she's done a runner,' Mery says. 'If she has more than half a brain cell, she must know we're on to her by now.'

I return to the master bedroom and open the doors to a walk-in wardrobe. The clothes and shoes are all arranged in neat rows. At the back are two sets of Louis Vuitton luggage, stacked in size order. None are missing, nor are there any obvious gaps in the clothes around me.

'If she's on the run, she hasn't taken much with her,' I say, and close the doors.

Karrion looks through the nightstand drawers. 'The Hamptens are loaded. They may have a bolthole somewhere else in the city.'

'That's true, but you forget that the woman we're after isn't Aleson Hampten. She may not know the full extent of the Hamptens' property.'

'This, lady and gentlemen, is what we call a mind fuck,' Mery says. 'Do we have any idea who she really is?'

'No, just like we don't know whose body was stolen from the morgue,' Jamie replies.

'Is it just me or has the Met's standards slipped while the wild chick sat in prison?'

Jamie offers us a grim smile. 'You're not wrong. What's even more worrying is that it was Yannia and Karrion who figured out we were dealing with imposters.'

'Fancy running New Scotland Yard?' Mery asks. 'The pay is decent, but the hours are unpleasant and the politics downright shit.'

'We'll pass, thanks.'

Beside me, Karrion nods.

'Should you call a SOCO team?' I ask Jamie. 'Although there are no signs of struggle, the open door is suspicious. Perhaps they can find something we've missed or a clue as to what happened to the Hamptens. They may even be able to shed light on the identity of the people we've been dealing with.'

'That was going to be my next move.' Jamie takes out his phone. 'Mery, would you like to start?'

'Whatever you say, boss.' Mery pauses in the doorway. 'On second thoughts, scratch that. It can only lead to madness.'

'I love you too, Mery.'

She shudders and gives Jamie the finger over her shoulder. While Jamie deals with the formalities, I follow Mery back to the lounge, drawn by the stacks of papers. There is plenty we can learn here without contaminating the scene any more than we already have.

Mery draws her fringe back, revealing a green eye that seems to emit a faint glow. Her aura quests out. Its feel is different from before, when she was gathering strands of power for a spell. Now she is searching for traces of magic, identifying the wards around the flat, and seeking anything out of the ordinary. I sense the edge of her awareness touching my aura, sliding along its edges, and venturing further but Karrion and I are not what she is interested in.

After a while, Mery turns towards a wall containing a row of five Japanese silk paintings. She cocks her head, as if analysing the images.

'What is it?' I ask.

'That wall. It's not real.'

'What wall?' asks Karrion.

'The one between the kitchen and the end of the lounge. Which bit is causing you trouble?'

'Only the bit where you said there's a wall there,' Karrion says, the feathers of his magic ruffling in irritation. 'It's floor-to-ceiling glass doors leading on to the balcony. I'd hardly call it a wall.'

Mery cocks her head. 'When did Shamans gain X-ray vision? Or are your bones infused with cold iron?'

'I honestly have no idea what you're talking about.'

'The wall is a Fey glamour. Which goes exactly no way

towards explaining why a Shaman like you would see through it.'

'Are you sure?' Karrion asks, ignoring the barb.

Mery reaches into her pocket and pulls out a thin torch. She clicks it on and shines the light in Karrion's eyes. He shifts aside with a wince.

'Would you mistake that for the sun?'

'Of course not.'

'Then trust me: it's Fey magic.'

I step closer to the wall. 'The question is, to what end?'

'No, no,' Mery says. 'Let's not allow ourselves to be distracted. Why does Karrion see through the glamour when we can't?'

'Even a Shaman like me has his ways,' Karrion says. 'Allow me to demonstrate.'

He draws his cold-iron necklace over his head, brandishing it before himself like a talisman. I take an involuntary step back. My dislike of cold iron has grown worse since the Winter Queen marked me and someone – most likely Pheonix – poisoned me. Karrion does not notice as he sweeps the necklace across the wall. The effect is immediate: what moments before was a solid wall wavers like a reflection on still water and dissolves into a view of the river.

The wall was concealing a narrow balcony, as Karrion said. Tall sliding doors offer a stunning view of the river and the South Bank. The balcony has just enough room for a small wrought-iron table and two matching chairs. There is nothing else out there.

Why bother hiding the balcony; and with Fey glamour, no less? What is Pheonix trying to hide?

'It's weird, right?' Karrion asks, tucking the necklace back under his collar.

'I was just thinking that.'

Through the glass, I hear a distant wail of sirens. They seem to be coming closer, though the echoes from the buildings make it hard to say for certain. Jamie strides in from the master bedroom.

'What the hell is going on?' he asks.

'We found a secret balcony,' I say, thrown by the alarm in his voice.

'I don't give a rat's arse about a secret anything. Dispatch just called to say that some genius thrill-seeker is climbing along the outside of this building.'

With a growing sense of dread, I yank the balcony door open. A small detached part of my brain notes that it was not locked, but I push the thought aside as I step out.

A breeze tugs at my clothes, bringing with it the scents of the sea. My head tilts back on its own accord so that I may better sample the air. I find the nose of a rat asleep in the rafters above the flat. With the keener sense, the scents unravel until I recognise each of them. They are like coloured strands in the air, and one tiny thread draws my attention. It is the colour of purple flames and smells of autumn leaves, overripe apples, frost-bitten sloes, and open fires. My head is drawn to the right.

The first thing I notice is the decorative ledge that runs the length of the building. It is barely wide enough to stand on. A flutter of movement snaps my attention further along, and I swear.

Aleson Hampten stands on the ledge, her cheek pressed against the bricks. Beyond her, grinning as if he has not a care in the world is Pheonix. His customary morning suit and top hat look out of place, but his eyes burn with familiar flames. Our gazes lock and his grin widens as he lifts his hat in mock greeting.

'Shit.' Karrion has followed me out and his word indicates that he, too, has spotted Pheonix.

The sound of the sirens grows loud enough that I have to resist the urge to clap my hands over my ears. They cut off suddenly. A glance down to the street shows a growing collection of emergency vehicles and curious onlookers. From various cameras pointed upwards, it is clear members of the press are also present. It is the last thing we need.

'Aleson,' I call out, trying to keep the fear and panic from my voice. 'Can you move this way? We don't want you to fall.'

She turns her head quickly to glance back, but I am left with the impression that she does not see us. Her attention returns to Pheonix, and she takes another shuffling step towards him.

'Fucking hell, she could fall any minute,' Mery stays, standing close enough that I can smell the cigarette smoke clinging to her clothes.

'Is there something you can do?' I ask. 'A spell that could slow her fall or stick her to the side of the building?'

'If I could get closer, perhaps I could decrease her weight or weave a web beneath her. From here, I'm not sure how much I'll be able to do. In any case, creating a spell powerful enough will take time.'

'Why don't you start and we'll see what we can do about buying you time,' I say.

'You're hot when you're bossy.'

I cast a sharp glance at Mery, but she is staring at the space beneath Aleson, a slight grin on her face while she gathers power to her.

Pheonix dances backwards along the ledge, as confident as if he were on the pavement far below us. Aleson shuffles forward. He is speaking to her, the words too faint over the noise of traffic and the shouts from below, though I catch the hypnotic lilt of his Irish accent. She is in his thrall, and I fear nothing short of brute force will snap her out of it.

'Give me your necklace,' I say to Karrion, a reckless idea beginning to form.

Karrion does not argue and hands me the protective string of cold-iron disks. I take it, careful to position my fingers as far from the metal as possible. Bracing my free hand on the balcony railing, I climb over it and on to the ledge.

The wind is stronger, tugging at my clothes in angry gusts. I fix my eyes on Aleson's back and draw upon my inner reserves of power to give me the balance of a squirrel. This is no different from climbing the high branches of the towering oaks and sycamores at the conclave, or so I tell myself.

Behind me, Jamie swears. 'Yannia, what the hell are you doing?'

'I need to break the glamour before she falls.'

'Who falls?' Jamie's voice is growing angry.

'Can your spell hold two, Mery?' Karrion asks, ignoring Jamie.

Mery coughs. 'Depends on how much time Yannia buys me.'

Skeins of power gather below me as Mery weaves a web of magic, using the very air to save us from a lethal fall. I inch along the ledge, reaching towards Aleson with the hand holding the necklace. All I need to do is touch exposed skin with the cold iron and the glamour will break. But one wrong move on my part or a jolt of waking from an enchantment, and Aleson falls.

'You are almost there, my dear,' Pheonix says to Aleson. 'A few steps more and we will be in the clear.'

At last I hear Pheonix's words and the slight hiss takes me back to a cold November night, when we spoke by a Fey Mound. His glamour had snaked its way through my defences, amplified by Baneacre's corruption spreading over Old London. He was certain of his master's victory that night, just as he is certain he will win now. His tail whips behind him in hypnotic patterns that threaten to distract me from the task at hand. I shake my head and force my attention to Aleson.

'Please, Aleson,' I call out. 'Look at me.'

Pheonix skips backwards, and now he appears to be standing on thin air, his arms open in clear invitation. Behind me, Karrion curses.

'That's not on. Why does the creepy fairy get to fly?'

Two more steps, and I can reach Aleson. My knees are shaking, my right hand gripping the side of the building until my joints ache. Any notion of safety has long fled my mind, but I am not prepared to give up, not while there is still a chance I can save Aleson. I shuffle along, but as I am holding out the necklace towards the back of her head, she moves towards Pheonix.

'Damn it.'

I sense the net of magic below me, but it is too far to the right, covering me but not Aleson. Mery is weaving more strands to expand it, which causes unpredictable gusts of wind to lash at me from below. One almost sends me tumbling head first off the ledge. Beyond Aleson, Pheonix grins, revealing two rows of sharp teeth.

'Please, Aleson,' I say, and lean towards her. She is so close, but again she moves out of my reach.

'Come now, little fly,' Pheonix says, his amethyst eyes glowing. 'Time for us to speed away.'

Aleson is at the corner of the building. Ahead of her is only thin air, and yet she leans forward to take Pheonix's hand. It's as though she expects there to be an invisible bridge or a walkway connecting the building to its neighbour. In her hesitation, I see that some part of her is resisting the glamour, but will it be enough?

It is now or never. I must act, even if it means risking my life.

I draw in a deep breath, calling upon the grace of a pine marten, and take three quick steps towards Aleson. My fingers brush the back of her collar just as she strides forward. One of the cold-iron disks connects with the back of her neck, and a shudder runs through her. She twists, eyes widening with fear, and the hand that was holding on to Pheonix closes around air. He has grown insubstantial and he lifts his top hat in a farewell before dissolving into a flurry of autumn leaves.

In a burst of magic that sets off an expanding pattern of bright lights across my vision, Mery sends strands of her web after Aleson. The air vibrates with power, but the structure is too weak to hold and Aleson plunges through it.

She screams all the way to the ground.

19

—————

STOLEN LIVES

It takes me several minutes to recover from the shock enough to shuffle back to the balcony. Once I am on solid ground, I slam my hand against the metal railing. Pain shoots up my arm.

'Yan, stop!' Karrion grabs my wrist, pulling me away from the railing.

'I should have been quicker!' I snap; a familiar taste of failure in my mouth.

'You did everything you could,' he says. 'My heart nearly stopped when you went after her.'

'I thought I could save her. There has to have been a way.'

'There was a way,' Mery says, none of her usual biting humour present in her voice. 'I should have created the spell quicker, should have anticipated that she might fall further along. I was so stupid.'

She kicks one of the iron chairs and curses, while I step back from Karrion's embrace. Below us, two Paladins are covering the body with a white sheet while several more are setting up a cordon to keep away the journalists and curious onlookers.

'Can someone please tell me what just happened?' Jamie

197

asks behind us. 'One moment she was stepping on to a walkway between the buildings, the next she fell. Did I miss something?'

Karrion frowns at Jamie. 'Only everything.'

Mery and I stare at him as realisation that Jamie, too, fell under Pheonix's glamour dawns on us.

'Have you ever considered buying something made of cold iron, heart copper, and true silver?' I ask.

'Like a protective amulet?' Jamie shuffles his feet, stuffing his hands in his pockets. 'Won't that interfere with... you know?'

'Interfere with what?' Mery asks, while I regret bringing up the subject in front of her.

'My innate magical talent.' Jamie speaks the words just loud enough for us to hear.

'I'd hate to break this to you, boss, but you're human. You don't have magic.'

'Not right now, but I've read that it can remain dormant in the blood and with the right training, manifest later in life.'

Mery's eyes flash as a grin forms on her face. Her gaze meets mine, and I shake my head, careful to keep my expression blank. She catches on quickly, and the amusement turns into pity.

'I'm sorry, mate, but like I said, you don't have magic. Humans never do.'

Laying a hand on Jamie's shoulder, I draw his attention to me. 'I think what Mery is trying to say is that it would be wise for you to take every precaution available. A cold-iron token kept next to your skin would offer you a degree of protection against Fey glamour.'

'Tinker Thaylor, a Mage friend of ours, does wicked designs,' Karrion says. 'It doesn't have to be a necklace either. If you want, I can perform introductions. She's pretty awesome, even if she does look a little like a beetle.'

Jamie nods, his whole being deflating a little. 'All right. I'll think about it.'

'Let's go back inside,' I say. 'We need to explain what just happened and I'd rather do it out of earshot of any reporters with magic at their disposal.'

Mery closes the sliding door behind us. She prowls around the lounge while I explain to Jamie everything he missed. Karrion remains leaning against the glass doors, his gaze fixed on the spot from which Aleson fell to her death.

'It doesn't make any sense,' he says when I finish speaking. 'Why would Pheonix have helped her this morning at the mortuary only to lead her to her death now?'

'Maybe he had no further use for her?' I suggest.

'That's cold.'

'This is one of the Fair Folk we're talking about, and specifically one from the Winter Queen's court.'

'Right, so cold is pretty much their trademark,' Karrion says.

Footsteps and voices approach in the hallway and a team of crime-scene technicians enter, all wearing protective white suits and blue shoe coverings. Without needing to be told, we file out of the flat, where a table with extra supplies has been set up, and don the protective gear. When we return, the lead investigator walks the flat with us and makes a note of everything we touched and moved during the brief time we spent at the scene. The rest of his team is already processing the flat. Mery takes a clipboard from one of them and makes notes about the spells present, while the rest of us stand back and let the technicians do their job.

'Here's something weird,' Mery says as she approaches us ten minutes later. 'This flat has two sets of wards.'

'Don't most Mage homes, especially the wealthy ones, have lots of active wards?' Jamie asks.

'Yes, but what's the point of duplicating them?'

'So there are two of everything?' he asks.

'Yep. All the usual suspects are present: sound, remote

viewing, perimeter alarm, harmful spells. But one lot of wards is active, whereas the other is dormant.'

'That makes sense, though, doesn't it?' I say. 'If the people who lived here over the recent months weren't the real Hamptens, it's unlikely they knew the activation words for the wards. They will have needed to set up their own.'

Mery nods. 'Pity that doesn't tell us anything about their true identities.'

'There's got to be something here that sheds light on that,' Karrion says. 'When can we start looking?'

'We're done with the dining-room table, though I expect we'll want to take most of the papers for further processing,' one of the SOCO team says. 'But you're welcome to look through them.'

'Great.' Karrion grins. 'I have a feeling those papers will crack this case wide open.'

I wince and, beside me, Jamie shakes his head.

Karrion shrugs. 'What did I say? Wait. I didn't mean "crack" like how Aleson died.'

'Way too soon, Bird Boy,' Mery calls out from the other side of the room.

Karrion's cheeks are pink as the three of us all choose different piles of papers and begin going through them. My first stack contains bank statements going back three years. I am about to set them aside, when I notice that many of the recent months have been annotated.

'Look at these. Someone has gone through every expense over the past twelve months and identified them, down to which are paid by standing order or direct debit and which require a cheque.'

'Maybe the Hamptens are careful with money,' Karrion says. 'Just because they're loaded doesn't mean they don't budget.'

'It's possible. But if you were trying to take over someone's life, wouldn't you want to know exactly what the outgoings are supposed to be and how to pay them?'

'And what money is coming in,' Jamie says, holding up a sheet of paper. 'Here's a balance sheet for the Hamptens and a list of monthly sources of income.'

'Yeah, okay. Their accountant ought to be in charge of all that,' Karrion says, leaning closer to Jamie. 'Especially as most of these have been added by hand.'

'Presumably when they came to the imposters' awareness. I have to say, this shows an impressive level of preparation.'

'What are you thinking?' Jamie asks.

'Whoever these people were, they must have done this kind of work before. There's no way your average person would wake up one morning and decide to take over the life of a millionaire Mage. A long con like this takes skill and practice.'

'Speaking of practice...'

Karrion draws two sheets of paper from the stack and sets them on the table side by side. They are both filled with signatures, one for Maerk Hampten, the other for Aleson. I pick one of them up and notice a series of pinpricks overlaying the first few signatures.

'What do you think these are?' I ask.

After inspecting the other sheet, Karrion grins. 'I remember seeing something about this on the television once. Apparently the easiest way to learn to forge someone's signature is to lay a sample over a piece of paper and prick holes through the main loops and whorls. That turns it into an exercise of connecting the dots.'

A memory tugs on the edge of my mind. It is something I saw weeks ago and it eludes me until I return to staring at Aleson's signatures.

'This explains it,' I say. 'When the woman claiming to be

Aleson hired me, the cheque she wrote me had already been signed. I thought it odd at the time, especially because the cheque below was signed too.'

'It's easier to forge signatures in the comfort of your stolen home, rather than under someone's watchful eye,' Jamie says.

We continue looking through the papers, searching for anything that might shed light on who these imposters are. In a pile of what looks like circulars and takeaway menus, I find a white envelope franked with the logo of a prominent Old London law firm. The envelope has been opened, and the papers stuffed back in haphazardly, so one corner is sticking out. My curiosity piqued, I open the envelope and begin to read. I get no further than the subject heading before I stagger back, a violent tremor shaking the pages in my grip.

'Yan, what's wrong?'

Ever sensitive to my mood, Karrion is at my side in an instant. I show him the letter and watch while his gaze skitters across it, at last landing on the subject line. His eyes widen.

'No fucking way.'

'What's going on?' Jamie asks.

'This letter is about the Cuckoo Trust.'

'Wait, isn't that the...' Jamie glances towards the SOCO team working around us, 'the settlement that Lloid had a connection to?'

'Yes, exactly.'

'What's the letter doing here?' he asks.

'Let me see if I can figure that out,' I say.

The tremors in my hands have settled enough for me to read the letter without any difficulties. It is several pages long and most of it seems to contain highly technical legal and tax advice. On the penultimate page are two tax computations, and my eyebrows rise at the figures involved.

'I can't claim to understand all the tax jargon, but the gist seems to be that it's highly inadvisable to add money to an existing settlement because it causes all manner of nasty tax charges, but since the Hamptens have already transferred two million pounds to the Cuckoo Trust, there's little the solicitors can do after the fact. There's a lot of tax to pay now, though I'm not sure who's going to pay it since both the Hamptens and their imposters appear to be dead.'

'Am I missing something?' Karrion asks. 'What's the connection between the Hamptens and the Cuckoo Trust?'

'Honestly? I have no idea.' I glance through the letter again. 'Though based on the dates in this letter, I don't think it was the Hamptens who made the transfer.'

'This is getting weirder by the minute.'

'I agree. Why don't we set this in the pile of things that don't make any sense for now and see what else we can uncover? Perhaps something else here will clarify things.'

'Detective?' a voice calls from the master bedroom.

We follow Jamie out of the lounge and to the en-suite bathroom. Even before we enter, I feel a brush of magic against my aura. Inside, a woman dressed in one of the white bodysuits stands, her arms spread wide. From the steely feel of the spell she has woven, she must be a Paladin, though I never realised they worked as crime-scene investigators.

'Take a look at this, sir,' she says, her voice tight with the effort of maintaining a spell.

An image of the floor is superimposed over the real one at the height of her knees. It shows the bathroom as I remember it from earlier, with one notable exception: there are purple symbols painted in a circle.

'Is that blood?' asks Karrion.

'Yes,' the Paladin says.

'Cool. Who needs UV lights when you can use magic?'

The Paladin glances harshly at Karrion over her shoulder.

'Don't worry, Bird Boy,' Mery says behind us. 'The Paladins have their sense of humour surgically removed when they take the oath to serve.'

'Sense of humour is not an organ.' The Paladin frowns.

'Case in point, ladies and gents.' Mery peers at the spell. 'Blimey. I can say with absolute certainty that this is where the ritual for the Death Mask was performed.'

'Do we know whose blood that is?' I ask.

'We'll collect samples from across the floor, but it appears that the bathroom has been cleaned many times since this ritual circle was created,' the Paladin says. 'A rigorous application of bleach will have destroyed the integrity of the blood.'

'The chick in white can spout technicalities all she wants, but I'd bet this month's wages on it being Aleson Hampten's blood.' Mery pauses, glancing towards the door. 'I mean, the real Aleson's.'

'How can you be so sure?' Karrion asks.

'The Hamptens lived alone, correct?'

'As far as we know,' I say.

'If the ritual needed Maerk Hampten's face, then the blood from the still-beating heart likely came from Aleson, unless Maerk was strangled just enough to knock him unconscious. But from what I remember about the ritual, it would be a lot easier to have the stiff whose face you wanted to steal ready at the centre of the circle and the blood donor cut open next to it. So assuming the Hamptens didn't have a live-in butler or maid who has mysteriously vanished, I'm putting my money on Aleson.'

The Paladin stares at Mery. Jamie, Karrion and I nod.

'I'm so pleased you agree,' says Mery. 'The real question is, what did the killers do with the bodies?'

Casting my thoughts back to our initial search of the flat, I try to imagine ways to dispose of one or more sets of remains.

There was no convenient rubbish shoot in the hallway, and the lift had a security camera, not to mention the doorman on duty in the entrance hall. The balcony is no more convenient, not when the road below is busy at all times of day and night.

Next to me, Karrion walks to the nearest wall and knocks along the tiles. The dull sound reveals no hidden compartments.

'No one who isn't completely doolally would consider hiding bodies in their walls,' Mery says, earning herself a glare from Karrion. 'The smell would be intense. The only reason they did that in medieval castles, apart from all the nobles being inbred lunatics, was because the stonework was so shoddy there was a permanent draft coming in through all the holes in the walls.'

'With that level of knowledge, you could be a history teacher,' Jamie says.

'And miss my calling to brighten each and every one of your days, boss?' Mery grins. 'No, thanks.'

'I think we're veering off to fantasy lands,' I say, ignoring the presence of a Paladin maintaining an active spell in the room. 'The Hamptens owned an import and export business. It would have been easy to order a few wooden crates to be brought into the flat and shipped out again the following day.'

'That makes sense,' says Jamie. 'I'll make some calls and see if we can't figure out where the bodies were taken.'

I stop him before he leaves the room. 'It would also be worth sending someone to the Mercury Deliveries office in Old London. Maerk Hampten must have left his fingerprints all over his room and we'll need them for comparison.'

'Good idea,' Jamie says. 'I'll sort it out.'

We spend the next two hours searching the flat, though much of it involves trying not to be in the SOCO team's way as they work through the rooms. One of them pulls out a small leather journal from a slit in the guest-room mattress, but it goes in an evidence bag before we have a chance to look through it. I am half tempted to ask Jamie if Karrion and I can accompany the SOCO team back to evidence processing, but given that we have only been reinstated for less than a day, it feels like pushing my luck. We will have to be patient and wait for the results, as usual.

By the time we decide that we have done all we can at the crime scene, we have long-missed lunch. Mery follows us out of the flat, and we bin our gloves, white suits, and plastic shoe-covers. While we have been searching for evidence, the death of the woman claiming to be Aleson Hampten had slipped to the back of my mind. But now, as we ride the lift down in silence, her screams echo in my memory.

'Anyone fancy a drink?' Mery asks as we step out of the building. Her tone is light, but her eyes keep sliding sideways towards the spot where the body hit the pavement, which is now hidden within a crime-scene tent.

'Not me,' Jamie says. 'Between the body that vanished from the mortuary and now this, I'll still be doing paperwork when I turn fifty.'

'All right.' Mery turns to Karrion and me. 'What about the wild dream team? Want to get wasted?'

I want to turn down her offer in favour of an early night, but I need not Wishearth's foresight to know I will end up spending the evening turning over the events of the afternoon and wondering what I might have done differently. Isn't it better to delay the inevitable, even by a couple of hours, especially if doing so will provide a measure of comfort for us all? I turn to Karrion, who nods.

'Sounds good, though I need to take care of my puppy first. Have you ever been to the Open Hearth?'

'Once or twice,' says Mery. 'It's a nice pub and best of all, walking distance from me. Shall I meet you there in an hour?'

'Works for us,' I say. 'Jamie, would you mind giving us a lift home on your way back to the Met?'

'Of course.'

We head towards the cars, ignoring the small cluster of reporters still lingering near the crime-scene tent. My hand is on Jamie's car door, when Jack Lincoln steps into view. A cold smile spreads over his lips as he directs his words at me:

'Yannia Wilde, are you concerned about how often people die around you?'

20

THE SOLACE AT THE BOTTOM OF A GLASS

Despite several hours alone, Sinta is reluctant to leave a bone I gave her earlier until she realises that the direction of our walk is taking us to the Open Hearth. She races as far ahead as her lead allows and jumps against the door, as if expecting it to open on her command. As soon as we are inside, I unclip the lead and Sinta rushes to greet Boris, who is sleeping by the fire.

Mery has arrived before us. She is paying for her drink when we join her at the bar. My eyes meet Wishearth's across the room. He raises his glass in greeting, but when he realises we are meeting someone else, his expression grows bored. It is a reminder that as friendly as Wishearth is with me and, by extension, with Karrion, he is slow to make friends and prefers to keep away from strangers.

'How's the food here?' Mery asks, once I have received a tumbler of brandy and Karrion is holding a pint of pale ale.

'Excellent.'

'Good, I'm starving. Shall we find a table?'

I lead the way around the bar. A table close to the fireplace is free, and I make a beeline for it. This way Wishearth can listen through the fire if he wants to, without having to share his space with a stranger.

My first instinct is to choose the chair furthest from the flames, but Wishearth's touch on the Fey mark last night lessened its hold over me. After a busy day, the heat of the flames will provide welcome relief from the pain, and I sit in the chair closest to the fireplace.

Sinta has abandoned Boris and trots past us to greet Wishearth. I watch her jump against his lower leg and bark. He laughs and picks her up, cradling her to his chest. She closes her eyes, tail wagging slowly against his side.

Mery has followed the direction of my gaze. 'Is this your pub?'

'What?' I force my attention to her. 'Why would you think that?'

'Your puppy seems to think she owns the place, unless all dogs mingle freely with the patrons here.'

'Sinta is a corgi, so by default she thinks she owns the whole world. But the owner, Funja, is a Dog Shaman and often looks after Sinta for me. She stayed here while I was imprisoned.'

'Handy, but also a pity.'

'Why?' I ask.

Mery grins. 'If this was your pub, I wouldn't have to pay for my drinks.'

We all laugh until a heavy hand squeezes my shoulder. I find Funja smiling at me, his eyes all but disappearing within the creases on his face. As usual, his thinning hair is pulled back in a ponytail, and he is wearing a stained apron over a black T-shirt and jeans.

'Yannia,' he says. 'It is good to see you.'

I rise and hug him. 'Thank you for taking such good care of Sinta for me.'

'Is nothing. She is family, as are you. Besides, Wishearth, he likes the puppy.'

Funja and I turn to look at Wishearth, who is still smiling at Sinta. A small crease appears between Mery's eyes.

'You will eat, *da*? You are always too thin, Yannia. Funja's food is good for you.'

'Yes, please. I'll have my usual, but hold the eggs.'

'Of course.' Funja nods to Karrion. 'I have a special dish for Bird Shamans. You like fish, *da*?'

'Love it.' Karrion grins.

Funja turns to Mery, who has been looking through the short menu.

'Do you have anything vegan?' she asks.

'Today's special is a red lentil dahl with vegan naan,' he says.

'Perfect.'

With a final pat on my shoulder, Funja takes the menus and heads for the kitchen.

'You're vegan?' Karrion asks Mery.

She sweeps a hand up and down her torso. 'What can I say? A temple of perfection like this needs to be looked after.'

'Then how come you smoke so much?'

'I said I was perfect, not a saint,' she says with a husky chuckle before turning to me. 'So that's Wishearth, eh?'

My surprise must register on my face, for Mery laughs.

'Are you a follower of the old ways?' I ask.

'No, not me. But Jamie's mentioned him once, twice, or about a million times. Apparently he's made quite the impression. I never expected him to be so...'

'Into day drinking?' Karrion suggests.

'I was going to say hot, but sure, that works too.'

To hide my smile, I take a sip from my brandy. When I dare glance in Wishearth's direction, he is watching me over the rim of his pint glass. It seems he is taking full advantage of the opportunity to eavesdrop.

'He's definitely the hottest person here,' I say to tease him a little, and I am rewarded with flames flaring in his eyes. 'He'd have to be, given that he's mostly made of fire.'

Mery throws her head back and laughs. 'It's official. We need to hang out more often.'

'I thought you preferred to spend your time in clubs where people wear leather and chains,' Karrion says.

He is sitting straight, slowly rotating the glass on the table in front of him. For someone usually so comfortable around people, he seems ill at ease in Mery's presence. I wish I could ask him why without drawing attention to his discomfort.

'There's a time and a place for everything,' Mery says, and winks at him.

We sip our drinks in silence. I am surprised to notice that my brandy is almost gone, and Mery motions to a passing waiter to bring us all a refill.

A tendril of heat from the fireplace brushes against my left hand, which is resting on my lap. I spread my fingers, and the heat splits into segments. They stroke my bare skin, as a lover might, and a thrill of desire runs down my limbs. I glance towards Wishearth. His eyes are closed, but his thumb moves in slow circles, and I can match the movement to the sensations along my skin.

'Yan?'

I snap my head up. 'What?'

'Are you okay?' Karrion asks. 'You looked like you were miles away.'

'Sorry,' I say, and the caress of flames slowly fades away. 'I was just thinking about stuff.'

Mery accepts a new gin and tonic from the waiter and downs half of the drink in a single swallow. 'I think we all are.'

The mood around the table changes from banter to seriousness as if someone flicked a switch. Mery's brow is creased and her blue eye, the only one not hidden by the uneven fringe, is narrowed. A realisation dawns on me, followed by a wave of sympathy.

'Is this the first time you watched someone die?' I ask, keeping my voice low to prevent our conversation from being overheard by the other patrons.

'Yeah.' She keeps her attention on her glass. 'I normally turn up long after the body's gone cold or, if I'm lucky, after the stiff's been carted away.'

'I'm sorry,' Karrion says, and some of his discomfort melts away. 'I didn't realise.'

'You guys must be used to it by now, but I can't stop hearing her screams or the sound her body made when it hit the pavement. It's stupid, really.'

Acting on an impulse, I lay a hand on Mery's arm. 'It's not. The day you grow accustomed to witnessing death is the day you've lost a piece of yourself.'

The image of Baneacre appears before my eyes, reminding me of the pain and outrage in his expression moments before I killed him. He is followed by Cathwulf cowering on the ground while Karrion reminded me that she was no longer a threat. We have witnessed so much violence and death in the past few months, I'm frightened of the effect it may have on us.

'Also, for the record, we're not used to any of it.'

Karrion nods.

'I just feel so stupid,' Mery says. 'If I'd begun the spell at the far end, I might have caught her. Years of studying and spell-casting meant nothing when someone's life was at risk. I panicked like a first-year acolyte.'

Opposite me, Karrion lets out a hollow laugh. 'You're not the only one. What good is a Bird Shaman who can't fly?'

'We all have our regrets,' I say. 'As much as you both wish you could have done something more, I was the one on the ledge with her. If anyone could have saved her, it should have been me.'

Karrion looks like he wants to argue, but I silence him with a shake of my head.

'But ultimately the only person responsible for her death was Pheonix. We may wish we could have done more to save her and our regrets may haunt us for a long time, but he's the one who lured her on to the ledge and off it.'

'You are a woman of great wisdom,' Mery says, but in the brittleness of her smile, I see she is not yet ready to believe me.

Funja approaches with a large circular tray and distributes plates, bowls, and condiments around the table. As he places cutlery wrapped in a napkin by my meal, he pats the back of my hand.

'Good for the body and the spirit,' he says. 'Enjoy your meal.'

Mery spoons some of her curry on to a piece of naan bread and bites into it. She grins as she chews.

'I think I'll be the one who needs to acquire a share of this pub. The food is amazing. Is the owner looking for a business partner?'

'Funja is a great cook, but I don't think so.'

'Damn. Well, that just means this has to become my new local. I have no need to bother shopping for groceries or wasting time cooking when I can eat food as good as this.'

'In that case, we may run into each other more often,' I say as I cut into my gammon steak. 'This is my preferred pub too.'

The corner of Mery's mouth lifts. 'Even better.'

Karrion snorts, but he covers it with a cough, keeping his focus on the plate in front of him. Funja's Bird Shaman special appears to be seafood four ways: fried cod, breaded scampi, whole fried whitebait, and a coil of smoked salmon. It is served with chips, mushy peas, and garlic sauce.

'Did you always know you wanted to be a PI?' Mery asks once the edge of our hunger has dulled.

I hesitate, wondering how best to answer the question without giving away too many Wild Folk secrets. The truth is that it had never been a particular aspiration of mine, but rather a profession that didn't require an advanced education that I thought I might be good at, given my innate magic. Now my Wild Folk instincts urge caution. Although Mery has worked on several cases with us, I barely know her, certainly not well enough to reveal information that concerns more than just myself.

Before I can formulate an answer, Karrion comes to my rescue.

'I met Yan shortly after she moved to the city. Straight away, I knew she was the coolest person I'd ever met, and that was before she told me about her new PI business. After I graduated from uni, I temped for a while, but I knew I wasn't likely to become a world-famous painter anytime soon. So I blagged an apprenticeship out of Yan, and the rest, as they say, is history. I like helping people. Sure, standing in shadowy alleyways for hours on end can be a bit boring, but solving crimes is awesome.'

'Yan?' Mery directs the question at me. 'Is that a nickname anyone can use?'

'Nope,' I say, and smile at the flash of pleasure in Karrion's eyes. 'It belongs to Karrion alone.'

'All right. I guess I'll have to come up with one of my own.'

I cover my surprise with a laugh and focus on my food. When I next look up, Mery is still watching me, her expression unreadable. Perhaps it is the warmth of the fire behind me, but heat creeps across my cheeks. I reach for my glass and straight away regret not ordering something other than brandy. The alcohol sets my throat on fire, and the flames pool in my stomach. In the low light of the seating area, Mery's blue eye seems to glow, like it does when she is using her power. But I sense no expansion of her aura now. There is only her, as she is, and nothing else.

Karrion clears his throat, and I realise I have been staring at Mery. Now I am certain I am blushing and I yank my gaze away. While I was distracted, Sinta has returned to our table. Karrion feeds her a piece of fish from his plate. Once she has licked his fingers clean, she turns to me, expectation clear in her brown eyes.

'Sorry, baby girl,' I say, and pat her. 'The gammon is way too salty for you, and I don't think you'd enjoy the pineapple.'

'So you're an artist?' Mery asks Karrion. Whatever moment we shared has reached its natural conclusion.

'Yes. I'm not just a pretty face, but gifted too,' he says with a grin. It pleases me that he is beginning to relax in her company.

'Gifted I can believe, but pretty? I'm not so sure. What's the look you're going for? Are you a tortured artist, as in someone has tortured you by making holes in your face, or are you trying to be the emo heartthrob that all the teenage girls fall in love with?'

'Not just his face,' I say, while Karrion shoots me a warning look.

'What's that?' Mery asks.

'The holes are not just in his face.'

With her lips curling into a lascivious grin, Mery looks him up and down. 'I'll say. Do you have personal experience?'

I laugh at the same time as Karrion makes a face.

'We're friends and business partners,' I say. 'That's it.'

'Yeah, Yan is like a sister to me.'

Mery raises her hands. 'Can't blame me for being curious. I never could quite figure out the vibe you two have.'

'Well, now you know,' Karrion says.

For the rest of the meal, Mery and Karrion swap stories from their university days. Although I have no wild tales to contribute, they both have a way of speaking that includes me in the conversation. The warmth from the fireplace, the good food, and the company all help insulate me against the screams of a woman falling to her death, and for that, I am grateful.

When the conversation reaches a natural conclusion, we drain the last of our drinks and walk to the bar to pay. Sinta had fallen asleep at my feet and she now totters after me on unsteady paws. I pick her up, and she sighs against the crook of my neck. Wishearth is watching us with a smile, and I wonder if he will rise from the flames of my fireplace again tonight.

'Well, this was nice,' Mery says as she stuffs the receipt in her pocket. 'A dead body aside, we should do this again sometime soon.'

Karrion and I both agree. Mery takes a step towards me. For a brief moment, I wonder if she is going to kiss me, but all she does is pet Sinta. With a final wave of goodbye, she strides out.

We are slower to leave, but as I set Sinta down outside the pub, I find Karrion grinning at me, his eyes dancing with mirth.

'What?'

'I don't know, it seemed like the two of you shared a moment earlier.'

'What moment?' I ask, feigning ignorance as I gently nudge Sinta away from several discarded chips next to a bin.

'Come on, she was practically undressing you with her eyes at one point.'

'I don't know what you're talking about.'

'No?' Karrion laughs. 'Then I suppose you wouldn't be at all interested to know that Mery slipped her number in your pocket before she left.'

FRIDAY

21

TO CON A CON MAN

I wake up early the following morning, a hint of a hangover causing a band of tightness around my head. Jamie and Karrion have agreed to come by for another breakfast meeting, and I've volunteered to supply the food. After walking and feeding Sinta, I stroll to the small supermarket nearby.

Deciding that we have had enough bacon rolls for a while, I fill my basket with a bag of bagels, smoked salmon, cans of tuna, salad, and cream cheese. In a fit of optimism about being able to take a lunch break, I also add pasta, a jar of tomato sauce, and mozzarella. At this rate, Karrion may accuse me of being a responsible adult, but it is a risk I am willing to take.

My good mood evaporates while I am queueing to pay and my eyes land on the headline splashed across the front page of the *New London Courier: Old London's Disgraced PI Stands by While a Woman Plunges to Her Death.*

Next to the words is a photo of me standing on the ledge, watching as Aleson falls. My anger flares, and although no one looks at me twice, I walk home feeling like someone has painted a target on my back. It is one thing for me to be publicly acquitted of the murder charges, quite another for people to forget that I stood to face judgement in the first place. The likes of Jack Lincoln seem intent upon making it as difficult as possible.

If this is the end of Wilde Investigations, what will I do then? The cash in the bank account will not support me indefinitely, and my skills are not suited to city living. Will this be what decides my future? That I must return to the conclave not because my father has died but because I failed at building myself a life in Old London? Am I to submit to being Dearon's mate and nothing more?

A tremor of pain shoots up my shins. I have been stomping along, kicking the ground with each step. After drawing in a few calming breaths, I slow down. Returning to the conclave should be a choice, not a necessity, otherwise I will become embittered and resentful. Dearon deserves more than a mate who shares his life because she is forced to. I deserve more too, no matter what my father thinks.

Back at home, I make a pot of coffee and set about preparing fillings for the bagels. Sinta rushes to the lounge door a moment before I hear the lock turning downstairs. I take that as my cue to slide the bagels under the grill to toast. Two sets of footsteps sound on the staircase. Sinta is whimpering and when the door opens, her claws scrabble on the floorboards as she launches herself forward.

'Morning, Yan!' Karrion calls out. 'Just so you know, your puppy has turned into a missile.'

'Clearly your siblings have been a bad influence.'

'You're not wrong,' Karrion says as he comes to the kitchen, Sinta cradled under one arm. Jamie hovers behind them.

Karrion's eyes light up at the sight of smoked salmon. He reaches forward to snag a piece, but my Wild Folk reflexes are faster and I slap his hand away.

'Wow, you're mean this morning.'

'Be patient,' I say.

'Can't. I'm starving and Bird Shamans can't resist salmon.'

'Now is the time to learn. Can you set the table? Though if we're going to make a habit of these meetings, I may have to invest in a third chair.'

'Way ahead of you,' says Jamie from the lounge.

I glance over my shoulder to find him unfolding a wooden chair and setting it by my small table. When I raise an eyebrow at him, he shrugs.

'The stool isn't all that comfortable,' Jamie says, 'and it doesn't feel right to force someone to sit on the floor.'

'By someone, he means me,' Karrion says. 'Much appreciated, mate.'

The smell of toasting sesame seeds alerts me to the fact that the bagels are ready. Karrion sets Sinta down and carries mugs and plates to the lounge. My table is just large enough to fit bowls of fillings, our plates, and coffee mugs.

'Thanks for breakfast,' Jamie says, and spreads tuna mayonnaise on his bagel.

'No problem,' I say as I pour coffee. 'You've bought breakfast plenty of times. I figured it was my turn.'

'Have the lab elves cracked the case yet?' asks Karrion. He piles his bagel high with smoked salmon and tuna.

'Lab elves?' Jamie asks.

'That's what they basically are. You know, those underappreciated people who analyse all the stuff we find at crime scenes and make sense of it all. It's a form of magic, or so it seems to me.'

'By elves you mean trained Metropolitan Police employees.'

'I don't know,' Karrion says. 'In my head the labs are filled with pixies and brownies and actual elves with colourful hats and boots that curl upwards.'

'You spent far too much time watching television while I was imprisoned,' I say.

'What else was I supposed to do? Life's boring without you, Yan.'

'It's nice that someone thinks so.' I look at Jamie. 'Semantics aside, Karrion's question was good. What news from the Yard?'

'Let me see.'

Jamie takes a tablet from his briefcase and unlocks the screen. He scrolls through a list of documents until he finds the right one. The screen fills with text.

'The good news is that we have one body in our custody and we matched her fingerprints with an old identity theft case. Aleson Hampten, or rather the woman impersonating Aleson, was called Lenda Haert. At least, that's as far as we know.'

'What do you mean by that?' asks Karrion.

'At the time of the earlier case, that was the alias she was operating under, but all her IDs were fake. So she could be anyone. Unless we get a partial DNA match to someone whose identity we can verify, it's likely we'll never know for certain who she is.'

'What about the body stolen from the mortuary?' I ask.

'Could be anywhere by now. We weren't able to follow the route of the hearse on the city's CCTV network, so that's a dead end.' Jamie winces. 'Pun not intended.'

'They must have disposed of the body,' Karrion says, reaching for another bagel. 'I mean, that's what I'd do. Destroy the evidence as quickly as possible.'

I set my half-eaten bagel down on the plate. 'You're right. I can't think of a reason for Pheonix to hang on to the body. And whatever Lenda wanted is a moot point, since Pheonix killed her.'

'We've asked the Paladins and police patrols to keep an eye out for the body,' says Jamie, 'though I doubt Pheonix will have disposed of it in the city. There are plenty of ways to destroy evidence once you're out of London.'

'There could be a simpler explanation,' I say. 'They put the body in a hearse. It's likely the funeral directors who supplied the vehicle also organised the body to be cremated. That's much less conspicuous than driving out of the city to dig a grave or take the body out to sea.'

Jamie jots a note on the tablet. 'I'll ask people to look into that too, though if you're right, the body is probably gone for good.'

'Perhaps we'll get lucky.'

'Are you feeling particularly lucky?' asks Karrion.

'Not recently, no.'

'There are two other things that were interesting,' Jamie says. 'The SOCO found a small Dictaphone. On it was a recording of a woman calling for help, over and over. We also discovered a string of emails on the Hamptens' computer confirming an order of trained guard dogs to be delivered to the company warehouse the day you went there.'

'If that's not absolute proof that Yan was set up, I don't know what is.' Karrion sets his plate down with a clatter.

A detail that has previously eluded me clicks into place, sending a shiver of ice down my arms.

'I've been wondering about the purpose of the dogs,' I say, 'but I think I finally understand. Pheonix knew I was scared of the Fey hounds, and it makes sense that he would have wanted to simulate them as closely as possible. Luring me into a room where I'd be surrounded by dogs and then hitting me with a Fey glamour was all that was needed to complete the illusion. If I knew I was about to be attacked by the Winter Queen's pack, I would have let my instincts take over and fought with everything I had.'

Again, the jumbled images of the night flash before my eyes, and the hairs at the back of my neck prick up. There was so much noise in that room; snarling dogs and voices raised in anger. It is a miracle the whole building did not shake from the force of the sound.

Or did it?

'You said you didn't hear any dogs barking, didn't you?' I ask Karrion.

'That's right. I didn't hear anything at all from inside the warehouse.'

'It makes sense that the recorded call for help was too quiet for anyone without Wild Folk senses to hear it, but the dogs were loud. Jamie, did the Paladins find a soundproofing ward in the warehouse?'

'Not as far as I know, but I don't think they would have been looking for one. Don't forget that for most parties concerned, it was a clear-cut case. Perhaps if they had called in a Mage, we might have more information–'

'But they didn't, as we now know,' I said, finishing the thought for him.

'They were blinded by the obvious,' Jamie says, regret in his eyes.

'Everyone except me.' Karrion reaches for another bagel, but drops his hand without touching it. 'Only no one listened.'

'If it had been someone other than me in that warehouse, would you have been so quick to declare my innocence?'

Karrion looks at me like I had just told him we had chicken for breakfast. Yet again, my heart fills with love at the sight of his loyalty.

'We've been on the side of the innocent before,' he says at last.

'Yes, though we've seen plenty of guilty people too. I thought I was guilty. Hell, I may still be guilty. That's how good the set-up was. But for now, the more important questions are who and why. It would have taken time and money to set it all up. To what end?'

We all sit in silence. Karrion's brow is furrowed, and his teeth clink against his lip piercing. Sinta paws at my shin, and I feed her a small piece of tuna off my plate.

'It's got to be Pheonix, right?' Karrion says. 'He killed Lenda or whoever she was. So surely it's him?'

'There's no question that he's playing a major role in all this, but I still don't understand why. If he wanted to avenge Baneacre, he could simply kill me. Or if he's forbidden from doing so, he could give me nightmares of Fey hounds. It's not like I can surround myself with cold iron to keep away Fey glamours. Cold iron wouldn't kill me, but it would make my life miserable.'

'But wait, if the Winter Queen doesn't let him kill you, how come you came close to being executed?' Karrion asks.

'Good question. Though from what I know of the Fair Folk, it could be a question of semantics. Pheonix may not be allowed to kill me himself, but if I happen to be executed for a crime he framed me for, then that's little more than an unfortunate consequence.'

Jamie stares at me. I replay my words and hear the coldness of them. When did I start living in a world where death can be so easily dismissed?

I am losing my humanity. Parts of me have been chipped away by violence, death, and more pain than I could ever have imagined. At this rate, will there be anything left of me in a year or two, or will I truly become one of the Winter Queen's pack?

As the weight of the question settles, Karrion reaches out to me at the same time as Sinta paws at my ankle. I cradle her to my chest, breathing in her sweet puppy smell, while lacing my fingers with Karrion's. They anchor me to this moment, shielding me from the world outside. Even Jamie, with his longing for power he will never be able to understand, is a spark flaring in the darkness.

Yet the fear of losing myself remains. Perhaps it is a good thing, a reminder of what it would mean to give up and admit defeat. I have resisted the Elderman's orders for years, so is this any different? In both cases, my sense of self is at stake. On my own, I might face an impossible battle. But despite my imprisonment, none of my friends have abandoned me. I have allies, and only with their help will I succeed.

'Are you okay, Yannia?' Jamie asks.

I realise I have been staring at the fireplace, expecting to see a figure beyond the flickering flames. Sinta squirms on my lap, and I set her down before smiling at Jamie.

'Fine, or as fine as I can be, all things considered. Has anything else come back from the crime scene?'

Jamie scrolls through pages on the tablet, before pausing. He reads, his lips pursing.

'They found a notebook hidden in the guest room,' he says, looking up.

'Stuffed inside a mattress,' I reply, and he nods.

'Apparently, it's filled with pages and pages of numbers. Each one has two columns and at the bottom of the page, it notes whether the columns agree or not.'

'What's the point of them?' Karrion asks.

'I'm not sure. But it says here that some of the pages are dated and they span about two years. Each dated page has a series of letters on the top. The most recent is from two months ago and the letters are AMH.'

Karrion sticks out his bottom lip. 'Are mice hunted? Ardent mountain of hubris? No, that doesn't work. Armed messy humans? Aesthetics means humility? I don't know. Yan?'

I think for a moment. 'Aleson and Maerk Hampten.'

'How boring is that?' Karrion says with a huff.

'It may be boring, but it's also likely. What if they were keeping track of the money they were making through each con?'

'If that's the case, why two columns?' Jamie asks.

Karrion half rises, a grin forming on his face. 'What if it was only one of them keeping track? What if the whole point of the notebook was to prove something was wrong?'

Pride insulates me against the Winter Queen's chill as much as Wishearth's touch did. I nod at Karrion, but remain silent, waiting for him to carry on. He stands, all but bouncing on his heels.

'Okay, what if those two have been partners for years? But if you're a con man, it must be hard to trust others like yourself because you make a living by lying and cheating. So, what if one of them became convinced the other was scamming them? What if that book was proof of it?'

'Who do you think figured it out?' I ask, content to let him make the deductions.

Karrion paces to the kitchen doorway and back. I wonder if it is a habit he's picked up from me, or if we share an instinct to move while working on a puzzle.

'Probably the bloke, let's call him Hampten for ease. He realised his partner was skimming money off the top and set about proving it. She realised it, and had him killed before he could put a stop to her double scam.'

Karrion turns to me, an expectant smile on his lips. I remain silent, and his expression falters.

'Did I get it wrong? I got it wrong, didn't I? What did I miss?'

'What about Pheonix?' I ask.

'Obviously he's in on it,' Karrion says.

'But to what end?'

He tilts his head back as he thinks, and the morning light

catches on the blue highlights in his hair. 'He agreed to help Maerk, but after Lenda killed Maerk, Pheonix killed her in revenge.'

Before Jamie or I have a chance to say anything, Karrion raises his hand, eyes still fixed on the ceiling. 'Wait, I'm missing something.' He whips around so fast that I worry he's going to pull something in his neck. 'The Death Mask.'

'How does it fit into it all?' I ask.

'It doesn't, that's the problem. I mean, it doesn't fit into my theory because it shows premeditation. If Lenda killed Maerk in self-defence, she wouldn't have disguised his identity.'

I smile, my brain working in tandem with Karrion's. 'What does that tell you?'

'It must have been the other way round. Lenda worked out that Maerk was scamming her, so she enlisted Pheonix's help in killing Maerk. They cooked up a plan to frame you for the murder, tied up loose ends by getting rid of the body after you were acquitted, and then Pheonix killed Lenda so she couldn't spill his secrets.'

Karrion looks from me to Jamie, who nods slowly.

'That seems like a good working theory,' Jamie says. 'However, proving it will be another matter.'

I draw my feet up, resting my chin on my knees. Karrion notices and returns to his seat.

'You don't agree, Yan?'

'For the most part, I do. But the Death Mask still bothers me.'

'How come?'

'I just think it's odd that if the real Maerk Hampten was killed two months ago, Pheonix and Aleson didn't use it straight away to set me up. Why wait all this time?'

'Didn't Mery say that the Death Mask can be stored for quite a while?' Jamie asks.

'She did,' I reply. 'Obviously, since there was a delay between the two events. But it makes me think that the Death Mask wasn't necessarily for framing me. I expect creating the spell would have been a two-person job even if the fake Maerk as a Dog Shaman wouldn't have been able to help with the ritual itself. There must have been a reason why they chose to work complex magic instead of simply murdering the real Hamptens.'

'Like what?' Karrion asks.

'Perhaps they had a plan to fake the real Maerk Hampten's death long after he had died, thus giving the con artists time to figure out what he owned and how best to funnel the assets to themselves. Or perhaps they had intended to frame someone else and the events of Samhain caused Pheonix to persuade them to target me instead. All we have at the moment are theories and assumptions.'

Karrion stretches his legs, nudging my mattress with the toe of his shoe. 'Then what do we do?'

I rise and set my mug on the empty plate before me. 'We speak to the one person who's still alive. We find Pheonix.'

22

AMONG FLUFFY MURDER BALLS

'How are we going to find Pheonix?' Karrion asks while he helps me clear the table. 'Are we going to hang around coffee shops until he waltzes by?'

'No. The way Pheonix used his glamour to fool the mortuary staff makes me think this wasn't his first time engaging in illegal activities. Just because rumours of his reputation haven't reached me doesn't mean he isn't a member of Old London's underworld. If my hunch is correct, other people in similar professions may know more.'

'Oh, come on, you're not seriously thinking about asking–' At my warning glance in Jamie's direction, Karrion chooses his words with more care. '*Her.*'

'Why not? She has a far greater network of contacts than we do.'

Karrion crosses his arms. 'Yes, but she's so... slinky.'

'Nothing wrong with that,' I say, and ignore Karrion's eye-roll.

In the lounge, Jamie is sliding the tablet back into his bag. 'I'd better go. There's a team meeting in half an hour, and the last thing I need is to be late.'

'We'll catch up later,' I say. 'Can you see if you can find out anything more about the Cuckoo Trust? I still can't figure out how the Leeches fit into all this.'

'Yes, that's on my list for this morning. Now that the trust is connected to two murders, the trustees should be more forthcoming about the other beneficiaries. Or, they may bury us in red tape and legal paperwork for months.'

I let Sinta outside and lean my hip against the windowsill. 'Let's hope they won't.'

With a wave, Jamie sees himself out. While Sinta chases a curious pigeon around the garden, Karrion and I put away the leftovers and we wash up. I spread peanut butter and yoghurt on a lick mat for Sinta, and we leave her among her toys.

'Do you want to take the bus?' Karrion asks as we ascend the stairs to the street.

I hesitate. How many people in Old London read the *New London Courier*? Have other newspapers picked up on Jack Lincoln's vendetta against me? The investigation will be many times harder if people will stare at me wherever we go.

'Let's drive,' I say, and immediately feel like I have lost a battle.

'Shall I take the wheel?'

'I'm still working up the courage for that.'

'Hang on, I drove you to Lady B's yesterday.'

'You did, and fortunately I was almost unconscious at the time.'

'Why do I get the feeling that you don't trust me?'

'I do trust you, I'm just worried about all the immobile objects in the city, such as gravestones.'

'Didn't we agree never to speak of that again?' Karrion asks with a groan.

'Not that I recall.'

'Crap.'

Steering him towards my car, I pat his shoulder. 'You'll get over it.'

'When?'

'In ten, perhaps twenty years.'

It feels good to laugh at Karrion's pained expression, and the decision to drive no longer seems so bad. The worst of the rush hour has eased, and we find a parking spot in front of St Andrew's Church, next door to Felix Felis, the home for homeless cats.

Exiting the car, Karrion shoves his hands deep into the pockets of his long leather coat. There is no sign of the damage Cathwulf inflicted on the coat and which I subsequently had arranged to be mended. The new enchantments woven into the fabric should keep Karrion safe, or safer than he was before, though I fear the spells will offer meagre protection against a Fey as powerful as Pheonix.

'I still can't see why we couldn't ask Tinker Thaylor, or Wishearth, or basically anyone else,' Karrion says as he trudges towards the cat shelter's door. 'I bet that creepy librarian at the Royal Exchange would know where Pheonix lurks.'

'Not everyone who seems creepy is a criminal.'

'No, but I bet he is.'

Refusing to be drawn into a discussion about every strange person we have encountered over the course of our investigations, I draw open the door and usher Karrion in.

We are greeted by the scent of ginger and apple cake. To our right, the cat café is busy, with most of the tables occupied. Several cats prowl around the room, pausing to rub against a pair of legs or an outstretched hand. The same woman who looked after the café when I was here in October smiles at us from the counter.

While Karrion peers at the café with a mixture of curiosity and apprehension, my eyes are drawn to where a matching room houses the cat shelter. Fria lies on a shaggy rug, laughing as several grey kittens climb all over her. She is dressed only in leggings and a T-shirt, and I cannot help admiring her lithe figure.

Fria glances in our direction, and several expressions flicker across her face, too fast for me to catch them. With gentle hands, she detaches a kitten from the collar of her T-shirt and stands. As she approaches, the kindle of kittens follows her. They trot forward, ignoring me to circle Karrion. He steps back, lips twisted in annoyance.

'Get your fluffy murder balls away from me.'

Fria's left eyebrow rises in a perfect arc. 'What harm could tiny kittens do to a bird as fearsome as you?'

Crossing his arms, Karrion glares at her. 'I don't know, but I reckon they're up to something.'

'Cats usually are.' She takes a step towards him, lips curving into a wicked smile. 'Are you here to adopt a kitten?'

'Hell, no,' Karrion says, before realising he's spoken out loud. He turns to me, grimacing.

'We're after some information, actually,' I say, coming to his aid. 'Perhaps we can talk in private?'

Fria looks from Karrion to me with an inscrutable expression. As if sensing the change in her mood, the kittens all follow suit, staring at us with pale-blue eyes. The colour reminds me of the frozen streams from my waking dreams in the cell, and I suppress a shiver.

'All right,' Fria says after a while.

She gathers up the kittens and carries them to a crate. Shutting the door triggers a chorus of outraged cries, which she ignores. She motions to us, and we follow her through the door at the back of the shelter, past a small clinic, and to her tiny office.

The piles of papers I remember from my last visit have not

moved and if anything, they have grown taller. Trying to move them seems futile, and Fria settles on closing the door behind us.

'What do you need?' she asks without preamble.

'Do you know of any Fey living in Old London?'

Fria scoffs. 'Why would one of the Fierce Folk choose to live in a mortal city?'

Her name for the inhabitants of the Unseen Lands is unusual, but not unjust. For are the Fey not as fierce as they are fair?

'Assume they had their reasons.'

'I've never heard of one,' Fria says with a shrug. 'Though isn't that what you needed a gun and cold-iron bullets for last year?'

'This is a different Fey.'

'Be that as it may, there's no one like that as far as I know.'

'What about a Feykin?' Karrion asks. 'When we first met him, that's what we thought he was.'

The left side of Fria's mouth twists into a slanted smile. 'You're going to have to be more specific than that.'

'Whenever we've met him, he's had purple eyes and wore a top hat,' I say. 'We know he has criminal contacts and he's connected with several crimes.'

'Is he a fence?'

'I doubt he'd limit himself to just moving stolen goods.'

'A fixer then.' Fria stretches, her T-shirt riding high. I watch while Karrion stares at the exposed stretch of taut abdomen. He swallows.

'Maybe,' I say. 'But one that has few scruples.'

Fria rubs her temple with the back of her wrist, like a cat performing ablutions. 'I may know of someone. Have you ever visited the Music Man of Leadenhall Market?'

I think back to my visits to Old London's ancient magical

market, but nothing relating to Pheonix springs to mind and I shake my head.

'If you have a problem, he'll help. With smaller things, he accepts payment in gems or rare musical instruments. With bigger jobs, the cost can quickly become high and the payment may not be what you'd expect.'

'Can you give an example?' I ask.

'It's a story that has gone through a number of iterations, but supposedly there was a man who needed to get rid of a Mage curse that most people wouldn't touch. The Music Man demanded payment in blood and the man agreed, but once the curse was broken, he tried to go back on his word. He ran, but didn't get far before the Music Man caught him and took the blood he owed, directly from his heart.'

'That's sick,' Karrion says in a hushed tone.

'The story doesn't tell whether the man survived or not and the details may be wildly exaggerated, but I don't think anyone has tried to double-cross the Music Man since.'

'What about him betraying his clients?' I ask.

Fria tilts her head as she studies me. 'I haven't heard of anything like that, but who would dare to spread rumours of his treachery?'

'Or, more likely, no one has lived to tell the tale,' Karrion says.

'It sounds like you know more about him than the usual rumours.' Fria leans closer. 'Anything you would like to share?'

'Aren't you concerned about drawing the attention of a powerful Fey?' I ask.

'I could ask you the same thing.'

'We are already inexorably linked to him. He knows it as well as we do.'

'Again I ask, would you explain?' Impatience has crept into Fria's voice.

'Perhaps once we have solved our current case.'

Fria huffs. 'You're even worse than Tinker Thaylor when it comes to information.'

I bite my lip to hide a smile. 'That's odd, when I've always found her open and forthcoming.'

'If that's the case, you have hidden skills I would dearly like to learn,' Fria says.

'I could say the same about you.'

Our eyes lock, appraising and assessing one another. There is none of the heat I experienced with Mery last night, but rather the respect of a meeting of two equals. I am serious about wanting to learn from Fria. She has plenty of skills that could help me in my profession.

'For the record, I'm happy with my current level of learning,' Karrion says.

Fria's lips twitch. 'That's good. Most birds are too busy harassing old ladies for bread to bother learning new things.'

'Perhaps when I have more spare time, we can come to an agreement about sharing our knowledge and skills,' I say before Karrion has a chance to think of an angry retort. He is making it too easy for Fria to tease him.

'I would like that.'

To my surprise, Fria extends her hand towards me. The gesture is oddly formal, especially in light of such a nebulous suggestion, but cats are nothing if not unpredictable. I take the offered hand. Fria's skin is soft and warm, but when she draws back, she rakes her nails gently across my palm.

'Did you want anything else?' she asks, already turning away with an air of disinterest. Her mood is mercurial enough to rival Wishearth.

'No, what you told us is most helpful.'

'Good.'

Opening the door, she leads the way towards the public

areas of the cat shelter. As she walks, her hips sashay with the calm confidence of a cat patrolling its undisputed territory. Beside me, Karrion's neck reddens. For the second time during the encounter, I do my best to hide a smile.

By the cat shelter's counter, Fria turns to me. 'You would do well to take care. It appears that you've made an enemy of a journalist. In your line of work, as in mine, it won't do to spend too much time in the public eye.'

'I know,' I say. 'Trust me, if I could stop that man from writing about me, I would.'

'Perhaps you ought to think harder about ways to discourage him.'

'Are you suggesting I threaten him?'

Fria widens her eyes with feigned innocence. 'Far be it for me to suggest anything that would be against the law.'

'Yeah, right,' Karrion mutters.

'I will say this,' Fria continues, ignoring Karrion, 'sometimes leverage works better than threats.'

'Do you have something in mind?' I ask.

'Figuring that out is your job, not mine.' She takes a step closer, dropping her voice to a conspiratorial whisper. 'Unless of course you'd like to hire me. Though I should warn you, my charges are steep.'

'I'll remember that, should the need arise. Thanks for your help.'

'You're welcome,' Fria says, already turning away towards the crate with the kittens.

'It's been super fun, as always, but we'll leave you to your murder balls,' says Karrion. He tugs me towards the door as the kittens tumble out of the crate. They make a beeline for him, but Fria steps in to block their path. After waving goodbye to Fria, I allow Karrion to lead me out.

'Are you sure you didn't want to grab a cup of tea and a slice of cake at the café?' I ask.

'I'm sure. The cakes are probably filled with crushed baby birds.'

I make a face. 'That doesn't sound like a popular flavour.'

'Who cares about popularity? Anyone working with cats is at least nuts but more likely homicidal. Those things kill anything and everything in their path.'

'Not all bird species are that friendly. Just think of what cuckoos do to the birds whose nests they invade.'

Karrion turns to glare at me. 'Whose side are you on?'

'While I'd like to say yours, it's hard when you've veered so far away from common sense that it's but a tiny speck on the horizon.'

Running a hand through his hair, Karrion offers me a weak smile. 'Sorry. When I'm around cats, I can't help myself. And Fria, she makes me feel all cross and foolish at the same time.'

As much as I would like to point out the obvious reason for his behaviour, I keep quiet. When it comes to Karrion's personal life, he should reach epiphanies at his own pace.

'Suspicious cats aside, at least the visit was helpful,' I say. 'We have another lead to follow.'

'I take it that we're going straight to Leadenhall Market?'

'Yes. Let's see if we can't lure out this mysterious Music Man.'

23

THE MUSIC MAN

While we walk towards Leadenhall Market, Karrion nudges me, his eyes sparkling with mirth.

'So... What do you think about Mery?'

The question throws me off balance. I stuff my hands in my jacket pockets, only to have my fingers close around the business card she slipped me at the end of our meal last night. Although I looked at it before going to bed, I left it in my pocket for reasons I am not yet ready to examine.

'I think we saw a different side to her yesterday. If we can trust her, and my feeling is that we can, she could be a useful ally.'

'Useful ally?' Karrion steps in front of me, forcing me to stop. 'Come on, Yan. Is that all you're interested in?'

'Given the recent blow to my reputation, maintaining what few allies and friends remain seems eminently sensible.'

'All right, I'll give you that much. But do you *like* Mery?'

'I don't know,' I say, answering with the truth. 'But I don't think I need to decide that until she brings a rabbit carcass or two to my door.'

'Wait, what? A rabbit carcass?' He grimaces.

I dodge around him and continue walking.

'At the conclave, dead animals are equal to flowers and chocolates elsewhere in the world. If a guy likes you, he brings you a dead rabbit or a pheasant. When he kills a deer in a solo hunt and carries it to your doorstep, you know he's serious.'

Karrion grins. 'So has Dearon brought you a whole menagerie of dead things over the years?'

I look away. 'He's never had to. I was given to him the day I was born.'

'He gets an F for lack of effort. You're worth at least a dead dragon.'

His outrage is enough to bring a smile to my face, and I brush my fingers against the back of his hand. 'Thanks.'

'I mean, there are better ways to ask a girl out than lob a corpse at her. Haven't you guys ever heard of Tinder?'

'It's not restricted to men. If a woman wants to express her interest in a potential mate, she does the same.'

Karrion stares at me, a slow smile lifting the corner of his mouth. 'There's something seriously hot about the thought of a woman drawing a longbow and bringing back the fruits of her hunt.'

'Steady on,' I say. 'With your luck, she'd bring you a dead pigeon.'

'Even so, you don't happen to have any younger cousins, by any chance?'

It is my turn to grin. 'Even if I did, I'm not sure you could handle a Wild Folk woman.'

Karrion's eyes widen, but try as he might, I refuse to elaborate on the point. At least he is distracted from the topic of Mery, which gives me the freedom to avoid figuring out how I feel about her.

We walk the rest of the way to Leadenhall Market in silence. I keep turning the various facts of the case over and over in my mind, trying to make sense of them, while every newsstand triggers a sliver of fear at the prospect of seeing my name in the headlines.

We are admitted through a gilded gate with elaborately curving and twisting metal bars and into the covered marketplace. On both sides of the walkway, display windows entice potential customers with everything from Feykin-made furniture to enchanted jewellery. Above the red and gold shop fronts are silver and brass sculpted dragons, which breathe gusts of colourful smoke. They leave the air smelling of a mixture of leather, cinnamon, freshly cut grass, and sandalwood. The mixture should be strange, but instead the scents combine in a way that invites exploration. Above us, the glass ceiling shows the rise and fall of the sun and the moon.

Leadenhall Market has been an important trading spot in Old London for almost a thousand years. What began as a regular fair that allowed witches to sell potions and Mages to show off their enchanted trinkets has grown into one of the finest places in Europe to purchase magical items. Unlike One Magic Change, there are no workshops here, no stalls selling spell crackers and other cheap items, and no food court that caters to the whims of tourists.

Near the entrance, a small crowd of children are gathered in front of a window. Karrion steers me towards it. The only item on display is a large grey rocking horse. The only thing that distinguishes it from other similar toys is a pair of downy wings. It moves on its own accord and after a couple of rocks, the horse spreads its wings and rises to the air. After flying in a tight circle, it returns to the ground and resumes rocking.

'Come, I want to show you something,' Karrion says as he pushes open the door to the shop.

The entrance resembles a castle portcullis, and we walk through an echoing stone tunnel to reach a castle courtyard; far too large to fit inside the small shop. There are toys and children everywhere, and their sounds create a cacophony of joy.

Without giving me an opportunity to examine the strange and colourful things around the courtyard, Karrion steers me to a small alcove near the window. Displayed on a low wooden bench is a toy castle populated by figurines of knights, gowned ladies, dragons, and magicians. As we stop in front of the toy, the small figures begin to move, going about the tasks of their lives with little regard for us.

While I admire the precision of the details, Karrion is fiddling with a small box connected to the castle's moat. He presses a button, and the stone walls disappear in a shimmer of magic only to be replaced by a wooden fortification of raised aeries encircling a small copse and a pond. Here, too, are figures, this time dressed in the greens and browns appropriate for their new surroundings. A figure climbs on top of the palisade and leaning over it, morphs into a bird that flies to the pond. A gasp escapes my lips.

'It's pretty awesome, isn't it?' Karrion says, his grin reflecting my delight. 'And it has a surprising number of Shaman features given that it's a Mage-made toy.'

'The only word to describe it is extraordinary.'

'That's what I thought too. I've already started saving so I can buy the brood one of these for Christmas.'

For the first time, my eyes are drawn to the price tag and my eyebrows rise.

'This is one way of hinting that you need a raise.'

'That wasn't my intention,' Karrion rushes to say.

'I know, but you do deserve one, especially in light of everything you've done over the past few weeks.'

'As much as I appreciate the sentiment and will certainly

welcome more money for my Christmas savings pot, maybe you should hold off on making such grand gestures until we get more paying clients.'

'*If* we get more paying clients.'

We both sigh and leave the toy shop without daring to look back at the wondrous castle.

Leadenhall Market is not large, and we take a bit of time out to explore. At the far end of one of the avenues, situated against a backdrop of steel and glass office buildings, is a small shop called Charmed Melodies. Karrion and I share a glance.

'Could it be that easy?' he asks.

'What better place for the Music Man than this?'

I push open the door, and the bells above it ring in a complex tune. There are various antique musical instruments on display. At first glance, there appears to be nothing magical about them, but a thrum of power vibrates through me. There is far more to this place than meets the eye.

Behind the counter, a young woman with deep-brown curls and round glasses is polishing a silver flute. She looks up when we enter, but the mechanical movements of her fingers never cease.

'Can I help you?' she asks.

Walking closer, I borrow the nose of a dog trotting past the shop. The scent of nectar, cherry blossoms, and meadow grass confirm what I already suspected: she is a Feykin. Of course. If this is Pheonix's shop, who would he trust other than one of his kin?

'We're looking for the Music Man,' I say, wishing I'd thought to ask Fria whether there was a secret greeting or a password I should use.

'What do you want with the Music Man?'

'Rumour has it that he can help with... problems.'

The Feykin scrutinises first me and then Karrion. I allow my aura to quest out, but I sense no active spells nearby, nor is the shopkeeper using magic in her inspection of us. She sets the flute and the cleaning cloth down on the wooden counter.

'He's not here right now,' she says at last, her fingertips tracing random patterns on the polished wood.

'Do you know when he'll be back?' I ask.

The woman laughs. 'I work for him, not the other way round.'

'Does he come to the shop most days?'

'Sometimes, if he's not occupied elsewhere.'

'Are there other shops like this elsewhere in Old London?' asks Karrion, his eyebrows furrowed as he stares not at the Feykin but at her fingers.

The shop assistant laughs a second time. 'I guarantee there's no other shop like this anywhere in the city or the country.'

There seems to be subtext to her words, but what it might be, I cannot tell. Despite her outward helpfulness, I know we will gain no further information from her.

'Thank you for your help,' I say.

'Would you like me to pass on a message?' she asks.

Our eyes meet, and hers shine with a challenge. Nothing here feels genuine. It is as though we have stepped into a play rehearsed to perfection, and we alone don't know our lines. I shake my head.

'No, thanks. I'm sure our paths will cross with the Music Man's when he so desires.'

As I turn to leave, my attention is drawn to a narrow table with a display of music boxes of all shapes and sizes. One of them catches my eye, though I cannot tell why that is. I pick up the silver music box. It is smooth and polished, about twice the size of my cupped palms, and its weight surprises me. The metal is ice cold despite the warmth of the shop. Only a key at the top gives a clue to its purpose.

Unable to curb my curiosity, I twist the key until it turns no further. As soon as I let go of it, a simple melody weaves around me, drawing all my focus to the box. The smooth surface ripples as figures emerge from the silver. They are hunters on huge steeds, carved in such detail that I can see the stretch of the horses' muscles and the flapping of the riders' cloaks. A figure at the head of the hunt raises a horn to her lips. A mournful note sounds above the pounding of hooves. In response, enormous hounds overtake the riders, their heads lifted to bay the signal for prey in sight.

From somewhere, be it the confines of my memory or the music box, comes the hissing voice of Pheonix.

'*Once upon a time, there was a queen who needed hounds. Twice upon a land, they hunted and all cowered along their path. Thrice upon our memory, their bays strike fear into the hearts of mortals.*'

As the hounds bay a second time, the music box slips from my fingers. I watch it turn as it falls towards the floor, the hounds still baying. The melody has sped up, and it now matches my thumping heart. I brace for its abrupt end while I imagine delicate cogs exploding across the floor. A desire to see the thing destroyed flashes through me.

A moment before the music box hits the floor, deft fingers pluck it out of the air. The shop assistant has moved to stand next to me while I was distracted. She now straightens, the music box in her outstretched hand. She looks at me with eyes too knowing to be disapproving.

'You should be careful with the merchandise. Everything here is very expensive.'

'Sorry,' I say, though the word is no more genuine than her reproach.

'Remember, Yannia Wilde, that hounds are made, not born.'

Her words are almost identical to those Pheonix said to me next to the Fey Mound last year. I stumble backwards, only Karrion's arm around my waist stopping me from falling. The Feykin smiles, exposing sharp teeth that remind me of Pheonix, and replaces the silver music box on the table.

'Do call again,' she says, and returns to the counter.

Karrion leads me out of the shop and around the corner to the centre of the market. Once there, I lean against an alcove and gulp in cinnamon-scented air. Little by little, the numbing fear relinquishes its hold on my limbs.

'Do you think that was the right place?' Karrion asks. 'I mean, I assumed the woman was a Feykin and they are tricksy, so she could have lied about that being the Music Man's shop.'

'It was definitely the right place.' I shake my head to banish the baying still echoing in my ears. 'I'm sure Pheonix and the Music Man are one and the same.'

'Okay, but what do we do now? He's not just going to walk up to us and ask what we want from him.'

'No, he's not, but I don't think he can stay away either. If this is all about avenging Baneacre, then Pheonix is going to come after us soon.'

Karrion's hand goes to the cold-iron necklace he keeps hidden under his shirt. 'That's not a comforting thought.'

'I know, but it's the truth, at least as far as I can predict him.'

'So what now?' Karrion asks.

'Let's find a café where we can keep an eye on the front of Pheonix's shop and talk in private.'

We choose a coffee shop across the road from the market. From this side, the entrance to the market is shrouded in bamboo scaffolding. People in hard hats and high-visibility vests swarm up and down the levels, carrying roof tiles and panes of glass nestled in protective packaging.

Karrion reserves seats by the window while I buy coffees and slices of chocolate orange tart. Climbing on to a tall stool reminds me of a similar meeting almost a month earlier, when we were only just beginning the Hampten case. I try to imagine how differently things might have gone if instead of rushing in by myself, I would have waited for the Paladins with Karrion. But knowing Pheonix, it's likely he would have found another way to entrap me.

'Let's think about what we know,' I say, keeping my voice low. 'The Hamptens died two months ago and a Death Mask ritual was completed at the same time. One of the con artists, probably Lenda, figured out that her partner was scamming her, and with Pheonix's help, arranged for her partner to be killed while I was framed for it. Then when the Herald acquitted me, Lenda and Pheonix stole her partner's body from the morgue so we wouldn't be able to identify him. Pheonix lured Lenda to her death to tie up another loose end. But we can't prove any of that and it's likely Pheonix isn't done with seeking revenge, though we have no idea what he's planning.'

'Well, when you put it like that...' Karrion rolls his eyes. 'Don't forget that the Paladins and the police wouldn't know half of that without us.'

'You did most of the work.'

'Are we going there again? I thought we agreed that this, like all our cases, is a joint effort.'

'Fine. But there's one thing I don't understand. How do the Leeches fit into it all? Why would the con artists masquerading as the Hamptens transfer two million pounds into the Cuckoo Trust?'

'Is it possible they might benefit from it?'

'How could they, when I know for sure that neither was a Leech? What are we missing, Karrion?'

'I don't know, but I reckon we should focus on one problem

at a time. Let's worry about Pheonix first and then sort out the Leeches later.'

'Sounds like a plan.'

My phone rings, Jamie's name flashing on the screen. When I answer, he skips the greeting to go straight to the point.

'Yannia, can you talk? I have news.'

24

THE LIFE OF A LEECH

'What's going on, Jamie?' I ask.

Beside me, Karrion leans closer. I tilt the phone to help him hear both sides of the conversation.

'First things first, we found the Hamptens' wills. Would it surprise you to find that Maerk Hampten left everything to his wife, while she bequeathed the bulk of her estate to the Cuckoo Trust?'

'We keep coming back to the Leeches,' I say.

'You know, before you rang me to ask for the Braeman case file and drew me into your investigation, I had never heard of Leeches. Now it seems everywhere we turn, there the damned people are.'

'Trust me, we know the feeling, mate,' Karrion says.

'What's curious, however, is that Maerk Hampten's will was dated two years ago, whereas Aleson's was changed only last week.'

'Actually, that makes sense to me,' I say to Jamie. 'Let's assume that part of the con for Lenda and her partner was always to fake the Hamptens' deaths. Their fortunes would be left to the con men in whatever convenient way they chose.

While taking an inventory of the Hamptens' home and papers, they probably came across copies of their victims' wills. It wouldn't surprise me if the terms mirrored one another, so whoever died first left everything to the surviving spouse. Was there a contingency clause to say what happened if Aleson predeceased her husband?'

'Yes, everything apart from the company would go to charity.'

'What about the company?' Karrion asks. 'The Hamptens had no children, right?'

'No, they didn't. The company was to be given to the present employees in shares determined by their length of service.'

Karrion takes a sip of his coffee. 'Wow, that's pretty generous.'

'I suppose it was a way for the Hamptens to give back,' I say, pushing crumbs around my plate with a fork.

'What about the other will, then?' Karrion asks.

'Right,' said Jamie, 'so the con artists knew what the will said and probably decided that Maerk Hampten would die first. That way, they could leave his original will in place and thus reduce the risk of anyone spotting that the signature was forged. Following on, all they'd have to worry about was Aleson's will. That should have left everything to Lenda and her partner.'

'Only, it didn't,' Jamie says.

'No, and that's weird. But it wouldn't surprise me to find out that Aleson Hampten changed her will twice in the past three months: once for the benefit of the con artists and then a second time in favour of the Cuckoo Trust.'

'Yeah, what's up with that?' Karrion asks.

'I don't know, but it's clear there's a connection between the con artists and the Leeches of Old London. We just don't know what it is yet.'

'And that brings me to the other bit of news I wanted to share with you,' Jamie says. 'We managed to persuade the trustees of the Cuckoo Trust to release some information without a court order. Apparently, being connected to two different criminal investigations could be viewed as bad for business. They confirmed that the trust was set up by Gideor Braeman, like we thought. But they also gave us the names of the beneficiaries.'

'Any familiar names?' I ask.

'Oh, yes. The first was Gerreint Lloid, but we already knew about him. Then there is someone called Patreck Fenthon. Does that ring any bells?'

I glance at Karrion, who shakes his head. 'Not to either of us.'

'Me neither. But you'll never guess who the third name is.'

The tremor of excitement in Jamie's voice tells me it's someone important. I rack my brain, trying to recall every Leech we have been in contact with. The list is so short it barely qualifies as one. I am about to admit defeat when an image of a woman sitting on a stone pillar floats up from my memory. During my imprisonment, I had all but forgotten about her.

'Eiva Langden,' I say.

'Damn it, Yannia. Does anything escape your notice?'

I smile at Jamie's grudging respect. 'Plenty, but you gave me a pretty big hint.'

'Still, of the two of us, I'm the trained detective. Stop making me look like an amateur.'

Karrion chuckles, but I silence him with a quick shake of my head.

'So, Eiva is part of Braeman's inner circle,' Karrion says. 'That's not a huge surprise, though, is it? I mean, why else would a Leech decide to impersonate an Elder? It's not like raising one of those pillars is easy or fun.'

'Karrion is right,' I say. 'Why risk being found out if you don't have to?'

'I know this doesn't concern *my* London,' says Jamie. 'At least not as much, but I have to ask: what was Braeman planning before he died?'

'There's one thing politicians and Leeches have in common,' I say. 'Power. That was all he ever wanted. Remember, he conned his way to the top of the Light Mages and the High Council. Can you imagine how much dedication and hard work that took, especially when all the power required had to come from somewhere else?'

'Also, can I add something?' Karrion jumps in. 'Jamie, you say it concerns your London less, but I'd argue you're thinking of the wrong London. Given how much time and effort you put into keeping Old London safe and free of murderers, it seems to me like that is your London, not the other one.'

The line goes silent. Karrion winces and raises an eyebrow, but I can only shrug. I am about to ask if Jamie is okay, when he clears his throat.

'Thank you, Karrion. That means more to me than you can imagine. I've always felt like Old London is where I belong, so it's an honour to keep the city safe.'

I need not warn Karrion to be careful how he responds. He has seen Jamie's obsession with magic and obtaining power of his own as well as I have. As much as Jamie wishes to be one of us – a wish the ramifications of which he will never truly understand – he was born a human. It is impossible to awaken the power in blood that contains none. But no matter how many times I have tried to gently explain this to Jamie, he is not yet ready to listen. Perhaps he never will be. I can only stand by him and be his friend while he gropes towards the truth.

'Yan has now exposed two Leeches within the High

Council and the Circle of Shamans,' Karrion says. 'How likely is it that there'll be more?'

'Not very. I've checked almost everyone off my list and the few stragglers are all low-risk. It's more likely that if Braeman's plan included other Leeches, they are lower along Old London's power hierarchy, possibly ready to step into high positions when the opportunity arises.'

'Do you think this Patreck person is one of them?' Karrion asks.

'Probably.'

'You'd have to vet everyone in Old London to know for sure.' Karrion's expression brightens. 'Any chance Lord Ellensthorne would pay for that?'

'Unlikely,' I say. 'In fact, I'm fairly sure I'm fired as it is. With my reputation in tatters, there's no way the Speaker of the High Council will want to associate himself with me, even through an intermediary.'

'At least he doesn't know about Eiva.'

'About that...' Jamie clears his throat. 'Eiva's gone.'

'What?' Karrion and I say in unison.

'I'm at her home now with two Paladins. We were going to ask her to accompany us to the Brotherhood of Justice to answer some questions about Lloid and the Hamptens, but the door had been forced and there are signs of a struggle.'

'We'll be right there,' I say, and end the call.

Since we left my car by Felix Felis, we take a taxi to Barbican, where Eiva lives. The grey block of flats is no different from a dozen others along the nearby streets. Nothing about the area speaks of the affluence of an Old London politician, but I remind myself that the Shamans are not considered as powerful or influential as the Mages. It stands to reason that their salaries reflect that.

We are also not far from the home of Phillep and Roselind Marshell. My consciousness twinges at the memory of their anguish as they spoke of their daughter, Thina. It has been over a month since she was kidnapped, and we have made no progress in finding her. A cat's eyewitness account of two men carrying her out of the flat is not much to go on, and Black Beauty's reference to shadows does not necessarily mean the culprits were Shadow Mages. But I cannot help thinking that Phillep losing his seat on the Circle only days before Lord Ellensthorne asked me to vet the Council and the Circle was not a coincidence, nor is his daughter's disappearance a random kidnapping. As much as everything seems to lead back to the Leeches, the same is true about Lord Ellensthorne.

Jamie is waiting for us inside the entrance to the building and he leads us up the stairs to the sixth floor. The corridor floors are worn and almost black along the edges, and the air smells of old grease. A Paladin is standing guard by a door near the far end. He hands us barrier clothing and steps aside to let us into the flat.

Having been in Gerreint Lloid's home, I was expecting to see something similar here: modest on the outside, quietly luxurious on the inside. Nothing could be farther from the truth.

Eiva's home is a small one-bedroom flat. The walls are covered in a faded floral wallpaper that shows darker outlines of previous pictures. A beige carpet looks like it may have been a different colour once. An open-plan kitchen shows chipped salmon-pink units and a cooker that is at least fifteen years old. All of this registers in the periphery of my mind.

The whole flat is filled with rabbits. There are cheap bunny statues on the bookshelves, photographs of rabbits and hares on the walls, and even the cushions on the cracked leather sofa have fluffy ears. The only thing missing from the décor is an Easter bunny costume hanging on the door.

'Wow,' Karrion says, summing up my thoughts too. 'She must really like rabbits.'

With a glance towards the door that remains ajar and the Paladin within hearing range, I choose my next words with care.

'It stands to reason, given that Eiva is a Rabbit Shaman.'

'What?' Karrion begins, but he follows the direction of my gaze and catches on. 'Yeah, I mean, I love birds and all, but you don't see my room decorated as an homage to an Alfred Hitchcock movie.'

'Given that Eiva lived and worked in the city, which doesn't have a wild rabbit population, this could have been her way of keeping alive the connection to her spirit animal.'

'Granted, but has she no taste?'

'I didn't call you here to discuss her interior decoration skills,' Jamie says. 'Come and take a look at this.'

He leads us to the bedroom, which continues the theme of bunnies. The double bed, which is the only piece of furniture that looks fairly modern, has pillows and blankets arranged in what looks to me like a nest. Whatever else may be going on, Eiva was certainly committed to keeping up the appearance of her deceit.

'I don't think we can be overheard here,' Jamie says, but he keeps his voice low. 'Is it just me, or is all this rabbit stuff weird?'

'It could have been a way for Eiva to stay in character,' I reply.

'Ignoring the bunnies for the moment, there's something I'd like to know,' says Karrion. 'How is Eiva powering the raising of the pillar at each Circle meeting? Shamans don't use mana gems. She can't use stored Shaman power the same way as she could if she was impersonating a Mage.'

'That's a good point, Karrion. Let me see.'

I send my aura outward, seeking other magical people nearby. The room around me fades away as I concentrate. Karrion's aura remains weak, and again, it sends a sliver of unease through me. For now, though, I ignore him in favour of continuing the search. I find the Paladin in the doorway to the flat and on the far side of Eiva's bedroom wall, there are several people, all possessing power. What the power might be, I cannot tell without their scent.

As I am pulling my consciousness back, another aura touches my awareness. It is one I recognise: Mery is approaching the door. A flush rises to my cheeks as I wonder whether she will act any differently given our dinner last night and the fact that she slipped me her number.

'Yan, anything?' Karrion asks.

'Nothing conclusive, for now. Did you have something to show us, Jamie?'

'Yes. Here.'

Jamie leads us to the side of the bed closest to the wardrobe. An open sports bag is partially obscured by a duvet hanging over the edge of the bed. I can make out a glint of metal inside the bag.

'May I?' I ask.

'Yes, but be careful.'

I draw the bag out. The glint of metal I noticed is a small pile of gold jewellery that has been dumped on top of clothes. Taking care not to disturb anything too much, I look through the contents. The bag contains enough clothes to last a couple of days, plus a passport and a white envelope with several thousand pounds in cash.

'Looks like Eiva was going somewhere in a hurry,' I say.

'If that's the case, why leave all this behind?' asks Karrion.

Before Jamie or I have a chance to reply, we hear the rustle of barrier clothes in the hallway and Mery stops at the bedroom door.

'Oh goodie, the gang's back together. You know, we really should do this more often.'

Jamie frowns. 'It's been less than a day since we were last at a crime scene together.'

'I know how to read a clock as well as you do. But once a day just isn't enough of your sparkling company.'

'Duly noted.'

'So, why am I here?' Mery asks.

'We have a potential missing Elder of the Circle of Shamans,' Jamie says. 'The door was forced and there were signs of struggle.'

'And you want to know if part of the struggle was magical?'

'That's the idea.'

'All you had to do was ask.'

Jamie draws in a deep breath. 'This is me, asking you to check for magical spell residue.'

'All right, is your thong chafing again?'

Mery turns away without waiting for Jamie's response, which no doubt would be rude. She sweeps back her uneven fringe as her magic expands in searching tendrils, much like mine did earlier.

While we wait for her initial thoughts, I look around the bedroom again. Nothing looks out of place. At first, I think it's all as it should be, but then I reconsider. If Eiva was packing to leave in a hurry, why is the bedroom so tidy? Why are there no open drawers or extra clothes discarded on the bed? It's as though someone didn't want it to look like she was intending to go anywhere. If that is the case, why was the bag left?

Moving slowly so as not to disturb Mery, I walk to the door and look at the room. If someone had walked in, intending to clean up any sign of Eiva's hasty departure, what would they do? The obvious answer is that they would close any open drawers. Could it be that they missed the bag by the bed? No, I correct myself. The bag was almost under the bed. Did Eiva move it there? Did she know she had run out of time and this was her last attempt to hide what she had planned to leave? Or could it be that it was intended as a message to whoever noticed her absence from the Circle?

A familiar tightness is forming behind my eyes. Am I approaching this as a Leech might? If she thought getting caught was only a matter of time, wouldn't she have a bag packed and ready? Could it be that she only needed to throw in the money and the jewellery, but even that took too long? If that is the case, who did she fear enough to go to such lengths?

'Well,' Mery says, turning back to us and letting her fringe fall back into place. 'This is certainly interesting.'

'What did you find?' Jamie asks.

'This room is dripping with spell residue. Someone cast a Shadow Mage spell intended to stun and disable a person. I'm also detecting hints of a North Mage wind lullaby, but it's so weak it may not have put the target to sleep. Beneath it all, though, is some really weird shit.'

'Weird, how?' Jamie steps closer to Mery.

'It feels... off. That's the best way I can think of to describe it. And it reminds me of something, but I can't think of what.'

Jamie, Karrion and I look at one another in silence.

'Hang on,' Mery says. 'Why is my sceptical side telling me none of this is a surprise to you?'

When none of us answers her, Mery throws her hands in the air.

'Oh, come on. After everything we witnessed yesterday, you don't think I deserve to know whatever secret you three are keeping?'

'Keep your voice down,' Jamie says. 'We don't want the Paladin outside to hear you.'

Mery looks like she is about to object loudly, but she shuts her mouth and pulls out a packet of cigarettes. She counts those remaining in the pack before shoving it back in her pocket.

'This unusual residue,' I say. 'Are you detecting old spells in it, or is it an echo of the people who've lived in this flat over the years?'

'Definitely not an echo. I recognise those, no problem. This isn't my first rodeo. But if the residue was left over from spells, they're unlike any I've ever encountered before. But I'm sure I've sensed this somewhere else.' Mery looks at me, her eyes narrowing. 'You were there, so was your trusty sidekick. We haven't been to that many crime scenes together. It shouldn't be hard to work it out.'

I look to Jamie, who shrugs. The only thing I can think to do is try to derail Mery with another question.

'Is there any chance it could be Fey–'

'The Lloid crime scene!' Mery grins, triumphant. 'I knew I'd work it out.'

'Is there any chance it could be Fey magic?' I ask again, refusing to acknowledge her conclusion.

'No chance. I haven't come across one of the Fair Folk often, but their magic is close enough to the Fey that it's easy to recognise. This is something different, I just don't know what it might be yet. But the more interesting question is why aren't any of you surprised about the connection?'

'Maybe we should discuss this back at the Yard?' Jamie asks.

Mery crosses her arms. 'Why am I getting the feeling that you're trying to fob me off?'

'On the contrary,' Jamie says. 'What you've told us is very useful. We suspected the occupant of this flat may have been kidnapped and your initial analysis seems to corroborate that.

We should organise a SOCO team to sweep the flat to see what else we might find.'

Mery turns to me, and I see hurt in the eye not covered by her fringe. 'So you really don't trust me enough to share?'

My conscience twinges as I try to figure out how to let her down gently without admitting that I don't, in fact, trust her enough to explain what we know.

'It's dangerous,' I say.

'In that case, it's all good. I wouldn't want a damsel in distress like me to get into any more trouble, especially when there isn't a PI in shining armour willing to ride in and rescue me from the evil dragon.'

Mery turns on the spot and strides out, calling over her shoulder, 'If you need me, boss, I'll be at my desk doing paperwork like the good girl I am.'

Jamie sighs. We stand in silence while we listen to Mery's retreating footsteps and the muttered words she exchanges with the Paladin. When we are certain she is out of hearing range, Karrion swears.

'That wasn't fun,' he says.

'No, it wasn't,' agrees Jamie. 'But what choice did we have?'

'Do you think we could trust her?' I ask.

'I'm not sure. We've worked together for several years and she's always struck me as someone who puts their money where their mouth is. She may have no filter, but she also refuses to play the politics game, which is a big point in her favour. But... I just don't know.'

When I begin to reply, Jamie holds up a hand, his brow furrowed. 'Why now?' he asks at length.

'What do you mean?'

'Why was Eiva taken *now*?'

'Any number of reasons,' I say. 'But I don't think it was

anything we did. I never told Lord Ellensthorne and Mr Whyte about Eiva.'

'No, you didn't.' Jamie clenches his fists until the knuckles turn white. 'But I logged her as a person of interest in the Lloid disappearance. And that was after I'd done some digging into her past.'

Understanding dawns on me. 'Could they have worked this fast?'

'If we're right and Lloid was framed for his girlfriend's murder and kidnapped, they worked bloody fast that time too.'

We all turn to face the door. Karrion voices the thought that occurs to me too.

'Do you think the Paladins are in on it?'

25

HIDDEN SECRETS

'Surely not,' Jamie says, but I note that he keeps his voice close to a whisper. 'They're Paladins of Justice. Shouldn't that mean that they're incorruptible?'

'Need I remind you of Brother Valeron?' I ask.

'I remember. But after what happened with Marsh, I would have thought the Paladin General would tighten whatever ways they have to screen for corruption.'

'It's possible. However, we know the General to be a man who will weigh the good of Old London against any potential cost to an individual. Just two months ago we agreed that when it came to the Leeches, we would let him decide the best course of action. What if he's already done so?'

'Do you think he knows about the vetting we've been doing for Lord Ellensthorne?' Karrion asks.

'He might. It's even possible that Lord Ellensthorne has told him and together they've devised a plan to contain any Leeches we find.'

Karrion holds up his hand. 'I could believe that the Paladins are prepared to lock up Leeches with minimal publicity, but there's no way they would have framed Lloid for murder.'

Jamie nods. 'Karrion is right.'

'I know, the theory doesn't hold much water,' I say. 'Especially since Mery told us that the major spell used to stun someone, likely Eiva, was Shadow Mage magic.'

'How do we prove any of this?' Karrion asks.

'We need to search this flat before the SOCO team arrives. I think it's safe to assume that anything processed by New Scotland Yard in the cases involving Leeches won't be reliable.' I offer Jamie a crooked smile. 'No offence.'

'None taken. As much as I hate to admit it, I suspect you're right. We're on our own.'

Together we search the flat, starting in the kitchen and living area. Most of the worn books on the shelves are about politics, economics, and city planning, and many still bear the stickers of second-hand bookshops. The fridge is full of vegetables and not much else. Karrion stares at the contents, unimpressed.

'Was she hoping to *become* a rabbit?'

We finish our search, but find nothing out of the ordinary. As we return to the bedroom, Karrion twists to look back.

'You know, there's something odd here.'

'What's that?' I ask.

'I get that the Elders don't get paid as much as members of the High Council, but they still receive a decent salary. Plus, we know that Eiva was paid five grand a month from the Cuckoo Trust. But this place looks like she's on the poverty line, way worse than me and Mum, and we're pretty broke.'

Karrion shares a small three-bedroom flat on Bride Lane with his mother and three siblings. Despite working two jobs, Aderyn keeps the flat meticulously clean. They may not have much in the way of luxuries, but all the children are fed and clothed. Their financial situation has improved since Karrion became my apprentice, and it occurs to me for the first time that if my business fails, Karrion's family will also suffer a financial loss.

If there is a way to salvage my reputation and the Wilde Investigations, I must do it, for their sake as much as mine.

'Yan?'

I am shaken from my reverie by Karrion's hand on my arm and I have to think back to what he said last.

'That's true, but it wouldn't be common knowledge that Eiva receives sixty thousand pounds extra a year,' I say. 'Could this be a way for her to make it look like her only income is the Circle salary?'

'They're bound to pay more than is reflected here.'

Pausing in my examination of the wardrobe, a small half-buried detail niggles at the back of my mind. I chase it until it leads to a memory of a red lollipop and bunny slippers.

'Remember Crysthal, the dominatrix who frequently saw Lloid at the Sensual Pleasures? We speculated that Lloid was stealing power from her rather than Leina.'

'How could I forget?' Karrion says. 'That place was bizarre, what with the geisha stuff and the dude in a wizard's robe.'

'Crysthal said that Lloid kept asking her to punish him. It could be "normal" sub/dom stuff, but what if it went further than that? What if Lloid hated living a lie and felt he deserved any punishment available?'

Karrion shrugs. 'Okay, but what's that got to do with Eiva?'

'Could it be that her living below her means is a self-imposed punishment for a similar reason?'

'I never knew Leeches could be so moral,' Jamie says.

'It would be wrong to assume that they're all like Braeman or Jans, just as it would be wrong to say all Shadow Mages are evil because Lord Ellensthorne is a thoroughly unpleasant man.' I shut the wardrobe doors. 'Jamie, you said you did some digging into Eiva's life. Did you find anything of note?'

'No,' he says, opening the top drawer of the dresser. 'It's like she didn't exist until five years ago, when she appeared in Old London.'

'Doesn't that sound a lot like Lloid?' Karrion asks. 'Though we did eventually trace him back to a village in Wales.'

'It stands to reason that any Leeches who are impersonating Mages and Shamans in the city's political structure would be using fake names,' I say. 'That goes hand in hand with the secretive trust payments.'

'Take a look at this,' Jamie says.

He pulls out a framed photograph from beneath a stack of T-shirts. It depicts a young girl who bears a strong resemblance to Eiva, but with a darker skin tone. She looks to be six or seven years old.

'This could explain why Eiva is living so modestly,' I say. 'Perhaps she's sending money to her daughter and whoever is looking after her.'

'But why keep her picture hidden in a drawer?' Karrion asks. 'It's clear from the flat that she lives alone.'

I picture Eiva standing by the dresser, staring at the photo, and then tucking it back in its hiding place with a furtive glance over her shoulder. The only thing that surprises me is that the photo isn't in the pre-packed bag, though perhaps it was the last item Eiva was planning to take with her.

'She was afraid,' I say. 'There's no way of telling whether she's always been like this, but in recent months, she had every reason to fear for her life. First, Braeman is murdered and then Lloid disappeared. She must have known there was a good chance she'd be next.'

'If that's the case, why didn't she leave Old London and go into hiding?' Karrion asks.

'I don't know,' I say, still staring at the photo in Jamie's gloved hand. 'Perhaps she thought she was being watched, or perhaps she needed the trust payments and they were contingent on her remaining in the Circle. Or perhaps she simply ran out of time.'

Karrion pulls on the row of hoops in his left ear. 'We need to catch whoever is behind all this.'

Jamie and I nod, then resume the search. He puts the picture back where he found it.

We go through the bedroom and bathroom without finding anything else of significance. The source of Eiva's power still bothers me, but the flat offers no insight. I'm about to declare the search complete when a small dent in the wall next to her bedside cabinet catches my eye. It could be nothing, but the edge of the cabinet is pushed as close to the skirting board as possible. Is it neatness or something different?

Careful to keep the cabinet doors shut with my knee, I tilt it forward and peer behind it. My hunch proves correct when I find a folded piece of paper taped to the back. Despite an instinct warning me not to disturb any evidence, I carefully peel back the tape. I put the cabinet back.

The paper I detached feels heavier than it should, and my fingers trace something hard inside its folds. I put it on the bed and unfold it to reveal a key. It has no tag attached to it, but it is nevertheless familiar.

'This looks like the key we found in Lloid's study,' I say.

'Did Scotland Yard figure out what it was for?' Karrion asks.

'I'm not sure it was even bagged as evidence,' says Jamie. 'There was nothing to suggest it was in any way connected to Leina's murder.'

'Damn, I thought we were finally getting somewhere.' I turn my attention to the paper and unfold it further. 'Never mind, I take that back.'

Scribbled on the piece of paper is an address in Chertsey.

'Where's Chertsey?' I ask.

'It's in Surrey, along the Thames,' Jamie says. 'My aunt lives there.'

'Why would Eiva have a key and an address in Surrey?' asks Karrion.

'I bet it's part of the Leeches' exit strategy, especially if this key matches the one in Lloid's flat. They must know about each other and protect each other, so it would stand to reason that they'd keep a bolthole somewhere out of the way. And what better place for one than outside of Old London, since our first instinct would be to look within the city.'

'Yannia is right,' Jamie says. 'Surrey also has the added benefit that Paladins only venture there when they have cause to do so.'

'Leeches can easily fool human police, but Paladins are trickier,' I say, finishing the thought for him.

'While it's unlikely that Eiva left this flat of her own volition, I think we should investigate the address as soon as possible,' Jamie says. 'I'll alert the Paladins.'

'Can we trust them, though?' Karrion asks.

'We'll have to trust someone,' I say, 'and Paladins are far more experienced in apprehending dangerous people than we are. I struggled against Jans. Though thinking about it, Jamie would be the best person to arrest any Leeches we encounter, so long as you and I keep our distance. We don't want to give a Leech access to our magic.'

'Hang on.' Karrion approaches the dresser. 'Before we rush off, let's just make sure we haven't missed anything else here. It's clear Eiva is smart about her secrets. If I tip this forward, Yan, will you look behind it?'

Without waiting for an answer, he braces the drawers with his body and pulls the dresser away from the wall. I switch on the torch in my phone and peer in the gap. Even so, I almost miss the slim dark object.

'There is something behind it.'

Kneeling, I reach into the tight space between the plywood backing and the wall. My fingers grasp the edge of something, but it separates into several items. I tug at the closest one and hear the sound of ripping tape.

One by one, I pull out three plastic document wallets. None of them bears a label, but each is secured with a rubber band. Pieces of tape still stick to the edges of the folders where they were attached to the back of the dresser.

'If those contain state secrets, none of this was my fault,' Karrion says. 'I don't want to go to prison for treason.'

'Why would they be state secrets?' I ask.

'Because this day has been so weird it's the only logical conclusion at this point.'

'Did you watch any conspiracy theory movies while I was imprisoned?'

'Maybe, but that's not the point.' Karrion lowers his voice to a whisper. 'The police are already after us.'

Jamie clears his throat, but Karrion waves a hand in his direction.

'You don't count.'

'I don't know whether to be relieved or insulted,' Jamie says.

'How about being sensible for a moment?' I pull the rubber band off the top folder. 'If what I find inside confirms that the royal family are vampires, I promise not to tell you.'

'You know, that would explain a few things,' Karrion says. I silence him with a pointed look.

I open the folder to reveal a small stack of newspaper clippings from various Old and New London newspapers. Every one of them relates to the murder of Leina Parez and the disappearance of Gerreint Lloid. Although the case attracted some publicity by default due to Lloid's position in the High Council of Mages, many of the details were never released to the press and the reports I skim through are far tamer than the actual crime.

Karrion manages to contain his curiosity for almost a minute before leaning over my shoulder to see the clippings. His enthusiastic smile soon fades.

'Well, that's disappointing. But I guess it makes sense that Eiva would be keeping track of cases that relate to other Leeches.'

'Sorry that real life is rarely as exciting as you hope,' I say.

'I'll live,' he replies with a put-upon sigh.

The next folder contains a thicker stack of newspaper clippings, all of which relate to the murder of Gideor Braeman. The focus of many of the articles is on Braeman and his rise to the top of Old London's political hierarchy, rather than on Marsh's judgement.

'Did she have a thing for murderers, or is she just obsessed with her own kind?' Karrion asks.

'More likely the latter. It ties in with our theory that she's keeping a close eye on anything that could expose her deception.'

'If that's the case, I reckon she's hiding somewhere near Lord Ellensthorne's home as we speak.'

'What about the third folder?' asks Jamie.

I open it and draw out more newspaper clippings. Before the headline of the top sheet registers, I try to recall any other prominent cases involving Leeches. Instead, I see the words *Beast of Old London* spread across the front page of the *New London Courier*. A tremor running down my fingers sets the clippings rustling. I lay them on the bed, hoping to find some among them that relate to something other than my recent disgrace. My hope is in vain.

'Why would Eiva have a folder of clippings about you? You're not a Leech,' Karrion asks.

'I don't know.'

'Wait a second.' He pulls back with a dramatic widening of his eyes. 'You aren't a Leech, are you?'

Ever since I tasted Cathwulf's blood and felt power coursing through my veins, I have wondered about the origins of Leeches. The book I read on the subject speculated that they may have originally been Leech Shamans intent upon gaining more power, or human followers of Vlad the Impaler who learned to absorb magic by drinking the blood of their victims, but no one seems to know for certain. My personal theory is far more disconcerting. If Wild Folk can enhance the power they glean from nature by consuming people, who is to say that somewhere in our long history, there weren't those among us who chose to become cannibals? Perhaps their practices were such that they lost their connection to nature and became a separate species.

I have no proof, one way or the other, and for that I am grateful.

'Of course not, for no other reason than how could I use Wild Folk magic without having someone to draw power from?'

'You're pretty enterprising. For all I know, you might have Dearon tied up in the broom closet of your flat.'

'My flat doesn't even have a broom closet.'

'So it's a secret cubby-hole somewhere. You're clever. If you set your mind to it, you'd find a way.'

The image of Dearon tied up in a cupboard invades my mind. I cannot decide whether the idea of having him at my mercy is ridiculous or curiously appealing. Shaking my head, I banish the thought.

'If you're quite done with this particular mad tangent, can we get back to the puzzle at hand?' I ask.

Karrion leans closer to sniff me. I spot laughter dancing in his eyes despite his best efforts to keep a stern countenance.

'What are you doing now?'

'You said Leeches smell funny.'

'Yes, to a Wild Folk.'

'That's your attestation.'

I turn to Jamie in the hopes that he might restore some sanity to the conversation.

'The Paladins had Yannia in custody for more than three weeks,' he says. 'Don't you think they might have noticed if she wasn't a Wild Folk?'

Karrion deflates with maximum flair. 'All right. She's not a Leech.'

'Your original question had a point, though. Why would Eiva have a folder of newspaper clippings about Yannia's arrest if the others specifically relate to Leeches?'

'There could still be a connection.' I silence Karrion with another pointed look. 'I'm the only one who can sniff out a Leech in Old London. Others may feel a vague sense of unease as well as weakness around one of them, but my Wild Folk abilities are foolproof. That by default makes me a threat to every Leech in the city.'

'Well...' Karrion begins.

'What?' I ask.

Tugging on the row of hoops in his ear, Karrion shifts his weight while avoiding eye contact.

'If you can accuse me of being a Leech, I should think you can say whatever is on your mind.'

'Your Wild Folk senses aren't completely foolproof,' he finally mumbles. 'Jans fooled you for months by dousing himself in a bucket of cologne every time he left his flat. It was only when he attacked you and you managed to catch his scent without the smelly disguise that you realised what he was.'

Karrion is right. How could I have forgotten? It has been four months since Jans broke into my flat and his pungent cologne had slipped from my memory. I try to tell myself that a lot has happened since and that it's natural to have pushed him out of my thoughts after a Herald declared him guilty.

'That's a good point,' I say. 'And here's a question we probably should have thought about sooner: if someone or a group of someones is kidnapping Leeches in Old London, is Jans where he's supposed to be?'

'Wasn't he imprisoned outside of Old London among human prisoners?' asks Karrion.

'That was my recommendation. Keeping him away from magic users would minimise the risk of him stealing power, though I also suggested that he be collared in case any of the human prisoners have magical blood they don't know about.'

Now that I have experienced the Paladins' magic-nulling collar for a longer period than a brief prison visit, the thought of having to wear one for years without any reprieve fills me with revulsion so strong I regret the snack I ate at Leadenhall Market. If Jans's experience of power is anything like mine, each day cut off from it must be torment for him.

I feel an unexpected flash of pity. Who would have thought that I would ever feel sorry for the man who tried to drain me of magic? While forgiving him for his actions will be difficult, at least until I regain a feeling of safety in my home and my everyday life, my imprisonment has offered me an insight into what it is like to be cut off from power. Had the roles been reversed, would I have been able to resist the temptation?

'He's in prison, has been since last October,' Jamie says.

'Do you think you could make some discreet inquiries?' I ask. 'Unlike Lloid and Eiva, Jans was known to be a Leech. That could put him in greater danger.'

'But wouldn't the fact that he's imprisoned keep him safe?' asks Karrion. 'Who's going to get at him from behind bars?'

'Someone with enough resources to frame a person for murder,' I say.

Lord Ellensthorne's arrogant sneer comes to mind, but I have no proof that he's behind any of this, only suspicions. He has been playing political games longer than I have been alive. How will I ever get the better of him?

26

BOLTHOLE

We leave Eiva's flat as the scenes of crime officers are arriving and discard our barrier suits in a white plastic bin. As we do so, a door to the flat beside Eiva's opens and a woman steps into the corridor, followed by three children. The faint scents of grass and earthen burrows reach my nose. They are a family of Rabbit Shamans. Suddenly a possible source of power for Eiva becomes apparent. If Jans was able to siphon power from me through walls, it stands to reason that Eiva could do the same.

By an unspoken agreement, none of us says anything until we step outside the building. While we were searching the flat, clouds have gathered in the sky and fine rain wreaths us in a damp veil. Karrion tugs the collar of his leather coat up.

'Are we heading to Surrey now?' he asks.

'First, we must speak to the Paladins,' Jamie says. 'We need reinforcements, preferably with magic-nulling chains.'

'So we're taking a chance on them?'

'We have to trust someone,' Jamie replies, and I nod. 'The Paladin General seems like a good bet.'

Tilting my head to the side, I breathe in air heavy with winter scents. 'I'd like to stop by my place to let Sinta out.'

'Shall I give you a lift there?' Jamie says.

'If you don't mind, could you drop us off near St Andrew's Church instead? It's where I left my car. We walked to Leadenhall Market.'

'Of course. Did you find out anything there?'

During the short drive, I describe what little we learnt about the Music Man and our visit to Charmed Melodies, keeping the source of the tip vague. Jamie listens without interrupting, his hands gripping the steering wheel a little tighter than necessary. I am surprised he does not spend all his money on magical curiosities such as those sold at One Magic Change and Leadenhall Market. Or does he? I have never been to his flat. For all I know, it could be a colourful mirage of magic in the grey landscape of New London, the power almost within his grasp, yet always out of reach.

He drops us off by my car, and we promise to meet him at the Brotherhood of Justice in half an hour. Karrion's stomach growls on the drive to my place, and I glance at the dashboard clock. It is gone two o'clock, and we have missed lunch.

'There are leftover bagels back at mine,' I say. 'Perhaps you can make us sandwiches while I sort out Sinta?'

'Is there any smoked salmon left?'

'Did you eat it all this morning?'

'I tried, but you kept trying to impale my hand with a fork,' Karrion says.

'Then there's smoked salmon left.'

We park in front of the building, and my eyes stray to the top-floor windows. It has been more than two months since a Snake Shaman couple moved into Jans's old flat, yet I still expect to see him hurrying down the road. At least with Drake and Lyn, I have checked that they are who they say they are as far as their magic is concerned.

While we have been out, Sinta has managed to nudge my wardrobe door ajar. A pair of green socks lies in ribbons across the floor. Sinta rushes to me, a long thread still hanging from her mouth, and makes every attempt to look innocent. Despite trying to be stern, I cannot help laughing.

'Should I take this to mean that you don't like my clothing choices?' I ask the squirming puppy.

'It wouldn't hurt for you to get a few more black bits,' Karrion says. 'I get that you have a whole natural tones look going on, but you'd blend into the shadows better.'

'You did your best to sort that out while I was in the hospital after the car accident.'

'It's good you clarified which time because for someone so young and fit, you spend way too much time being sewn back together.'

'No comment.'

I carry Sinta to the window and set her down outside before tidying up the mess she created. Once the floor is clear, I move one of the armchairs to block the wardrobe to discourage her from further destruction of my clothes.

Karrion makes our sandwiches and fills travel mugs with coffee. My conscience twinges at the thought of leaving Sinta again. Our life together consists either of days spent at home or days of absences. I wish there was a way to strike a balance between the two, but I dare not take her with me to Chertsey when we have no idea what we will find there or how long the trip will be. She will be safer here, especially as I know Wishearth will check up on her even without a lit fire.

Sinta barely notices our departure, too intent is she on the enrichment toys I have left out for her. I take one of the travel mugs from Karrion and breathe in the smell of fresh coffee.

During the short drive to the Brotherhood of Justice, I drink half the coffee, but resist the temptation to tuck into the bagels.

I park the car next to the courthouse. The white marble façade and the statues of mounted Paladins flanking the entrance glisten from the fine rain. I hesitate, reluctant to leave the safety of the car. A patrol of three mounted Paladins passes us on the other side of the wrought-iron fence. It may be my imagination, but their gazes seem to linger on me. Do they recognise me? Did any of them undertake guard duty during my imprisonment? Did they see the feral creature I became, or did they watch me make offerings before a feeble fire without ever receiving a response?

As much as I now know Wishearth responded to my call every time, the recalled bleakness of thinking he had abandoned me to be executed alone freezes my insides with the same efficiency as the Winter Queen's kiss. How long will it be before the sting of his imagined rejection no longer wounds me?

Karrion's hand covers mine. 'Are you okay being back here?'

My first instinct is to lie, but I stop myself. There is too much we leave unspoken, too many things we have brushed aside. If I expect him to open up to me, I must do the same.

'No. A Herald may have declared me innocent, but that doesn't hold the same absolute certainty these days. What if the Paladins decide the Herald was mistaken and put me back in that cell? What if that's what I deserve?'

'The Heralds are infallible, remember?' Karrion holds up his hand to stop the words I am about to speak. 'Even if the circumstances surrounding the judgement are dodgy, the Heralds are never wrong. We proved that to be the case. As far as the Paladins are concerned, you're as innocent as I know you to be.'

How will I ever express my gratitude for his undying faith in me? Even now, when I suspect myself to be a killer, he doesn't.

'Between the judgement and Jack Lincoln's articles about me, I feel like someone has painted a target on my back,' I say, aiming my words at the steering wheel.

'So what? Let that arsehole take his best shot. Despite the shit his editors choose to print, you're back working with the Met and figuring out stuff the police missed. Every day, you're proving that you deserve to be on the case. If Old London doesn't know enough to appreciate a PI of your calibre, then the city doesn't deserve you.'

'But if Wilde Investigations fails, I'll have to return to the conclave.'

'No way.' Karrion squeezes my fingers. 'You always have a choice. If you decide that you love Dearon and want a life with him, then go back to the conclave. But if you'd rather be free, you'll find a way to rebuild your business. Don't forget, you still have allies in the city. Robbert Craichton has hired you twice already and you haven't pissed him off.'

'True, but if he's serious about going into politics, he's unlikely to want any association with a social pariah.'

Karrion clicks his lip piercing against his teeth. 'I reckon he's free-thinking enough not to be too worried about that.'

'Let's hope so. I can't see Lord Ellensthorne giving me repeat business.'

I spot Jamie stepping out of the main Brotherhood of Justice building. 'Come on, Jamie is waiting.'

We meet him halfway across the car park, Karrion carrying our lunch. I turn my back to the Brotherhood's buildings.

'Are we getting backup?' Karrion asks.

'Yes,' Jamie says. 'A section of Paladins will accompany us to Surrey.'

'What did you tell them?' I ask.

'Not a lot to the Paladins themselves, but I explained more to the Paladin General.'

Karrion raises an eyebrow. 'You got an audience with the big boss?'

'The guards were reluctant at first, but when I mentioned a connection to Gideor Braeman, they escorted me into his office so fast I was almost running to keep up.'

'How much did you reveal?'

'I told him that we suspect Braeman had set up a trust to finance political careers for other Leeches and that one of them was Lloid. He knew of the murder, of course, and he was concerned about the potential connection to Eiva. I had barely finished explaining about the address we found before he ordered the section of Paladins to report to the captain of the guard for briefing.'

'Were you there for the briefing?'

'No, but the Paladin General said he would explain that the Met was investigating a politically volatile situation involving a Leech. He assured me the Paladins would take every precaution.'

A grey van bearing the sword and scales logo of the Brotherhood of Justice emerges from the access track leading to the barracks behind the public buildings of the compound. The driver's window slides down and the Paladin waves to us.

'That's our cue,' Jamie says. 'I told Silah, the Paladin in charge, that we'd follow in my car.'

We are turning towards his car when movement in the corner of my eye draws my attention elsewhere. Beside a Toyota in a faded gold colour, a camera with a long-range lens is pointed in our direction. I frown and beside me, Karrion follows the direction of my gaze.

'What the hell?' he mutters.

When the photographer lowers the camera, I recognise him: Jack Lincoln. He must be after his next story about Old London's disgraced PI.

'Let's go,' I say to Karrion.

'No way,' he replies. 'It's time that moron learned a lesson about spewing lies.'

'Don't.' I lay a hand on his shoulder. 'As much as I'd love to watch you peck his eyes out, we don't need any more negative publicity.'

Karrion looks like he wants to argue, but he exhales slowly and follows me to Jamie's car. As soon as the doors are closed, I turn to Jamie.

'We need to go, and fast.'

'Why?'

'Jack Lincoln is here. That reporter. He probably noticed the Paladin waving to you. If he thinks there's a chance that following us could lead him to a big story, he'll do so. The last thing we need is a human reporter breaking a story about a Leech hideout.'

Jamie swears, unlocks his phone and passes it to me. 'Find Silah in my contacts and call her to explain we are shaking a tail and will meet the Paladins at the designated spot.'

While I scroll through the contacts, Jamie switches on the flashing lights of his unmarked car and speeds off in the opposite direction of the Paladins' van. As we pass the gates, I look up long enough to watch Lincoln rush around the car with the camera still in his hand. There is little chance he can catch us, or so I hope.

We cross the river to New London. Jamie keeps the siren on until we are well past Big Ben. The road dips in and out of sight of the Thames. I watch London landmarks go by while I take reluctant bites of a smoked salmon bagel. Seeing Jack Lincoln for the second time in two days has robbed me of what little appetite I had.

How long will he continue writing about me before losing interest? How long until another scandal draws his attention away?

The crowded streets of the city gradually give way to the suburbs until Jamie steers us on to the motorway. From there, the journey goes faster.

Light is fading in the western sky as we drive slowly through the centre of Chertsey, past small shops and a pub called the Crown. The streets are busy with people wrapped up against the chilly February evening. I watch the well-dressed pedestrians, wondering whether any of them are Leeches.

'Why did they pick this place?' I ask no one in particular.

'Maybe it's as good as any,' Karrion says from the back seat.

'Could be. Do you know whether there's a particularly large population of magic users living here?'

'No clue,' he says. 'But I couldn't even have told you where Chertsey was.'

'Perhaps they picked it purely because most people here are human.' Jamie turns right. 'Wouldn't that make it a better hiding place?'

'It would, assuming Leeches don't need regular access to magic.'

'Isn't that what mana gems are for?' Karrion asks.

Jamie's satnav directs us to a long street of detached houses. They are all almost identical, with black or white doors and small front gardens dotted with plant pots. Cars are parked on both sides of the road. Nothing here suggests it's an ideal hiding place, but perhaps that is the point.

The Paladins' van is parked near the top of the road, a hundred yards from the house we are after. Jamie pulls up as close to the van as possible. Upon seeing us, four Paladins climb out and open the side door to access equipment lockers. They don their Kevlar armour and enchanted swords. One of them draws out a black sports bag. The contents give a metallic clink, and I draw back a step.

'My name is Sergeant Silah,' one of the Paladins says. 'This section is under my command and from this moment on, so are the rest of you.'

I begin to introduce Karrion and myself, but Silah waves away the introductions.

'We all know who you are.'

Nothing in her expression offers clues as to whether they know me from the Marsh investigation or the more recent events. I see no disapproval on the Paladins' faces, but they show no warmth either. It would not surprise me to learn that the Paladins would have preferred to investigate our lead without a Wild Folk, a Bird Shaman, and a human getting in their way.

'When we go inside, you three will stay well back and obey any of my commands without delay. Is that clear?'

We have little choice but to nod.

'Should we discover any individuals on the premises, I trust you will be able to determine whether any of them is a Leech?' Silah asks me.

'Yes, so long as I am close enough to smell them.'

'Good. We will secure the suspects first and then you can sniff to your heart's content.'

Her tone is dismissive enough that my hackles rise, but I swallow back any objections I might have. Antagonising four armed Paladins will achieve nothing.

'Are you all ready to proceed?' Silah asks, directing her words as much to the other Paladins as to us.

We all murmur our agreement. Silah locks the van and leads us across the road. A man on a scooter slows as he passes us and almost crashes into a parked car. I imagine this is the first time the neighbourhood has seen armoured Paladins walking down the street.

'Ready protection spells.'

Without waiting for a reply, she whispers a short incantation. A soft brush of magic tickles my cheek, though I cannot tell how or from where Silah drew her power. While I am slowly beginning to understand Mage magic, Paladins are an unexplored mystery.

In response to her words, a blue gem in Silah's sword hilt begins to glow, the illumination spreading to her arm and across her body. Soon, she's bathed in dim blue light. The other Paladins follow suit.

Karrion leans closer to my ear. 'Check that out. We have Paladin glow sticks.'

I shush him, worried the Paladins will have heard, but I cannot help grinning. It eases some of the tension tightening my muscles.

Yet, when faced with the prospect of coming face to face with a cornered Leech, I am reluctant to approach the house.

Silah knocks on the door. Loud barking erupts from inside. There comes a thump of paws against the wood. Whatever dog the owners have, it is a large one.

A voice inside issues a muffled command, and the barking subsides. The lock clicks and a middle-aged woman opens the door. Her eyes widen at the sight of four glowing Paladins on her steps. Each Paladin has a hand on his or her sword hilt, but the weapons remain sheathed. Nevertheless, none of us needs to see the enchanted metal to understand the severity of the situation.

'Madam, are you the owner of this house?' Silah asks.

'Yes. What's this about?'

Behind the woman, a large Doberman is leaning over a baby

gate, a low growl issuing from its throat. For the moment, the dog appears content to wait for a command, but a single leap will see it upon us. Unease pricks up the hairs at the back of my neck. Last time I was close to an aggressive dog, I woke up next to a dead man.

'Are you the sole occupant of the property?' Silah asks, ignoring the woman's question.

'No, my husband is working a night shift.'

'By the order of the Paladin General of Old London and New Scotland Yard, I am to detain you while your property is to be searched.'

'What for?' the woman asks, her voice rising in panic.

'Evidence for crimes committed in Old London.'

'I don't know anything about that.'

Silah shifts aside, motioning for the woman to step out of the door. The Paladin with the bag removes a length of chain with a collar and manacles. A soft whimper escapes from the woman's lips.

'The restraints are a precaution,' Silah says. 'They will not hurt you, and you will be released as soon as possible.'

The woman allows herself to be chained. From the way the Paladins' glow reflects from her eyes, I see she is close to tears. Once the restraints are secure, Silah motions me forward.

'Sniff.'

My temper flares at being spoken to like a dog, but I lean closer and borrow the nose of the growling Doberman. The woman smells of tea, sausages, and coconut oil. Some of the tension leaves my muscles.

'She's human,' I say.

'Of course I'm human. What else would I be?'

Silah says nothing, while the chains are unlocked and put away. The woman draws her wrists close to her chest, rubbing the skin that touched the metal.

'Madam, what is your name?' Silah asks.

'You come to my house, issuing orders, and putting me in chains, but you don't know who I am. What sort of police are you?'

'Please answer the question, madam.'

'My name is Donna Ballard.'

'Besides you and your husband, Mrs Ballard, does anyone else live in this house?'

Donna hesitates. 'Well, no.'

'Are you certain?' Silah asks.

'Yes, I mean, no one else lives here. Except for Cypher.' She nods towards the dog. 'But we do rent out the top bedroom.'

'Is your tenant here at present?'

'No.' Donna hesitates again, frowning as though she is trying to remember something. 'In fact, I've never even met him... or her.'

A thrill of excitement runs through me. I shift a little closer. Jamie must think along the same lines for he stops beside me and shows Donna his Scotland Yard identification.

'I think this is a conversation we had better have indoors. The presence of armed Paladins is already going to cause a stir.'

Donna pauses on the threshold, arms gripping the sides of the door. It looks like she is going to block our path, but after a glance towards the stairs behind her, she steps aside. Cypher's growl intensifies.

'Settle,' Donna says.

The change is instant. Cypher's growls cease and he lies down on the kitchen floor, his muzzle pressed against the bars of the gate separating him from us.

'That's impressive,' I say. 'Do you or your husband compete in protection sports?'

'No.' Donna stares at me. 'Why would we?'

'I simply wondered because you've trained your dog so well.'

'We didn't train him.'

'Then who did?' I ask.

'We bought him from a company that specialises in supplying ready-trained guard dogs.'

'Why?' asks Jamie. 'Forgive my curiosity, but do you have any reason to fear for your safety?'

'None that I know of, but it was a condition of the lease for the top bedroom.'

There it is again, a whisper at the back of my mind that tells me we are closing in on something important. Could Cypher have come from the same place that supplied the dogs for the warehouse?

'Do you remember the name of the company that sold you Cypher?' I ask.

'Not off the top of my head, but I'm sure we have a note of it here somewhere. Is it important?'

'It could be,' I say.

Donna leads us past the small kitchen to a spacious lounge. Sliding glass doors afford a view of a small garden, though there is little to see in the winter dark. A large green leather sofa faces a wall-mounted television, while an oval dining-room table is tucked in the opposite corner. Next to it is a raised dog bed.

Silah asks Donna about her husband's work schedule. From above me, I catch a faint sound of a creaking floorboard. It could simply be the house shifting with the dropping temperature, but my wild instincts rise, alerting me to the presence of... what? Is it a predator or prey that waits for me upstairs?

I look around to see if anyone else heard the sound. Two of the Paladins are guarding the front and back doors, while a third stands by the stairs leading up. Silah and Jamie are with Donna, who has taken a seat on one of the dining chairs. Karrion is watching Cypher from a respectful distance.

The sound comes again, and this time I am certain it is more than the natural noise of a house. Even the Paladin by the stairs appears to have heard nothing, which shows that my Wild Folk senses are keener than hers.

Karrion nudges my shoulder, an eyebrow raised. I glance up.

'Did you hear something?' he whispers.

'Yes. Did you?'

'No. Was it someone calling for help?'

'Not this time. I think someone is upstairs.'

I walk to the lounge doorway and wait until there is a lull in the conversation.

'Mrs Ballard, are you sure there's no one else here?' I ask.

Donna frowns. She looks like she wants to reply straight away, but something holds her back. After a moment, she nods.

'Yes, I'm sure.'

'The tenant who rents your top bedroom. You said you weren't sure whether they are a man or a woman?'

Again comes the hesitation. Donna presses her arms against her chest, her fingers clenching and unclenching.

'No, I'm not certain. I'm sure my husband would know.'

'How long have you been renting the bedroom?'

'Over two years.'

Jamie looks up from his notebook. 'And in that time, you've never met your tenant?'

'No.' Donna shifts back in the chair. 'That's odd, isn't it?'

'Very,' I say. 'Do you have a tenancy agreement?'

'We must do. Mustn't we?'

Donna is growing more confused by the minute. Jamie looks at me, a question in his eyes, but I can only shrug. Silah kneels in front of Donna.

'May I try something?' she asks, her voice gentle.

'What's that?' asks Donna.

'A simple spell to check whether anyone has cast magic around you. It won't hurt, I promise.'

Donna looks like she would like us all to leave, but to my surprise, she nods.

Silah places one hand on Donna's shoulder and the other on the side of her face. The magic that connects them is soothing like a favourite lullaby, gentle as the touch of moth wings, and warm as the fading embers in a fireplace. Donna shudders, trying to shake off Silah's hands, but the Paladin retains the link. After a few moments of futile effort, Donna's body relaxes and she slumps forward.

Letting her hands fall as her spell fades, Silah rises to her feet. Donna stays where she is, only the gentle rise and fall of her shoulders indicating that she is still alive.

'She has been made to forget. The spell was powerful, but it's broken.'

Donna gasps. She looks up, first at us and then at the ceiling. All colour drains from her face.

'There's someone in the house,' she whispers.

27

THE LAST STAND

Silah draws her sword. The other Paladins look to her for orders, and she motions for them to stay where they are.

'Are you sure?' she asks Donna.

'Yes.' Donna's voice shakes and she grips her cardigan with bloodless fingers. 'Someone came earlier today. He did something to me and I forgot about his arrival.'

'Whoever it is, they're still here,' I say. 'I heard the creak of a floorboard.'

'Sister Maika, you're with me,' Silah says to the Paladin by the stairs. 'Bring the chains. Sister Ales and Brother Rhees, you guard the front and back doors.'

She moves towards the stairs, Maika beside her. Jamie, Karrion and I try to follow, but Silah stops us.

'No. If there's a Leech upstairs, I will not endanger any of you.'

'My senses are better than anyone's here,' I say. 'Let me come as far as the middle floor and see what I can hear. Trust me, I have no desire to get close to a Leech again.'

Although she looks like she wants to argue, Silah nods. 'No further than the middle floor.'

'Oh, come on,' Karrion huffs behind me. 'How come you have all the fun again?'

A meaningful glance from me silences any further objections. Karrion crosses his arms and leans against the hallway wall. Behind him, Jamie bends to murmur to Donna.

Without another word, Silah climbs the stairs, her sword pointing the way. Despite the full armour, she is light on her feet and chooses the edges of the steps where they are less likely to creak. Maika goes second, the bag of chains in one hand and her sword in the other, while I bring up the rear.

The middle floor has a bathroom and three bedrooms. At the far end of the landing, a further set of stairs leads up to where the loft has been converted to another room. Thick carpet muffles our footsteps, but I find the silence oppressive. It is as though the entire house is aware of our presence and is poised to attack.

At the foot of the next staircase, Silah pauses and turns to me. She need not speak to convey a question.

Rather than finding Cypher again, I draw upon my inner reserves of power to borrow the hearing of a barn owl. I focus on the stairs and the room above me.

All is quiet. I concentrate harder. Silah and Maika's breathing become gusts of storm wind, but beyond them, I detect the steady breath of another being. They are calm, which gives me hope that they may not be aware of our presence. Perhaps they assume that the spell was enough to deter further exploration of the house.

I hold up one finger and point up. Silah nods. The glow surrounding her intensifies. She ascends the stairs, Maika a few steps behind her. I creep as far as the end of the landing, but go no further.

A whisper of hinges is all the warning I receive before darkness blasts down from above. Silah, who had reached the turn midway up, is hurled against the wall. The last thing I see before the shadow reaches me is her glow blinking out. I hear a thud and the clatter of a sword sliding down the stairs.

No longer concerned about preserving my magic, I call upon the sight of a wild cat. Nothing happens. The darkness surrounds me, settling over my shoulders like a heavy blanket, encouraging me to lie down. The air seems to be growing heavier, and I struggle to draw a breath.

The creak of a stair distracts me from labouring lungs, but before I have a chance to move, a weight slams into me. I stumble backwards and fall, my head hitting the floor hard enough that bursts of light flare beneath my eyelids.

Before I have time to think about sharpening my senses, the sour tang of spoilt milk and rotting meat envelops me. I have to fight back the urge to vomit.

'I have you now,' a hoarse voice hisses near my ear. 'At last we have our revenge.'

As hands clamp around my neck, several images flicker through my mind: Cathwulf's prone form beneath mine, Baneacre reaching to stroke my cheek, Tem licking my blood off his blade, the hulking forms of the Fey hounds, Melissa urging her illusions to attack, Reaoul Pearson standing in the middle of a maelstrom of light, and Jans's hands choking Ilana. Above it all, I see the man in the warehouse lunging towards me, a pack of dogs closing in around us. A spray of blood splatters across my face, shockingly hot, and where the blood touches my lips, it sends a thrill of power through me.

It is that shiver that jolts me back to the danger at hand. I try to twist my head to bite my assailant, but the angle is wrong. My nails scrape across his wrists. I dare not call upon the claws of nature for fear of him stealing them. Human nails have little effect. Instead, I try to claw at his eyes, but I cannot see anything in the darkness.

Strength is slipping from my limbs while I struggle to draw breath. My lungs burn and my throat is on fire. Fumbling around for anything I could use as a weapon, I draw out the small torch Karrion gave me. I switch it on, but the beam cannot penetrate the magical darkness. The torch handle contains a short blade of cold iron, but my numb fingers struggle to release it.

The roar of blood in my ears is fading. If I could see, I imagine my vision blurring. The fingers digging into the sides of my throat no longer hurt. I have no more than a few seconds left before I pass out.

With what little strength I can muster, I slam the handle end of the torch upwards. It meets flesh, eliciting a yelp of pain from my attacker. A few droplets of foul blood land on the side of my nose. The grip around my throat loosens. I gulp in a breath, doing my best to ignore the blinding pain blocking my airways.

The weight on me shifts, and I buck. My attacker slides partly off me. My groping hand finds his upper arm, and I feel the sharp edge of Velcro. A memory of Gerreint Lloid's study comes back to me. Could it be? I grip the Velcro with my fingers and yank.

Straight away, the steady pressure of a spell against my aura falters. Shafts of yellow light begin to penetrate through the darkness. A shape looms over me, hands reaching for my throat again. I react with animal instincts and bite down on the closest fingers. Reaching up sends blinding pain across my throat, but I ignore it as I lock my jaws. My attacker yells in pain, thus giving me an opening to rip the mana-gem holder from his other forearm.

Light floods back into the hallway. Beside me, connected by his fingers and my teeth, looms a man I have never seen before. His blond hair is plastered to his forehead and his eyes burn with hatred so strong I almost loosen my bite. At the foot of the stairs leading to the loft room, blocked partly by the man's body, I can see the crumpled form of Maika. The black bag is on its side and loops of chain have spilt on to the carpet.

The man raises his free hand and punches me. His fist connects with my temple and the starburst of pain in my skull is enough for me to gasp, thus freeing him. He pulls his hand back, blood dripping from his fingers, and fumbles for the mana gems. Power begins building again, and this time I am certain the spell will do something far more dangerous than causing temporary blindness.

'I'm going to crush you,' he says between gritted teeth.

Beneath me, the floor vibrates from approaching footsteps. Caught between the pain in my head and throat and the rising power, I cannot tell from which direction the steps are coming. I have perhaps a few seconds before the spell is complete, but I have no idea how to defeat a Leech without magic.

But if he is building a Shadow Mage spell, that means he is not focusing on draining my power. The only thing that can save me is speed.

I reach within for what little power I have left. The memory of the agony from the cursed cold-iron token flashes through me, separating me from my magic. For a fleeting moment, I am once more an empty husk, hollowed out without the power that defines who I am. I grope for the wildness within, but it slips through my fingers, just as my wildness has gradually been tamed by Old London.

Pheonix has won, for I have no defence left against the Leech that would see me dead.

Frost floods my veins. Rather than eliciting the fear that it once did, it calms my racing thoughts. I force my trembling fingers to obey and they find the invisible mark on my forehead. The cold intensifies, my breath forming a cloud in the air above my face. But the Winter Queen's mark has done its job. It connects me to the Unseen Lands, takes me back to the moment when I knew I would die and I opened all of myself to the wildness of that land.

Now, I find that connection again and invite the power in. Magic flows through me, the wave of it so powerful that my spine bends and my heels drum against the floor. My sudden movement distracts the Leech briefly, and that is all the opening I need.

Instead of calling upon the strength of a bear, I become the bear, and my fury knows no bounds. With a swipe of my paw, I slam the Leech against the wall. The mana gems scatter across the floor, but they are nothing to me. I lumber to my feet, intent on finishing off my prey.

The Leech reaches out to me, some of his hatred replaced by hunger. He wants my power. His slimy grip slides along the edges of my aura, seeking purchase, and I swipe it away. His eyes widen. I growl, lifting a paw for a killing blow.

There comes the sound of running footsteps, and a bird in a man's body skids to a halt. I turn my head to warn him to keep away from my prey. A circle of metal, which burns and freezes and poisons me all at once, clamps around my paw. My magic disappears so suddenly I jerk and contort in the air, landing on my side on the floor, the breath knocked out of my lungs.

Silah stands above me, holding the chain connected to my wrist with one hand and pointing her sword at the Leech with the other. Blood drips from her nose and ears, but it does nothing to hide her fury.

'Don't move,' she says.

The remaining two Paladins push past Karrion. Ales draws her sword and points it at the Leech, while Rhees drops to his knees beside Maika. While Ales guards the Leech, Silah opens the manacle and frees me. She then untangles the rest of the chains. The magic-nulling collar goes around the Leech's neck, followed by manacles around his wrists and ankles.

The little power I had left when Silah cut me off from it has faded. I allow my head to rest against the hallway carpet. My body is a mass of pain, and each breath brings fresh agony. Karrion kneels beside me, smoothing hair away from my face as he leans closer.

'Yan, can you hear me?' he asks.

I try to nod, but any attempt to move my neck proves too much. Next, I try to speak, but the words are too large to fit through my bruised throat. All I can do is reach out and take his hand.

'We need a medic,' Karrion says, looking past me at the Paladins. 'Please tell me you brought medical supplies?'

'Sister Ales,' Silah says, and the other Paladin sheathes her sword and hurries past us.

Silah wipes her face, but the action only smears the congealing blood across a larger area. Someone groans near me, but Silah never looks away from the Leech.

'What's your name?' she asks him.

The Leech, now cut off from all the power around him, sits against the wall, cradling his wounded hand to his chest. He glares at Silah with sullen defiance.

'Allow me,' Jamie says, coming into my field of view for the first time.

He searches the Leech with practised efficiency and pulls out a wallet from the inside pocket of the man's coat. Jamie checks through the cards inside.

'His name is Patreck Fenthon.'

So this is the third Leech.

He shows no reaction to the sound of his name and instead he switches to watching me, the unchecked hatred flooding his eyes once more. It strikes me for the first time how strange it is that someone I have never met hates me so.

'Patreck Fenthon, I hereby detain you for multiple assaults until you face judgement by a Herald of Justice,' Silah says. 'The police will also wish to question you in connection with the disappearances of Gerreint Lloid and Eiva Langden.'

At last Patreck stirs. He bares his teeth at Silah.

'They didn't disappear. They were taken.' He points at me with his unwounded hand. 'Because of her.'

28

PAWN

Silence falls in the hallway as we all absorb Patreck's words. I would like to argue that he's mistaken, but I still cannot speak. Something in my expression must convey my confusion, for Karrion says what I wish I could.

'No way. Yan had nothing to do with it.'

Patreck scoffs. 'She's as much responsible as if she'd forced them into a black van herself.'

'You're insane,' Karrion says.

'Before she moved to Old London, we were safe here. Now Gideor is dead and three of us are missing.'

Three? Through the haze of pain, I go through my mental list again. Eiva and Gerreint are both Leeches and both are missing. I have vetted the High Council of Mages and the Circle of Shamans, and there are no others. In fact, I am not certain how Patreck fits into this all. Could it be that he's someone climbing the political ladder and, had my assignment from Lord Ellensthorne continued long enough, our paths would have crossed?

Even so, surely he cannot mean himself? Who is the third Leech? Braeman's settlement only had three beneficiaries.

Could it be that he made other such trusts, choosing to limit those who could receive money from each trust to preserve their anonymity? If so, how are we ever going to find them all?

'What do you mean, three?' asks Jamie.

Patreck glances at him, huffing dismissively. 'Call yourself a detective, Jamie Manning?'

'You know who I am?'

'Of course we know who you are. How could we not when you've chosen to align yourself with our enemy? Your obsession with magic makes you more pathetic than even the most desperate of my kind.'

Jamie flinches. I wish I could come to his aid, but the words cannot be unsaid.

'Who's the third?' Karrion asks, his voice tight with anger.

'Figure it out, Bird Boy. Or have you wasted your intelligence as well as your power chasing after a hopeless obsession?'

Karrion draws in a sharp breath. I tilt my head as far as I am able to watch him. It takes no more than a second for him to school his expression into impassivity, but Patreck's words hit a mark. But what does it mean? How can it be that Patreck knows something about Karrion that I don't? Why won't he trust me?

'Go fuck yourself,' Karrion says, and Patreck laughs.

'Spoken like a true professional PI. That is what you want, isn't it? To be just as brilliant as your boss. I have news for you: it will never happen. You're not good enough. She hasn't yet had the heart to tell you that, but one day soon, she will. Then you're out of a job again and your siblings will have to go hungry. What sort of a bird can't even feed the fledglings?'

Karrion turns to me, anger and desperation warring in his eyes. I try to speak, but my throat is coated in ground glass.

'See, she's not even denying it,' Patreck says with a laugh.

I reach out and grip Karrion's hand. Blooms of pain blossom

from the finger joints, but against a backdrop of agony, it barely registers. Karrion stares at me, and I will him to understand that Patreck is lying, manipulating us with the information he has gathered. How he knows so much about us is something to be examined later.

'You make a fine pair, really. Only a loser whose life skills consist of painting pretty pictures would consent to working with a barely civil barbarian. Or are your duties limited to hiding your boss's opioid addiction from the rest of the world? I can't say you're doing a very good job of it. But fear not, it's not forever. Sooner or later, she'll be forced back to the deepest, darkest north to serve her mate and birth crippled beasts. It's all she's good for.'

A low growl reaches my ears, and it takes me a moment to realise the noise is coming from me. It reignites the fire in my throat, but I am beyond caring. Karrion presses a hand against my shoulder.

'Don't, Yan,' Karrion whispers. 'He's not worth it.'

The thud of footsteps signals the return of Ales. She hurries down the hallway, carrying two large bags. One of them she sets down next to me and the other she hands to Rhees. Gathering her magic, she casts a spell over me that is like the stroke of my mother's hand on fevered skin. The entire world seems to hold its breath for just a second before the magic fades away.

Ales opens the bag and spreads out supplies. She selects a vial containing liquid that shimmers like trapped starlight. Unstoppering it, she brings the vial to my lips.

'Drink.'

I try to protest that I cannot, but the liquid slides down my throat with no effort, bypassing the agony that still smoulders there. Straight away, a cooling numbness begins to spread over the area. I draw in a deep breath, relishing the abundance of oxygen.

While I am still enjoying the abatement of pain, Ales opens a large jar and spreads thick salve over my throat and temple. By its scent, I identify it as a healing unguent the Paladins use to reduce swelling and bruising. It is a sure sign that I have been too careless with my safety in recent months that I am becoming this familiar with Old London's healthcare methods.

Now that I can breathe more easily, I shift on to my elbows. Karrion supports me while I shuffle until my back is against the opposite wall from Patreck. Ales offers me a second vial, this one filled with deep-green liquid. Again, I recognise it as fast-acting pain relief and swallow the vial's contents without a protest. Straight away, a blanket of numbness settles over me. I relax.

Ales turns her attention to Patreck and bandages his bleeding fingers without a word. His shirt is torn across one shoulder and blood drips from the scratches my claws left. None of them looks deep.

Maika groans as Rhees helps her sit up in much the same way as Karrion did me. Blood still drips from her nose and ears, but the first aid acts fast and she is soon on her feet.

'Why...?' The word stings my throat, but I refuse to give up. 'Why do you think I'm responsible for the disappearances?'

Patreck laughs past Ales. 'You serve the leader of Old London.'

'Hardly.'

'Are you not his personal bloodhound, sniffing out scandals and purging those who don't belong? Did you think he ordered you to do it for the good of the city?'

I hesitate. Was that not how I convinced Karrion we should accept Lord Ellensthorne's job offer? How often since have I wondered at his hidden agenda? In trying to do good, have I caused more harm instead? Would Leina still be alive if I hadn't exposed Lloid as a Leech?

'If the citizens find out about Leeches in the Council, there will be an uproar,' I say, but the words sound weak even to my ears.

'So what? Isn't there a different scandal every other week? Better to be exposed than exterminated.'

'No one is exterminating you.'

Patreck scoffs. 'Tell that to Gerreint and Eiva.'

I frown. Did he witness what happened to them?

'Do you think they're dead?' I ask.

'If they aren't yet, they soon will be.'

'How do you know?'

After a glance towards the Paladins, Patreck presses his lips into a thin line. I repeat the question, but he ignores me. I ask him about the third Leech missing. He doesn't even acknowledge me. It becomes clear that he has nothing more to say.

'Are you well enough to stand?' Karrion asks me.

'I think so.'

He grips my forearms and pulls me to my feet. After a moment of unsteadiness, I nod and he lets go. My muscles tremble like I have chased a deer across the length of the conclave lands and then carried it back without help. Reaching within, I find my inner power reserves depleted. I will need a trip to my beach or a visit to Lady Bergamon's garden to restore my magic.

Thinking about my power takes me back to the moment when Patreck reached for my magic and I deflected him. I could do no such thing when Jans attacked me. Is that, like my enhanced powers, a result of my trip to the Unseen Lands, or does the Winter Queen's mark afford me a measure of protection I otherwise wouldn't have?

I have no answers, only more questions, so I let it go for now.

Together with Jamie and Karrion, I climb the stairs leading

to the top bedroom. Now that the darkness spell has dissipated, I sense no trace of it. I wish I knew how Mages perceive traces of magic and active spells. Perhaps one day I will ask Mery.

The top bedroom is a loft conversion, which makes the space larger than a typical room. A key is inserted into the lock on the inside. The room is sparsely furnished with a wardrobe, a double bed, and a bookcase. Another door leads to an en-suite bathroom.

At first glance, nothing about the room suggests that it is the secret hideout of Leeches. The covers on the bed are rumpled, suggesting someone has slept here recently. Karrion crouches to check under it.

'Hey, there's a camp-bed tucked away here,' he says.

'Which means that at a push, this room sleeps three,' I say.

We keep coming back to that number, yet one unnamed Leech is unaccounted for. Who is the third person that has disappeared recently?

Jamie and I walk to the wardrobe. Rather than a rack for hanging clothes, it contains only shelves. There are changes of clothes for both men and women, and the lower shelves contain various snacks and canned foods that do not require heating.

'Looks like this place is intended for lying low.'

'Not just that,' Karrion says from behind us. 'Check out these books.'

The cheap shelves are bowed under the weight of spell books. Most of them relate to Shadow and East magic, but there are also several volumes on the theory of Shaman spellcasting. On one of the shelves are narrow black and green boxes. I open one of them to reveal a row of gleaming jewels nestled on velvet cushioning: mana gems.

'How much do you want to bet that the Leeches came here to practise passing as a Mage?' Karrion asks.

'I suspect you're right.'

Karrion checks one of the other boxes to reveal more mana gems. As he moves to put the box back, he stops.

'There's something behind these.'

We help him move the stacks of boxes to reveal white envelopes. Inside each is a passport, a driving licence, and bundles of cash. The names are all unfamiliar, but the photos are all of Lloid, Eiva, and Patreck.

'They had everything they needed to become their Old London personas and also to disappear,' I say.

'The fake IDs are convincing.' Jamie thumbs through a passport. 'These must have cost a lot of money.'

'If Braeman financed all of this, it would stand to reason that money was not an object,' I say.

'But someone is continuing to pay for this stuff,' Karrion says. 'I doubt it's his widow. So who do you think it might be?'

'It might be the trustees of the Cuckoo Trust. Or there could be another player out there we're yet to meet.'

'Maybe that's the third Leech Patreck mentioned?' Karrion suggests.

I cock my head. 'It's possible, if they were bankrolling this before they went missing. But there's nothing here that shows who that person was.'

We search through the rest of the shelves, but find nothing else of interest until we come across a pile of folders hidden behind clothes in the wardrobe. I open the top one and the first thing I see is a photo of me standing outside my flat with Sinta in my arms.

'What the hell?'

Moving to the bed, I spread out the contents of the folder. There are more than twenty photos of me, sometimes alone, sometimes with Karrion or Jamie. In one of them, I am sitting at Wishearth's table in the Open Hearth. Opposite me, Wishearth is lifting his pint to take a sip from it, but his features are slightly blurred, as if he moved just at the right moment. Another photo shows Karrion and I walking through a gate in a residential street. The house behind us looks no different from the one next to it, and I struggle to remember where it could have been taken. It is only when I focus on the wrought-iron gate that I realise it is familiar. This is Ivy Street and the house must belong to Lady Bergamon, only none of the plant pots occupying every inch of the front garden are visible.

Is this how the rest of the world sees Lady Bergamon's house?

'This is not cool,' Karrion says beside me, his voice trembling with anger. 'This is so not cool.'

At first, I think he is bothered by the photos of us together, but when I glance in his direction, he is holding one of the other folders. Fanned out in his hands are several photos of him with his mum and siblings. Fear drains the colour from his face.

'The Leeches know where I live. They know where the owlets go to school and where Mum works.'

Now Jamie picks up a folder to reveal photos of himself. Many of them are taken outside a terraced house that I don't recognise. It must be where he lives, though it occurs to me that I am not certain where that is. The last photo shows a woman in her early thirties leaving a restaurant hand in hand with a tall man.

'Apparently they know my ex-wife too, though they're welcome to have her,' he says.

In silent agreement, we look through the rest of the folders. The surveillance has been thorough. There are folders for Lord Ellensthorne and Mr Whyte too. At the back, we find sheets containing an alarming amount of personal information and descriptions of routines for each of us. It becomes abundantly clear that we have been under surveillance for some time.

'How long has this been going on?' Jamie asks.

I return to the photos in my folder. Many of them have a blurry quality that suggests they were taken from a distance. How is it that I never noticed someone tailing me? What kind of a predator is not aware of threats in her own environment?

There is one photo that draws my attention. Karrion stands in the doorway of my shed, an axe in hand. I am a few feet away, mostly turned away from the camera, but enough of my face is visible to show I am smiling. Nothing about the scene is unusual, for Karrion has made it his mission to ensure I never have a chance to chop the driftwood I gather, but it is the angle of the photo that gives me a pause. Dread slowly worms towards my heart.

The photo was taken from above, but not from the sky.

My fingers tremble while I search my memory. When did Jans move to the flat above me? Did he live there when I arrived in Old London, or did he appear only after I began advertising my PI business? Why didn't I pay better attention?

'Jamie,' I say, still staring at the photo. The autumn leaves in my garden glow red and orange. 'Where's Jans?'

29

LITTLE FLY

J amie looks up, frowning. 'In a prison outside of Old London. Why?'

'Are you sure?'

'Yes. He was sent there after a Herald judged him guilty of attempted murder and assaulting you and Ilana.'

'That's not what I mean.' Shaking my head, I force my focus away from the photos. 'Are you sure he's still in prison?'

'Where else would he be?'

'Think about it. Patreck said three Leeches had gone missing. We know of five. Braeman is dead, Patreck is here. That leaves Lloid and Eiva, who are missing. But what about Jans?'

'He could've meant someone else,' Karrion says.

'Not if they're missing because of me.'

Jamie draws out his phone and dials. While he waits for the call to connect, he paces to the narrow window. I sink to the floor beside the bed, the pain of my injuries settling over me like a blanket.

The weariness I feel goes beyond the exertions of the day. My imprisonment damaged something I cannot define,

305

unsettling my sense of belonging in the city. The weight of the Winter Queen's mark grows heavier with each winter day. My tripping pulse counts down the time I have left in Old London before Dearon comes for me.

I wish I could sleep until my equilibrium returns, but it would do me no good. This path has been mine to forge since I left the conclave, and I must accept the consequences of my actions, good or bad.

Karrion drops down beside me with a thump and laces his fingers through mine. I let my head fall against his shoulder while I breathe in the familiar scents of a Bird Shaman. He is my anchor, my guiding light, and I love him for it. The path I chose is lonely, but with Karrion by my side, it is easier to traverse. But that doesn't lessen the guilt I feel.

'Everywhere I turn, I find a new way I've messed up,' I say.

'That's not true.'

'It may be a little melodramatic, but it is true. We've been outsmarted time and time again.'

'Doesn't that mean we've both messed up?'

I shift to look up and find Karrion grinning at me, eyes filled with his usual warmth. 'Perhaps,' I say, 'but I'm the one who's supposed to know what I'm doing.'

'If we're a true partnership, we need to share the blame equally,' says Karrion. 'As much as I was suspicious of Lord Ellensthorne when he offered to hire you, I never thought we'd end up here.'

'We don't know he's behind all this—'

'Come on, Yan. Who else could have planned and executed it with such precision? We've been used from the very beginning.'

When I offer no reply, he runs a hand through his hair until the blue-black strands stick up in all directions.

'It's embarrassing when you think about it. A Wild Folk and

a Bird Shaman outsmarted by a mere Mage. Let's not put this in our marketing brochure.'

His words have the desired effect, and I chuckle. He squeezes my hand and presses a kiss against my temple.

'I know everything is a bit shit right now, but we'll get through this the only way we know how: together.'

'You're right. We've come this far, so that's clearly the way to go.'

'Besides, I was temping in a marketing firm before I blagged a job with you. As far as I'm concerned, this is a huge improvement.'

I nudge him with my elbow. 'When things calm down a little, we need to discuss you raising your expectations a little.'

Before Karrion has a chance to reply, Jamie returns to us, the phone still in his hand and his expression ashen.

'Jans was transferred from Belmarsh five days ago,' he says.

'Transferred where?' I ask, scrambling to my feet. My balance is off, and Karrion steadies me.

'That's the thing, no one at the prison can find any trace of the paperwork. But they said the transfer request was all in order. They had no reason to suspect anything was amiss until now.'

'So he's gone?' asks Karrion.

'Looks that way. The third missing Leech.'

'Patreck was right. And it is my fault,' I say.

'Don't be daft, Yan. What was the alternative to imprisoning Jans? Give him another chance to murder you?'

'I know he had to pay for what he did that night, but after Lloid went missing, we should have thought about Jans. We should have put some kind of safeguards in place to make sure he remained in prison.'

'How could we have foreseen this?' Jamie asks. 'And how do

you think you could have guarded him better than the prison staff?'

With a soft noise of derision, I take a few paces back. 'How many times in the past couple of months have we been in this situation? We fucked up again. We need to be smarter about everything.'

Karrion nods. 'Where do we start?'

'With Patreck,' I say. 'We need to make sure he stays safe. If we lose him, we lose the last remaining Leech that we know of and our biggest chance to set a trap for whoever is behind all this. Besides, I can't imagine anyone kidnapping Leeches for anything other than a sinister purpose, especially if they were prepared to murder Leina in the process.'

'But if they can snatch Jans from a prison, what are the three of us going to do?' says Karrion.

'Karrion has a point,' Jamie says. 'I'm almost certain people at the Yard are involved.'

'So we turn to the one person we know we can trust when it comes to Leeches: the Paladin General.'

'What about them?' Karrion asks, dropping his voice to a whisper and nodding towards the door. 'Do you reckon we can trust them?'

'I think we must,' I reply. 'We need their swords and chains to transport Patreck safely to Old London.'

Jamie nods. 'Agreed. If they were acting under different orders, I'm not sure they would've allowed us to come along.'

'But that doesn't mean someone else doesn't know about this place and what we've discovered. We need to make sure the Paladins keep this quiet until we've reached the Brotherhood of Justice and spoken to the Paladin General.'

'We'd better get going,' Jamie says.

As we move to leave, a corner of something red catches my eye in the gap between the bed and the wardrobe. After a few awkward moments of reaching with the tips of my fingers and nudging the object further underneath the wardrobe, I retrieve a small paper bag. Printed on to it in silver and scarlet letters is the name of Pheonix's shop: Charmed Melodies. In the bag is an item no larger than my fist, wrapped in shiny purple paper. Attached to it is a small gift tag with two words written in elaborate cursive: *Little Fly*.

My fingers tremble as I tear open the wrapping to reveal a small silver box. The surface is polished so well that my perplexed expression is reflected back at me, and the metal feels unnaturally cold beneath my fingers. On one of the four sides is a small key. I move to turn it, but Karrion stops me.

'Are you sure that's a good idea?'

'I think it's meant for me,' I say.

'That doesn't answer my question. Pheonix is bat-shit crazy. What if he's left you a magical bomb or a cold-iron grenade?'

'Is that his style? If he had laid a trap, he'd want to see me walk into it, wouldn't he?'

'Point taken.' Karrion crosses his arms. 'But let the record reflect that I don't like it.'

'Noted.'

After a steadying breath, I turn the key until it goes no further.

For a heartbeat, nothing happens. Then music begins playing, each note slow and funereal. Although I don't recognise the melody, it reminds me of the slow tango Pheonix danced around Baneacre's Fey Mound. The cold menace of Lady Bergamon's decaying garden returns to me, filling my veins with despair. I recall the stench of death and decay in Baneacre's breath, and feel the revolting promise in his fingers gliding over my skin. In the space between tortuous seconds, I am briefly his.

The melody picks up speed and the sides of the box split open. Darkness flows out of the box until I no longer see the hand holding it. A silver fly buzzes out of the blackness, pausing to hover a few inches above where the box should be. The shadows coalesce into strands that slowly rise and weave themselves into a web with the fly caught in the middle. It struggles briefly. Around the fly, the weft grows rigid as frost spreads outwards, forming the outline of an enormous spider. The strange vista hovers in the air for a few moments before fading away with the whisper of a fire going out.

Soon, I am left holding an empty silver box in my palm. Silence returns to the room as the magic fades. I am about to close the sides of the box when I notice three words carved into the inside of the lid with a looping script that makes it hard to decipher: *Freeze or die?*

'Pheonix is certainly not subtle,' I say as I shove the box back in the paper bag.

'That was beyond creepy,' says Karrion. 'Are you okay?'

'Fine.'

I keep my voice light, though in truth the display has triggered the anxiety at the back of my mind that has resided there since Samhain. A sharp pain lances through the Fey mark, reminding me of the favour I owe. As if I could ever forget the Winter Queen or the terrible awe she inspires in me. Even now, the thought of becoming one of her hounds and serving her for an eternity fills me with both longing and disgust.

'For a PI, you're a terrible liar,' Karrion says, but his face shows only concern, not anger.

'Am I rattled by such a blatant threat? Yes. But that doesn't mean I'm going to scurry off to hide in my father's cabin in the North Lands. In fact, his leaving a package here tells me that his plan hasn't been quite as infallible as he would have liked. Why threaten someone if you've already won?'

'That's all well and good, but what happens if he does try to kill you?'

'Then either he succeeds or he meets the same fate as Baneacre.' I shrug, though I feel anything but confident.

'How? You gave the sword back to Tinker Thaylor, didn't you?' Karrion casts a careful glance in Jamie's direction.

'For the sake of our friendship, I hope you haven't acquired another illegal handgun,' Jamie says.

'I didn't mean that I'm going to make a habit of shooting Fey lords in the middle of the city, but rather that I'll take steps to defend myself. To that end, it might be worth having a chat with Thaylor about how I might Fey-proof my home.'

'It's not like you can cover your doors and windows with cold iron since it affects you almost as much as the Fey,' Karrion says.

'That's true, but there are other things they hate that I don't. Yew oil, for instance.'

'Now I have an image of Sinta spending her days licking your skirting boards.'

'Not quite what I was going for,' I say. 'Though perhaps it would be better to take a two-pronged approach.'

'What do you mean?'

'As capable as I know Tinker Thaylor to be, I imagine that were she to combine her knowledge and talents with those of Lady Bergamon, my house would be far better protected.'

Karrion grins, his eyes lighting up. 'How awesome would it be to watch them work on a project together?'

'My thoughts exactly. Hopefully they'd be open to doing me a favour.'

'I'm sure they would, especially if you were prepared to break the habit of a lifetime and actually tell Thaylor what's going on.'

'Seems only fair,' I say, glancing at the paper bag dangling from my fingers. 'But that's a task for another day. Right now, our main concern must be Patreck and his safety. Then we'll have to figure out why Leeches keep disappearing and who's behind it all.'

'Under different circumstances, your concern for a man who just tried to kill you would seem strange,' Jamie says. 'But as things stand, I think you're right. There's more going on than we currently understand, and I don't like being in the dark.'

'How are we going to manage that?' Karrion asks. 'It's not like we can invite him to stay in Yan's flat while he waits for judgement.'

'We follow the plan we put in place after Lloid disappeared,' I say. 'We confide in the Paladin General and ask for his help.'

'About that,' Karrion rubs the back of his neck, 'it's probably best if I won't be there when you speak to him. I was pretty rude about the Brotherhood and their general competence after Lincoln managed to weasel his way into your cell. I don't think my presence will help our case. At all. In hindsight, I'm amazed that I didn't get arrested.'

'He came to see me during my imprisonment,' I say. 'I must have forgotten to tell you. Rather than be angry at you, I think he was impressed by your courage and loyalty.'

'Oh.' Karrion's eyebrows rise. 'In that case, I might be useful.'

I smile. 'You always are.'

30

BLINK TO MISS IT

The Paladins have finished their first aid and are packing away their supplies when we return from the loft room after pausing to lock the door. Patreck remains seated against the wall, chained and bandaged. The feverish hunger for power has faded from his eyes. Our gazes meet, and for a second, I am certain I see a flash of fear. Almost before the thought registers, Patreck has schooled his expression into neutral indifference.

'Silah, may we have a word?' asks Jamie.

She nods, and we move along the corridor to the stairs leading down. Jamie ducks his head as he leans closer to Silah to keep his voice low.

'We're concerned about Patreck's safety given that other people who have been identified as Leeches have gone missing. I think it would be wise to transport him to Old London as quickly as possible, so that we may consult the Paladin General on how best to keep him safe. Do you agree?'

Although Jamie has always expressed a dislike of politics, he has chosen his words with care. He has offered her the illusion of control, all the while making it clear that there is only one course of action available. Silah has little choice but to nod again.

'We are ready to leave,' she says.

'Excellent.' Jamie continues to speak quietly. 'I also think we should keep his arrest quiet until we reach Old London.'

At this, Silah's eyebrows rise. 'Why?'

'As I said, we're concerned for Patreck and want to do all we can to keep him safe.'

Silah's expression grows troubled and she says nothing as she turns back to the Paladins. After a brief indication from her, Rhees and Ales help Patreck up. Maika shoulders the first-aid kits and follows after the others. We file downstairs, filling the narrow hallway. Donna is in the lounge, the Doberman by her side. At the sight of us, Cypher lowers his head and growls again, but he stays where he is. Jamie goes to her and speaks in a low voice before offering Donna one of his cards.

The Paladins escort Patreck out, Silah at the lead with her sword drawn. Karrion and I follow them, eyes roving the quiet street for any sign of a threat. We see none, and I breathe a little easier once Patreck is secured inside the Brotherhood's van. The back holds four self-contained cells, and Patreck is locked into a seat in one of them. Jamie jogs across the road to join us.

'We'll follow behind you,' he says to Silah. 'At the first sign of anything amiss, call for help and let us know.'

Silah's expression is sceptical as she glances from me to Karrion and back, but she says nothing. The Paladins take their places in two rows of seats at the front of the van.

'Do you think that in addition to a vow of loyalty, the Paladins also have to swear to always be grumpy?' Karrion asks in a low voice as we walk to Jamie's car.

'Maybe it's us, not them?' I reply.

'No way. We're cool, even if people aren't smart enough to appreciate us.'

'It's good to know that we're an acquired taste,' I mutter as I walk around the car to the passenger seat.

'There's something that still bothers me,' Karrion says, leaning forward between the front seats.

'What's that?' asks Jamie.

'What is the connection between the Leeches and Pheonix?'

'They must have gone to him for help, possibly after Braeman was murdered,' I say.

'Okay, fine, but what's he getting out of all this? The con artists, presumably because of his influence, diverted a large sum of money into a trust to help the Leeches. We haven't found any payments to Charmed Melodies, so Pheonix probably didn't get paid for his services in cash. So what's his angle?'

We all consider the question in silence as Jamie navigates past a busy Sainsbury's.

'Between the cursed cold-iron token and the warehouse set-up, it looks like he's targeting you,' Jamie says, glancing at me. 'Perhaps he's doing this simply for revenge?'

'Braeman died over the summer,' I say, 'long before I ever crossed paths with Pheonix.'

'Yes, but maybe the Leeches didn't feel threatened immediately after Braeman's death,' says Karrion. 'After all, the trust was providing them with monthly income with zero involvement from Braeman, so they may have thought their plans were secure.'

'What changed?' asks Jamie.

I think for a moment. 'Lord Ellensthorne hired us to vet the High Council and the Circle. If the Leeches somehow got wind of our assignment, that would have changed everything for them. Based on the photos we just found, we've all been under surveillance for months.'

'No offence, Yan, but if I were a Leech trying to hide in plain sight, I'd put any Wild Folk in the city under immediate surveillance.'

'Exactly.' I nod to Karrion. 'It's possible that someone saw Lord Ellensthorne and Mr Whyte visit us and jumped to the right conclusion, especially when I then started spending time around Council and Circle meetings.'

'And that was around the time you first met Pheonix,' Karrion says, finishing the thought for me. 'Have you considered that it wasn't a coincidence that you ran into him in that coffee shop?'

I open my mouth to reply, but words fail me.

'Maybe this all goes back much further than I thought,' I say at last.

Jamie stops at a red light and turns to me. 'If Karrion is correct and Pheonix is doing this because he was hired as well as out of vengeance, it means you're in grave danger.'

There is little any of us can say to that.

We hit traffic as soon as we leave the centre of Chertsey, and our progress slows to a crawl. An accident on the motorway sends us along a diverted route. The further we drive, the more the queues melt away until we and the Paladins are alone on a country lane. Trees crowd over the road, blocking out any hint of star and moonlight despite the lack of leaves. The shadows seem to grow, blurring my consciousness along its edges. They are warmer and more inviting than I ever knew darkness to be. My body aches from the injuries I sustained and from having all but drained myself of power. I long to be on my beach, or in the unspoilt landscape of the conclave, but more than that, I want to sink into dreamless sleep so deep I lose myself in it.

My eyelids grow heavy. I yawn, grateful I'm not the one driving. The brake lights of the Paladin's van blur, swimming in and out of focus. I rub my eyes with a hand that seems to weigh a ton. The shadows have entered the car, wrapping me in a promise of rest and rejuvenation. All I need to do is give in.

I blink.

The gap between us and the van widens.

I blink.

The van is right in front of us.

I blink.

The van is gone.

I blink.

Everything is dark. I wave a hand in front of my face, but the blackness is absolute. My heart begins racing. Did Patreck do something that robbed me of my sight? Could this be an after-effect from the cursed cold-iron token that was poisoning me for weeks? How will I manage my life if I'm blind?

Before the panic has a chance to set in, I reach into my back pocket and pull out my phone. Activating the screen shows a faint glimmer of light. The relief that washes over me is so strong my hand trembles. In its wake comes a different kind of confusion.

If I am not blind, why can't I see anything?

A muffled sound reaches my ears. It is only then that I realise the only sound I can hear is the thumping of my heart. Is the car still running? I cannot tell, though I feel no engine vibrations. The sound comes again, too faint to tell whether someone is speaking or whether it has a different origin. I turn my head, trying to pinpoint its direction, but my efforts are futile. The shadows are soft and soothing, coaxing me to relax and surrender to their silent lullaby.

I open my mouth to call out to Karrion, but it's as though the darkness steals the voice from my throat. A surge of fear lends me power, and a wordless groan escapes my lips. The sound does not carry, as if the very air has turned to treacle.

A hand landing on my shoulder startles me, and I jerk forward, my momentum arrested by the seat belt. My limbs have grown leaden, but mustering my strength, I touch the hand. Slender fingers grip me gently, and I recognise them as Karrion's even before my exploration finds the spiked bracelet around his wrist. Whatever has happened, we are still together.

What about Jamie?

If he is still in the car, he must find the situation even more frightening than I do. As much as he works around magic, he will have little experience of being under the influence of spells. For that must be what the shadows are.

I fumble to my right, and my hand lands on Jamie's upper arm. He jumps much as I did moments ago. A muffled word reaches my ears.

'Yannia?'

The power that held us captive is beginning to fade. Gradually, the shadows melt away until the outline of the dashboard appears. Jamie has his back partly pressed against the car door and he is facing me. As more details become clearer, I see that his eyes are wide with panic. Twisting in my seat, I find Karrion is rubbing his face.

'Karrion, can you hear me?'

'I can now,' he almost shouts, then lowers his voice. 'Couldn't you hear me before?'

'Only barely. Are you okay?' I ask.

'Getting there. Whatever happened was beyond creepy.'

He sounds so like himself that I relax a little. I turn back to Jamie, who hasn't moved.

'How about you? Can you hear me?'

Jamie is slow to nod. One of his hands is gripping the gear

stick, the other the handle of his door. Was he worried something was going to snatch him from the car?

'Are you hurt?' I ask, keeping my tone gentle.

He shakes his head.

It is only now that I realise the car is no longer running. Just as well, since we could easily have driven into a tree or a ditch. Outside the windows, the darkness is absolute.

I frown.

The darkness is too complete. A clear night would allow some starlight through. When the weather is overcast, the clouds will reflect the light from the cities to provide illumination. Only in the wild lands of the conclaves have I ever experienced true darkness. Here in the south, we should be able to see something, even if it is just a glow of the van's brake lights ahead of us.

'Jamie, can you switch on the headlights, please?' I ask, still keeping my voice calm.

He looks at me, uncomprehending, his eyes wide with fear that has not yet faded. A stab of anxiety flashes through my compassion. Jamie shouldn't be so adversely affected by a spell, even if he hasn't experienced something similar before. Now that we can see again, his police training should kick in, but it is clear from his shallow breaths and white knuckles that so far that hasn't been the case. Could it be that he, as the driver, was specifically targeted?

'Everything is okay,' I say, laying my hand over his on the gear stick. The contact feels strange, for we rarely touch one another. 'The magic is fading and things are going back to normal. We can see and hear each other again. That means the spell has broken, and it's not coming back.'

Although I know he can hear me, Jamie doesn't respond. He is still trapped in some personal nightmare of shadows and terror, his breath coming in gasps. That gives me an idea.

Reaching into the inner pocket of my jacket, I fish out my torch. Rather than shining the light in Jamie's face, I bring my hand close to his neck and shine the beam in the direction of his gaze.

'See here, the shadows are gone. We're safe inside the car and if we switch on the lights outside, the darkness will recede from there too. As long as we stick together, we'll be okay.'

Slowly Jamie lets go of the door-handle and brings his hand up, fingers spread as if he was attempting to catch the torch beam. He rubs his fingers together, then runs them over his face. Some of the panic leaves his eyes.

'I was falling,' he says, his voice hoarse. 'There was nothing but darkness around me, no ground, nothing. I was untethered, spinning down and down. No matter how much I screamed, no sound came out. I knew, somehow, deep in my bones, I knew I would be trapped there forever.'

Anger flares in me at the thought that anyone would do this to Jamie. He is human, defenceless against powerful magic. While his job puts him at risk, he doesn't deserve this. No one deserves this. A spell like that could have broken a weaker mind. Perhaps that is what they wanted.

The secret corner of my mind, where rage and hatred slumber and which has been partially awakened by the Winter Queen, whispers that I must seek vengeance for my fallen allies, that the blood of my enemies must drench the ground before I am satisfied. Were I to step on that path, the dark hounds would run by my side, all of us one pack at last.

My mind shies away from thoughts of the Fey hounds. Somehow I brought the Winter Queen to me during my imprisonment. What if the same happens with the Cù-Sìth? Alone on a country lane, we would not stand a chance against my queen's pack.

'Can you feel the seat beneath you?' I ask Jamie, forcing my attention away from my spiralling fear.

'Yes.'

'Good. That's real, as is the floor beneath your feet. So am I, and so is Karrion. What you see, hear, smell, and touch is all real. The darkness that's now gone wasn't real, it was simply a trick designed to confuse you.'

Karrion knows me well enough to understand what to do without words. Leaning forward, he grips Jamie's shoulder. Between the torchlight and our touch, Jamie's breathing starts to even. He blinks and rolls his shoulders. Fear gives way to embarrassment in his expression as he looks from Karrion to me and back.

'Thanks,' he mumbles.

I shrug, trying to combine nonchalance with sympathy. 'We're a team, this is what we do.'

'True, but...'

Our eyes meet, and I understand what he leaves unsaid. He is older than us, more experienced than us, he is the detective inspector, while we are amateurs. What we have is magic, and that is what Jamie wants more than anything. If he had power, he would be complete. I have never been able to put into words how spells cannot plug the gaps in our lives, or provide instant and permanent happiness. Magic is like money, health, or family, unequally distributed and simply one of the many aspects that define us.

But for him, it will always be the Holy Grail, just out of his reach. Now, faced with a targeted magical attack, I can well imagine him feeling vulnerable in a way that he would not be if threatened with knives or guns. Yet none of us are immune to spells or their effects, and we fought them off together. I hope, in the days that come, that Jamie will remember that.

'Okay,' Karrion says, bringing my thoughts back to the car as he waves his hand around. 'What the fuck happened to us?'

Outside the windows, the darkness remains absolute. It

wraps us in an impenetrable cocoon, shutting away the world. No, not a cocoon, for that implies a measure of safety I cannot feel. Rather, we are three people huddled around a sputtering campfire, hoping the meagre flames will keep the dangers lurking in the shadows at bay.

'We were hit with magic,' I say. 'Not just any magic, but a Mage spell.'

'That was my guess, too.' Karrion tugs at the necklace of cold-iron disks he keeps hidden beneath his shirt. 'This didn't help at all.'

'Who would do this?' Jamie asks.

Karrion leans forward from the back seat, pointing at the blackness outside the window. 'Don't you think that's a clue?'

'Before we begin speculating,' I begin, diverting a potential argument before it gains momentum, 'why don't we start by focusing on breaking the rest of the spell? Jamie, can you switch on the headlights now?'

Jamie flexes his fingers, working the stiffness from them. His hand trembles as he reaches for the steering wheel and flicks on the lights.

For the first few seconds, nothing happens. The darkness remains impenetrable. Then a narrow shaft of light breaks through the gloom, then another. The shadows begin to lift, but it is gradual, like treacle dissolving into hot water. A patch of road appears before us, growing larger with every passing moment. The white line denoting the border between the lanes glows in the glare of headlights. Indistinct shapes of trees loom ahead. As slow as the spell was to break at first, the process is picking up speed. Then the world outside the car snaps into focus.

The Paladin's van is nowhere to be seen.

31

AMBUSHED

With the fading magic, the last vestiges of my fear melt away. I open the car door, adding to the light illuminating the country road. My legs are unsteady at first, but strength soon returns to them. The shadows are sliding away, skirting around the car, and I follow them. Painted on to the middle of the road is a small black sigil. As I watch, the last of the magical darkness is sucked back into it and the mark begins to fade. I fumble for my phone and snap a quick photo before it disappears.

This was a targeted attack. Someone knew we would be here and they set a trap for us. But how? We hadn't planned on taking this route. Were we followed? Or, and this worries me even more, is someone tracking us? Could we have been steered on to this deserted country road for the sole purpose of a trap?

That can be a question for later. Our priority is finding out what happened to the Paladins. Outside the sphere of light from the car, the darkness is absolute. I walk along the road until I am beyond the reach of the headlights, and I scrabble for threads of wildness from the trees around me. My body protests, sharp aches flaring from my injuries, and my power is so low that connecting to nature causes me pain. Since my PI business took off, I have been using my magic with wild abandon, but now for the first time, I wonder if I have gone too far. What if the cursed cold-iron token caused permanent damage and I'll never recover?

Threads the width of a pine needle questing along my aura distract me, and I open myself to the woods. A squirrel leaps from branch to branch, lending me its wiry strength. An owl glides between the trees, searching for prey, and I borrow its eyes. A colony of ants slumbers beneath the road, and I take a little of their endurance. A spider lends me patience, the trees their fortitude. I stand a little straighter. There is not enough wildness here to restore my depleted magic, but the tremors of exhaustion have subsided and my determination has returned.

Using the owl's keen eyes, I turn to follow the direction of the road. The night is no longer black, but merely shades of grey. I stare down the tunnel of trees, seeing far beyond the range of human vision, to where the road curves and disappears. We are alone. Relinquishing the threads of power, I shield my eyes as I return to the car. Karrion and Jamie are standing beside it, but I say nothing as I walk to the edge of darkness behind them. In that direction, too, the road is deserted, even when I enhance my sight. The sharper senses of wildness pick up the rumble of an approaching engine. I let go of the owl's vision before the headlights blind me and return to the others. A silver jeep drives past, slowing slightly as the driver stares at us. Silence returns to the road.

'The van is gone,' I say.

'I tried calling the Brotherhood, but my phone had no reception,' Jamie says.

Pulling out my phone, I check the display. The top of the screen informs me that I can only make emergency calls, but while I watch, the reception bar fills.

'Try again.'

Jamie makes another call, and this time, it connects. While he deals with the Brotherhood's switchboard, Karrion draws me away from the car.

'Do you think Jamie's going to be okay?' he asks in a low voice. 'He was proper freaked out earlier.'

'I hope so. Tonight has given him a taste of what magic can be at its worst. It's one thing to witness it from the sidelines or investigate it after the fact, quite another to be the target of an attack.'

'Could this be what puts an end to his obsession with magic?'

'Only time will tell,' I say, twisting to look at Jamie, who is pacing beside his car. 'Though perhaps it would be no bad thing. Can he ever truly find peace or happiness if he doesn't accept his place in life?'

Karrion opens his mouth to reply, but doesn't say anything. I know what he is thinking: does the same not apply to me and the promises that bind me to the conclave?

'I would say the plot thickens,' Jamie walks towards us, pocketing his phone, 'but I've now lost it completely.'

'How so?' Karrion asks.

'Two things: the Paladins' van is still heading towards London. They're about ten miles from here. And they received a message via the Brotherhood's dispatch that we'd suffered a flat tyre and that they should go on without us.'

'Clever,' I say as Karrion makes a surprised noise. 'The Paladins wouldn't have any reason to doubt a message that came from their own people. Whoever set this trap is smart. I suspect it was no accident we were diverted away from the busier roads to here.'

'Is it too soon to make wild accusations about certain Shadow Mages?' Karrion asks. When Jamie frowns at him,

Karrion throws his hand in the air in exasperation. 'Oh, come on. We were attacked by creepy shadows. Who else could have put something like this together in such a short time?'

'Karrion has a point,' I say.

He whips around to stare at me. 'Wait, what?'

I frown. 'What?'

'Nothing. I was sure you were going to tell me I'm paranoid and weird again.'

'What we experienced was a powerful Shadow Mage spell. We'd have to check with Mery, but I'm not sure someone from another school of magic could have cast it. That's a point in favour of your Lord Ellensthorne theory. Plus, we've seen first hand how cunning he can be. What concerns me is how he could have possibly known about Patreck. Were we being followed?'

'Not that I noticed,' Jamie says.

'I didn't see anything either,' replies Karrion. 'And I spent a good half of the drive looking backwards for that very reason.'

'That was my feeling, too. At no point did I notice anything suspicious, especially after we'd apprehended Patreck. We know the Paladins' van has a tracker, given that the dispatcher just told you where they were, and I'm guessing the same applies to your car and work phone. What I can't figure out is how they knew we'd found another Leech. We didn't tell anyone and you gave Silah explicit instructions not to. So why spring this trap?'

'Could they have guessed that was the reason for the trip?' asks Karrion.

'It would be a huge leap,' Jamie says. 'I was very careful to speak only of a suspect. At no point did I mention that the said suspect was a Leech.'

I look from Jamie to Karrion. 'So how did they know?'

'Could Donna have called someone?' asks Karrion. 'I mean,

we thought she was downstairs the whole time, but what if she eavesdropped from the staircase or something? We weren't all that quiet.'

'No.' I shake my head. 'If she knew Patreck is a Leech, she could have had him picked up at any time and we wouldn't have known anything about it.'

'Except that she was under some weird spell,' Karrion says.

'I'd forgotten about that. She didn't know who Patreck was, let alone his true nature. But I'm still not convinced she tipped someone off about him.'

'We can puzzle over that later,' says Jamie. 'But right now, I'd like to catch up with Silah's team and make sure Patreck is safe.'

A stab of guilt flashes through me. That should have been my priority. Why wasn't it? Is Patreck's safety less important because he is a Leech? Was I right to be distracted by the trap, or is that what someone hoped would happen? I rub my temples, once again feeling like I am missing vital pieces of the puzzle.

'Can you call them and ask them to wait somewhere for us?' asks Karrion.

'Worth a try. That would be easiest.'

Jamie dials again, and I listen to his one-sided conversation with the switchboard. When he is put on hold, he motions for us to return to the car. He hesitates by the driver's door, uncertainty written across his face. I imagine it will be some time before he can be near his car without remembering the effects of the spell.

When Jamie ends the call, the press of his lips tells me it didn't go as planned.

'Silah said that they're not allowed to stop while transporting a prisoner or slow down to allow us to catch up.'

'In that case, we'd best get going,' I say. 'They have quite a head start. Let's hope the evening traffic will work in our favour.'

'Or...' Karrion flashes Jamie a hopeful grin. 'This could be an opportunity to show off that siren of yours.'

Jamie looks like he wants to argue, but instead he lets out a weary chuckle. 'Twice in one day?'

'We didn't go that far earlier, so it barely counted,' says Karrion. 'If I remember correctly, there weren't even any cute girls swooning as we sped past.'

'Your priorities are messed up.' I flash Karrion a grin as he fastens his seat belt in the back seat. 'Shall I give Fria a ring so you can have a shag and focus better?'

'What?' Karrion sputters curses. 'Why would you even say something like that?'

I offer him my most innocent smile. 'It was just a suggestion.'

'Yeah, maybe if you're locked up in a loony bin,' he says, but his cheeks have turned pink and I take pity on him.

'Do you think we'll catch them?' I ask Jamie.

He starts the car and switches on the siren. 'I'll do my best.'

We are all lost in our thoughts during the drive. I keep turning over the pieces of this investigation, trying to make sense of the various aspects of it, trying to see what, if anything, we have missed. I have too many unanswered questions and yet again, I have a sinking feeling of failure. So many people have died or gone missing. What could I have done differently to prevent that?

Once we reach busier areas, the siren speeds our journey considerably. The Paladins have enough of a head start that we do not catch them until we are approaching Old London. They acknowledge our presence with a flash of the hazard lights, and Jamie switches off the siren. We escort them the rest of the way to the Brotherhood's compound, navigating a narrow alley to the back of the building, away from prying eyes. We park near a nondescript entrance that leads straight to the prison block. This is the way I, too, entered after my arrest, though I remember next to nothing about the journey.

Silah is scowling as she exits the van, her posture stiff with disapproval. She rounds on Jamie, who is stretching his legs after the tense drive.

'If you plan on escorting suspects in the future, you'd do well to ensure your vehicle is properly maintained,' she says.

Jamie stares at her. 'What?'

'This is why we,' Silah gestures to the other Paladins, 'do the real work in both Londons.'

'It wasn't a flat tyre that delayed us,' I say, and Silah redirects her glare at me. 'Someone cast a powerful spell on us to ensure we couldn't remain with the van.'

There's a pause while Silah considers my words. 'To what end?'

'So there would be fewer people guarding Patreck,' I say, fighting to keep my voice level.

'The three of you are hardly a threat.'

'Wasn't it Yan who subdued the Leech, rather than one of you lot?' says Karrion, not bothering to hide his irritation.

'That was more luck than skill,' Silah says. 'When it comes to protecting the citizens of Old London, we are the experts.'

'Which is why you locked up an innocent woman for three weeks,' Karrion says, and I lay my hand on his shoulder, shaking my head. He closes his mouth, but his glare equals Silah's.

I raise my hands in a gesture of appeasement. 'All of that aside, the fact is someone set a trap that was almost certainly designed to put Patreck in harm's way.'

'Then they failed,' Maika says. 'Our prisoner is safely where we put him.'

As if to demonstrate the truth behind Maika's words, Rhees

unlocks the van's back doors and pulls them outward. He takes half a step backwards, grabbing the edge of the door for support. A familiar dread creeps over me as we crowd around to see inside.

Patreck is gone.

'Impossible,' Silah says, several shades paler than before. 'How could this have happened?'

Rhees turns on his heels and jogs through the door of the prison compound, a hand gripping his sword hilt.

Ales steps into the van and touches the melted lock of the cell cubicle that Patreck had been secured in. 'An alarm sounds when the back door is forced open. Why didn't we hear it?'

'Did you stop at any point during the journey?' asks Jamie.

'We are not permitted to,' replies Silah, her voice sharp with annoyance and fear. 'Our priority must be safeguarding the prisoner.'

'Well...' Maika starts, before hesitating. 'We stopped at traffic lights.'

Silah huffs. 'Don't you think we would have noticed if someone opened the back of the van while we were waiting for a green light?'

'What about those temporary lights for the roadworks?' Maika's voice is quieter, but it holds a note of confidence. 'I remember staring at the red light and thinking that it was taking forever for them to change. Did you see any cars coming the other way?'

'There were none,' Ales says.

'Wait, where were the temporary traffic lights?' I ask.

'Along the diversion,' Maika says. 'We drove cross-country, through a forest, and the roadworks were right before we reached the next village.'

Jamie, Karrion and I share a look, confusion written across all our faces.

'We didn't see any temporary traffic lights,' Jamie says.

Silah crosses her arms. 'Then you must have taken a different route. Or you simply weren't paying attention.'

'No, we followed you,' I say. 'The traffic lights weren't there when we drove through the area.'

'You must be mistaken,' Silah replies, stubborn in her insistence that we are wrong. 'No one could have moved them in the middle of the night.'

'Actually,' Karrion steps in, his voice calmer now, 'to set that up, all someone needed were two signal posts with built-in batteries and a stack of traffic cones. As traps go, it's quick enough to lay and remove, especially if you can shove everything in the back of a van.'

I appreciate anew the trouble someone went to in order to capture Patreck. They would have needed two teams: one to delay us and another to target the Paladins' van. Both must have consisted of at least two people, possibly more. I will need to check with Mery whether the spell cast on us could be performed by one Mage or whether it would require a collective effort. An even more important question is how much power was required to sneak a prisoner out of Paladin custody without them noticing that anything was amiss.

Before Silah has a chance to argue further, Rhees returns with more Paladins. Two of them, dressed in the grey robes of the Brotherhood rather than in battle gear, stop by the back doors of the van and link hands. The hairs at the back of my neck prickle as the air becomes charged with Paladin magic. I have no idea what spell they are casting, but soon thick tendrils of darkness appear around the open doors, spreading outward to form a shield around the middle of the van. A yellowed leaf appears out of nowhere and floats down, disappearing before it reaches the ground. Inside the van, the door to Patreck's cell cubicle glows with the remnants of another spell.

'Strong Mage magic was wielded here,' one of the robed Paladins says. 'There is also a hint of something else, Feykin or Fey power, designed to blind the guardians, to distract the watchers. The spells came from outside, not from within the cell.'

That would mean that whoever – I am still reluctant to assign a name to my suspicions – set up this trap was working with a Fey or a strong Feykin. Could it be that Pheonix is working for both sides? Or is there an unknown player in the mix who is content to remain in the shadows for now?

'Someone helped Patreck escape,' Silah says.

'Or someone took him,' I add, earning another glare from her.

'Either way, the timing is weird. Who could have acted so fast?' asks Karrion.

I turn to Ales. 'Is there any chance Donna overheard something about Patreck being a Leech while you were guarding the door downstairs?'

'No.' She shakes her head. 'She never left the sitting room, and while the sounds of struggle were clear, the subsequent conversation wasn't. Unless she enhanced her hearing with magic, she wouldn't have heard a word.'

Jamie sighs. 'That takes us back to only the people in the two vehicles knowing about Patreck.'

'Not quite,' Silah says. 'I reported the arrest to the Brotherhood when we left Chertsey.'

Karrion, Jamie and I stare at her.

'Why would you do that, when I specifically asked you not to?' Jamie asks.

'I'm hardly going to disregard our regulations and procedures on the say-so of a human,' she replies, her tone cold.

'Wow, you sure know how to foster good working

relationships with the New London law enforcement,' Karrion mutters.

Silah doesn't appear to have heard him, and another shake of my head warns him against antagonising the Paladins further.

Over the next hour, we give our statements regarding the events of the evening. The Paladins question us closely, and I forward them a copy of the photo I took of the fading symbol on the road. After Silah's clear dislike of us, I was expecting more hostility, but everyone treats us with the same detached professionalism as in our previous encounters with the Brotherhood.

We exit through the main doors. A chill wind tugs at my clothes, and I breathe deeply, enjoying the cold air. It rejuvenates me after the stuffiness indoors. A section of Paladins on horseback rides out of the main gate. Beside me, Jamie's phone beeps. Having glanced at the screen, he groans.

'Great, I have to go explain all of this to my superiors now.'

'Haven't they heard of information sharing?' asks Karrion.

'When it comes to assigning blame, they like to have all the facts first hand.'

'Surely they can't claim any of this was your fault,' I say.

'I imagine they're going to try.' Jamie stuffs the phone back in his pocket. 'I'll say goodnight, then. Shall we meet up for lunch tomorrow?'

Karrion and I agree to do so and wave him off. As we head towards my car, my eyes are drawn past the fence to the street. Jack Lincoln's Toyota is in the same spot as before. I stare at the car, so intent on my thoughts that I stumble over a loose paving stone. Karrion catches me with practised ease before I end up sprawled on the ground.

'Watch out,' he says.

'Do you think it's odd that Lincoln's car is exactly where we saw it earlier?'

'So he didn't try to follow us when we left in a hurry?'

'It doesn't look like it. Or if he did, he came back to the same spot.'

'Maybe he was hoping to catch us when we returned?' suggests Karrion.

'If that's the case, where is he?'

We both look around the compound and the street running alongside it, but there is no sign of Lincoln. I should be relieved, but a feeling of unease worms its way back into my chest.

'A pee break, possibly?' Karrion shrugs. 'It would be pretty funny if he missed us because he had to duck into a pub to use the facilities.'

'Maybe...'

I veer away from my car and pass through the open gates to the Victoria Embankment. The evening traffic has slowed to a trickle, and joggers and dog walkers dodge past us as we make our way towards Lincoln's car. As I walk, I keep an eye on everything around us, in case Lincoln makes a sudden appearance and accuses me of murdering someone else.

At first glance, there is nothing out of place with Lincoln's car. It is only the lingering unease that urges me to take a closer look. Even so, as my attention is drawn to the camera with a telephoto lens tucked into the passenger-side footwell, I almost miss the message left for me.

'Look,' I say to Karrion.

Hanging from the rear-view mirror is a small silver fly. It turns slowly one way, then another. When I lean close enough, the tiny threads binding the fly become visible. At the top of the mirror, partially hidden where it attaches to the ceiling, is a black spider.

'Does that mean Pheonix has Lincoln?' asks Karrion.

'I think so. And that means he's in grave danger.'

Karrion lays a hand on my arm. 'You do know it's a trap, right?'

'I do.'

'Given all the lies Lincoln's written about you, all the half-truths he's twisted to suit his shitty agenda, no one would blame you if you walked away and let matters run their course.'

'I know,' I say, looking down at the fly. Various newspaper headlines about me rise from the confines of my memory, followed by Pheonix's swirling purple eyes. 'But I can't. If we let Lincoln die, Pheonix will go after someone we love next.'

32

DIGGING DEEP

We drive east along the river towards Leadenhall Market. The lights of Old London on our side of the Thames, and New London on the other, cast blurry streaks on the restless surface of the water. Karrion twists in his seat to look at me.

'Okay, boss, what's the plan?'

'Stop Pheonix before he murders someone else.'

'That's great, but it's a little light on details.'

'How am I supposed to come up with something better when I have no idea what we're up against?' I ask, and immediately regret the sharpness of my tone. 'Sorry. I wish I knew what to expect. Pheonix is a powerful enemy.'

'It's fine. We'll just wing it, as usual.' Karrion smiles.

'I'm not proposing we go in all spells blazing, especially given that we've struggled with plans in the past, but it's impossible to say anything for certain until we know more about what's going on. If Pheonix has Lincoln inside Charmed Melodies, we may need to be sneaky and emulate Fria.'

Karrion makes a gagging sound. 'Why would you want to do that?'

'She is the sneakiest thief we know. When planning a possible break-in, there are worse examples to follow.'

'You know what, I think we need to cultivate better professional contacts. Preferably ones that aren't Cat Shamans.'

I flash a grin in Karrion's direction. 'Wouldn't you miss her?'

He splutters objections. 'Why on earth would I ever miss her?'

'Because she's so... slinky?' I ask, fighting to keep a straight face.

'Shut up.'

'What's wrong?'

'Just shut up.' Karrion crosses his arms.

I laugh, but doing so flares up the pain from my injuries. As if opening the floodgates, the aches bring a crushing sense of fatigue. It has been a long day, and at no point since my release from the Brotherhood have I felt truly well. Now I wish I could sleep for a week, followed by a full day at the beach recharging my power. Or, perhaps Lady Bergamon would allow me to camp out in her garden until I have recovered.

At the next set of traffic lights, I lean my head against the window. 'I'm knackered. Utterly exhausted. I think now would be a good time to break out the emergency chocolate.'

'Wait, we have emergency chocolate?'

'Check the glove compartment,' I say, and ease forward in the traffic.

Leaning forward, Karrion rummages around and pulls out a handful of chocolate bars. He grins at me.

'It's official. You're the best boss ever.'

'A couple of chocolate bars was all it took to earn that title? Interesting.'

'What can I say?' Karrion shrugs. 'After my last temping job, where the office manager repeatedly tried to push his religion on to me, the bar is set so low it's basically on the ground. Now which of these do you want?'

I indicate my choice, and Karrion unwraps the bar. It restores some of my energy, though I know I am simply plastering over the cracks. What I need is proper rest, not sugary snacks.

'Feeling better?' Karrion asks once I have finished the chocolate.

'A little, but truth be told, I'm not sure I'm in any fit shape to take on a Fey.'

'Good job you've got me as backup,' he says, though the lightness in his tone is forced.

'I wouldn't be able to do this without you.'

Karrion's aura expands with delight, but I barely feel it. I am depleted, almost as low on power as I was when the Paladins removed the collar and I collapsed to the marble floor. A new fear chills my bones. What if I try to access my power in vain and someone gets hurt because I have no magic left? What if something happens to Karrion and I am powerless to help?

As if sensing something of my thoughts, Karrion squeezes my shoulder.

'It's two against one, remember? Besides, we have a secret weapon against him.'

'What's that?' I ask, wondering if he and Tinker Thaylor have built some sort of Fey death ray without my knowledge.

'Cold iron. I have my necklace and you have your torch. It's his kryptonite. If we can fling the necklace over his head, he'll be done for. Kaboom.'

'Kaboom?' I raise an eyebrow.

'It's a figure of speech. Sort of like what happened to Baneacre, only with no Lord Ellensthorne there to get in our way.'

I see before my eyes Baneacre's shrivelled, blackening body, feel the pressure against my temples that signalled an impending implosion. Only Lord Ellensthorne's magic circle saved us, and it was almost not enough. Handling Baneacre's decaying body caused severe burns to my palms. I owe the use of my hands to Lady Bergamon's healing, and the silvery scars left behind are a permanent reminder of my battle against a Fey lord.

'If you don't mind, I'd like to aim for a plan that doesn't leave you quite so vulnerable,' I say, rubbing my left palm against the steering wheel. 'If you miss, you'll have no defence against his glamour.'

'Like I'd miss.' Karrion raises his free hand before I have a chance to object. 'But point taken. Baneacre was so strong a single cold-iron token wasn't enough to protect me. While I'm hoping Pheonix isn't as powerful, we'll be no use to anyone if we end up under his thrall.'

'My suggestion is that we park in one of the side streets and approach Leadenhall Market on foot. That way we can see what's going on, hopefully without being spotted. Once we know more, we can come up with a more detailed plan.'

'Sounds good.' Karrion opens another chocolate bar and wolfs down half of it in seconds. 'Do you think we should give Jamie a heads-up?'

I think for a moment, then nod. 'He may have had enough of us for one day, especially if he's getting a bollocking from his superiors, but in the interest of openness and honesty, we should tell him.'

'Shall I text him?'

'Please. Say that we suspect Pheonix may have kidnapped Jack Lincoln and that we're conducting discreet surveillance to gather information. Once we know more, we'll call him to figure out what our next step should be.'

Karrion sends the text, and a few seconds later his phone

beeps. 'Jamie replied. He says "okay". Wait, he sent another message. "Keep me posted". A whole three words. I feel special now.'

'Good, because that's exactly what you are.'

'Why doesn't that seem like a compliment?' asks Karrion, and he slips his phone into the inside pocket of his leather jacket.

Instead of replying, I slow the car to a crawl and park behind a delivery van. The nearest Leadenhall Market entrance is around the corner, and I choose the side closest to Charmed Melodies. The unease I felt earlier returns when I step out of the car. I stretch my aching muscles and wince as the developing bruises around my neck make their presence known.

'Ready?' I ask.

Karrion nods and pulls down the collar of his jumper to reveal his necklace. He checks the cord, so it is easy to pull over his head, but keeps the disks against his skin where they can provide maximum protection. I lay my hand on my inside jacket pocket, where the small torch is safely hidden, and wish I had thought to bring the small bottle of yew oil I used to coat the cold-iron blade.

We head towards Leadenhall Market. As we approach the corner of the street which would afford us a view of our destination, something brushes against my aura, soft as dandelion seeds. My steps slow, and I look around. A Mage sigil painted on to a nearby bus shelter glows faintly. I reach out to touch it, and the air around me is filled with the smell of rotting rubbish. It is a prank graffiti, nothing more. Yet, as I move to carry on, the same sensation of dandelion seeds floating along my aura returns.

'Did you feel something?' I ask.

'I'm a bit nippy,' Karrion replies, buttoning his coat, but leaving himself unrestricted access to the necklace. 'And thanks to you touching graffiti you should leave well alone, my nose is stuffed with the stench of cat litter.'

'Sorry. But is that it? You can't feel anything on the edges of your aura?'

'No, and we've already established that I don't get the same vibes as you and your wild instincts.'

'That could be it, or...' My eyes are drawn to his necklace.

Following my hunch, I detach the handle of my torch enough to expose the small cold-iron blade attached to it. As soon as I touch the metal, familiar nausea rises from my gut, filling my mouth with bile. I swallow, straining to concentrate on my fraying aura. The soft brushes are no longer there, though whether it is because the cold iron blocks them or has dulled my senses, I cannot tell. I let go of the blade and close my eyes while I wait for the nausea to subside.

'Anything?' asks Karrion.

'Not sure,' I say, and tuck the torch away.

The pavement beneath my feet tilts, and I grab Karrion's arm before I lose my balance. He wraps an arm around my waist to take more of my weight and steers me to a nearby bench.

'Are you all right?' he asks once I am sitting down.

'No. What if Lincoln dies because I'm too exhausted to save him?'

'I know it's not what you want to hear, but I doubt he'd be greatly missed,' Karrion says, and raises a hand before I can object. 'Not funny, I know. But we can't do more than our best.'

Closing my eyes, I massage my scalp. 'True. Pity we don't have a bag of mana gems to help us out.'

'They'd only slow us down since neither of us can use them.'

I want to agree, but I have sensed the power within the gems, barely beyond my reach. There must be a way to access it, to draw it out like opening a deer's vein and collecting the blood. But now is not the time to be distracted by another puzzle.

'Here,' Karrion says when the silence has gone on for a while. He hands me a half-eaten bar of chocolate. 'Since I have neither mana gems nor a Wild Folk power battery pack, you'd better finish this off.'

'Thanks.'

Chocolate and caramel form a sweet film in my mouth, flirting with the edge of nausea that has not quite gone away. I swallow back bile, hoping that the sugar will grant me a burst of energy. If it won't, Pheonix will meet minimal resistance when he comes to kill me. In a moment of dark despair, I am not certain which would be worse.

'Feeling any better?' Karrion asks.

I shrug, uncertain of the answer. The brush against my aura comes again, soft as spider silk, and something clicks into place.

'He knows we're coming.'

Karrion does not question my certainty, but he lays a hand on my knee. 'We can still walk away, you know.'

'No.' I shake my head. 'We can't. If Lincoln isn't enough to lure us into his trap, he'll find someone else as bait, someone who matters to us.'

'In that case, come on.' He stands, offering me his hand. 'We have a Fey lord to stop.'

It is the warmth of his hand, rather than the chocolate, that gives me the strength to rise from the bench. Side by side, we round the corner.

33

SPIDER'S WEB

Shadows crowd over the entrance to Leadenhall Market. The lights are dimmer than they should be, their glow like that of the blood moon on the night of Samhain. Although none of the dragon decorations points towards the entrance, purple smoke is billowing out of the market. It spreads across the road, stretching its tendrils towards us. I am reminded of misty autumn nights at the conclave, when everything was still enough to blur the veil between the worlds. In the restless dance of mist over calm waters, I caught glimpses of the Fey host assembling for a hunt. Now, similar hints of shape and movement within the smoke send a shiver of fear through me.

Could it be that the Winter Queen's court will soon ride through the streets of Old London?

No. I dismiss the thought with a sharp shake of my head. We are months past Samhain, when the veil between the worlds is at its thinnest, and the vernal equinox is not yet upon us. Pheonix may be powerful in comparison to the average citizens of Old London, but surely he cannot create a portal to the Unseen Lands and hold it open for the host to ride through. Or could he?

The smoke reaches us, enveloping us in the combined scents of campfires and fresh blood. They should take me back to the familiar landscape of my childhood, should offer a measure of safety, but instead they set my teeth on edge. Everything here has been set up by Pheonix. He is waiting for me somewhere in the smoke, poised to begin a dance that will end my life or his, while the Winter Queen watches on with her lords of war and cruelty.

Beside me, Karrion swears. I tear my eyes away from the restless smoke. He points beyond the entrance. 'Is that him?'

Tendrils of the smoke are curling up along the bamboo scaffolding, undulating in a wholly unnatural way. A figure is moving along the lowest level, partially hidden in the haze. My heart jumps, certain that Karrion has spotted Pheonix and provided us with a fractional advantage, but I soon realise my mistake. The movement of the figure is fumbling, too clumsy for the elegant Fey. It is too late for construction workers. Is it Jack Lincoln?

'What's Lincoln doing up there?' I ask.

'Probably looking for a better vantage point for spewing his poison,' Karrion mutters.

'No, I don't think so.'

While we watch, Lincoln reaches the ladder leading to the level above. He begins to climb, his movements slow as if sleepwalking. My fear returns tenfold. While the details are not an exact match to the scene at the Hamptens' flat, there are enough similarities for me to guess the outcome. Beside me, Karrion swears.

'Shit, is he going to leap off the top?'

'Not if we can stop him,' I say. 'Come on.'

The smoke has thickened, turning into a sticky substance that slows our steps. It slides along my exposed skin and leaves behind a crawling sensation that has me wishing for a shower.

Instead, I scratch the back of my hand until a flaring pain indicates I have drawn blood. I stare at the crimson bead welling in the wound, my thoughts drifting away like the dandelion seeds I felt earlier. My fingertips prickle with cold as ice begins to flood my veins. Dark figures move within the smoke, creeping closer as the Winter Queen's hold on me tightens. A growl begins forming in my throat, signalling my transformation into one of the Fey hounds.

'Yan.'

The name is the bay of a hound, both distant and familiar. It means nothing now, for in a landscape of falling snow, I am no longer myse–

Fingers close around my wrist, hard as yew, hot as cold iron. They yank me away from the world of frost and death to one of glass and concrete and steel. My vision clears, though the smoke still dances around us. Karrion is staring at me, eyes wide with alarm, his other hand clenched around the necklace.

'Yan?'

'What happened?' I force the words out from a throat that would rather growl.

'You stopped in your tracks and let out a howl, like you were pretending to be a wolf. Proper creepy, that was. I tried talking to you, but it didn't seem like you heard me.'

'I didn't. It's the smoke, I think. It's messing with my head.'

Now that the glamour's effect on me has lessened, I notice that while the smoke is circling Karrion, he stands in a clear space. The disks of his necklace glint in a flicker of light reaching us from Leadenhall Market. He is much better prepared for Pheonix's trap than I am. At any other time, the thought might fill me with pride, but all I feel is despair. I should be the one setting an example, not him.

My fingers tremble as I reach into the inside pocket of my coat and draw out the small torch. The thought of holding something made partly of cold iron brings bile to my mouth, but I swallow back the revulsion, careful to hold on to the steel handle when I withdraw the short blade.

The smoke shifts away from me, as if cut by the blade I hold. The pressure of the glamour against my senses eases further. With my mind clear, I muster my remaining strength.

'Come on,' I say. 'We don't have much time.'

Together we hurry to the scaffolding, and the smoke parts before us. When I glance back, the shops on the opposite side of the road are hidden behind the haze. A shiver runs through me. I hope no humans stumble within the spell's grasp, for they will surely become lost. But the quickest way for us to help people is to stop Pheonix's plan, whatever it may be.

Karrion reaches the ladder to the upper levels first. He steps aside to let me go in front of him, but I shake my head.

'You're in better shape than I am,' I say. 'Just be careful.'

'Should we check each level as we go up? Visibility is shit, thanks to Pheonix.'

'No. Knowing him, he'll force Lincoln to climb as high as possible so he'll have farther to fall.'

Karrion shudders at my words, then nods.

While I give him a head start, I text Jamie to let him know that we will be needing backup and to not go anywhere near the smoke without cold iron.

We climb slowly, mindful of dangers lurking within the coils of smoke. I am soon out of breath, and my damaged throat burns with each inhale. My arms shake from the effort, but I force myself to keep going beyond the reserves of energy to a place where I can only rely on the strength of my will. Soon, nothing exists but the aching fingers clinging on to the rungs before me and the bamboo beneath my feet. Then, I am at the conclave, working on an endless series of chores while the nameless agony consumes every part of me. All I have left is survival.

When Karrion helps me on to the top level of the scaffolding, I sink to my knees, half blind with exhaustion. Over the roar of blood in my ears, I catch snatches of a tune. It sounds like a lullaby. Rubbing my face with the hand not holding the blade, I stand up on shaking legs. Ahead of us, half-hidden in a shroud of smoke, a figure is moving. The vibrations from his steps send a tingle up my calves. When we move, he will feel us too. But will he notice or care?

The lullaby grows stronger as we approach the figure. Its notes coil around us like the smoke, but the cold iron keeps the song from gaining purchase in our minds. Yet the more I listen, the more snowflakes begin to dance on the periphery of my vision. I shake my head, not daring to touch the blade to banish them.

Three more steps bring us close enough to see Lincoln approaching the edge of the scaffold. During the climb, I never paused to calculate how high we are, but a glance down is enough to assure me of the danger we are in. If Lincoln jumps, he will not survive.

Beyond Lincoln, the smoke parts to show Pheonix. Tiny purple flames outline him, and his tail stirs the roiling clouds around him. His hair, which seems an extension of the flames, floats like a mantle of otherness. He is the embodiment of autumn, with the power of the Unseelie court behind him. Around him, shadows take shape and fade away again: felines, canines, hunters on steeds.

What chance do two exhausted mortals have against a Fey lord? Once Pheonix has killed Lincoln, what will he do to Karrion and me?

What if we left?

We could back away, climb down, and leave the insidious

smoke for the safety of the dark streets of Old London. Jamie is coming with reinforcements. What would be the harm in leaving this to the authorities? And if a life is lost will anyone mourn a man like Lincoln, just as Karrion suggested?

I glance down. The silver Fey scars are visible around the blade's handle. Over the past few months, I have been marked inside and out. I have been angry, calculating, and cruel. I have been frightened, desperate, and determined to protect everything I hold dear. Every decision I have made has moulded me into a person I sometimes struggle to recognise. With one death already weighing heavily on my conscience, will I survive another? I couldn't let Lord Ellensthorne die, so is this any different?

Tightening my grip on the blade, I narrow my eyes to block out the snowflakes. Lincoln is not far. All I need to do is take a few quick steps forward and yank him away from the edge of the scaffolding. If I can touch his bare skin with Karrion's necklace, the cold iron will break Lincoln out of Pheonix's glamour so we can help him back to the street.

A step brings me level with Karrion. With a nudge of my head, I indicate that we should move forward. The bamboo is uneven beneath my shoes, and I slide my feet along its surface to maintain my balance.

We have not gone far when Pheonix's eyes flick from Lincoln to me, and he smiles. The lullaby changes from soothing to sinister. Lincoln turns, his speed taking me by surprise after his sluggish movements. He launches himself at me, hands raised.

Karrion steps forward, throwing a punch that sends Lincoln reeling. As Lincoln does so, his flailing hand connects with mine, and the torch flies from my grip. It bounces on the uneven bamboo, falling through the opening in the floor, and landing on the level below.

Immediately the lullaby becomes a roar in my ears as I am engulfed by a blizzard. I cling on to the railing while the bamboo slowly turns to ice under my fingers. The Winter Queen's hand strokes my cheek, her lips are on the Fey mark on my forehead, she is inside my mind, whispering an invitation to join her frozen kingdom as a loyal servant. I want to yield, more than I have ever wanted anything in my life, and I sink to my knees, ready to serve my queen.

'Here,' Karrion's voice comes from the far side of the storm, 'take this!'

At the touch of cold iron against my skin, the glamour is cut off so fast I pitch forward. I manage to put a hand out before my face collides with the floor, but the nausea that comes from the proximity to Karrion's necklace has me retching.

'I'm sorry, Yan. But of the two of us, I'm in better shape to retrieve your torch.'

As much as I want to tell Karrion's retreating form that I understand, all I can do is focus on not hurling the necklace over the side of the scaffolding. Adjusting my grip so I am no longer touching the cold-iron disks helps, but even proximity to metal is enough to drain away whatever power reserves I have left. I reach past the depleted well of magic to that inner place made of galvanised steel, which kept me going through years of pain at the conclave. My exhausted body protests, but I force myself to rise by sheer willpower. Seconds drag by, but at last I am standing once more.

A few feet away, Lincoln stirs, hand rising to cup his jaw where Karrion hit him. He stands in a movement that is wholly inhuman, as if pulled up by invisible strings. The chill of winter settles over me as I realise we are alone on the top level of the scaffolding. I brandish the necklace in front of me; my only defence against him and Pheonix. Beyond Lincoln, Pheonix laughs with the hiss of an extinguishing fire, and a few seconds later, Lincoln copies him.

'Cold iron has no sway over mortals, little fly,' Pheonix hisses.

He is wrong, but my protest dies in my throat as Lincoln comes at me again. This time, his movements are more measured, held in check by the Fey's cunning. I retreat as he advances, my fingers aching from the death grip I have on the necklace. The little cold-iron disks send the fog swirling around us, but it offers no concealment or protection.

Lincoln lunges, and his fist connects with my stomach. I double over, managing to yank my head to the side as he lifts his knee. Unable to retaliate with a blow, I throw my weight at his legs. The move sends him off balance and he grabs for the handrail. My momentum carries me towards the wall of smoke beyond the scaffolding, but a hand closing around my ankle keeps me from going over the edge.

Karrion pulls me back, and I wince as the uneven bamboo presses on to the area where Lincoln hit me. Once I am further from the edge, Karrion takes the necklace from me and hands me the torch, before helping me up.

'Thanks,' I say.

Lincoln has straightened himself and now faces us both. His eyes flicker from me to Karrion. Beyond him, Pheonix's tail changes the pattern of its hypnotic dance. Lincoln's expression goes blank. He turns towards Pheonix and takes a hesitant step forward, then another. My stomach drops.

I act on instinct and thus I am already moving as Lincoln begins to run. My muscles protest, the last of my strength draining away. I do the only thing I can and hurl myself forward with everything I have left, my arms outstretched. While my fingers seek purchase on Lincoln's clothes in vain, the short cold-iron blade sinks into his right buttock. He screams, losing his footing and crashing on to the floor, his head hanging over the edge. I land partly on top of him, though I manage to twist to the side enough to avoid forcing the knife deeper. Lincoln writhes underneath me, whimpering in pain, but at least he is no longer trying to leap off the scaffolding.

Pheonix growls his displeasure, and the press of the glamour against me intensifies. I reach for the knife, careful to keep its blade in the muscle to protect Lincoln, but it offers me scant protection now I am Pheonix's main target. Already I can feel the suggestion is worming its way into my brain, whispering that I should approach my master and follow him like the loyal dog I am. Hissing laughter coils around me.

'Why?' I force the word out.

'I was to be the Knight of the Dying Lands, second only to my cyning, and free to do as I pleased. Yet, because of you, I remain beholden to the Unseelie Cwēn. She will be displeased when you die, but her anger will not last forever.'

His words erode my resistance, urging me to give in. Gathering what remains of my willpower, I bring my legs up so I am crouching over Lincoln. The position reminds me of a hound guarding a kill, but I push that thought aside in favour of another. Here is my chance to ask the question that has haunted me for weeks.

'Did I kill that man in the warehouse?' I ask, unable to keep the desperation from my voice.

Pheonix bares his long, sharp teeth. 'I'll never tell.'

The anger that blazes through me burns away the exhaustion and the pain, leaving behind only the rage of nature. Tightening my grip on the blade, I ready myself for the leap that will carry me to Pheonix. I will sink my weapon into his flesh, watch it burn him while he screams, even if doing so means that I will fall to my death. More than anything, Pheonix deserves to burn.

Before I can launch myself off the scaffolding, a hand closes around the back of my coat's collar. In one fluid movement, Karrion steps in front of me and throws his necklace at Pheonix. It strikes him in the face and neck. Straight away, his skin begins to blacken. The cold-iron disks stick to his flesh, sinking into his bones. Pheonix screams, and the sound slices through my skull, blurring my vision around the edges. One moment he is thrashing mid-air, the next he bursts into an incandescent ball of fire, leaving behind nothing but a glowing trail of purple ashes.

34

———

ASHES

Karrion and I remain frozen to the spot, staring at the space where Pheonix floated moments ago. A drop of blood lands on my upper lip, then another. I wipe the blood away, ignoring the tiny thrill of power as I lick my lips, and try to shake the orange spots from my vision.

Beneath me, Lincoln moans softly. With Karrion's help, I scramble up, away from him. The blade is still sticking out of his buttock. He cranes his neck to look over his shoulder, eyes widening.

'You stabbed me.'

'Would you have rather I let you leap to your death?' I ask as I unwind my scarf.

Lincoln moans again, rubbing his forehead. 'What am I even doing up here? Everything is a blur.'

'This is what you get for meddling in the affairs of magic users,' Karrion says. 'Now hold still. This is going to hurt.'

He braces Lincoln's pelvis while I pull out the knife. A trickle of blood runs from the wound. Lincoln howls. Without bothering to give him any warning, I shove my scarf down his trousers to stem the bleeding until he can receive proper first aid.

'How did you get the Herald to declare you innocent when you clearly killed Maerk Hampten?' Lincoln asks.

Anger surges through me, but Karrion lays a hand on my shoulder.

'Let's go, Yan. Jamie will want to know what happened and we should check on Pheonix.'

'Right.' I stand on shaking legs, grateful for Karrion's arm around my waist keeping me upright. 'Though this may take a while.'

'Take all the time you need.'

'Wait,' Lincoln calls out after us. 'What about me?'

'Make your own way down,' Karrion says.

'Can't you see I'm bleeding?'

'Then stay up here. I don't give a pigeon's fart either way.'

'Bravo,' I mutter as we make our way to the ladder.

'Can you manage the steps?' he asks.

'I think so. Besides, I'm keen to get as far away from Lincoln as possible.'

It takes us a long time to reach the ground and by the time we do, I am shaking so much I struggle to hold on to the ladder rungs. Once my feet touch the pavement, I sink to my knees, gulping for air. Karrion crouches beside me.

'What can I do?'

'Can you find me something to eat? Preferably something sugary.'

'No problem,' he says, already hurrying away.

The smoke glamour has cleared during our descent, and the entrance to Leadenhall Market looks no different from any other night. Further along the street, a Paladin van pulls up next to Jamie's car. Two armoured Paladins approach me, their swords drawn.

'Are you injured?' one of them asks.

'Not really, just exhausted. But there's someone at the top of the scaffolding with a shallow stab wound. He's human.'

One of the Paladins sheathes her sword and jogs back to the van. She returns moments later with a first-aid kit and begins climbing the scaffold.

'What happened?' the remaining Paladin asks.

'The human was under a strong Fey glamour and was about to jump off the top. I tried to break the glamour with my cold-iron blade and accidentally stabbed him in the process.'

'Where is the Feykin now? Detective Inspector Manning warned us about dangerous smoke contaminating the area, but it appears to have dissipated.'

'It was a Fey, not a Feykin who was behind it all. As for what happened to him, I'm not sure.'

Karrion returns and hands me a paper bag containing three pastries as well as a bottle of orange juice. I eat an almond croissant without the taste registering, and drink half of the juice in long gulps. The shaking in my limbs begins to ease. I savour the cinnamon swirl a little more and split a blueberry muffin with Karrion. By the time we have finished eating, I have regained a measure of energy. Karrion helps me up for what feels like the tenth time this evening.

Together we walk to the far end of the scaffolding, where we last saw Pheonix. On the ground is a pile of ashes. Among them are the cold-iron disks from Karrion's necklace, now twisted and scorched.

'Did he die?' asks Karrion.

'I don't know. But it wouldn't surprise me if he was like a Cat-Sìth with nine lives.'

'You may be right, but if he tries to rise from the ashes, I'm covering the bastard with cold iron.'

'Be my guest. I'll cheer you on from a distance.'

Karrion sighs and nudges one of the blackened disks with his boot. 'I'm going to have to order another necklace from Thaylor.'

'The business will pay for it, since this one was destroyed during office hours.'

'Thanks, Yan. Though I'm interested to find out that we're supposed to have office hours.'

'Ours are the flexible kind.'

'Thought so.'

A mint-green VW Golf pulls up in the middle of the road and stops with a belch of black smoke. Mery climbs out of the car and after a brief discussion with Jamie, they both approach.

'Have you been having all the fun without me again?' Mery asks, and gives me the once-over. 'Wow, you look like shit.'

'Thanks.'

'Anytime, darling. I heard rumours about a wicked Fey glamour. The air is thick with magic residue, like someone has sprayed the whole area with heather mead and then set it on fire. So what the hell happened?'

Karrion and I explain everything that transpired since we said goodbye to Jamie at the Brotherhood. Once we reach the end, Mery laughs.

'You gave him a literal pain in the arse because that's exactly what he is. Now I know why I like you.'

Beside me, Karrion tries to mask a chuckle with a cough, while I am grateful for the relative darkness of the street as a flush rises to my cheeks.

Mery crouches to inspect the ashes. When she looks up at us, her mismatched eyes glow in the light of the lamp-posts.

'You two make quite the team. Two Fey destroyed in less than a year. Carry on like this and you'll have to watch your back with the city's Feykin.'

'There is that,' Jamie says. 'Though personally I'm just

amazed that you called for help before everything went down the shitter rather than afterwards like you usually do.'

'I feel personally attacked,' Karrion says.

'Good, you were meant to. Do you have any idea how much paperwork an accidental stabbing is going to cause? Especially since the victim has been writing some very unpleasant articles about Yannia.'

'It's at this point that I'd like to remind everyone that *I* didn't stab Lincoln,' Karrion says.

I nudge him with my elbow. 'Way to throw me under the bus.'

'In all seriousness, Yannia, you'll have to come back to the Brotherhood to make a statement. It helps that Karrion was there to witness what happened, especially since Lincoln attacked you first.'

'By this time tomorrow, I'll have a bruise to prove it,' I say, and lay a hand over the sore area of my stomach.

The scaffolding behind us creaks as the Paladin helps Lincoln down the remaining steps. He walks with barely a limp, which goes some way towards soothing my twinging conscience.

'Well, if it isn't Mr Nice Guy,' Mery says, stalking closer to Lincoln with a glare. 'Always chatting up the ladies at the front desk, hoping for a juicy lead or a bit of gossip to twist into a sensational headline. Well, I have news for you: keep well away from New Scotland Yard. I'm going to make sure no one there will ever lower themselves to speak to you, you slimy, immoral wanker.'

'I was just stabbed,' he replies, though his voice lacks the indignation from earlier. Mery can be a fierce sight to behold.

'Like I give a fuck. Be grateful you're still breathing instead of being splattered across the pavement for someone else to clean up. Because that's what you're best at: making a mess and leaving others to take care of it. From now on, consider yourself done with Old London and the Met. We don't want you.'

Mery turns back to us, but cannot resist making one more comment. 'I hope you said thanks to the woman who saved your life.'

Over her shoulder, my eyes meet Lincoln's. The message is clear: he will not thank me, nor apologise for the lies he published, while I will not forgive him. The best I can hope for is that our paths will never cross again.

It is well past midnight before I finally step through my front door and make my way upstairs, each step taking its toll. Karrion comes with me long enough to collect a squirming Sinta and her things to give me a day in bed to recover from my injuries. He presses a kiss on my temple before carrying an indignant Sinta out.

Giving our statements to the Paladins took longer than I expected and towards the end, even Jamie grew frustrated with the delays. At least everyone agreed that no further action would be taken against me over the stabbing.

The pastries I ate earlier have triggered nausea, not helped by the fact that we found no time for dinner. It has been too long since I last took any medication, and the pain that has settled in my legs is crushing the bones and corroding my joints with acid.

My home is quiet without Sinta. When I step on one of her toys, the squeak sounds too loud in the silent room and I regret agreeing to Karrion's suggestion that he take her. I switch on a lamp and carry on to the kitchen. Brewing Lady Bergamon's pain-relieving tea is too much effort, so I settle for taking the strongest dose of medication available and washing the pills down with a glass of milk. Although I have little interest in food, I force myself to eat a banana so the nausea doesn't grow worse. All I want is the oblivion of sleep.

I walk to the fireplace and sweep it clear of aches. My log basket is almost empty, but there is enough wood for a small fire. I strike a match and light the kindling, but do not make an offering. Even the words of my childhood prayers refuse to go beyond a blockage in my throat. So instead, I pace to the window to stare at my flickering reflection.

What little satisfaction I gleaned from saving Lincoln has faded, leaving behind the ghost of uncertainty. I look at my hands, remembering the stickiness of blood covering them. No matter how much I try to cajole my memory, I still cannot recall what happened in the warehouse. I must resign myself to the fact that without going before the Herald a second time, I will never know for certain whether I am a murderer.

How will I carry on? How can I reconcile the uncertainty with the way I try to lead my life? Is this the beginning of the slide down to a place where I become the kind of savage killer so many people in Old London have accused me of being? How long before I no longer recognise the woman staring back at me in the glass?

The silence in the room grows oppressive. I turn to the fireplace, a name already on my lips.

'Wishearth.'

He materialises out of the flames in an instant, as if he was waiting for my call. We stand facing each other, but all thoughts of discussing the case with him slip away. They are replaced by the fear of being alone, of waking up in a tiny cell with a collar binding my magic. I am frightened of falling asleep, lest I return to the nightmare.

His eyes are drawn to the darkening bruise on my temple. Two hot fingers come to rest over the tender area, and some of the pain fades under his touch. He does the same with the bruises around my throat. I wish he would engulf me in his fire and burn away every shadow and ghost that drags me down.

'Plenty of people are drawn to the flames,' Wishearth says, as if reading my mind. 'But only a few are brave enough to catch fire and burn.'

'It's ice I fear, not fire.'

'I know.'

Wishearth steps closer. Silence settles between us as his pupils are engulfed by flames. It is perhaps the most beautiful thing I have ever seen. I reach up to touch his cheek, but pause millimetres from his skin. He lays his hand over mine, closing the distance. I stroke his cheek with my thumb and slide my fingers along his jaw, encountering smooth skin instead of stubble. We stay like that for what feels like an eternity, until at last, Wishearth kisses me.

His lips are almost too hot against mine. I refuse to pull back and soon get used to the heat. Wishearth's warmth sinks into me, easing the pain and kindling a fire that turns into a blaze. The scent of smoke strokes my skin. It triggers tremors that leave me shaking in his arms. He hugs me closer. One of his hands cradles the back of my neck, the other slips under my shirt to splay across my lower back. The crushing agony in my legs fades away.

I am safe in his arms and some restless, wild part of me finds peace. The stillness spreads over me, as comforting as Wishearth's warmth. My fears and doubts melt away until this moment and Wishearth are all I need. All that I am is his, for he demands nothing of me, only accepting that which is freely given. As part of the daily offerings to him, along with prayers and faith, I also gave him myself.

The kiss becomes more insistent, and desire mingles with the stillness. He bites my lower lip, and even his teeth are warm.

His heat insulates me against the rest of the world, shutting out everything but this moment. Any thoughts not relating to Wishearth slip away when he parts my lips and deepens the kiss.

This is not the first time I have made love in front of an open fire, but Wishearth *is* the fire, the flames, the light.

We end up on the bed with me on his lap, though later I cannot quite recall when we moved. Wishearth has lost his coat, and I slip my hands under his woollen jumper. His skin is hot and smooth, inviting further exploration. Wishearth nips my ear, causing me to arch against him. A wicked smile curls the edges of my mouth upwards as I lean back enough to run my fingertips across his stomach and up his sides. He shivers, whether from pleasure or from being ticklish, I cannot tell. His chest is smoother and softer than Dearon's and devoid of scars...

Dearon.

I break the kiss, leaning back to catch my breath as my hands still on Wishearth's chest. He pants against my neck, close enough that a shiver runs through me. The fingers stroking my back are too hot for a mortal, for Wishearth is not from this plane. How often has he reminded me of the fact, speaking with a measure of regret about not having the same needs as me? I am nothing more than a mayfly in his long existence; here one moment, gone the next. Wishearth cares for me, of that I am certain, but he cannot give me what I need, what I still hope I may find with Dearon, nor can I be what he wants.

When his lips brush along my jaw, I pull back further.

'Wait. I'm not sure this is a good idea.'

The flames disappear from his eyes so quickly that I wonder if I imagined their existence. He stares at me, his expression stony.

'It's because I'm not *him*, isn't it?'

Before I have a chance to protest or explain, he vanishes in a cloud of acrid smoke, taking the flames from the fireplace with him. Off balance, I pitch forward on the bed, the agony returning in a rush of pain, and I am left alone in my cold, dark home.

THE END

ALSO BY LAURA LAAKSO

Fallible Justice

Echo Murder

Roots of Corruption

Wildest Hunger

The Doves in the Dining Room (a Wilde novella)

ACKNOWLEDGMENTS

Thank you, as ever, to the whole Bloodhound team for helping me turn my manuscripts into books. Huge thanks must also go to Louise Walters, the best editor I could ask for. She knows the characters almost as well as I do and puts up with all my bizarre shenanigans with her usual good cheer.

My deepest thanks always goes to Andrew Rogers, who saw bits of this book completely out of order and loved it just the same. Thank you to all my friends for their support, especially when it comes in the form of baked goods and hot chocolate. My mum keeps telling me to write faster so she has more books to read, so hopefully this will satisfy her for a while.

Thank you to readers near and far for continuing to ask what happens next.

Finally, my love goes to Halla and Usva, who fill my days with joy and dog hair. Sinta taught you both well.

www.ingramcontent.com/pod-product-compliance
Lightning Source LLC
Chambersburg PA
CBHW031304210726
48287CB00005B/1413